CATACLYSM

"A momentous and violent event marked by overwhelming upheaval and demolition. Broadly: an event that brings great changes."

By

R.J. SMITH

A Storyteller Novel

(MMXIV – 01)

First Edition June 15, 2014

Published by:
Storyteller Entertainment, LLC
United States of America

In collaboration with RJ Smith Productions

Copyright © 2014-2016 by RJ Smith

ISBN: 978-0989675369

Represented by

JRK Literary, USA
Robert Snow, U.K. Agent
Glenda Findley, U.S. Editor

Cover Design

Richard K. Green

"If aliens ever visit us, I think the outcome would be much as when Christopher Columbus first landed in America, which didn't turn out very well for the Native Americans."

Stephen William Hawking
Professor of Mathematics
Theoretical Physicist

Chapter 1

EARTHQUAKE

THE ISLAND of La Palma was deadly.

It was the fifth largest of seven Canary Islands hosting a hundred thousand residents.

That meant trouble.

The volcanic ocean landmass contained three ridges. One of these, Cumbre Vieja, towered four miles from seabed to summit and it was a slumbering demon.

Locals supposed the volcano was primed for catastrophe, believing one day the beast would awake in a noxious, fiery explosion of ash and lava.

When that transpired, everyone would die.

Home to the world's most sophisticated telescopes, the William Herschel stood majestically atop the caldera with its optical near-infrared reflectors monitoring the heavens.

If E.T. existed, this lens would make contact.

Through a layer of wispy, fibrous white clouds, a Beechcraft Baron twin-engine plane lined up for landing on a short blacktop runway. It belonged to the U.S. Geological Survey and ferried scientists to the volcano.

"This is a hot blooded monster," Dr. Tish Harriet stated exiting the plane and leading her team of six men into a bunker. "It could take out the United States."

They'd been watching the Old Summit closely due to alarming steam vents which had recently erupted.

"The data is disturbing," Professor Chris Grossman agreed checking the latest AFM readings on his tablet. "If we have lahar activity, this could very well mean massive slippage of the ridge."

"We need to get down to the monitoring poles," Tish answered. "See if the data confirms our suspicions."

Tish was lead volcanologist and had spent her entire life studying stratovolcanoes' tall, pointed summits... built up by countless layers of hardened lava, tephra, pumice, and volcanic ash.

Suddenly, an alarm erupted.

Beeeeep
Beeeeeeeeeeeep–Beeeeeeeeeeeep

"We have a problem!" Chris shouted, glancing at a seismogram display. "This is huge activity."

Seismograms were registers produced by seismographs that calculated the location and magnitude of a quake.

On the graph, lines began spiking spiked.

"Damn," Tish yelled hurrying to the monitor.

Installed along the volcano's ridge, the seismographs detected, amplified, and recorded ground vibrations before sending signals back to the bunker during earthquakes. They were securely mounted in the earth... so when the ground shook, the unit wobbled with it. As it vibrated, the device recorded motion between itself and the rest of the instrument, thus recording ground motion.

"A minor tremor," Chris muttered watching the spikes elevating on the screen. "3.3 is the current reading."

Then, it shot up.

Each second, it rose higher, until passing through 5.5. Nobody here sought to openly proclaim a prediction of doom; yet privately, they made escape plans.

"Maybe Sam is right," someone whispered.

Dr. Samuel May was the premier researcher of volcano doomsday theories and prophesies... who, up until this moment... was the laughingstock of volcanology. So, for the last few years, he'd been secreted away in the isolated wasteland of Iceland.

Up there, in the middle of nowhere, his public predictions of disaster could be silenced.

And everyone could breathe a sigh of relief.

That was, until the bunker shook violently.

That caused Tish to glance out of a fortified window where the dome of the William Herschel collapsed. With a tired shrieking roar, it gave up its ghost and plummeted to the ground with a thunderous crash.

"Notify the Hazard Center," Tish shouted. "Send out an immediate satellite dispatch!"

The team was clustered around an array of computer screens struggling to balance themselves. Rows of florescent lights flickered. An alarm whooped, a siren shrieked, and shelves of research equipment fell from the cracking walls.

"It's going to erupt!" Chris hollered glancing to the wall of video screens. The room shook again, and a three-foot wide monitor blinked 8.9. "Look at the size of this! We may have flank collapse! Notify GDACS and locate Sam, immediately!"

Tish rushed to a satellite phone and punched her finger onto its dial pad. "This is the Palisades Hydrophone Station at Cumbre Vieja Volcano! We are experiencing a major earthquake!"

Then, suddenly, the ceiling cracked, bowed, and collapsed around the researchers. The monitoring displays broke free of their hangers and crashed to the floor.

Above their heads, and one by one, the florescent lights exploded, thrusting the chamber into darkness.

Chapter 2

ACT OF GOD

TOM ANDERSON was the network's fluff man.

He was the correspondent Network News tossed across the globe when *the package* was a sidebar of public interest. His assignments were filler for dead air... to thistle down the violent coverage pouring in from around the globe. Syria, Iraq, Afghanistan... that's where the *real* news was, hidden away in tempestuous countries where violent threats of terrorism were everyday occurrences. Unlike this event of the newly elected pope, and his attendance at:

Nothingville!

This was filler, capital-F for fluff.

> "Good morning from the Canary Islands," Tom smiled into the camera as the *Emissary of God* stepped from the pope-mobile surrounded by cardinals and Swiss Guards. "The popular Spanish Pope, Callixtus the Fourth, just three weeks from his elevation by the conclave of cardinals, has arrived here at the Patron Saint of the Canary Islands for what has been dubbed the seaside salvation of souls."

The pope cut his hand through the air and made the sign of the cross, a humble expression lining his face. He'd traveled to *Basilica of Candelaria* to attend and celebrate the famed apparition of Mother Mary on the Island of Tenerife. According to legend, a statue of The Virgin appeared on this beach in 1392 bearing a child in one hand and a green candle in the other. How that came to pass… a statue sloshing from the ocean… that little detail was never fully explained. But, it happened all right, just as sure as the day is bright.

There were eyewitnesses.

Two Guanche goat herders claimed they saw Mary trudging from the sea, dragging her feet along the frothy sand. Approaching, one of the men tried to throw a stone at her, but his arm became paralyzed. When the second man attempted to stab *The Virgin* with a knife, he ended up wounding himself.

They were stories and lore.

"Papa!" an old woman cried falling at the pope's feet. "Bless me, Father!" Beside her loomed nine bronze Guanches King Statues representing the aboriginal kings. These were the Menceys of Candelaria mounted along the seashore beside the basilica. Some claimed they had worked alongside people from another planet centuries before to build this paradise.

"Bless you all," Callixtus muttered to the thousands of onlookers lining the route. "Go with God, my children."

Alongside the pope strolled Cardinal Jonathan, the pontiff's handsome Italian personal assistant. He grinned while explaining the significance and antiquity of the bronze sentinels.

Yet, Callixtus was Spanish and knew the history.

Then, thousands of Eurasian Sparrow Hawks flapped into the air from nearby trees, filling the sky with shrieking, echoing cries. They were small, bluish-gray *birds of prey* who specialized in hunting woodland birds.

Now, they fled in fear of something else.

"Oh, vaya, mira thos criaturas hermosas!" Callixtus exclaimed at the sight.

"Sì Padre, sono belle!" Cardinal Jonathan nodded. "They are beautiful, aren't they?"

"Strange," Callixtus muttered in broken English. "I've never seen them in such a panic before." Glancing at the television reporter, he watched him point into the distance.

"A flock of sparrows have jolted from their nearby perches. They're soaring over the guardian sculptures lining the shore. With their backs to the sea and facing the basilica, these eternal monuments watch over the faithful in attendance today, just as they have for an eternity."

Unexpectedly, the statues shook as the earth quaked.

It reminded the reporter of Universal Studio's Earthquake Ride in Orlando. "It's an earthquake!" he yelled into the camera as pandemonium broke out around him... the people sprinting for their lives.

"Watch out!" someone shouted. "The church is collapsing!"

Unpredictably, the statue's stone foundations crumbled and the Guanches toppled to the pavement.

"The cathedral is shaking," Tom yelled into the camera. "Behind me, you can hear its bells gonging oddly inside the twin stone towers of the old stone apostolic."

At that second, a loud screech escaped the pylon and stones and brocks collapsed in a giant cloud of crumbling cement. Piece by piece, the tower released its clutch on history and sent its enormous brass bells plummeting to the ground with a thundering roar.

"Look out!" a priest screamed. "Everybody run!" They were the last words the holy man would offer, as one of the mammoth carillons crashed onto his head and sent his soul to heaven for a much awaited meeting with Saint Peter.

"Oh, no!" Callixtus bellowed to the sky while studying the scene. "Not yet! I haven't had enough time!"

"We have to get you out of here, Holy Father!" Cardinal Jonathan shouted as Swiss Guards frantically ushered them towards the motorcade.

"Quickly! Get to the vehicle, Your Holiness!"

However, Heaven had other plans.

The destruction of faith was underway.

Belief was being tested.

Just a millisecond before Callixtus reached the safety of his pope-mobile, an enormous sinkhole swallowed the holy chariot into its cavernous jaws.

Oh, Dios Mío! Callixtus thought as the guards pulled him to safety. *The dismantling of the world has begun!*

Chapter 3

MR. VOLCANO

GRÍMSVÖTN VOLCANO hulked over Iceland.

Its icecap, Vatnajökull, loomed magnificently on the northwestern ridge and boasted the highest eruption frequency of all volcanoes in the country. Because most of its mass lay beneath ice, its eruptions were sub-glacial.

That's what held the attention of researchers the world over... deadly, fiery, magma... bubbling deep below the surface. It brought survey grants because sleeping giants like this one had the ability to end a lot of things.

It threatened life on planet Earth.

Everybody agreed that a super-volcano explosion could marshal in a new ice age when ash from the eruption would travel the globe and block out sunlight for years.

And, without the sun, crops would fail... plant life would perish and food would become scarce. That would bring famine, the breakdown of civilization and, quite possibly the end of mankind.

In 2011, an eruption began here that lasted four days. Spewing plumes of ash and lava into the atmosphere, it accompanied several earthquakes resulting in the cancellation of nine hundred flights in Iceland, the United Kingdom, Greenland, Germany, Ireland, and Norway.

Planes were forced to land, and international travel crawled to an economy crushing halt.

The airports became parking lots.

Some said it was the beginning of the end.

When natural disasters like that happened–directing airliners to their nearest tarmacs–money poured in and prominent researchers the globe over assembled.

Those prophecies of fear are what brought a research team to Geological Base Camp Fireside to lead the way.

The plan: to save the world from total destruction.

One of the team members was American geologist, William Squire. On this bright sunny morning, he celebrated his forty-eighth birthday by staring into a hole in the ground. This is what he lived for, science.

"Good morning, Sunshine," he muttered to an Acoustic Flow Monitor lying exposed in the excavated earth.

Will specialized in the study of solid and liquid matter that constituted the Earth, the processes and history that shaped it, and all things related. When compared to other scientists, he was more exposed to the outdoors than those in laboratories.

He treasured the frontiers of hazard and thrived on the forefront of natural danger and global disaster warnings.

His thing was studying earthquakes, volcanic activity, tsunamis, weather storms, and the technologies used to warn governments of those events.

Sometimes, that works just fine, he considered glancing to the towering icecap and then looked back to the hole. *And sometimes, all hell breaks loose.*

At that instant, the rumble of an engine brought his attention out of the hole. When he peered across the tundra, he smiled at the sight of a muddy Jeep Wrangler Rubicon. In the background, far beyond, the volcano, superheated steam spewed into the brisk morning air.

As the Jeep slid to a stop in a patch of mud beside the excavation, a British man winked at Will and stepped to the soggy ground. He was Dr. Samuel May, a rugged crackerjack of a man, steady as the volcanoes he studied.

"You don't look a day over forty, Will."

"Is that right?"

"Right as can be, dear boy!" Sam snickered, slapping his junior researcher on the back before pointing his thumb back towards the volcano. "She's all mouth and no trousers, I tell you; day six of moaning and groaning!"

"That's what you get when you mess with women."

"Huh? What's that, Chap?"

"Never mind, Professor," Will waved dismissively. "Women are women, even when they're volcanoes!"

"Oh, yes, dear boy. You have learned a thing or two."

Interrupted by the sound of an approaching helicopter, Sam raised his hand to block the glare of the sun cresting over the summit of the icecap.

"Bollocks! What the hell is this tosh, the newsies again? Haven't you told them to stay out of our testing area?"

A white United Nations helicopter then swooped out of the clear blue sky, landed, and deposited a man wearing a United Nations GDACS bomber jacket.

Crouching beneath the blades, he hurried to Sam.

"Professor May, I'm Oscar Thomas, from the United Nations Global Disaster Alert and Coordination System here in Iceland."

"Is that right?" Sam chuckled pushing out his meaty hand. "You must be new at the post; your accent sounds like you spring from the Caribbean."

"The Virgin Islands, Sir, my friends call me *V.I.* for short, and yes I am from St. Thomas."

"No kidding? Well, Mr. Virgin Islands, you must be out of your element here in Iceland!" Motioning towards the excavation, he introduced Will. "Professor Will Squire and I know the U.N. well. Besides, that bird you sprang from gave you straight-away. How're the lackeys back at GDACS, huh?"

V.I. shook his head. "Not good, I'm afraid. We received word from Secretary Soma that the U.N. requests your immediate presence in New York!"

The mention of his longtime frenemy brought a grin to Sam's face. "Karin dispatched you all this way to pull my chain, eh? What's biting her rump these fine days?"

"It's Cumbre Vieja, Professor."

"The Old Summit?" Will snorted. "What's happening in La Palma, Spain?"

"The U.S.G.S. Volcano Hazards Program has confirmed seismological data on the ground. They have catastrophic seismic activity in the Canaries and are concerned the western flank of the volcano might be unstable."

"Son of a gun!" Sam exclaimed. "They've finally realized their cock up and have come to their senses? Are they actually talking about collapse?"

"Yes, Sir," V.I. stated pointing at the chopper. "I need to get you to New York at once; we have a plane standing by at the airport."

"Should we deactivate the AFM monitors?" Will asked, pointing to the hole in the ground.

"There's no time, Dr. May!" V.I. urged. "If your past predictions of Cumbre Vieja are true, Africa could only have hours!"

"Leave the equipment to the elements, William," Sam ordered. "Grab our bug-out bags. We have to move with the wind, dear boy."

Gathering their belongings, which were always ready for immediate escape, they hurried beneath the helicopter's spinning blades and climbed aboard.

"If the summit fails," V.I. asked, "Is there anything that can be done to save the Atlantic shores?"

"When she erupts," Sam answered as the chopper lifted, "the only thing we can do is get out of her bloody way!"

Chapter 4

JUST THE FACTS

THE U.N. chopper was a battleship.

V.I. pointed to a string of bullet holes peppering the floor. "This MI-24 was one of the choppers that took on heavy gun fire in the village of Kinshasa."

"Bob's your Uncle!" Sam scoffed. "It flew the Democratic Republic of the Congo? Why're bullet holes still visible in the airframe?"

V.I. shrugged. "Repairs cost more than retiring it for missions like this in non-hostile sectors of the world."

"And yet, it still has guns attached to the exterior," Will nodded out the window. "Worried about an invasion?"

"It's a dangerous world," V.I. observed. "We never know when a rocket propelled grenade will streak its way up from the ground."

That forced Sam to consider the ramifications of such an event. "In that case, we'd be a bit shanghaied, would we not?" Following world affairs with a keen eye, he recognized disasters and military upheavals often dictated his own survival while traversing the globe's most treacherous environments.

"The U.N. security council," V.I. continued, "activated a squad of these attack-helicopters to knockout insurgent positions in the eastern Congo in 2012, after they gained ground in heavy fighting."

"It's a testy planet," Sam granted. "Nobody seems to recognize we're all on this planet together. We're fighting each other when we should be focused on one unique enemy, you know?"

William cut into the conversation. "What did President Ronald Reagan say to the U.N. about the human race and aliens? He stood before the U.N. in 1987, stared across the Great Hall and said: 'How quickly our differences worldwide would vanish if we were facing an alien threat from outside this world.' How do you like that for disclosure?"

"Aliens exist," Sam affirmed. "I could tell you stories. Their elongated skulls have been found in tombs on too many of my digs"

"I've read your papers," V.I. quickly changed the subject. "In college I heard about the possibility of flank collapse and read your theory on Cumbre Vieja. Do you really believe an earthquake will cause a tsunami?"

"It could. I was concerned in 2011 when officials on the smallest Canary Island, El Hierro, had to evacuate civilians following a series of quakes. They experienced over eight thousand tremors during two months, and I feared a major disaster would happen back then."

"But it didn't."

"No, it did not."

"Do you think this quake will cause an eruption?"

"None has taken place on any of the Canary Islands since the Las Palmas in 1971, but my team has been warning the international community that a La Palma eruption could take place when her magma rises to the surface and produces a series of ruptures."

Will pulled an iPad from his bag and showed it to V.I. "We don't know if magma will break through the crust, cause an eruption, or worse." On the screen was a computer generation of what might happen if an eruption did cause flank collapse.

"This is the cause?" V.I. asked staring at the video of the volcano ridge splashing into the ocean.

"It is," Sam muttered. Then, motioning for Will to turn the display off, he turned to V.I. and peered into the man's eyes. "So, what do we know so far?"

"La Palma had an 8.9 early this morning. Of the thousands of swarm tremors recorded since, only twenty or so have been noticeable to residents. However, Spain is reporting the quakes are continuing across all seven islands. The volcano itself has not seen an eruption, but the Spanish have raised the eruption risk-level to red, the highest alert since the swarm began."

"Bonkers!" Sam grunted. "All seven islands are experiencing quakes! An 8.9 is enormous, it might have displaced La Palma already!"

"But there hasn't been an eruption," V.I. argued.

"Not yet," Sam contended glancing out the window at the mountain peaks below. "But it's coming, my friend, just as sure as we sit in this bullet ridden deathtrap. Has anyone heard from my wife, Dr. Tish Harriet?"

V.I. reluctantly frowned. "The last we heard was an alert she sent out from the Palisades Hydrophone Station."

Chapter 5

PREDICTION OF DOOM!

KEFLAVÍK INTERNATIONAL was the largest airport in Iceland and American tourism was big business.

After landing in the chopper, the men hurried across the tarmac and approached a Lear Jet bearing the olive branch seal of the United Nations.

V.I. stood at the top air-stair. "Whenever you're ready, Sam, the pilot has indicated we're clear to push off."

"Thank you, Mr. Virgin Islands," the volcanologist smiled politely staring toward the end of the runway. "I'll be a few more minutes." He was at the bottom of the stairs speaking animatedly to Will. "We have to lay it all out again to the United Nations. Show them our data and the flank failure model. Convince them to close the London Underground and evacuate America's East Coast."

"Good luck with that!" Will grunted. "Do you really think they'll take our work seriously now? The U.S. Congress practically laughed us out of The Beltway the last time we went to Capitol Hill warning of this very issue."

"It's those Republicans," Sam sighed. He had stressed to the American Congressmen that the eastern coastline of the United States was under threat from a monster wave of Hollywood–and Biblical–proportions when the volcano finally collapsed and crashed into the ocean. He thought that perhaps bringing God into the equation might have helped–though he really didn't believe in such an entity.

"Maybe this time they'll listen," Will hoped.

Sam grinned. "This quake should bring them around." Yet, deep down, he wasn't convinced the White House could be persuaded the earthquake would cause a massive landslide sending a 300-foot wave across the Atlantic.

Will shook his head in disbelief. "We've issued countless warnings to the U.S.G.S. predicting that, in the best-case scenario, a tsunami would destroy the east coast from Florida to Maine."

"Maybe now they'll listen," Sam stated glancing towards an Icelandair commercial plane leaping from the runway and bursting through the sky.

"Don't hold your breath. People in Washington wait until the last minute to do anything."

Sam knew this was true.

Actor Samuel Jackson had even gone on the Discovery Channel and warned that of the top five natural disasters facing the globe, a volcanic collapse from Cumbre Vieja was one of them.

The problem was this: although Hollywood loved end of the world disaster predictions, they were slow to climb onboard another disaster, thanks to the Mayan 2012 lunacy. That END OF DAYS prediction claimed a catastrophic event would occur on December 21, 2012, and Earth would cease to exist thanks to a collision with Planet X. Some even suggested the North and South Poles would reverse bringing on worldwide earthquakes that terminated all life.

That prophecy expired on December 22nd 2012.

Sam shrugged as he emerged from his thoughts of disaster. "Washington's elected officials are not going to jump onto another prediction of catastrophe. Especially one that calls for a tsunami generated by a mountain twice the size of Britain's Isle of Man crashing into the sea following a volcanic eruption."

Will grunted. "We have to make them believe."

"I remember," Sam chuckled glancing at his colleague, "the first time I told U.S. officials a 500-mile-per-hour wave would wipe out the east coast."

"They were a bunch of grouchy, whining broods," Will recalled. "The National Weather Service smiled politely, and showed your British rump to the door."

Not one U.S. Senator or Congressman believed it would happen. They practically threw Sam off Capitol Hill.

But Sam's team all believed.

"What about Admiral Brancor?" Will asked, a smile stretching out the corners of his mouth, remembering the saucy American Admiral. "Is he going to be at the U.N. council meeting?"

Sam snorted and pushed his hands into his pockets. "I've got a two-finger salute for that chap!"

"What's that?"

"It's similar to the American middle finger, dear boy."

"I didn't know the British were so vulgar."

"Well, now your doorbell has been rung," Sam smiled hurrying up the air-stairs. "We'll put some welly into our arguments to the global community. They have to understand the severity of the crisis."

"We'll give it all the muscle we have."

"Cheerio, then; off we go," Sam ordered stepping onto the airplane. As the door closed, he wondered if he'd ever see Iceland again.

This might be the beginning of a deadly journey.

Chapter 6

THE BIG APPLE

THE SKYLINE of Manhattan was a beacon of hope.

We'll need lots of hope, Sam thought, stepping from the helicopter that had ferried them from JFK to the 34th Street Heliport on the east side of Manhattan.

Nobody–including the President of the United States–entered New York City in a helicopter without landing here. Known as the Atlantic Metroport, it provided charter, commuter, and sightseeing flights, replacing the heliport atop the Pan American Building, which closed in 1968.

Now, as Sam led his entourage across a blacktop landing strip, he was surrounded by armed federal agents.

"Welcome to New York, Dr. May," an agent stated extending his hand. "I'm Agent Gordon Holland, but you can call me Gordy, I'm with the Secret Service and am the head of your security detail here in the States."

Sam was dismayed. "Well, Gordy, this is cracking, isn't it? Why do we need government security?"

"It's at the order of the President."

"That's barking mad! Why in the Queen's name is the President protecting us?"

"To shelter you from the masses... so, if you'll follow me, I'll transport you to the U.N. building."

Sam stared, bewildered at half a dozen armed agents standing beside black SUVs. He knew the ride to the U.N. was only a half-mile and wondered what rambled through the President's head going to all this trouble. Secretly, however, he supposed his warnings were finally taking up residence in the leader's mind. So, as he climbed into an armored vehicle, he pondered his words to GDACS and tried to relax.

"They're sure taking our visit seriously," Will winked confidently to Sam.

"You're the men of the hour," V.I. proclaimed. "The entire General Assembly will be in session for your address and recommendations."

"Well, that's the bee's knees, isn't it?" Sam sniggered. "Imagine a lowly researcher and his junior colleague being treated as knights!" Peering out the window, he squinted toward the U.N. skyscraper rising from the bank of the East River as the SUV rolled to a stop.

Pulling open the door, Gordy watched his agents surround Sam as he stepped to the pavement.

"Easy, boys," Sam jested. "It's just a meeting, after all."

The U.N. complex served as the official headquarters of the world since its construction in 1952. Its 18-acres were home to representatives of Earth's six billion people. Those reps had long traversed the globe to attend discussions of peace, justice, and the social well-being of the planet.

Wait 'til they hear what I have to bark, Sam thought. He suspected there'd be heated bickering and angered ramblings as members debated the veracity of the day.

"Right this way, gentlemen," Agent Holland directed, pointing down a concrete sidewalk leading to the entrance of the massive complex.

Glancing to Will and V.I., Sam nodded and hurriedly followed Gordy down a footpath lined by member country flags flapping in the brisk breeze. He knew there were one hundred and ninety-six countries in the world and caught himself counting the flags. Regarding V.I., he nodded to the poles. "Why doesn't Taiwan have one swaying in the breeze along with the rest of the world?"

V.I. grinned. "Although Taiwan operates as an independent country, most nations refuse to officially recognize it because China considers Taiwan a breakaway province and countries who want to do business with China have to sever formal relations with Taiwan."

"Politics is codswallop," Sam huffed walking through the grand entrance and bypassing rows of metal detectors. "It's a load of tosh, a bunch of baloney!"

New York had become a military state since the terrorist attacks of September 11[th,] 2001. Security was everywhere–hidden just out of view–and Sam suspected that somewhere deep in an NYPD Operations Center every move he made was being analyzed.

Not just his moves, but everyone who walked the street.

V.I. interrupted those thoughts. "The United Nations has three additional regional headquarters located in Geneva, Vienna, and Nairobi. Of course, they won't be in your meeting today."

"Who is attending?" Sam asked.

"All the Atlantic Ocean countries, Britain, Ireland, France, Spain, Brazil…the Caribbean nations and Africa."

Sam often joked about the interest the U.N. had in Africa. Although the United Nations helped represent global interests, facilitating diplomatic activities, and enjoying certain extraterritorial privileges, millions starved to death on that forsaken continent… and death by hunger didn't show leadership in his eyes.

"What is your biggest worry right now?" V.I. asked.

"Morocco," Sam groaned. "It'll get walloped first,"

Agent Holland wasn't so sure. "You talk about this disaster like it's a foregone reality."

"It's not a question of if, Gordy…"

At that instant, a middle-eastern man appeared holding a portable phone. "Dr. May! I have an urgent call from the Canaries!"

Gordy stopped the man in his tracks.

"Stay where you are, please!"

"It's all right," V.I. assured. "He's an attaché with the U.N. Global Disaster Office."

Sam grabbed the phone. "Who is it?"

"Doctor Harriet."

Sam placed the phone to his ear and stared into a screen of a Galaxy Tablet that V.I. handed over. On its screen were live news reports of the quake's aftermath in Tenerife.

"Sam, honey!" his wife Tish said. "It's begun, we are experiencing flank displacement!"

She was the only woman Sam ever loved, and now, he detected fear in her voice. "What are the AFM readings?"

On the tablet, he stared at the news reports showing the collapse of the basilica and a reporter pointing to the pope-mobile lying in a sinkhole.

Chapter 7

IT'S GETTING HOTTER

SOMETHING STRANGE was in the air.

Dr. Tish Harriet couldn't quite place her finger on it–*but it was there*, tugging at the corners of her mind–a sense of impending doom.

Since the earthquake ceased, an unnerving calm had filled the void; the normal cacophony of birds chirping on tree branches... *they were gone*. The woods on the volcano were dead-quiet, nothing climbed through the brush.

When Tish had swiftly directed the team out of the collapsing research bunker, they were stunned to see the William Hershel Telescope lying crumpled on the soil.

That was then...

Now, it was nothing more than a folded piece of astronomical wreckage littering the quaking caldera.

That vision of the destroyed telescope was five hours old; an eternity of time that now brought the researchers deep onto the summit where saplings were heaved from the earth, pitched aside like discarded toothpicks.

Holding a satellite phone to her ear, Tish listened to Sam back at the United Nations.

"It's getting hotter as we snake our way through the canopy," Professor Chris Grossman stated navigating a foot trail up ahead. "I can feel a drastic change in temperature!"

It *was* getting hotter... a scorching heat escaped the saturated ground, like a pot of water boiling on a stove–*its steam rising*–fighting for escape to cooler air.

"Sam," Tish barked into the phone. "We're making our way down the ridge to obtain a manual reading from the transmitting pole because the quake knocked out the station's AFM monitors."

CATACLYSM

They relied on a series of stations installed downstream from the volcano. Each one consisted of a seismometer detecting ground vibrations of an approaching mudflow.

Lahars had the potential to be extremely destructive, running tens of yards-per-second they destroyed everything in their path. The most destructive lahars had been the *Nevado Del Ruiz* in Columbia and *Mount Pinatubo* on the island of Luzon, near the Philippine province of Zambales.

Each killed thousands of people.

So, AFM monitors, and the microprocessors that analyzed their signals at the station, were essential in receiving information from the base station.

But that bunker was now gone and here they stood.

Tish shrugged off those thoughts and led the team down the dense, steep ridge. They carried foldable shovels, packed in shoulder bags slung over their throbbing shoulders that contained testing tubes and small rock picks to excavate the hard soil. The team pioneered the study of pyroclastic volcano deposits, ash beds, and mudflows.

Dr. Tish loved deciphering the eruptive histories of volcanoes and knew the pyroclastic rocks were the product of volcanic explosions where fragmenting shards of rock were violently ejected from steam vents.

That turned her on.

Now, continuing down the muddy, heated ridge, she suspected an eruption might not be far off. Glancing ahead, she watched Chris navigate the path. He was a forty-five-year-old seismologist who studied earthquakes and the spread of elastic waves through Earth. The field encompassed examination of seismic activity properties, such as tsunamis and seismic sources such as volcanic, tectonic, oceanic, atmospheric, and artificial processes such as explosions.

Yet, Tish knew, it was the study of *landslides* and the direct impact of a possible *tsunami,* which brought Chris to her team at La Palma.

"Tish!" Chris suddenly shouted pointing excitedly towards an enormous erupting steam vent. It was the size of *Meteor Crater* in Arizona. Down the center of its vent ran a crack blasting superheated steam through trembling trees.

The steam whistled like a signal along a railroad station.

"Jesus!" she shouted. "That fault line has got to be one hundred feet wide!" It was the western flank of the volcano separating west from east. The temperature in the air rose suddenly to a hundred and fifty degrees. "Sam? Sam! Can you hear me? It's begun! The ridge is failing!"

The ground violently trembled beneath their feet and the team ran for their lives.

Time was of the essence if surviving was the goal.

At that moment, as they sprinted for safer ground, a titanic explosion rocked the ridge and projectiles shot from multiple new steam vents.

"It's going to explode!" Chris warned sprinting with all he had to escape the steam venting in a circle around him.

"We have to make it to the plane!" Tish urged. "There's very little time now!"

But… time was the *least* of their worries.

Chapter 8

GENERAL ASSEMBLY

THE GLOBAL Disaster Alert and Coordination System was a joint initiative of the Coordination of Humanitarian Affairs and the European Commission.

GDACS usually convened in the U.N. Security Council Chamber where it served to consolidate the dissemination of disaster related information to advance the direction of international assistance efforts.

But, when the *shit* hit the fan, member-nations gathered in the General Assembly Hall.

Established in 2004, GDACS was a multi-hazard disaster monitoring and alert system for earthquakes, tsunamis, floods, volcanoes, and tropical cyclones.

That meant their business howled down Sam's bailiwick and he wasn't about to be pushed around by policy makers.

Sometimes, committees just get in the way.

Approaching the hall, he shouted into his cell phone. "Well, get your rump off that rock, Tish!" At that precise moment, the cell connection was lost and he turned to Will. "Bloody things are absolute tosh! In ten years we'll discover cell phones cause brain cancer!"

"That's already been discovered," Will answered.

"You ready to take them on?" V.I. nodded towards heavy walnut doors bearing the seal of the United Nations.

Shoving the cell phone into his pocket, Sam nodded and marched into the General Assembly Hall, the largest chamber at the U.N. with a seating capacity for eighteen hundred people.

"It's bigger than I expected," he whispered, scanning the interior before setting his eyes on two abstract murals hanging on either side of the Hall. They were designed by

French artist Fernand Leger and were donated through the U.N. Association of the United States. "The pictures give life to the staleness of the place, don't they?"

"The General Assembly is the central structure of the U.N.," V.I. advised trooping into the chamber. "It's where all Member States gather to discuss the unyielding glitches of our time, most involving countless continents and requiring international cooperation. The resolutions passed here are not legally binding, however, through recommendations, we can focus world attention on significant matters generating international cooperation and, in some cases, the conclusions we reach can lead to legally binding treaties and conventions."

"Where does that leave my disaster?" Sam chuckled. "My twigs and berries are flapping in the fire!"

"You have an uphill fight," V.I. agreed.

Suddenly, a notification alert erupted from Sam's tablet and when he glanced at it, he whistled.

"Is everything all right?" V.I. asked glancing at a video playing on the screen.

"Hydrothermal vents are erupting on La Palma," Sam winced. "My team has to dash off the ridge! It could blow at any moment!" Hurrying through the chamber, he scanned the faces of the international representatives and military personnel filling rows of seats.

Ahead sat a staged horseshoe shaped dais hosting representatives of the United States, Britain, Morocco, Portugal, France, Ireland, the Bahamas, Cuba, and Venezuela.

"It's show time, William!" Sam muttered heading for an English man garbed in a cheap, wrinkled, Seville Row suit. It had been quite some time since he laid eyes on Dr. Jack Robbins, a sixty-year-old British scholar and Sam's lead benefactor who now spoke excitedly to an African-American woman seated on the dais.

In Jack's hand a red laser pointed to a huge video monitor displaying a satellite image of the Canary Islands.

"That is why University College London has committed such time, energy, and, let me remind this body, money that it costs us to run such research!"

"Yes, yes, of course." Secretary Karin Soma interrupted. "But tell me one thing, what of the real catastrophic issue of the day? Be my hero, Dr. Robbins, will *this* volcano erupt or not?"

All heads turned when Sam cleared his throat, held up the Galaxy tablet and said: "It's not a question of *if* Cumbre Vieja collapses, Madam Secretary. It's simply a question of *when!*"

The representatives' gasped while watching Sam rush down the green-carpeted aisle towards Dr. Robbins.

"Oh, Samuel, thank the House of Lords you've arrived! The wankers have been eating me alive!"

"Darn buggers, aren't they? I'll *cow bosh* the bastards from here." He was about to dampen the mood; to spoil everything the assembly wanted to hear.

"Dr. Samuel May," Ms. Soma smiled respectfully. "Good to see you again. Please, come forward and let us hear directly from the horse's mouth, as it were."

Jack whispered into Sam's ear. "She is heading this *cataclysm* for the Office for the Coordination of Humanitarian Affairs."

It was a big title for an administrative role, Sam knew. They'd tangoed once or twice before on disaster preparedness. "Let me have at the duffer," he whispered glancing to his friend with a smile.

"Good day, Karin. It's unfortunate we must cog the system with un-pleasantries today."

"Drop the nonsense, Samuel," Karin growled. "If your disaster predictions prove true, we don't have time to waste on pleasantries."

Stepping to an unoccupied seat at a conference table, he placed the tablet on the table and grabbed the laser from Jack. Pointing it at the smallest island up on the screen, he bellowed, "Madam Soma and international representatives, we await the birth of a cataclysm like modern man has never dared imagine! I predict the collapse of the volcano Cumbre Vieja, an active ridge, on Isla de La Palma."

The Hall erupted with excited protests as he fingered the tablet sending computer-generated simulations to the hall's huge screen. There, CGI animations showed the volcano exploding in ash and lava, and soon after, crashing into the Atlantic Ocean.

That brought screams of damnation.

"The United Nations will soon be underwater!" Sam yelled over the uproar. "The East Coast of America will be wiped off the face of the Earth and London will drown beneath a surge!"

Chapter 9

PUSHING ASHORE

SANTA CRUZ de la Palma sat shrouded in a heavy layer of black smoke along its eastern shore.

Its highest peaks loomed 5,900-feet above sea level and offered fantastic sloping panoramic views.

Those vistas carried in the cruise ship sightseers.

They'd march along ancient cobbled streets, reach deep into euro-lined pockets and spend millions on offbeat arts and crafts. Here, they'd soak up the glorious sun while street peddlers hawked handmade cigars.

But, on this day, the port lay in ruins, an unsuspecting victim of the massive earthquake. Its cobblestoned streets were nothing more than rubble; the steppingstones heaved from the earth that once held them captive. The historic shops had collapsed, raging fires leapt through the hillside, and the once scenic coast was little more than a war-like scene of wreckage and shattered memories.

In the harbor, a tall ship was sinking, its crew leaping from her bow where they splashed through warm summer seawater reeking of diesel fuel.

Beside that listing ship, seamen on a pilot boat tossed life preservers to survivors desperately treading water.

"Nadar! nadar! Agarrar el salvavidas!" a Spanish sailor yelled. He wanted them to *swim* for the life preservers.

But those in the sea were unprepared tourists and hadn't a clue what he hollered. So they flailed their arms, panic settling in their stares, the realization that death chased their souls in the once beautiful island paradise.

Then, a horn loudly blew and the pilot boat sailors peered towards a massive cruise ship with *Valencia* painted on her side.

That's where a bald Hawaiian captain stood on its bridge staring through a pair of large binoculars.

He was Captain Grayson Maka, a fifty-two-year-old storied officer with Atlantic Cruise Lines who'd made his career on quick, precise assessments with the safety of his passengers in mind.

"Unbelievable!" he grunted to his crew. "Take a look at this chaos!" He recalled, just then, the worst passenger ship disaster since the sinking of the Titanic.

The Italian cruise ship, *Costa Concordia*, had partially sunk after running aground at Isola del Giglio, in Tuscany. With forty-two-hundred people aboard, the ship was on the first leg of a voyage from Civitavecchia, Italy, when it plowed into a reef during a near-shore salute to locals.

Dumbass, the captain thought. *Diverging from the ship's computer-programmed route, claiming he was familiar with the local seabed.* When learning of that wreck, he was off the coast of Spain commanding a five-day cruise. He'd never allow such atrocities to occur on his voyages.

To him, commanding meant maintaining control.

His thoughts were interrupted by his First Mate, Fern Noord, a thirty-year-old Swedish mariner, who busily pushed buttons on the navigation control panel.

"Are we going straight through to Tenerife, Captain?"

"Set a course, Fern," he answered, lowering the binoculars. "This port is devastated, we can't disembark passengers. Let's head straight on, full speed ahead!"

"Aye, aye, Captain," Fern replied. He was proud to be *First Mate* on the Valencia and wouldn't want any other assignment. If he knew anything about his captain, he understood when disaster struck this was THE CAPTAIN to right the ship.

But nobody believed a disaster would find them.

Through the bridge window, the captain scanned the shattered shoreline and took in the sight of the raging fires leaping across the rooftops.

Heavy plumes of smoke swirled into the thin air.

"It's going to be some time before ships return here," Fern mumbled in disappointment. "It's a tragedy, that's what this is."

In the distance, desperate screams of agony confirmed that assessment. The taking of life was underway.

What nobody knew, but everyone would soon find out, was the worst was yet to come for Valencia.

Chapter 10

ANGELIC WINGS

TENERIFE'S NORTH AIRPORT was one of two international airfields connecting the island to the world.

The worst aviation accident in history happened here.

It occurred in 1977 when two Boeing 747s collided in heavy fog and exploded.

Nearly six hundred people died.

Today… the airport lay in ruins.

The terminal's rooftop buckled onto thousands of unsuspecting passengers. Gas line explosions finished them off, ripping apart their bodies, as the modern building detonated in a spray of shattering glass.

Out on the runway, sinkholes swallowed jumbo jets which only moments before prepared for takeoff. Injured travelers wandered the demolished taxiways, their faces blackened by smoke; the clothes hanging tattered from bleeding bodies… pools of bright red blood staining the shattered concrete ground.

It was a scene from *Dawn of the Dead.*

There were few survivors.

On a clear patch of taxiway, an Italian Navy Agusta Bell SH-3D helicopter sat surrounded by Swiss Guard as a line of SUVs crossed the airfield, stopped at the chopper, and deposited Pope Callixtus and his entourage of cardinals.

"Lord Jesus!" the Holy Father exclaimed passing beneath the chopper blades. To either side of the bird, lifeless corpses lined the field.

"How many have we lost to this tragedy?" one of the elder cardinals asked, glancing toward the bodies.

"The numbers are said to be great," Cardinal Jonathan mumbled and climbed onto the airframe strapping Callixtus into his seat.

They had just journeyed along the devastated seashore, leaving behind the demolished basilica and thousands of dying and deceased worshippers.

"I feel as though I must do something, say something," Callixtus muttered glancing out the window.

"And, so you shall," Jonathan nodded.

"Unacceptable," the pope grunted glancing at the cardinals and Swiss Guard crowding the cabin.

They were his closest advisors and protectors who now stared at him grasping the gold papal rosary while muttering a prayer.

As the helicopter lifted off, Callixtus regarded the fractured landscape below. The once beautiful homes that had peppered the shoreline were now flattened, the roads leading up to them all disappeared into sinkholes, and the wounded homeowners wandered amongst their once storybook lives.

Nothing remained in Tenerife except memories.

"Are you okay, Papa?" Cardinal Jonathan asked.

It's all gone, Callixtus thought, ignoring his assistant. *Why have they forsaken me? Why didn't they give me more time?*

Just four weeks into his papacy, the fledgling pope had deep reservations about being elected to the papacy. He didn't want the job and didn't expect to be elevated as the leader of a billion Catholics.

In fact, Cardinal Carlos of Spain was the *longest* of long-shots for being named pontiff. Nobody believed a 45-year-old could get the votes needed to lead a broken church into the next century.

Scandals, lawsuits, sex-allegations... they all tarnished the image of the Catholic Church.

But here Carlos was... dressed in white papal vestments in a heavily fortified helicopter flying above a shattered landscape far away from Rome. Arriving into the priesthood young, he moved up the ladder fast. By the age forty, he was named Cardinal of Barcelona and quickly became known as a tireless trailblazer in human rights and a tireless advocate of the poor.

That's exactly what the conclave of cardinals voted for, it's what they needed, to reinvigorate the globe with a groundbreaker who'd relate to the average JOE who was struggling to feed his family.

VATICAN ELEVATES 'EVERYDAY MAN'

Barcelona Cardinal Named
Callixtus the Fourth

That was the headline in the New York Times.

Cardinal Carlos of Barcelona was now the pope.

But none of that mattered now.

Watching the shattered landscape fade to the deep cobalt sea off the Santa Cruz coast, the inexperienced Holy Father questioned his very being.

What is my purpose, God? I need a purpose to see me through this upcoming madness!

He knew there was a conspiracy in the church and understood that he must be the one to reveal their ancient secrets. But, he was too late. The planet was facing destruction; the environment had been destroyed by years of abuse by mankind... Earth's weather patterns had changed, natural disasters were trending across the globe, and nobody was paying attention.

Connecting the dots was an easy undertaking for anyone willing to draw the lines of common sense, but humanity was a selfish entity.

The ecosystem of Earth is dying...

Then, the pope's thoughts were traumatized by the imagery of splattering blood. "Good God!" he mumbled and came back to his senses, staring at the bloodstained Plexiglas. Then, something slammed into the aircraft.

"Holy mackerel!" Cardinal Jonathan whined glimpsing the horror of the blood upon the window.

"Cardinal Jonathan!" the pope screamed.

However, before he could utter another word, a bird slammed straightaway into the window, and then another. Unknown to anyone on board, they were the same Eurasian Sparrow Hawks that had taken flight from the basilica. After being frightened by the earthquake, they took flight for this collision with the chopper's jet engine.

Suddenly, the airframe began to shudder, its engine droned piercingly, and thick black smoke billowed past the cabin windows.

"Shepherd One," a voice boomed from the cockpit. "We have a Bird Aircraft Strike Hazard. Mayday! Mayday! We are going down!"

"Roger, Shepherd One," a static-filled voice responded. "We have radar tracers on you, over!"

"I need a landing zone!"

Callixtus peered through his bloody window at the outline of a vessel making way through the Atlantic Ocean.

"Down there! I see a cruise ship!"

At that moment, the cabin aggressively quaked and the airframe dropped more rapidly.

"We're going down!" the pope cried. Grasping his rosary, he whispered a plea to the heavens. *I submit my will to thee, for what comes next, I accept that circumstance.*

"Sweet Jesus!" Jonathan exclaimed.

Then, the engine coughed, the chopper dropped.

Shepherd One was going down.

Chapter 11

ROTTEN PEACHES

ATLANTA'S HARTSFIELD-JACKSON International Airport sprawled seven miles south of downtown.

Meteorologist Mark Langford had carried his bones through the check-in counter hundreds of times. He was a middle-aged frequent flyer with a million miles logged in the great blue sky. With e-tickets and the convenience of checking in from the Global Airlines app on his iPhone, he wasn't bothered in the least by the inexcusably rude TSA troglodytes.

People at a funeral are happier.

Perry Whitson didn't like airports. He was old school and remembered when jumbo jets crashed frequently… back when Eastern Airlines and PAN AM would either get you to your scheduled destination on time, or plummet to the Earth in a fiery explosion.

You see where those airlines are now? he thought. *Out of business, sold off to the highest bidders with safer flight inspections and better trained pilots.*

Perry was the senior producer and editor at Atlanta's WATL Channel 5 News. *Five on the Scene* was their tagline, but most often, they were the last to show up at news scenes. Part of an aging dinosaur of news organizations, they had a ton of debt and an ever dwindling viewership thanks to social media and downloads.

Nobody watches news anymore, he thought. *They all browse the internet. What a racket! Impression advertising, cost per clicks. What a bunch of horseshit.*

Biting into a peach he'd just bought, he found it rotten.

"Aw, shit," he grumbled turning to Mark. "Even in Georgia I get screwed by rotten fruit? What is it with peaches, anyway? They're either too hard to bite or rotten in spots you can't see! How often do you find a really good peach anywhere?"

Mark chuckled as they approached the Advanced Imaging Technology security scanner.

"Aw, shit," Perry whined staring at the peach.

"I rarely eat them," Mark shrugged. "Besides, did you know Georgia isn't really the Peach Capitol of the World?"

"It's not?"

Shaking his head, Mark grinned. "Although our state calls itself *The Peach State*, Johnston, South Carolina actually grows a lot more peaches and they love exposing Georgia as the fraud that it is."

"I should've gotten my peach there, then," Perry griped. "Funny what we learn nowadays working in television. All the useless trivia gives me headaches. What happened to real news? Like C.I.A. assassination conspiracies and billionaire investment bankers running off with grandma's retirement fund? Now it's all shootings and murder."

"That's all on Al Jazeera," Mark answered. "The network that used to show Americans being beheaded by the Taliban now has a U.S. channel. Can you believe it? And, our station is more interested in bullshit news!"

Perry sighed. Changing the subject, he brought his ire back to his peach. "Does anyone really eat South Carolina peaches?"

"Sure," Mark fondly recalled. "In April, the wife and I went to Johnston's annual Peach Blossom Festival. The town holds it every year on the first Saturday. We were treated to homestyle food, browsed handmade crafts and then took in a free music festival. It's one of the prettiest towns we visit in spring."

"No, shit, huh? A festival surrounding baskets of peaches? What a racket that is!" Watching a group of TSA agents searching an elderly woman's wheelchair, he noticed they were forcing her to stand while inspecting the chair seat like it hid some device from a Ray Bradbury Novel. *Hello! Does she look like an Afghani with a backpack bomb?* He considered the ridiculous obtrusive searching of American citizens at airports something similar to Nazi Germany street seizures.

Stepping into the scanner, he raised his hands over his head, placed his thumb and forefinger together in the shape of a spade and waited for the see-through technology to search his bowels. The machine could literally detect anything inside the human body.

It put drug smuggling mules out of business.

Of course, the TSA would take milk from a baby.

Waiting for Mark to follow him through the scanner, Perry proceeded to the conveyor belt and grabbed his shoes, belt, laptop, and personal effects.

This was his least favorite part of the screening process, being half-dressed in front of god knows who, while running for a plane about to depart the gate.

Thinking of the Police State America had become, he couldn't help but recall a piece of artwork at Denver International Airport showing a Nazi-like soldier pointing an assault weapon towards passengers.

"Hey, Mark, remember that twisted painting at DIA?" he asked while slipping on his leather shoes. "The soldier dressed in a Nazi uniform with that weird symbol on his hat, the face covered by a gas mask while weeping parents clutched their dead babies? The mothers were crying, with their kids lying dead on the bricks, the corpses showing no visible signs of injury, almost as if they were killed by lethal gas descending from the rainbow?"

Mark nodded and pulled his belt through the loops of his Levi 501s. Recalling the brutality of the painting's imagery, he winced. "It's a ridiculous painting for an international airport, huh? That soldier holding a rifle in one arm, and a steel sword in the other piercing the body of a dove, I remember that; who could forget?"

Slinging laptop bags over their shoulders, the two made haste along the concourse to the departure gate.

"That's not the only weird thing about Denver airport," Perry went on, his sense of a story coming on. "I've spoken to some people who believe there's an alien base beneath the airport which will bring in a new world order."

"Is that right?" Mark chuckled. "What did corporate say when you proposed that story?"

"You know what the spit-shiners did? They laughed me out of their steel and glass skyscraper and asked me to tone down the rhetoric... spelling it, R-H-E-T-O-R-I-C... just like that. The VP of Programming didn't care about the apocalyptic horse with its glowing red eyes welcoming the airport travelers. They shrugged off my descriptions of the sick demented paintings, and don't get me started on the indecipherable words embedded in the floors."

"Ha-Ha-Ha! You aren't going to be spreading this at the conference in London, are you?"

"Ah," Perry waved him off. "You non-believers think you know everything. There are things unexplained in the world you know... everything's not so cut and dried. Did you know a million people disappear every year in the United States? Poof! Just like that, gone!"

"You're about to retire next year," Mark offered and glanced at their gate. "One more calendar turn and you can chase down those conspiracies in your big RV."

> "Global Airlines Flight 2291," a boarding agent called out on a microphone, "would like to invite our Gold Member Elite passengers to proceed to the Jetway for our direct service to London's Heathrow International Airport."

Walking to the agent, Perry scanned the barcode on the screen of his phone and led Mark through the breezeway and down the ramp.

It was time to fly the friendly skies.

Chapter 12

RUN FOR YOUR LIVES!

TISH SCRAMBLED along the quaking ridge.

The steam vents pugnaciously blasted scorching air, soil and rocks from the sopping earth. Trees shook themselves free of their roots and plummeted to the ground.

It was hell on Earth.

"We have to make it to the plane!" She shouted moments before a colossal explosion assaulted the hillside.

The thundering blast shifted the ridge just behind her… and when turning to peer towards the painful pleas for help, she helplessly watched the ground swallow five researchers into an enormous sinkhole.

Darting thoughtlessly in their direction to help, a massive vent expelled huge boulders from the soil.

It's useless, she thought, stopping in her tracks.

"Run for your lives!" she howled in horror, dashing for safety …seemingly *in slow-motion*… like a sight from a disaster movie set right after the director yells ACTION!

But, Chris didn't need to be told when to haul ass. He ran with all he had, leading the last remaining researcher away from the blowing sinkhole.

That's when a boulder the size of Mount Rushmore blasted from the vent, tore through the hillside, and plummeted back to Earth where it crashed atop the last absconding researcher.

Chris tripped over fumbling feet and collapsed on a patch of scorching, wet sludge. Balancing himself on one knee, he was frozen in fear at the sight of the dead researcher's mangled arm protruding from beneath the boulder just feet from where he knelt.

It was the only evidence he'd ever lived.

"Professor!" Tish screamed, scrambling to her shaken colleague. His stare was blank and he trembled in what looked like shock. Grabbing his arm, she pulled him to his feet. "Chris! Snap out of it! We must reach the plane!"

They hurried through the disintegrating hillside, dodging fragments of rock and bark, shielding their eyes from projectiles blasting through the ridge like wayward bullets.

And then, just up ahead, only a stone's throw away, they glimpsed a clearing that led to the safety of the airplane, and perhaps, an opportunity to escape the exploding volcano. So, they ran, for all they were worth, battling through the trembling hillside, until *finally,* they cleared the collapsing tree line and bounded onto the fracturing blacktop runway.

"The plane!" Chris shouted in relief at the sight of the Beechcraft. Darting for its passenger door, he climbed into the cockpit and strained to catch his breath. "Get this thing started and off the ground!"

Tish shrugged off her backpack and tossed it into the back of the cabin while pushing the ignition button.

Nothing.

"Come on… start!"

"Oh, my God!" Chris cried, panic blazing in his eyes. "It's not going to start!"

She ignored his panic and frantically pushed the start button again.

The engine *coughed...* the propeller blades *spun twice* and then *stopped dead.*

In the background, the volcano thundered, spewing hellish steam and spreading thick gray ash into the air.

Tish flipped a few control panel switches and again pressed the start button.

The engine turned over, coughed, and then failed.

"Jeez, Tish, come on!"

"Start, you son of a bitch!" she growled, slamming the palm of her hand against the instrument panel, and punching the button again.

The engine *moaned*, turned over, and *roared* to life.

"Yes!" Chris cried in delight.

Pushing the throttles, she shouted encouragement to the airframe. "Move your ass! You old piece of junk!"

The ash covered plane responded.

It sped down the blacktop, cutting a path through the ash-covered airstrip. That's when the western flank of the volcano exploded and released a bursting flow of lava that raced down the ridge towards the fleeing plane.

Chris went into a panic pointing through the windscreen at the advancing lava flow. "It's going to cut off our path!"

Fiery orange magma flowed onto the blacktop.

Chris sniveled. "We're not going to get off this rock!"

"Yes, we are!" Tish insisted, pulling the trembling yoke... and grinning in triumph when the plane's nose lifted skyward.

Then, the lava flow swamped the blacktop and popped the tires. But they were airborne.

"You did it!" Chris clapped. "We freaking made it!" Glancing at the island below, he watched the magma drowning the telescopes and setting everything afire.

At that moment, the ridge exploded in a spray of dirt and rocks... peppering the fleeing fuselage.

"What the hell!" Tish questioned at the sound of debris smashing into the underbelly of the plane.

Suddenly, the aircraft began losing altitude.

"We're going to crash, Tish! We're going down!"

As the airframe plummeted for the rocky ridge and certain death, the last thing Professor Chris Grossman thought was this: *I should have kissed my wife goodbye.*

Chapter 13

KEEP 'EM DRINKING

MSS VALENCIA was on her maiden voyage.

She was the largest cruise ship in the world.

When Captain Maka brought the ship into its home port of Fort Lauderdale three months earlier, he recalled how the sight wowed awaiting media.

They were stunned with Valencia's supreme elegance.

Standing on the bridge now, he stared at the sea. "It's a great ship," he muttered to his first mate.

"It's the best in the world, Skipper," Fern agreed glancing to a wall of video monitors that surveyed a replica *Statue of Liberty*, encircled by cafés and specialty shops where performers entertained the passengers.

A regeneration of the *Empire State Building* rose through the courtyard where a magnificent glass elevator ferried passengers to the sundeck's pools. There was a realistic looking recreation of *Central Park* hosting the first living botanical garden at sea.

"This ship is incredible, Captain!" Fern stated in appreciation. "I'm grateful you chose me as your First Mate."

"You deserve it," the skipper grinned. "You've paid your dues and climbed the ranks in Atlantic Cruise Lines."

It was true… Fern *had* fought the mighty sea for ten years, working his way up from a stateroom steward on a three day Bahamas itinerary to this ten-day transatlantic.

Staring back to the sundeck monitor, Fern scanned the *Water Park* featuring a sloped beach with real sand… numerous pools and three surf simulators that produced waves.

"How're the passengers getting on?" the captain asked.

"I was *astern* earlier; it's a real party back there."

"What's going on?"

"The waiters are selling thousands of Lava Flows... the little umbrella glass toppers are littering the pool deck."

The Hawaiian drink got its name from its vibrant red and yellow colors–*from strawberries and bananas*–and the way it appeared in the glass.

"Valencia's skilled bartenders," the captain chuckled, "sure know how to layer that concoction in our chilled glasses, so the liquefied strawberries look like they're flowing down the inside of the glass."

Fern laughed. "The passengers are lined up like cattle."

"Keep them drinking," the skipper sniggered. "That's the motto of a happy Captain." Moving on to more important business, he changed the subject. "Did you make an announcement about the earthquake?"

"Yes, Sir, I announced we're headed to Tenerife."

"That's good, because this FAM is jam-packed to capacity with fifty-five hundred cruise agents and travel writers from around the globe. This *trip* is designed to give them a genuine feel for the voyage, so they recommend Valencia to potential customers back home. And if alcohol helps make that sale, Atlantic Cruise Lines will be glad to provide an ocean of liquor."

The ship was now five days into its cruise with ports in the Canary Islands, Barcelona, Marseille, Naples, and Rome.

But the earthquake in Santa Cruz changes things.

The skipper was lost in his concerns of the tremor when a radio operator shuffled up beside him.

"Sir, we have a chopper coming in hard for an emergency landing on deck-one and you're not going to believe who's onboard."

"Well, try me."

"It's Shepherd One."

The captain shrugged. "What is Shepherd One?"

"It's the Pope, Skipper."

"Jesus, Mother Mary and Joseph!" Fern bellowed moving beside the radio operator.

"No, just the Pope," the radio operator grinned.

Picking up his binoculars, the captain peered into the sky and observed the outline of the helicopter trailing heavy plumes of smoke.

"Son, can you raise them on the radio?"

"Sure thing, Captain, what should I say?"

"Tell them they're cleared for an emergency landing."

Chapter 14

THE CHAMBER

THE GRAND HALL was silent.

Sam flipped through photos on his tablet. As he did so, images of the volcano ridge appeared on the enormous screen in the hall. "Hydrothermal explosions are occurring within Cumbre Vieja. During the 1949 discharge, Duraznero, San Juan, and Hoyo Negro vents opened and fiery lava poured out during two earthquakes that fractured the western flank shifting the ridge towards the Ocean."

"Yes, of course," Karin interrupted. "But that was a long time ago, Sam. There's been none since then, right?"

"Wrong. There was the '71 discharge at the Teneguia Cinder Cone volcano vent. That eruption was strombolian in style and lots of lava erupted."

"We're talking forty plus years ago," Karin shrugged.

Sam flipped through the photos, selected one and sent it to the Grand Hall's screen. There, a gigantic photo showed a snaking fracture scarring the ridge of Cumbre Vieja, presenting a fault line similar to California's San Andreas.

"Will today's quake cause ridge failure?"

"Like none we've ever witnessed," Sam assured. "The process will be caused by pressure of rising superheated water trapped inside the volcano. That liquid will heat to a point where it cannot absorb thermal energy in the available space. Thus, the volcano must expand, and the only way *that* can happen is for the ridge to move."

"When you say move, Dr. May –"

"The earthquake will shake La Palma so critically," he interrupted. "The unstable western ridge of the volcano will collapse along the fracture and crash into the ocean."

At this juncture, Will handed Sam a can of Coke.

"Look at this can," Sam shouted holding it up for everyone to see. "It's merely a simple aluminum can containing carbonated water, right?"

"Yes," Karin smiled. "It's just water."

Nodding agreement, Sam shook the can.

Popping a pen into its side, the liquid exploded from the puncture in a violent spray of foam and gushing soda.

"Just like this soda, the water inside our volcano has nowhere to escape unless it blows apart."

The video changed to a CGI simulation of the ridge exploding and sliding towards the ocean.

Gasps erupted from the delegates, and then, dead silence filled the chamber as everyone stared towards the imagery on the enormous screen.

Aiming his stare across the Great Hall, Sam spread his arms in a sign of helplessness.

"I don't know what else to say here today other than to stake my reputation on the fact this volcano will explode; the detonation will cause the ridge to fail and crash into the Atlantic Ocean. Once that transpires, tons of displaced seawater will push a tsunami towards several seashore nations."

"What of the warning systems?" Karin shouted above the cacophony of human voices arguing the circumstance. "How long do we have from first notice of the collapse?"

Sam shook his head. "My team has already received first warnings. Within the last hour a lahar detection system has indicated displacement has begun."

The chamber erupted in heated arguments.

"Order! Order!" Karin yelled banging a wooden gavel on the tabletop. Glancing to an American military contingent, she pointed to their leader. "I'd like to defer to the U.N. Security Council committee on natural disaster preparedness. Admiral Brancor, take it from here."

Lew Brancor was in his late fifties and was the American President's 'Man in Charge' when it came to natural hazards and oceanic catastrophes. Standing from his seat, he marched over to the volcanologist.

"Sam, here we are again. Haven't you been suggesting this cataclysmic event would occur for the past fifteen years? I've heard this argument twice before."

"Somewhere around there, Lew, maybe a bit less."

"Aren't you barking out your ass again with this *maybe, possibly*, once upon a time, BS story?"

"Spare the rod, Lew, you know I don't bark. This volcano will explode, and that tsunami will impact Morocco, Portugal, the East Atlantic and then, the United States and all your naval ships."

Unexpectedly, the Great Hall doors slammed open and a Paige hurried in. "Madam Soma," the excited female called. "The Global Affairs office just received urgent notice that the volcano has erupted!"

That's when Agent Holland jumped from his seat, hurried to the admiral and handed over a cell phone.

"What's this, Sir?" Lew asked.

"It's the President of the United States."

Chapter 15

WE'RE ALL GONNA DIE!

THE BEECHCRAFT BARON cost the United States Geological Survey a million dollars.

It was a respectable airplane with the ability to carry five passengers nine hundred miles on a tank of petroleum.

There had never been a *problem...* until now.

Chris stared through the cockpit windows at a *two-mile-long* crack along the western ridge of the volcano.

It was widening!

"La Palma tower!" Tish shouted into the Denali Dual Input Stereo Headset. "This is BC-122, come back!"

There was no answer.

"The volcano is failing!" Chris shouted realizing his life's work was about to be proven true.

The plane had dropped more than 1,500 feet towards the jagged ridge after the debris struck the fuselage.

"Pull it up, Tish! Pull back the yoke!" His face was drenched with sweat, the blood running through his veins boiled. A heart attack threatened to explode in his heaving chest.

Tish fought, struggling with the yoke, desperately trying to pull out of the dive. Pushing the throttles to full power, the twin-engines roared. "Crap! Come on, piece of crap!"

But, nothing happened.

The aircraft continued towards the jagged cliffs.

"Grab your yolk, Chris, and pull with all you have!"

"I don't know how to fly!"

She cursed him, recalling the day he'd requested extra funds to lengthen the fuselage in order to increase space for scientific equipment. Everyone had warned that overequipping the prop-plane with thousands of pounds of monitoring devices would cause issues.

And here they were, fighting for survival.

That extra weight in the back might cost us our lives.

"Mayday... Mayday! La Palma control, this is BC-122 announcing an immediate air emergency!"

Nothing, only static filled the cockpit.

Tish considered the flight thus far. Upon escaping the erupting volcano, they flew due west towards Santa Cruz. Yet, just as the airframe made the turn for the coast, an air pocket sucked the aircraft towards the ridge.

Air compartments were deadly for small airplanes.

They were caused by an updraft or downdraft of air and were usually a weather related phenomenon.

But *this pocket* was a downburst, *a microburst*, and it was deadly and difficult to predict. A similar one had caused Delta Flight 191 to crash on final approach at Dallas Fort Worth in 1985. That incident prompted the FAA to deploy storm detection radar stations at major airports.

But in the Canaries, those systems hadn't been installed.

The pocket causing the Beechcraft's dive was more likely caused by volcanic gases rising into Earth's atmosphere following the eruption.

And that is deadly for the twin-engine.

Shaking that thought from her mind, she glanced towards Chris grasping his co-pilot's yolk.

"Come on, you Sonuvabitch!" he hollered.

Below, they saw chaos gripping Santa Cruz.

People were fighting for their lives with lava chasing close behind.

Then, a warning system beeped.

"What is it, Tish?" Chris pointed to the gas gauge. "Are we running out of fuel?"

Glaring at the gauge, Tish scowled at the sight of the needle moving towards E. Looking out the window, she regarded the wing where fuel was escaping a small hole in the thin metal. "We're losing petrol!"

"We're gonna die!" Chris howled.

As pathetic as it seemed, she supposed he wasn't much off the mark. Death now seemed likely.

Chapter 16

IT'S A BIRD!

MIKEY COOK was an average sixteen-year-old Irish boy from New York City.

Transplanted to Delray Beach, Florida, at the age of ten, he was a fan of the *NY Yankees* and *Miami Marlins*–and he wasn't afraid to tell people about his favorite players.

That was especially true if *they* were from Boston...

The Red Sox suck the big banana.

With a Yankee cap tilted backward on his head, he lounged in the whirlpool on Valencia's sundeck slurping coke through a cheap plastic straw. The blazing sun scorched his fine pale skin and his mom busily applied a thick layer of sunblock to his shoulders.

"Ma! Give me a break with that crap, will ya?"

"You have to wear the sunblock, Honey. You're turning into a tomato!" Distracted by a passing Filipino waiter, she picked up an empty plastic margarita tumbler and waved to the attendant. "Yoo-hoo! Hello! I need another margarita, and make it a double!"

Next to Patty–*they called her that in her office at iCruising Corp*–her husband, George, held a Corona bottle to his lips while eyeing younger bikini-wearing twins splashing in a nearby pool.

That's when Mikey glimpsed something barreling through the sky trailing thick black smoke. The speck was so far off, it resembled a black dot.

"Mother! Check it out! It's a UFO or something!"

"It sure isn't Superman," a tipsy retiree mumbled stepping from the whirlpool and shielding his eyes. "What the heck is that?"

"Mom! Mom!" Mikey squealed. "What is that thing on fire in the sky?"

"What's that, Mike?" Patty mumbled, handing over her *Sail & Sign* ship card to the waiter. "You're going to make it frozen, right?"

The plastic card resembled a credit card imprinted with the passenger's name, photo, and assigned dining room. It allowed guests to charge purchases and was connected to a credit card on file with the cruise line.

"Yes, Madam," the man smiled while swiping the card on a mobile reader. "A double shot of tequila will be in the drink." Ripping a receipt from the machine, he handed it over and watched her sign the $16.00 authorization.

"C'mon, you guys are making a killing!"

Mikey rolled his eyes and shook his head. *They never pay attention to me, especially when alcohol was in their vicinity.* Glancing to his father, he saw dad winking at the girls.

"What's that?" Dad mumbled without looking.

"Pop! C'mon! Look in the sky!"

His father sighed. "Leave your mother and me alone, Mike, we're on vacation."

Patty smiled at George... *and then* noticed him flirting with the girls. Moving beside her husband of twenty years, she whacked him on the head. "What the hell are you doing, huh? Don't pull that Brooklyn street corner crap on me you no good son of a bitch!"

"What? This is Spain and we're on the best cruise ship in the world!"

"What's that got to do with anything?"

"It's a little wink, that's all I'm saying."

"Are you kidding me right now, a little wink?"

The waiter returned with the frozen margarita, handed it over and watched the spectacle unfolding.

"It's just a wink," George chuckled motioning to the drink. "Sip your attitude changer, will ya?"

Mikey, eyeing the approaching fireball, leapt from the whirlpool, trooped to his parents and pointed to the now clearly visible helicopter barreling towards the ship.

"Pop! Mom! Look! It's a freaking helicopter!"

Glancing into the sky their faces filled with panic.

"This wasn't in the *FAM* brochure," George mumbled, forgetting all about the girls and bringing his attention to his family. Pulling them through a mob of screaming passengers he peered nervously at the chopper.

"It's a helicopter!" someone yelled.

"It's going to crash!" a kid screamed.

Shepherd One *was* headed directly for the ship.

Pandemonium broke out.

The passengers scrambled along the deck, pushing and shoving one another with panicked shrieks escaping their lips, much like b-list actors in front of a green screen.

"Holy shit!" a brunette screamed, "we're all dead!"

And that's how it looked.

As for Mikey... he wasn't afraid, but wanted to experience the disaster up close! He belonged to a generation of PlayStation III and X-Box gamers. *Maybe I'll catch a video clip for my Facebook friends and YouTube channel.* "Whoa, this shit is way too cool!"

Chapter 17

A LOAD OF TOSH!

GORDON HOLLAND had been a Navy SEAL.

Up until two years ago, he hiked through Forward Operating Base (FOB) Restrepo in the Korengal Valley of Afghanistan. He had been attached to the Second Platoon, B-Company, 2nd Battalion, and 173rd Airborne Brigade Combat Team of the United States' Red Blooded Army.

The unit had stalked the mountains in search of Taliban leaders and *public enemy number one…*

Gordy remembered the deck of cards he'd kept in his fatigues with that face printed center on the Ace of Spades.

Osama hole-in-the-head, Bin Laden.

He now slept with the fishes….

Recently, the whispers around the White House supposed Gordy was part of the *A-team* who led the raid on the Pakistan house. He might've even killed the 911 mastermind. Nobody knew for sure.

That kind of stuff was top-secret information known only to a few CIA operatives with top level security clearances. What everyone did know was that Gordy was later handpicked by the President himself, and somehow got assigned as the President's *body man.*

"Right this way, fellas," he motioned to the Great Hall doors of the United Nations. "You guys have an appointment in Washington."

He was also the *Agent in Charge* of a special detail that provided physical protection to the nation's highest priority government bureaucrats–at the president's personal order.

"Where are you taking us?" Sam complained. "Don't we have a say in our own movements about America?"

"Not today, Sir."

In order to safeguard his unenthusiastic clients, he never revealed specific methods of security procedures, not even when those decisions directly influenced the freedom of his charges.

Today is no exception.

Sam, Will, and V.I. were now high priority guests of the United States of America.

"It's *a load of tosh*, that's what this is!" Sam bitterly complained as agents moved them through a doorway and down a long hallway.

"Right this way, Sir," Gordy pointed. "The President is awaiting your team in the PEOC."

The President's Emergency Operations Center was buried beneath the East Wing of the White House. It was capable of withstanding everything except a direct nuclear blast and was the president's evacuation point.

In general, Gordy was permanently assigned to protect POTUS and FLOTUS–the president and first lady.

But occasionally, *during a national crisis*, President Powell would dispatch him to grasp hold of an object of national interest.

That's what now brought him to push Sam and his team onto the streets of Manhattan.

Admiral Brancor approached. "I've been ordered back to the White House. Can you give me a lift?"

"Yes, Sir, Admiral," Gordy answered.

"Lew, what right does the President have to latch hold of us?" Sam complained. "It's kidnapping, I dare say!"

"You may dare anything you like, Samuel," Lew nodded to the door of the SUV. "But you've apparently been issued *Temporary Protective Status* here in country, much like any high profile candidate or foreign dignitary afforded temporary assignment from the Secret Service."

"You're a scoundrel!" Sam spat in aggravation to Gordy who busily buckled him into a seatbelt for the five-minute drive back to the 34th Street Heliport.

Gordon smiled. He'd been called worse by bigger men and now recalled another type of scoundrel he'd protected not long ago. The memory followed him like a hungry lost puppy at a Texas barbeque. It was a humid September evening at JFK Airport and he was just home from Afghanistan, when then Iranian Premier, Mahmoud Ahmadinejad, stepped from his plane leering at journalists, bureaucrats, and secret agents peppered throughout the pulsing crowd. It was Holland's first stretch working an Iranian dual-surveillance detail.

He shook his head now, lost in mental images of President Powell informing him to stay close enough to place a bullet between the Iranian's eyes if such an order was given.

"Why would the President want us in the White House?" Sam demanded, shaking Gordy back to the present. "If I were him, I'd be heading for the mountains of Camp David right about now!"

Lew snickered. "Tell him that when you meet."

"Bonkers, that what this is!"

The fact was… POTUS wanted Sam to explain one thing, and one thing only.

How could the White House save millions of Americans who lived along the eastern shores of the Unites States?

The president couldn't rely on human resources in local communities when designing a coastal evacuation that nobody really understood.

"I have to hear it from his own mouth," POTUS had advised Gordy earlier that morning. "Go fetch this British doomsayer from the U.N. and let's have a look at him."

That's how Sam found himself in *protective custody* against his will. He *was* the man with the plan, the numbers guy, and the lone ranger when it came to life saving factoids about the predicted *cataclysm*.

Gordy glanced at the frazzled volcanologist now staring out the window, seemingly lost to his miserable circumstances.

After all, when the secret service had your ass strapped into a bullet proof SUV, what were the alternatives?

"Lew, has there been any word on my wife?" Sam asked, his tone less aggravated, a streak of concern and hope ringing clear as a bell.

The admiral was speechless. He could say what he knew, or sit silent as the president had ordered.

"Come on. Surely information about the well-being of my wife is not a matter of national bloody security!"

But it *was* just that. A *secret*... a tidbit of information designated for *"eyes only"* or *"need to know."* Or, to be more truthful, it was a trading chip for the White House; a *tit-for-tat* bargaining tool to grasp the information the professor held deep in his brain.

"I'm not privy to such information," Lew lied. He knew all-too-well the latest dispatch. The FAA had sent word on order of the chief of staff that the Beechcraft transponder was reporting its position over the Atlantic Ocean just off the coast of Santa Cruz.

And that meant only two things, Lew considered. *Sam's wife was onboard or...*

"She's dead, isn't she?" Sam tearfully grunted staring into the admiral's eyes. "Tell me the truth, Lew."

As the armored vehicle pulled alongside a black helicopter, Gordy unlatched Sam's seatbelt and pointed to the door. "Perhaps they'll have news at the White House."

That's when reporters began to shout questions as Sam and his team stepped onto the concrete helipad.

"Dr. May! How long do we have?"

"Will a tsunami wipe out New York?"

"Suddenly, we're no longer quacks, huh?" Sam angrily spat at the leeches pointing cameras into his face, microphones desperately awaiting his words of impending doom. "My opinion now means something to you?"

"Congress calls your predictions ridiculous," a FOX News reporter yelled. "They allege this is all a conspiracy to trample the constitution and take away guns."

Sam turned on the reporter and laughed.

It wasn't a chuckle or a wayward snicker... this was a loud bursting fit of laughter right in the man's face.

"It's all a horse and pony show for you people, isn't it? I'm a segment of ridiculous entertainment for your political pundits!"

But before they could answer, Dr. May was pushed aboard the chopper behind Will and V.I.

As the chopper lifted above the hulking cityscape, Sam wondered how many millions in the concrete jungle below would perish when the wave came. *They can't save everyone. Some have to die for others to live.*

That was the order of the universe.

"God help us!" V.I. whispered.

"There is no God, my friend," Sam answered, lines of apprehension dancing on his face like a jigsaw puzzle.

"You have kids over there in the islands?"

"Four boys, they live in Orlando, Florida. I haven't lived in the islands for years."

"Disney World is sixty miles from the Atlantic," Sam shrugged. "They're safe that far inland. But there'll still be chaos in the Goofy Land."

"Why is that?"

"Looting and chaos, millions will flee to Orlando in order to escape death along the Atlantic Ocean shoreline."

"Shit."

"A big pile of it," Sam agreed.

Chapter 18

GNASHING TEETH

SHEPHERD ONE crash-landed in a ball of flames onto the crowded deck of Valencia.

Its scorched rotor-blades whipped through the crowd of ensnared passengers, the steel finding its deadly mark slicing through drunken flesh like a Ginsu knife.

"For Chrissakes!" Captain Maka shouted in shocked surprise at the gore playing out before him.

Bodies soared overboard and splashed into the ocean, bait for ravenous predators that lucked out on a free meal.

Running to the balcony rail and looking to the water fifteen decks below, the skipper cringed at the spectacle of tiger sharks circling screaming bodies.

Screams echoed through the air.

"Help me!" a man begged, hopelessly treading water, one of his arms ripped from its socket. He was gasping for air... wishing he'd booked a different cruise on another ship at a different time.

Then, in a scene right out of JAWS, the jagged teeth of a great white burst through the surface and chomped the screams to silence.

"Poseidon's ass!" the captain bellowed scanning the bloody water. Turning back to the raging fire engulfing the helicopter, he shouted to the deck hands to put out the fire.

They glanced briefly at their commander.

And then, the captain realized the reason for their cold glares. For just inside the chopper, quite probably, the leader of the Catholic Church lay dead.

Burned to a crisp, nice and toasty.

Then, right in the middle of that consideration, he overheard his second in command.

"Son of a gun!" Fern shouted running onto deck.

A dozen bodies were sprawled in pools of blood…and that was just the beginning of the horror.

"Get that helicopter door open!" the captain barked, approaching the smoldering airframe.

The painted seal of the Vatican was lost to the fire, and only blackened, charred metal remained. Unexpectedly, from somewhere inside the cabin, panicked voices erupted a second before the door exploded from its frame, soared overboard, and splashed into the sea.

Unknown to the captain, the detonation was the result of a light charge fixed to the molten door by the pope's security detail.

Surprisingly, through the curling smoke, a group of Swiss Guard appeared, jumped onto Valencia's charred wooden deck and pulled the pope from the chopper.

"Sorry to drop in like this, Captain!" Callixtus coughed. "I'm sure you understand, man plans and God laughs."

"Right this way!" the skipper nodded, pointing across the deck to a corridor leading into the ship.

"It's a miracle!" a passenger screamed.

Fern glanced at the woman standing beside a boy wearing a Yankee cap.

"Get a tender into the water," the skipper ordered. "Go find survivors!" The moment he uttered the words, he regretted them, knowing full well the sharks had feasted.

Patty made the sign of the cross above her heart and glanced to her son. "See Mikey? God watches out for those who believe!"

Mikey was posting a video of the crash on YouTube. "I've never seen anything like that! Not even in a Dwayne "the Rock" Johnson movie!"

His father chuckled. "Even the Pope has problems!"

"You're going straight to hell!" Patty grunted. "You know that, right, George? Do not pass go, no two hundred dollars… *straight on* to the devil's doorstep!"

"Why am I going to hell?"

"For talking about a Saint like that!"

"Who's talking about a saint? That's the Pope, and he's a man, not a saint. Now, *John Paul the Second*, him they made a saint."

She shook her head in amazement.

If Satan walked the Earth, she believed George was him. As far as she was concerned, Pope Callixtus was a saint.

On this day, few would argue that point.

Chapter 19

THE WHITE HOUSE

THERE WAS only one helicopter authorized to land on the South Lawn of the White House.

And that was *Marine One*.

It was the call sign of any United States Marine Corps aircraft carrying the President of the United States and symbolized a chopper operated by the HMX-1 Nighthawks Squadron.

They were the bad-asses of the sky.

And they ruled the night.

Gordy knew that sometimes rules were destined to be shattered. That was especially true when the country was at risk of destruction. So, at order of POTUS, clearance was granted to the black secret service bird and they went wheels down.

"Right this way!" Gordy directed everyone as they approached the West Wing.

Will and V.I. were in awe.

Before them, just beside the entranceway, a single U.S. Marine stood sentinel, his spine stiff as a board, the glare of his eyes displaying the seriousness of the storied post.

"This is incredible," Sam muttered. "He's absolutely brilliant, I say!"

Lew glanced at the Marine. "You like him, huh, Sam? There are four of our Marines on duty serving at the pleasure of the President. Each one works the door in thirty-minute shifts."

"It makes a strong first impression. They have quite the job, don't they?"

"You bet your scientific ass, they do. Notice how this Marine stands on gray stones and not the carpet leading to the door?"

Just then, a man emerged from the entryway and Sam watched as the Marine pivoted, held open the white door, and stood firm on a piece of black floor stripping separating the rug from a stone walkway.

"They do it the same way every single time," Lew nodded proudly to the Marine. "This is Corporal Appleton, one of my favorites. How are you, Son?"

"Sir, I'm standing tall! Good to see you again, Sir!"

"At ease, Son," Lew ordered, returning a rigid salute.

"They do that all the time?" Sam asked, spellbound by the formality and the snap of the soldier's wrist.

"As sure as the red, white, and blue blood that courses through their veins."

Passing through the doorway and into the West Wing, a tall jittery man approached. "The President is running behind a few minutes, Admiral. We're all set up in PEOC."

Motioning to Sam, Lew introduced his guests. "Robert, this is Dr. Sam May and William Squire from the Hazard Research Centre in London."

Then motioning to V.I., he nodded.

"And that's the U.N. guy, Mr. Oscar Thomas."

"Sure, sure," Robert replied shaking hands. Turning to Sam, he said. "I'm Robert Laslow, the White House Chief of Staff. My office informed me of your prior warnings and we spent time watching the documentary."

The Discovery Channel hour-long film spotlighted Sam's forecast of the catastrophic volcano collapse, and the lack of response from the United States government.

"Glad you saw it," Sam grimaced. "I'm unhappy it took this event to bugger an official response."

Leading them through a series of turns and then down an elevator, Mr. Laslow hurried along a corridor where they emerged in a tunnel beneath the White House.

"Are the satellites in position for a pass-by?" Lew asked. "We have a small window of opportunity."

The chief of staff nodded. "The Pentagon has the uplink; everything is green-lighted on our end."

They passed several joint service military officers and NCOs before continuing through a steel vacuum-sealed door with a brass plaque embossed with this:

Inside, Sam observed a group of staffers standing behind leather backed chairs encircling a large walnut conference table. On that table, before each chair, sat laptops and binders with *Project Cataclysm* printed on their covers.

"What in bloody hell does Project Cataclysm mean?"

The chief of staff turned to Sam. "The President has been following a string of predicted global natural disasters and this is the first major event on the list."

Sam grunted and flipped open the cover. "That's a tad dodgy, wouldn't you say? How could anyone know in what sequence cataclysms occur?"

"It's a matter of national security," Laslow responded.

National Security, Sam thought dismissively, *what does an earthquake in Spain have to do with that?*

"On the screens," Laslow stated pointing to TV displays; he rapidly changed the subject. "We're playing news stories from around the world."

Turning to a giant screen and a news report from Candelaria, he marched over to it.

"What's the current status of the quake?" Lew asked.

"There is massive loss of life," the National Security Advisor, Steven Richards, answered. "Many more are dying on all seven islands in the Canaries,"

"What about the volcano?"

Quiet.

And then, after Lew nodded approval, the national security advisor, spoke up. "The AFM monitors your team buried on that volcano have indicated slippage of the western ridge."

That's when President Powers marched through the door with his Vice President, Foster Logan, and an overweight Director of FEMA at his heels.

"Have a seat everybody," POTUS ordered. "Let's get this thing on the road and see where she leads." Collapsing onto an oversized leather chair, he flipped open a binder embossed in gold with the seal of the president.

Glancing up, he pointed to the TV news report.

"The V.P. and I were watching network coverage up in the oval office. Things aren't looking good." Glancing to Sam, he spread his arms. "Tell me, Sammy, that I'm not going to have to evacuate the east coast."

"I couldn't possibly advise you of such, Mr. President."

A hush extended around the conference table.

"What's my best shot here, then?" the president grunted. "Give me your gut feeling. If you were sitting in this seat, what would you advise the country?"

Sam peeked at the TV, and then stared back into the president's glare. "I can tell you what I personally believe, but it surely won't make me any friends in this room."

The president smirked. "Sam, thirty-five-million people *LIKE* my Facebook page, and I don't know any of them. Trust me, some friends are overrated."

"What the President needs to know," Steven Richards offered, "is which cities we must focus on evacuating in order to save the most lives *if* this thing really collapses."

Sam shook his head. He couldn't believe they still doubted. "Mr. President, make no mistake, Sir! Every American coastal city and town from Miami to Maine faces certain destruction *WHEN*... not *if*... Cumbre Vieja crashes into the Atlantic."

"That's not good, Sam! I knew you'd say that."

It was the wake-up call he expected.

America was facing certain destruction.

Chapter 20

THEY'RE DOOMED!

TISH STARED at the Beechcraft's gas gauge.

It was close to empty.

The earsplitting *whirr-RRRR* of the failing engines rattled the glass cockpit as unsecured objects flew through the cabin behind them.

Flying at 500 feet, she peered to the shattered landscape where lava flows flattened the hillside.

"We're running out of fuel!" she exclaimed, an expression of fatigue and astonishment twisting her expression.

The sight was devastating.

Gone were the elegant postcard scenes that once littered Santa Cruz, replaced by fiery fingers of molten rock pushing everything towards the seashore.

"We should head to Gran Canaria Airport!" Chris bellowed. "It's the only safe airport!"

But that wasn't true.

The research team had run multiple evacuation scenarios at Palisades Hydrophone Station over the years and, Tish knew when Cumbre Vieja failed, Sam's tsunami prediction model would prove true.

And that meant two things.

First, within thirty minutes, everything on the western shore of the Canary Islands would vanish.

Second, everything along their eastern shores would be flooded by the resulting surge.

So, landing anywhere in the islands is not an option, she realized. "I wanted to try for Africa, but we don't have enough fuel to make Casablanca, and even if we did, an hour from now, a three-hundred-foot wave might crash into the shore of Morocco."

Africa's long draught was about to end.

"Then, what're we going to do?" Chris worried placing a pair of binoculars to his eyes and staring to the Aeropuerto de Buena Vista. Planes were lined-up for take-off, *one after another*. Crowding the runway, the jets leapt into the sky eastward, like a funeral procession. "There's nowhere to land down there. Commercial aircraft are on every runway!" Looking for a landing strip, he observed lava snaking its way towards town.

"We have to make it to Gran Canaria!" Tish sighed.

"We're losing fuel, we won't make it!"

"I have to try," Tish argued. "Landing here will be the death of us for sure." As the plane struggled for altitude, she stared below at the fiery death creeping down the hillside.

"Those poor people," Chris groaned. "They're doomed to a scorching demise!"

It wasn't the first time the city faced a crisis.

Raided by pirates in 1493, the locals reconstructed and fortified their homeland against future attacks. Over the centuries, there had been multiple economic crises that caused the population to drop to 11,000.

In the future there'd be a sign that read:

Santa Cruz de la Palma: Población – 0
Population Zero

The coastline would be *gone…* washed out to sea by a river of lava guaranteed to drown the grand hotels and flamboyantly painted seaside homes.

"Look at all those people down there!" Tish pointed.

Realization of death caused men and women to dash along a long wooden dock jutting into the sea. At its end, they jumped onto overcrowded pleasure boats.

Fistfights broke out over the right to live.

That's when a woman pulled a gun and shot a man dead in broad daylight!

"Oh, my, it's so sad!" Tish moaned glimpsing a splash from the corner of her eye as the plane buzzed the docks.

Just below, an overweight man pushed an old woman into the water, started the engine of a stolen Sea Ray, and pushed into the marina in a desperate attempt of escape.

But he didn't get far. Half a dozen people leapt onto the boat and overtook control of her wheelhouse.

"Look!" Chris pointed excitedly.

The coastal town hosted the only port on the island with ferry routes to ports in Spain. That ferryboat was now congested with folks occupying its roof and sideboards.

As Chris and Tish stared at the heaving boat, it suddenly rolled to starboard and began to sink. And then... the Beechcraft was out to sea, flying over shipping lanes, the shore left behind to chaos that overtook its people.

The propellers stopped, the fuel line not delivering gas to power the twin-engines.

"We're going down, Chris!" Tish screamed. "We have to land on the water!"

Just ahead, the outline of a ship appeared.

"It's a vessel dead in the water!" Chris bellowed in disbelief. Peering through the binoculars, he saw the blackened, burned-out shell of a helicopter.

Along the side of the ship was painted:

THE VALENCIA

"If we set this deathtrap down," Tish hoped. "Maybe they can send someone out to help us!"

"Can you raise them on the radio?"

"What's the name of the ship?" she asked dialing in the VHF radio's transmitter to Channel-16.

It was an international channel used for distress calls.

"The Valencia."

"BC-122," she shouted into the radio, "this is an emergency broadcast to the cruise ship Valencia, do you copy, over?" Secretly, waiting in static noise, she wondered if the captain would think her crazy when he learned of her plan. "Valencia, come in. This is an emergency! We're declaring a crisis!"

Chapter 21

WE HAVE A SITUATION!

PRESIDENT POWERS had listened to the prophecies of disaster for over an hour.

"We have ourselves a situation!" Vice President Foster Logan interrupted Sam's prediction.

"That's an understatement!" Sam replied walking to the large screen displaying a Network News report of Tom Anderson seated in the cockpit of a helicopter.

The chopper was filming Cumbre Vieja's angry volcanic eruption. Lava covered the entire caldera; its blazing magma twisted its way down the elevation. In the sky above the island a mammoth ash cloud hovered.

The poisonous hulk consisted of pulverized rock fragments, minerals, and volcanic gases.

"What exactly is this?" the chief of staff asked. "It appears to be a mere volcano eruption."

"It is tephra," Sam answered. "And it forms during explosive eruptions when dissolved gases inside the magma expand and escape violently into the atmosphere. The force of that gas shatters the magma and propels it into the atmosphere where it solidifies into fragmented shards of volcanic rock and glass. The ash is produced when the magma comes into contact with water during phreatomagmatic eruptions, causing the water to explosively flash to steam leading to the shattering of magma."

"Yes, sure," the V.P. grunted in confusion. He didn't want to seem stupid, but the science was beyond his knowledge of a life in politics. "But, how is this eruption going to cause a tsunami here?"

At that moment, the voice of Tom Anderson interrupted. On the TV the volcano's ridge showed the gigantic, gaping fault line widening.

> "For our viewers at home watching this natural disaster unfolding, we've just gotten word from the United Kingdom Hazard Research Centre that this fault will cause half the volcano to crash into the sea creating a huge tsunami. That will swamp the west coast of Africa, and within hours, the wave will reach southern England before crossing the Atlantic where, scientists say, it will wipe out the East Coast of America."

"There is your answer, Mr. Vice President!"

"Okay, Sam," POTUS pitched in. "You have my full attention now."

"That fault line, Mr. President," Sam excitedly shouted, "is ripping the island apart! The whole western ridge is in the process of slipping into the sea, triggered by the earthquake and eruption."

"We have to evacuate the east coast!" the FEMA director stated reaching for a secure line.

"Hold on, Tommy!" the president ordered rising from his chair and walking to Sam who stared at the TV. "Sammy, how long do we have before the ridge fails?"

"There's no way to know."

"An hour? Two? Perhaps, three or four? What?"

"It could happen in minutes, hours, or days. I just can't predict when it will fail. Ultimately, it will happen."

"Sammy, once the volcano hits the ocean, how long before the wave reaches the east coast?"

"Seven hours, Mr. President."

"Jesus," the V.P. grunted.

The president looked to Lew. "Mobilize the National Guard and all branches. I want every city from Maine to Key West evacuated."

"Should I set up a conference call," the FEMA Director asked, "get all the city mayors on standby?"

"Yes, Tommy," the president answered. "And get the governors on the horn." Looking over at the TV and La Palma exploding, he sprung from his seat. "We're going to have pandemonium in the streets. Get the press assembled."

The PEOC exploded in a rush of excited phone calls to every state house in the country.

There is very little time, Sam thought.

Indeed, unknown to anyone in the room, all hell was about to break loose in cities across America.

"Sam," POTUS said pulling Sam aside. "I have a mission for you if you choose to accept it."

How could he say no?

Chapter 22

POPE ON A BOAT

POPE CALLIXTUS had never been aboard a cruise ship.

Standing beside Captain Maka, he glanced through the bridge thinking the hectic scene reminded him of a war room. It was a hive of activity with seamen, technicians, and navigators working desperately to determine the damage to the ship.

"What's wrong?" Callixtus muttered.

"When Shepherd One buzzed the top of the deck," the captain calmly explained, "the bottom of the chopper clipped our RADAR hardware knocking out the Electronic Chart Display and Information System running our advanced Integrated Bridge System."

"Good heavens!" Callixtus frowned.

"What does this mean?" Cardinal Jonathan asked.

"Basically, we're sailing blind. The twenty navigational computers of the ECDIS system would normally share hundreds of data inputs ensuring the absolute highest level of navigation."

"And now?" Callixtus asked.

"We'll not be able to navigate to shore," First Mate Fern Noord nodded. "We could run aground on uncharted rocks causing us to sink."

"But," the captain cut in. "Our communication specialists have sent a distress signal to the Naval Command of Santa Cruz de Tenerife. Hopefully they'll send a cutter with a pilot boat to guide us into port."

"If there is a port,' Fern mumbled.

That worried Jonathan. "We must get the Holy Father to Rome! The world will be panic stricken to learn their Pope is lost at sea!"

Fern pointed towards a wall of blank 27-inch widescreen monitors. "Without the exterior RADAR hardware, we cannot access our five scanners, bow or stern. Those are what enable the *Vision Master* system to inform the navigators of the ship's position."

An officer hurried to the captain and shook his head.

"Captain, there's no response from the Spanish Navy."

The captain grunted. "We'll have to utilize Doppler to find a path for us."

The officer shook his head.

"I'm afraid none of the DOP logs are working."

"What of the other systems?"

"Nothing, Sir," the navigator helplessly shrugged. "The acoustic anemometers, satellite-positioning sensors, depth sounders, fiber optic gyrocompasses... none of the navigation systems are operational!"

"Captain!" a radio operator shouted from his communications panel. "I have something on the distress channel you need to hear!"

The captain nodded. "Put it on the intercom system."

As the operator dialed in the frequency, a woman's voice filled the bridge.

"Mayday! MV Valencia, this is a USGS aircraft. Break. Position 29.43832 North 18.27026 West."

Glancing to a chart officer, the captain shouted. "Where is she hailing from, Son?"

"That's over our position, Sir!" the young navigator shouted staring at the coordinates on a handheld GPS positioning device.

Captain Maka picked up his binoculars and peered into the sky where the Beechcraft dove towards the ocean.

"USGS, this is MV Valencia," the radio operator answered, "what is your actual emergency?"

"This is Dr. Tish Harriet with the Hazard Research Center. We were forced to flee La Palma due to a catastrophic eruption of the Cumbre Vieja volcano..."

"USGS flight," the radio operator answered. "How can we assist you?"

"Our plane is going down, we are in imminent danger!"

The captain handed the binoculars to Fern and hurried to the operator snapping his fingers. "All hands, ready the crew for an emergency rescue at sea!"

Fern picked up a red phone and shouted a command. "Attention! Attention! The Captain has declared a general emergency. Prepare a tender vessel for rescue measures!"

As the signal blew, Callixtus huddled with his cardinals and stared at the plane diving for the water.

"Is she going to crash?" Cardinal Jonathan asked.

"Don't worry," Fern calmed. "We'll do our best to get our men out there to rescue any survivors!"

"Of course," the captain confirmed. Picking up a headset he stared at the aircraft. "Dr. Harriet, this is Captain Grayson Maka aboard Valencia, I will send out a rescue team when you put down at sea, over?"

But only static answered as the Beechcraft hit the ocean, pitched into the surf, and flipped into the depths.

Chapter 23

UP & AWAY

THE AIRBUS A380 was *on time.*

The monster jet was a double-deck, wide-body, four-engine jumbo and the world's largest passenger plane.

It caused many airports to upgrade outdated runways to accommodate its size. Originally baptized the A3XX, the manufacturer designed the airplane to contest competitors' domination in the large aircraft marketplace.

It was a big, monster plane.

The deck extended along the entire length of the fuselage and provided seating for 525 people in a three-class configuration. Having left Atlanta's airport, it would make the 4200-mile transatlantic, eight-hour flight... to London's Heathrow.

It was easy-peasy!

"Nice plane, huh?" Mark remarked, reclining into a business class aisle seat.

Commonly referred to as *The Whale,* the aircraft was powered by Rolls-Royce turbo-fan engines with noise reduction technology.

Most enjoyed the ride... but not Perry.

"Ah," he shrugged glancing out the window. "I personally prefer the Boeing 777, there's just something about an American twin-jet that rocks my flipping boat."

"Bitching and moaning doesn't suit you."

Sometimes, his producing editor was a handful.

"Let me have another drink, will you?" Perry asked a friendly *acting* flight attendant pushing down the walkway.

"What're you drinking?"

"Crown Royal," he sarcastically answered pointing to three miniature bottles situated atop a pull down tray.

"Same as the last three times I asked you… straight-up, one cube of ice and no stale pretzels."

"Sure thing, handsome," Jeanne replied with a wide smile. She was a ten-year veteran of making smart-assed tongue-snappers happy.

She knew how to handle the herds.

Perry recognized she was faking it… *the see-through happiness phony-baloney.* He suspected Miss Maybelline, *too much makeup*, was giving just enough pleasantries to make it through another foot aching, bank account swindling trip.

These attendants always plaster deceiving half-hearted smiles on their painted faces, baiting fliers like me to swipe nearly maxed-out credit cards for a taste of heaven.

He despised the onboard marketing, too.

The constant harassment and peddling of high-interest credit card applications.

Frequent flier bonus plans, my ass!

He wouldn't line up like a lamb for fleecing; he was smarter than that! Of course, as long as they continued to serve booze, he'd play along.

"What about your friend?" Jeanne asked, glancing to Mark who'd just swiped the digital front page of the Atlanta Journal-Constitution on his iPad 2.

SEVERE WEATHER ALERT
87° / Atlanta, GA

"Looks like bad weather back home," Mark mumbled. Then, realizing Perry and the attendant were staring, he comprehended he'd missed something. "I'm sorry; did you ask me a question, Miss?"

"Anything to drink?" she sighed with a *hurry-up and give me your order* kind of look. "Soda, coffee, maybe something stronger, I also have more pretzels?"

"Smart ass," Perry grunted.

The attendant grinned and winked.

Perry snickered. "You never run out of those stale things, do you? How about some top shelf caviar and a side order of goat cheese and tiramisu for desert?"

"Seriously?" she grinned. "What do I look like, some sort of miracle worker?"

"Nothing for me," Mark smiled and turned off the tablet. "I think I'll get some shut-eye before we land on the royal British soil."

"Okay," she winked turning to Perry. "I'll be right back with your Crown Royal, Mister High and Mighty."

Watching her rump disappear, Perry turned to his friend. "What a piece of work. Have I ever told you my joke about the guys who went to hell?"

"Let me hear it," Mark agreed turning off the overhead light and pushing back into the seat.

"There's an Irish guy, Spanish guy, and black guy riding in a brand new sports car. Suddenly, without warning, the tire blows out and the sportster rolls over and explodes."

"Why would that happen?" Mark asked.

"I don't know... who cares?"

"Okay, go ahead..."

"Anyway," Perry continued, "they all die and go to hell where the Devil sits waiting on a chair of brimstone."

"The Devil? Does he meet everyone when they arrive?"

"Just let me tell the joke, will ya, hard ass?"

Mark playfully chuckled. "All right, okay. Go on, Jimmy Fallon; let's hear your Tonight Show monologue."

"So, the devil says, '*Welcome to hell, I'm going to give you guys a chance to have a do-over and go back to Earth and live out your lives to old age.*'"

"How would that really happen?"

"All they have to do is put their balls on the devil's hand and if their nuts don't melt, the Devil assures he'll give them their lives back."

"And what if the nut-sacks melt?"

"Then they're stuck in hell for eternity."

"You've been drinking too much Crown Royal."

"So," Perry went on. "The red headed Irish guy pulls his peanuts out, lays 'em on the Devils hand and sizzle, sizzle, sizzle, they dissolve. The Spanish guy lays his walnuts out and they explode. But when the black guy does it, the baseballs don't freaking liquefy. They still bulge heftily in Satan's palm and nothing happens."

"Why did his balls not fry?"

"That's what Mr. Evil wants to know, so he asks the kid. You know what he says?"

Mark shook his head. "Tell me."

"The black guy looks into Satan's piercing red eyes and says, '*Look sucker, you want my balls to melt? Chocolate melts in your mouth, not in your hands.*"

Everyone in the surrounding seats laughed for what seemed like eternity, some even glancing over their seatbacks to look at the crackerjack jokester.

"I swear to freaking God, it really happened."

"You're going to hell," Mark said, "you know that?"

With the cabin practically in tears, Jeanne arrived with Perry's drink and handed it over amidst the waning chuckles.

"What's so funny? Clue me in, will ya?"

"Chocolate melts in your mouth, not in your hands," Mark said before cracking up uncontrollably.

"I know," she said. "I love M&M's."

That was it! Almost everyone in business class split their guts in a delightful momentary sliver of time.

It just couldn't have worked out better.

On that particular day, the joke killed!

Chapter 24

THE PRESIDENT'S MEN

DR. SAMUEL MAY grinned at the opulence in which American officials jettisoned about their country.

They know how to travel, he considered, glancing about the C-20G Gulfstream IV.

It was a long range, high-speed aircraft that accommodated twenty-five disaster response passengers and a crew of four.

The President of the United States was sending Sam on a mission to educate as many governors as possible.

"So," Gordy said, "the plan is to meet with the Governors of the Northern States. From there, we'll fly south to meet with coastal evacuation planners."

"Everyone forty miles from the ocean will need to be displaced." Sam insisted. "That wave will knock down skyscrapers."

Gordon unfolded a map of the eastern seaboard and ran his finger up the east coast. "That's millions of people. I'm not sure we'll be able to evacuate everyone."

"What about England? Has the Prime Minister been notified to close the underground? The Thames River will surge over the Barrier Gates and London will be drowned."

The barricade was the world's second-largest movable flood barrier located downstream of central London. Its purpose was to prevent the city from being flooded by exceptionally high tides and storm surges moving in from the sea.

This would be the straw that broke the queen's back.

Gordy glanced to the agitated British researcher. "The President will be calling 10 Downing Street, the French

Government, Lisbon, and every other country which lies in your predicted path of destruction."

Sam peered at the agent. He sensed a tone of disbelief in the man's voice... almost as if there was a hint of ridicule in his words '*your predicted path of destruction*'. "You still don't believe *this* eruption will cause a cock-up disaster in your country?"

"I'm not sure, Sam, it seems impossible."

"Bollocks!" He couldn't believe his ears. After all the *warnings*, despite having watched the news reports of the volcano *exploding*, the fault line *widening...*"

"From a military standpoint," Gordon argued, "moving millions of people and evacuating them from their homes and towns, on a *maybe...*"

"Are you bloody bonkers, man?" Sam snorted slamming his finger onto a red line he'd drawn down the middle of Florida. "Everything east of that line will be *wonky* and gutted, wiped from Earth, like slapping flies from the Queen's tabletop!"

That brought the attention of everyone.

Standing from his seat, Sam peered back into the plane. "Are all you Americans thicker than two short planks? You're all bells-ends!" Pointing to V.I., he shook his head at Gordy. "His home island, Sir, the Virgin Islands, will *be gone*! Bermuda, the Bahamas, Turks and Caicos, the eastern coast of Cuba... those places will no longer exist!"

Gordy tried to calm Sam. "I suppose I'm holding out hope you're wrong."

"Wrong? You've lost the plot, Sir!"

"Huh? I don't get what you're trying to say."

Sam stared the agent down. "You've gone crazy! A bit of a *nutter* you are... throwing a spanner in the works!"

Then, sitting back upon his seat with a sense of failure, Sam realized something. Millions of people would die if the president had any doubt of one thing.

A bloody monster was headed to America.

Staring at the map in Gordy's hand, Sam thought of the kids and considered the hopes of a young family sunning themselves on the beaches of Miami or Long Island... and then, he imagined the enormous wall of water that would come and...

"Sam?" Gordon interrupted. "We're going to follow the President's orders. Those coastlines will be evacuated. My personal opinion doesn't count."

That's when a man walked up. "We are about to taxi for take-off, Agent," FEMA Assistant Administrator of Logistics, Ray Gould, instructed. "We should land at JFK in an hour."

"Thanks, Ray," Gordy answered.

"Who is that chap?" Sam asked.

"Ray is the Federal man in charge of the Logistics Management Directorate which organizes the support structure, delivery of goods and other services in response to major disasters and other national emergencies."

Sam chuckled. "Might be better suited if he represented God himself, because nothing can respond to this disaster."

Maybe Ray did represent God, who knew?

"We're going to work this out," Gordy nodded, placing his hand on Sam's shoulder. "And if you turn out to be right, you'll be an international hero."

"If I believed in God, I'd ask him to send angels to forgive your stubborn government ass."

"I know, Sam."

As the jet leapt into the sky and punched through a layer of dark gray thunder clouds, he hoped something else, too.

That the American President got out of Washington.

Chapter 25

HOLY CONSPIRACY

CARDINAL PETRUS ROMANO ran Vatican City.

It was a landlocked sovereign city-state with eight hundred residents walled into a small hundred acre enclave.

That made it the smallest government in the world.

When the previous pope resigned and left a vacancy known as *"sede vacante"*... Petrus was called upon to serve as *Camerlengo*.

He was head of state.

That caused many to point toward a nine-hundred-year-old prophesy specifying the next pontiff would be Earth's final Bishop of Rome.

His reign was said to end in destruction.

And, his name was prophesied as *Peter the Roman*.

Petrus Romano.

He was a shoe-in who'd served silently as Cardinal Secretary of State beside three previous pontiffs. Having the votes to become the right hand of God, he knew the end of the papacy was near.

The Sky Gods would soon return; the planet would learn the *truth*... and religion would be finished.

However, the College of Cardinals elected Callixtus.

That shocked everyone.

The Knights Templar is alive and well, Petrus thought. *But, soon I'll have the last laugh.*

Gone were the assured prophesies of a *Last Pope*.

And, along with Callixtus' election came the severance of Petrus' hope of stepping into the most powerful position on the planet.

Now, as the sixty-year-old hung-up a white multi-lined telephone and pushed aside heavy golden curtains that looked down at Saint Peter's Square, he wasn't sure all was lost. Everything might work out after all.

It may all be coming true once more.

"What is it, Cardinal Secretary?" an archbishop asked, perceiving a change in liveliness.

"Has something occurred?" a monk whispered.

Petrus turned back to the weekly meeting and a room full of cardinals, priests, and monks watching his every move. "There's been an accident."

He looked pitiful standing there.

However, inside, deep down in the pit of his soul, he was *leaping, laughing,* and slapping his thigh in a fit of excitement. *An Accident! It's perfect! The pope lost at sea!*

"What's happened, Cardinal Secretary?" the archbishop worried, his fingers nervously tapping the arms of a plush, red satin chair.

The words brought Petrus back from his blissful mental farewell party... and, he realized just then, *I've got to let them see a somber reaction.* "Notify the cardinals to stand ready!"

An audible gasp went up among the clerics.

However, the archbishop merely sighed and bit his lower lip. *There was hell to pay and maybe now we'll get a chance at payback.*

A bishop stepped forward. "Cardinal, what shall be your message?"

Petrus glanced out the window at the faithful rushing into the square. "Tell them to prepare themselves."

"What for, Dear Secretary?"

Through the window, the cries of the flock could be heard. Word had gotten out; the globe's 1.2 billion Catholic sheep would all be glued to their televisions wondering if their pope was alive.

"Papa!" a woman screamed from the square.

"It is a tragedy, a horrible accident!" Petrus whispered to his loyal allies standing beside him.

"What is it, Petrus?' a Franciscan monsignor begged. "Is Callixtus the Fourth all right?"

Petrus stared at the burgeoning square below.

"Inform everyone that Shepherd One has crashed onto a ship... and tell the churches to pray for a miracle."

The sight below was incredible.

Thousands had already heard of the helicopter crash.

The people of Rome were shouting towards the empty papal balcony while waving their arms and praying for the rescue of their leader.

Petrus knew Callixtus was alive; he'd just spoken to Cardinal Jonathan, one of his trusted conspirators.

However, who was he to spoil the opportunity?

After all, he thought. *Isn't it I who should be the leader of the church?* This was an opportunity for revenge, the payback his little sect of schemers needed. There had to be a way... to get rid of the young trailblazing, know nothing, snot nosed, Spanish Pope.

Petrus would make sure the papacy came back his way.

That *they* remained a secret...

And, his henchmen would help fulfill prophesy.

With a little nudge in the right direction... they'd guarantee he'd be the last pope standing.

Pope Petrus would serve!

Before the ancients returned and ruined it all.

Chapter 26

BLOOD IN THE WATER

FIRST MATE NOORD had never seen anything like it.

The surf was littered with shredded, bloodstained clothing from the helicopter crash. A pair of Walmart jeans bobbed in an upsurge, one leg still holding the flesh of a victim eaten alive by the hulking depth dwellers.

A school of barracuda nibbled at the plump toes.

One at a time, Fern watched as the digits disappeared in a flash of gnashing teeth that eviscerated the foot of the once thriving flesh.

Now, only bone remained.

Glancing to the distance, he watched as the crashed Beechcraft rolled upon the sea, its frame pitching with each transitory upsurge of the waves. The engine of the tender roared behind him, and ahead, whitecaps broke over the bow, the seawater splashing across his face.

Then, one of his men turned to him, worry lining his brow. "We can only hope *El Gran Comedor* is not down below!" *The Great Eater* was a great white shark responsible for a string of recent carnages inflicted upon water sports attendees.

The Scuba and Snorkeling Commission had recently restricted programs in the Canaries for the remaining month of August.

Known for its size, the shark was said to be twenty-feet in length and weighed over five-thousand pounds. It was a streamlined swimmer, had a torpedo-shaped body with a pointed snout and flashed over 3000 razor sharp teeth arranged in several rows. But it was the first two that spread fear. Those were the shredders it used for *grabbing* and *cutting*…and then, dragging a body beneath.

"The Captain said he saw it!" one of the tender's rescue crewmen hollered. "He claims it was bigger than a bus!"

The shark was a storied legend in La Palma.

Fern scanned the sea, recalling a summer his fourteen-year-old eyes read *Jaws* by Peter Benchley, and soon after, hurried down to Blockbuster to rent Steven Spielberg's depiction of the eating machine.

Fern still didn't like getting in the water.

Everyone still believed–*just when you thought it was safe to go back in the water*–Spielberg's shark would come for *them* while on vacation.

"Nah," Fern dismissed with a grunt. "That shark is long gone by now." But in his thoughts, a whisper taunted.

What if she is down there?

"Last week," a seaman offered, "a champion Tenerife body-boarder was eaten alive by the white bellied beast."

Fern knew it was true.

According to the Tenerife News, the attack occurred Thursday afternoon off the coast of Las Teresitas beach, a popular destination located five miles from the capital,

BOY EATEN ALIVE!

> Conner Bidwell, 20, was killed yesterday afternoon when a great white shark severed his body below the hips.
>
> Bidwell's younger brother, Duncan, attempted to fend off the shark with his boogie board.
>
> But, the man-eater lunged at Conner twice before returning for the fatal attack.
>
> Duncan, who was not injured, rushed his brother back to shore on his board, but Conner lost too much blood by the time rescuers arrived.

It was a sad FRONTPAGE story.

Only the upper half of the body remained.

The article marked the end of the International Body-boarding Championships in the Canary Islands.

Some said the summer cancellation was way overdue.

Others complained it hurt business.

Another headline stated:

JAWS LIVES!

The Great Eater Is Feasting

"Are you going to dive for the rescue?" one of his men shouted, holding out scuba gear.

That snapped Fern back to the present as the tender chopped through the whitecaps, speeding towards the condemned sinking Beechcraft.

Well, are you going into the water? The voice whispered. *Or, are you just a First Class Pussy?* It was a challenge.

"Of course, I'm in on the rescue!" Fern shouted.

I dare you, Pussyboy! The voice chuckled. *You know you're just a scared little boy!*

"We'll see about that!" Fern responded, much to the surprise of his crew who shook their heads.

"How's that, Skipper?"

Realizing he'd answered a voice in his head, he strapped on the oxygen tank, stared at the plane, then plunged backward into the water.

I'll show that kid who the pussy is!

The rescue, *or a bloody slaughter*, was well underway.

Chapter 27

MEET THE PRESS

THE JAMES S. BRADY Press Briefing Room was a small theater in the West Wing of the White House.

It was located between the White House Press Corps and the Office of the Press Secretary. In 1969, to accommodate an increasing number of reporters assigned to the White House, *Tricky Dick* ordered the indoor swimming pool roofed and turned into press offices and a briefing room.

Nixon wanted to keep an eye on them.

In 2000, George W. Bush remodeled that room and renamed it to honor James Brady, the press secretary who'd been shot and permanently disabled during an assassination attempt on President Ronald Reagan.

The chamber buzzed now as the White House Press Secretary spoke to its forty-nine correspondents.

"Attention, everyone!"

Each seat in the room was assigned to a news organization, with the most prominent occupying the first two rows. That meant NETWORK NEWS... the *who's who* of blood sucking mongrels. The information men, the media mafia... there were many names for them, each having its own ring of truth. The lowly reporters who didn't have seats stood along the back wall. They were known as press pool correspondents.

The nobodies among somebodies.

"Listen up, people," the press secretary shouted. "The President is on his way down here for a live address to the nation. Inform your nets they're going to have to break programming on this one."

That morsel of red meat sent the room into a feeding frenzy. The sense of breaking news was palpable.

The reporters *lived* for this; moments when the president would grace their presence with his aura.

It was big stuff when *he* came down.

Someone yelled from the back. "Is the President going to confirm the tsunami prediction?"

The press secretary shook his head. "That's exactly why you guys are standing back there in the desert; you're always stepping out of turn." Behind him, a softly-lit screen bordered by fake pillars acted as the official backdrop, replacing the former drab blue curtain. Placing his hands on the podium, he glanced down at a video monitor. On its screen, a digital clock counted down from sixty. When it hit zero, POTUS would magically appear through a side curtain. Everything the president did was scheduled, every move, each step.

There was *one exception* to this rule, the bathroom.

Nobody controlled that.

"Wow," a White House Correspondent exclaimed, glancing to his iPad and a live video stream of the volcano exploding below a Network News chopper.

"Thirty seconds for the President," the press secretary informed, motioning for everyone to take their seats.

That's when an advance secret service team pushed through the curtain, dispersed into the room, and suspiciously eyed the reporters. When all seemed in place, an agent whispered into his sleeve and the president appeared followed by Admiral Lew Brancor, Defense Secretary Clark, and Will Squire.

Camera shutters clicked loudly over the scene, flashes erupted, and the whispers soon hushed to silence.

The entire nation was paying attention.

Moving to the podium, the president waited for his words to appear on one of three displays.

To the left, a flat screen television had this:

WHITEHOUSE.GOV

"My fellow Americans, this morning I was alerted to what was then believed to be a common earthquake on the island of La Palma in the country of Spain." Motioning to William with a nod, he read the facts. "The United Kingdom Hazard Research Centre Department of Geological Sciences, along with its director, Dr. Samuel May, has for many years warned that such an earthquake could, at some point, cause volcano Cumbre Vieja to collapse and fall into the Atlantic Ocean causing an east coast tsunami."

Silence, and then:

"Governments the globe over, including our own, scoffed at the notion. None believed the research, and in fact, many of us turned our noses up at the very thought of such a catastrophe. Today, it is apparent we were wrong to dismiss such forewarnings."

President Powers turned towards the flat screen and it came to life with a video of the volcano and its exploding caldera. The press was spellbound.

"These are live-feeds. They're from a Lockheed Martin unmanned aerial vehicle operated by the United States Air Force."

It was the age of drones.

"Initial examination of these scenes by the U.S.G.S. along with our military and the scientific communities of the United States, Britain, and South America is this: the western flank of this volcano is failing and will collapse! Questions?"

The room exploded with shouted queries.

To the president's right, at the end of the first row was Chuck Stodd, Chief White House Correspondent for NBC Nightly News.

"Let's take Chuck first," the president pointed.

Standing from his seat and glancing to his right at correspondents from FOX and CBS, the reporter said:

"Mr. President, are you telling the American people the east coast *will be* hit by a tsunami?"

Looking directly into the camera, the leader of the free world nodded. "That's exactly what I'm saying."

With that, everyone stared in shock.

To those watching at home, what followed must have seemed like a SITCOM in Prime Time Television.

The press didn't know what to say.

For a second, they just stared at the president.

Imagine that, President Powers thought.

Chapter 28

SEND IN THE CLOWNS

COLONEL ELMAR MEEDS knew The Guard had changed over the last five hundred years.

Yet, its core mission to protect the pope remained.

Except that wasn't his mission, *not this time.*

Now, as the specially trained Italian Special Forces *KILLER* stared down at the cobalt Atlantic Ocean, he recollected another time:

"I swear to serve the Pope, And give my life to defend him!" That was his oath ten years prior.

And he'd been prepared to lay down his life.

However, things change and people find excuses.

"Damn." The memory faded with the sight of a colossal pleasure vessel at the edges of his sight. He understood no one could guarantee the Holy Father's security, as proven true by the 1981 assassination attempt on *Pope John Paul II* by Mehmet Ali Agca in St. Peter's Square.

The ranks were routed after that humiliating day.

Memories of that failed attempt reminded Meeds of his oath and responsibility. Crouched beside him in the Agusta Westland helicopter were the best three commandoes of the 9th Parachutist Assault Regiment.

They were equivalent to the British Army's SAS.

Yet the commandoes know nothing of my task.

The official mission: to rescue Pope Callixtus.

The actual directive from the cardinal secretary:

"Wait for the Black Pope's order to eliminate the humble servant. At all costs, make it look like an accident."

Meeds knew the unthinkable would one day appear at his doorstep. *That sooner or later,* the society would activate his skill set against one of their own.

And on that day, his personal beliefs would be tested.
That day had come.

It banged now at his heart. Like a blacksmith's hammer. *Pounding...* it beat his faith into the anvil of his soul.

He was a member of the Special Forces, but had been specially trained by *The Illuminati Order*. It was a geo-political and male-only organization structured as a secret military operation. They conspired with a secret Vatican hierarchy who demanded clandestine oaths and complete obedience to the Superior General–*the black pope*–dressed in black and *standing in the shadow* of the white cassocked ruling pope.

"He's not one of us," Cardinal Secretary Romano had instructed Meeds. "I should have been Bishop of Rome."

That declaration occurred two hours prior.

The call had been placed from an ultra-secure line hidden deep within a secret stone chamber of the Vatican.

"It's not possible for anyone to guarantee one hundred percent security," the cardinal went on. "Callixtus is *not* one of us and I won't be deprived of my destiny."

There was outright anger in the ranks.

A coup d'état was underway.

The Vatican power structure was considering removing their gardener. It would be a sudden deposition by the governing Jesuit establishment to depose the extant pope and replace him with Petrus.

A coup d'état was considered successful when the usurpers established their dominance.

But this coup required *MURDER.*

The Cardinal Secretary forgets one thing, Meeds thought glaring at the burned-out shell of the helicopter atop Valencia's deck. *When the coup either fails completely, or succeeds, a civil war is a likely consequence.*

Everyone knew Callixtus didn't want to be pope.

In fact, the conclave only elected him to ruin Petrus.

Meeds knew Callixtus wanted to be called *Carlos* when speaking to friends and he seemed reluctant to call himself pontiff. After his first night in the grand papal apartments at the Apostolic Palace, he moved to the Vatican Hotel.

He rejected wealth and opulence and seemed in denial over his appointment as leader of the church. What nobody knew was something changed in Callixtus after his visit to the Room of Tears. That's where he changed into his papal vestments before receiving the pledges of obedience from his fellow cardinals.

In the room, he was handed a box that changed his faith.

"He's altering the idea of what it means to be Bishop of Rome," the memory of Cardinal Romano's conversation interrupted. "This *no-frills* style he cultivated in Barcelona has broad implications for the church across the globe."

Everyone knew that in the short time Callixtus was pope, he'd cast aside the trappings of the papacy and refused to wear the red velvet cape used for official occasions, deciding to keep the simple, iron-plated pectoral cross he used in Barcelona.

Meeds understood the young pope's desire to serve the worlds lowliest, *but washing the feet of inmates*, pissed off the society. Previous pontiffs had washed the feet of *priests* in Rome's most lavish basilicas.

So, here was the colonel, a contract killer, staring down at an Italian flagged cruise ship baring the name Valencia.

"Commander," a commando shouted over the *Whrrrrrr whap-whap-whap* of the helicopter blades, "we have to hoist that chopper off the deck in order to land!"

"Ready the hoist!" Meeds ordered. "Let's get on that ship and save our man!"

Chapter 29

LADY LIBERTY

JOHN F. KENNEDY International Airport controlled more traffic than any airport in North America.

The place was gigantic.

It remained *one* of only *two* airports in North America with flights to most inhabited continents.

Today, only one plane was cleared to land.

Everything else was an emergency departure.

"Okay, people," the Gulfstream Captain's voice blurted over the intercom. "The tower just cleared us for landing on runway 4R-22L, and since we're the only *arriving* aircraft we should be putting down momentarily."

Peering through his window, Sam stared at the Statue of Liberty rising from New York's Harbor. The robed statue represented *Libertas...* the Roman goddess of freedom, who displayed a torch and tablet evoking the law. Upon that tablet was etched the date of the Declaration of Independence: July 4, 1776.

At her feet, lay a broken chain.

She's an icon of freedom, or hell. As the statue disappeared from sight, Sam surveyed the skyline that replaced her. He recalled another time then; *it seemed so long ago...* when the once enormous Twin Towers crowded this view.

Now, only horrid memories remained.

Those remembrances were jam-packed with *screams, rubble,* and *clouds of ash* chasing people through Lower Manhattan.

"Bloody bastards," Sam grumbled.

"What's that, Dr. May?" Gordy asked, snapping the researcher back from his disturbing memory.

"I was just thinking about the World Trade Towers that once superbly rose into Manhattan's skyline."

"Yeah, that's something every American contemplates when flying into Manhattan."

"I don't believe your country has a monopoly on that memory, Gordy."

"It lingers with everyone. What *once was*… will *never* be again, and that includes a lot of things… and *brave people*… who gave everything for our way of life… for America's freedom."

Staring at the newly erected Freedom Tower which replaced the Twin Towers, Sam grunted. Change came and went, things moved on…

Moments later, the plane's wheels hit the runway, the rubber tires squealed, and the engines reversed thrust which pushed him forward in his seat.

"Welcome to the Land of Queens," the captain's voice informed, "the temperature is eighty-nine degrees with zero chance of rain here in the Big Apple."

Talk about coincidences, Sam considered. *The earthquake was an 8.9! The temperature in Manhattan is eighty-nine…*

Sometimes, life had a sense of humor all its own.

As the Gulfstream exit door pushed open, Gordy directed Sam and the others into a five-car motorcade which waited at the bottom of the air-stairs.

"Welcome back, Sam," Gordy smirked.

"Don't get your knickers in a twist. You have your work cut out for you, chap! What's the plan?"

"First, we'll get to Brooklyn where the Coalition of Northeastern Governors is anxiously awaiting your expert assessment of their coastal evacuation plans."

"Where do they hail from?"

Gordy read a list from his iPhone. "They're from Connecticut, Maine, Massachusetts, New Hampshire, New York, Rhode Island, and Vermont."

"What about New Jersey, Delaware, and Maryland?"

"No word from them, yet, we've not been able to get their offices on the phone. Maybe they'll show up."

"Maybe?" Sam griped. "Now is not the time for party line politics."

"After you finish here, we'll chopper back to the Gulfstream for an immediate departure to Miami. Once there, you'll meet with Governors of Virginia, North Carolina, South Carolina, Georgia, and hopefully Florida. The President will need you to assist with the federal evacuation plans for South Florida."

"Hopefully?" Sam grunted. "Why hopefully?"

"Party politics…"

Sam knew no one in Florida was safe. "Bonkers! Florida is only a hundred miles wide from Miami to Naples, and there are millions living along five hundred miles of shoreline from Key West to Jacksonville."

The weight of those numbers brought silence.

"Key West is surrounded by the Atlantic," he continued. "The people are condemned unless we can convince the Florida Governor to start moving them one hundred sixty miles north up US-1. This isn't a presidential election; long lines will kill people now." The *Overseas Highway* would be bumper-to-bumper traffic along its one hundred and twenty-seven miles through the Florida Keys.

Gordon glanced out his window. "They're working on the Governor from Florida."

Glancing towards the skyline, Sam considered the consequences of the mega tsunami that would push up New York Harbor. Saltwater would drown the Statue of Liberty, surge into Manhattan and swamp Central Park. Twenty floors of the Empire State Building would lie beneath the tideline. Lower Manhattan would never recover.

Hundreds of thousands would die.

"We're going to have ourselves a bloody mess," Sam grumbled pointing to Manhattan's skyscrapers on the horizon. "We'll need a ton of body bags. It'll make Hurricane Katrina seem like child's play."

"It's an American Armageddon." Gordon pitched in.

Even that is an understatement, Sam knew.

Chapter 30

DEATHTRAP!

THE BEECHCRAFT windscreen shattered on impact.

Warm seawater gushed through its frame and inundated the cockpit, the force of the current pressing Tish into her unyielding pilot seat.

The sound of *gushing* water filled her ears.

It was the unmistakable roar of cascading liquid... similar to the thunderous waterfall at Niagara Falls–*a pounding fist of H20*–crashing itself over rock and dirt in a torrent of natural energy.

It was the soundtrack of a childhood vacation.

But, *this* wasn't America's oldest state park, and the froth slapping her face didn't spawn from a dramatic apex of the Niagara River Gorge. This was a violent gush of saltwater in the middle of the Atlantic... and it filled the cockpit rapidly.

It was trying to kill her.

She *felt* the watermark rising... *inching* up from her ankles, creeping along the calves, thighs, and onto her lap.

"Oh, shit, I have to get out of here!"

The closing credits of life were rolling across her mind.

Fate always knew the outcome of destiny.

She imagined something then, locked in the fear that gripped her. There was a Machiavellian whisper taunting her considerations. It nagged her like a swarm of mosquitoes on a warm summer evening. It took its tone from her teenaged quarterback boyfriend who'd once thought he was Mr. It, a smart-ass country boy huckster from Austin, Texas. The son of the mayor, he was a meat eating, beer drinking, women abusing prick.

His words stung her like a wasp.

A bite *here*… a sting *there*… and then… *swelling*.

The reaper will find you, the whisper toyed. *This water is gonna fill up that sour mouth of yours like a pitcher of sweet lemonade.*

And then… it would be *nighty-night, sayonara*… bring in the marching band and send out the clowns.

Once you drown… the sadistic mumble purred, *you'll be chum for the man-eaters waiting just outside the plane.*

Truth lingered in that statement.

Monsters waited in the depths, circling the sinking aircraft, ready to attack… hammerheads, tiger sharks, and one big swallower… a great white called The Great Eater.

It had the scent of blood in its nostrils.

"It's a deathtrap!" she screamed with fright glancing to her friend. "Wake up, Chris!"

He was slumped onto the instrument panel; his head a blood spattered mess… a wide gaping slash unfastening his brow. Beneath that, the cranium lay exposed. The thick white bone had cracked open and brains were visible.

His face was unrecognizable.

The Beechcraft's shoulder harness mount had failed; a floor bolt had twisted its way free from fatigued threads.

"Goddamn it, Christopher, come back to me!"

But the professor wasn't coming back from anywhere.

He was *gone*.

Lost to the tunnels of *nevermore* where the grit of worldly things faded to black.

There, only lullabies and bright white light resided.

Pilots and co-pilots who didn't wear their *harness safety system* often croaked from massive head injuries like this one… suffered in similar crash landings.

The waterline reached Tish's nose then and she had just enough space between her flaring nostrils and the roof of the cockpit to breathe a few more gasps.

Better get a move on, Miss Class President, cheerleading heart breaker, the voice taunted. *There isn't much time before the grand finale marches right up your ass.*

Her trembling fingers clawed at the stainless steel harness release latch hidden beneath the waterline. Struggling against the fastenings, she rolled her eyes to the water entering her nose.

Soon... death will find you, my dear.

Panic set in with that cackling voice... and she knew the end was close. Death's horrid eternal clutch pulled at her considerations.

It taunted the anxiety of fate like a Hitchcock Masterpiece. Terror... *it was always there* ... lurking just beneath the surface of her concerns, prowling... like a slaughterer shadowing a victim on a dimly lit street.

Demise waited for us all in the end... as it has for centuries. *The Grim Reaper* hunted with its filthy murderous claws of infinity.

Death tugged at her sense of hopelessness and fright, inflicting the desperateness with whispers of condemnation.

Come on, honey! Breathe in the saltwater!

"Screw you!" she gagged.

In a burst of anger, her strong fingers caught the harness latch, pulled its release handle, and sensed freedom as water pushed up her nose and drowned the skull.

With a final glance at Chris' corpse, she pushed through the empty windscreen frame and swam into the Atlantic.

Through murky seawater, the image of First Mate Noord appeared with a scuba tank strapped to his back.

Reaching her side, he gave her the thumbs-up, and then, after she pointed to the cockpit and the sight of Chris trapped in his harness, she watched Fern point to the surface while swimming for the Beechcraft.

Stroking for the shallows, with long terrified strokes, she dug deep, pulling herself through the sea with all she could muster. That's when she saw the mammoth shark.

Its jaws hung open, just wide enough to give a sense of its jagged deadly teeth. It looked like the bastard was smiling. It was feeding time.

And Bessie the Beast was hungry.

Chapter 31

TIMES SQUARE

THE GREAT WHITE WAY was *the* place to be.

The center of the universe stretched from West 42nd to 47th Streets in the City of New York.

Broadway was instantly recognized around the world as the home of IT–and that meant BIG.

Stardom... *the shit, the bomb*... it all meant the same thing. It told the world you had *arrived* on scene.

You *were* the hot new *thing*.

If you had the IT factor, then your face would grace the masses, *it* would be *one* of a select *few* gigantic posters lining Broadway. Everyone else who stared up at those billboards... they were the *unknowns*, the sheep who laid down hard-earned sawbucks and followed IT.

Justin Bieber, Facebook, *things* and *people* like that...

And, all those *types* made a presence, sooner or later, *here* at the world's busiest pedestrian intersection.

TIMES SQUARE... the heart of Manhattan!

If you could make it *here*, well... *you know the rest.*

That's where thousands of sheep now stood, staring at the CBS Spectacular Jumbotron. Its HI-DEF screen displayed the national address of President Powers.

"In Spain," the president spoke from the massive display, "I just learned Shepherd One has crashed onto a cruise liner."

The screen split into three separate live feeds.

One showed the president, another displayed a *YouTube* video of Shepherd One's crash landing, and the third presented the exploding volcano.

The pedestrians stopped on the concrete sidewalks–*their jaws hitting the pavement*–and pointed towards the Jumbotron gasping in astonishment. It wasn't the president that caused them to glower and point... he was a nothing to them. He didn't matter to everyday folks, unless, someone did something *stupid*, like the idiots in Boston who bombed the marathon. When that went down, people wanted blood.

What made these Manhattan pedestrians stare was the exploding volcano. The imagery was something different, a unique occurrence during an ordinary summer morning.

President Powers went on. "This is the greatest test our nation will ever face. I've ordered temporary martial law under article H.R. 5122, also known as the John Warner National Defense Authorization Act. This allows me to take charge of National Guard troops without state governor authorization. Moments ago I ordered the Chairman of the Joint Chiefs, Admiral Lew Brancor, to put into effect mandatory evacuations along the eastern seaboard of our country..."

"Get outta here!" a man yelled to the screen.

"Fuhgettaboutit!" his buddy chimed. "We ain't going anywhere you elitist, prick bastard!"

Those surrounding the men frowned.

They were *out-of-towners*, mere bystanders.

Two of these were happily married Packers Fans who were giddy to have a story to tell their vacation-jealous friends back in Green Bay.

Cheeseheads loved Manhattan.

Suddenly, the volcano exploded on the screen and the island separated from the ridge and collapsed towards the ocean. Thunderous explosions rocked the landmass; trees, rocks, dirt and smoke rocketed into the sky.

"Oh, my!" the Wisconsin woman cried.

Beside Mrs. Cheesy-weesy, and wearing a *throwback* Brett Favre jersey, her gruff-looking husband hugged her tight. "Don't worry, that's a world away!"

Gasps went up from the street.

ALL eyes were on the Jumbotron.

Then, the volcano's ridge hit the water.

Staring at the screen, everyone watched the big splash. It was bigger than anything they'd ever seen and it rose so high... the news chopper camera filming the scene went black. And, that caused silence to overtake the street.

The couple from Wisconsin realized the constant sound of yellow cab horns *stopped* blaring. People *stopped* pushing, and *for just an instant*, there was peace.

Go figure.

But then, mere seconds later... not more than a heartbeat following the momentary harmony... *Chaos erupted.*

Up on the Jumbotron, secret service agents surrounded *The Prez* and grabbed his elbows.

"It's time to go, Mr. President."

And that was the end of the presidential address.

Cutting away from the White House Press room, the live shot shifted to talking heads at the network studio.

As for the Green Bay Packing Cheeseheads, they shook their heads and moved off down Seventh Avenue.

There was shopping to do.

Nothing could stop the tourists.

Except, maybe, lunch at Bubba Gump's and the eventual end of the world.

Chapter 32

SHARK BAIT

FIRST MATE NOORD was chum.

Chumming was the practice of luring *sharks* by throwing fish chunks and blood into the water to entice their keen sense of smell.

Fern was *the* bait, and he knew it.

They don't just nibble on the eyes down here, his boyish voice chuckled. *No, no, no way! Here, razor sharp jaws strip flesh like wood-chippers.*

After indicating for the woman to swim for the surface, he stroked to the sinking plane and the man trapped in the co-pilot's harness.

Not looking good for this guy. He's a bloody, deceased mess of stink!

And that meant the *GOBBLERS* would come.

Stalking, they'd circle the plane and flash thousands of pearly white daggers in a grin of slaughter.

The forewarnings of Fern's mind shook him. He was frightened; the supposing whispers might become certainty.

Pulling himself into the sinking airframe, he felt a sense of danger. Tingling fingers of anxiety crept up his spine, arms, and legs… goose bumps trailed along his neck.

They reminded of his fear of spiders! The uglier they were, the worse his dread. He was twenty-eight at first contact with the appalling species. And, he remembered it like yesterday.

The incident–*that's what he called the occurrence*– happened on a storming spring evening, his body exhausted from an 18-hour shift working the Port of Miami, training on a new vessel at the cruise terminal.

Walking into his apartment, he'd plopped onto a ratty Rooms-to-Go faux leather couch to watch the Miami Dolphins game on a *half-assed* Sony television.

They LOST the game! What else was new?

The Dolphins sucked.

The winning days of Quarterback Dan Marino and Head Coach Don Shula were long gone. Super Duper didn't track down the field anymore. Nowadays, the *logo-changing losers* had become a thug-club of rags-to-riches millionaires who showed up for *a maybe.*

Kids these days!

Fern couldn't recall how *the spider incident* happened; he couldn't place his memory on the exact moment he dozed off during the post-game breakdown of *loser-land!*

But, within minutes, he was out cold. The eyelids twitched, and behind them, his eyes danced their *REM* party.

He's sleeping! Attack!

That's when a Brown Recluse spider crept through the window, scuttled onto the sofa and CRAWLED up his face sinking its venomous fangs into his eyelid.

The eight-legged spider didn't fare well that night and would never see old age. The Recluse was as common in Miami as Cuban Nationals washing ashore on rubber tubes before stumbling onto the white sandy beach.

"América! Inicio de los valientes!" they'd scream... *screw you, Fidel Castro!*

In any case, on the night Fern was bitten, Jackson Memorial Hospital put him in a hyperbaric chamber to keep his face from melting off.

A scar still reminded of that fateful evening.

Here, diving in the Atlantic, while lost in *these* thoughts, a huge dark shadow moved across his peripheral vision, and that snapped him *right back* to the here and now.

There she is, Bessie the Beast is here in the depths stalking your skinny European ass!

His breathing accelerated; blood raced through the veins. It was astonishing, the sounds he could hear underwater. His heartbeat pounded in his head, the heaving sounds of respiration, the air bubbles releasing from the dive gear, a propeller moving somewhere above.

But, the *things* Fern wanted to hear and see…

They were silent.

Reaching to his belt he drew scuba shears from a black sheath. Working quickly–*more out of fear than trying to save anyone because he knew the man was a cadaver*–he cut the insipid corpse from the harness and pulled him through the broken frame.

That's when something *bumped* him.

Here they come… You better watch your back, big bro!

He released the professor and thrashed wildly in the murkiness. His panicked movements caused ripples in the sea, a telltale signal to predators that something in distress deserved immediate attention.

You know better than that. Now the big 'ole hungry ones will come for a lookie-loo seeking dinner!

Fern's vision cleared. There *were* no monsters lurking, their teeth *weren't* chomping at his flesh.

Only small fish swam before his eyes.

But, then, out of nowhere, just as he exhaled a flurry of relief bubbles, thousands of red, yellow, and blue Parrotfish raced past. Before he could think of a reason for the hyperactivity, schools of larger agitated fish zipped past.

There were Skipjack Tuna, Atlantic Chub Mackerel, and then, a pair of Blue Marlin hightailed it for deeper-waters.

And, if *they* were on the run… something much bigger might be chasing them.

Maybe it's already arrived, Fern considered.

Remembering he'd released the dead man, he peered back into the murkiness, glimpsed the sinking body and started towards it. At this precise moment, the biggest fish he ever witnessed appeared through the shadowy water.

The *GREAT WHITE SHARK* had enormous gloom filled eyes, and for an instant, Fern thought the creature stared at him. But the beast zeroed in on Grossman.

Jesus Christ! Fern thought, stroking for the surface with terrorized screams raging through his mind.

Swim, you sorry excuse of a seaman!

Fern flew through the water.

An Olympian wouldn't catch him on that day!

But, maybe something else might.

Chapter 33

A BLOODY HAZARD

THE UNITED KINGDOM Hazard Research Centre's Department of Geological Sciences was Europe's leading threat assessment center.

And they had balls the size of basketballs.

Some said they were British *snobs*.

Well, the losing green-eyed monster of jealousy always raised its head to degrade #1.

Every Book Junkie knows that.

Based at University College London, *The Centre* included three departments: *Disaster Management, Meteorological,* and *Geological Hazards.*

It all meant one thing… *cataclysm.*

Asteroid impacts, hurricanes AND volcanoes.

Not to mention the Polar Vortex!

They all came full circle to Death & Destruction.

And, that was the finality of humanity.

It was the *big kahuna,* the *grand finale* leading to:

When first responders left a disaster scene, and the rescue became a recovery, meat wagons arrived to carry off the sightless ones who'd lost their lives.

Inside the vehicles laid exterminated bodies.

These guys sought to prevent the coroner from going out in the first place. As far as they were concerned, the meat wagons should stay parked in the garage.

Everyone who was anyone was here glaring into wall-mounted televisions and sitting at enormous banks of computer stations. The research students did the grunt work; the tireless, thankless, non-ending data reviews.

Moving through the room was a rather heavy *bugger* about to offer his two cents. He was the man in charge; the headmaster of this crowd of modern-day Albert Einstein *wannabes*.

"Somebody, give me something, anything!" Professor Wild Bill shouted to the room of braincases.

He was *large and in charge!*

But… only when Dr. May was out doing fieldwork.

The field is where they all *wanted* to be.

Anywhere but here!

That was their slogan.

Nonetheless, Bill knew *on-site digs* were incentives, something for him to hold over the heads of the data-slaves. It was something for them to work towards… a big orange carrot! It hung there, above their keyboards, like a Piñata of papier-mâché, pottery, or cloth; decorated and filled with a field-dig *freedom ticket* to a smoldering, volcanic ridge!

Who would get to swing at that Piñata?

Being out in the midst of hazards was the stuff of *Indiana Jones & the Spewing Volcano!*

They all envisaged *THE* dream.

Yet, Bill knew that sometimes… reveries turned to nightmares. Like this one: *The tsunami from hell!*

Stalking the great Indiana Jones adventure… that would come later in their long-suffering careers.

Right now, he had to find Tish.

Wild Bill glanced around the room. "What do we have on the Beechcraft in Las Palma?"

"The plane went bloody-down!" a young student assured the unadventurous scholar. "The Beechcraft Baron plunged off the radar; we've lost all tracking satellites."

"That's a crapper, Bob the Knob-head!" Wild Bill grumbled. "This is Dr. Harriet and Professor Grossman you've dammed to the fishes!"

The room grew silent at the mention of Sam's wife and their longtime professor. Nobody wanted to buy into a worst-case scenario.

"You daft cow," Wild Bill continued. "Are you proposing the airplane carrying Tish and Chris was demolished above the exploding ridge of Cumbre Vieja?"

"It could have happened," Bob shrugged. "The data is the data, and the electrical monitoring system we installed on the aircraft sent a three minute stream indicating a sudden loss of fuel, an abrupt descent towards the ocean and then nothing!"

"Rubbish," Bill protested pointing a stern finger at the young bloke. "You think you know your onions, eh? They are alive, you'll see!"

None were taking bets to that melody.

The communication apprentice was just about to voice a protest when a flashing red light blinked on over their heads. It was a signal that the European Space Agency's Satellite Earth Observation satellite was seconds away from offering them a live look at the volcano's caldera.

"Brilliant!" Bill shouted and clapped his hands. Summoning everyone to gather around a 70-inch wall mounted monitor, the images caused him to gasp.

Cumbre Vieja was gone, and a wave taller than Big Ben rolled out from the island in the form of a tea-saucer.

"Ring-up 10 Downing Street!" Wild Bill yelled. "And, find out where the Americans have ferried Samuel! The city will be under water in hours, people will be running through the streets of London to find death!"

"Blimey Church of England!" a researcher bellowed. "The Prime Minister's office will be arse-over-tit when they see this!"

"Get your knickers twisted, everyone!" Bill shouted. "Send out alerts to the House of Commons. We have an end of life situation headed to the Kingdom!"

But, it isn't really a KINGDOM, is it? Bill thought.

For as long as anyone remembered, a queen ran the show, and that made England *QUEENDOM-Land.*

Either way, the room burst into energetic activity.

Bob, however, was busy zooming in on the images. He saw something the others had missed.

"What is that?" Wild Bill squinted.

Zooming in as far as the computer would allow it became clear what they peered towards.

"It's the cruise ship from the newsies," Bill regretfully sighed, "the vessel with the Pope onboard."

Zooming back out, they watched as a wall of water barreled towards the unsuspecting vessel.

"How far is it from that ship?" Bill asked.

"Less than one hundred kilometers," a human calculator answered. "They'll have impact in minutes."

Chapter 34

BLOODBATH

DOCTOR HARRIET plunged through the surf, gasped for oxygen, and screamed.

"Help me! Help! Help me!"

The seamen aboard the tender boat stared in horror at the trembling, terrified woman bobbing in the rolling whitecaps.

"I'll get her!" a seaman shouted, seizing a life preserver and jumping into the water. Yet, what he *splashed* into… *that* was something *more* than saltwater and frothy waves.

It was a cocktail of *blood* and *seawater*.

And, if he didn't hurry, the Great Eater would have a good old-fashioned happy hour.

It would be an *eat one–get one* kind of deal.

No coupon or dinner jacket required.

Back on the cruise ship, the human *COWS* would call that a smorgasbord… a fat-filled *buffet*.

All they can eat, anytime they wanted.

But, here in the ocean, sloshing above the waterline were chunks of bloody flesh *plopping* from beneath.

Everyone heard it, the subtle…Bluuuup–Plop–Bluuuup–Plop That's what the chunks of *meat* sounded like when they surfaced. Surrounding the body parts *popped* dozens of pinkish air bubbles. It was the sound of fear and reminded the crewmembers of what gum sounded like when teeth exploded a bubble they'd blown between their lips. But these bloody air bubbles indicated something else.

Chow Time!

The banquet had begun in the Atlantic.

Bluefish and a school of Barracuda showed their ugly mugs now, and their thrashing teeth didn't distinguish between dead or living.

They just wanted in.

Like a *PAC-MAN* game, the flesh-rippers munched on everything in their path, ripping the epidermis, swallowing the flesh and scrambling below before anyone saw the damage.

"Maldita bastarda!" the rescuer yelled pushing Tish to safety aboard the tender. He was swatting at the surface of the sea where a school of jaws tore at his body.

"Help him," Tish yelled, "pull him outta there!"

The two crewmen looked at one another. They weren't jumping into the washbasin of demise. No way! They hadn't signed up for death by consumption.

The water resembled a washing machine of blood, as thousands of sharp teethed fish jutted for position.

"Dios me libre!" the crewmember screamed from the water, his flesh disappearing from his bones.

"Are you kidding me?" Tish hollered pointing at the man who'd saved her life. Then, she realized it was too late. Within seconds, only his bones remained.

And then, the skeleton sunk.

He was gone; lost to the sea creatures.

Before anyone could mourn his death, Fern broke the surface about twenty-five yards off starboard. He was stroking through the surf with urgency, almost as if he'd seen the devil himself.

"It's the Great Eater!"

It was one of many names.

Everyone heard the tales during late nights drinking at local taverns hidden along the town's cobbled alleys. There, seafarers stumbled through with cheap cans of Dorada Spanish beer spinning yarns of a giant shark lurking in the Canary Islands.

"El Gran Comedor!" a crewman worried and pointed.

Tish saw the 30-foot monster surfacing. Right there, in grayscale... before her very eyes. From nose to tail, she glanced over the dark gray creature as it circled Fern swimming the race of his lifetime. "Oh, hell, look out!"

Fern didn't see it.

But, the tender crew saw it, and they yelled.

"Swim Comandante!"

"Que hay en el agua! Nadar!"

They were howling in Spanish, for Fern to swim. However, the warnings never made it into his ears. He was underwater and his eyes were locked on hell.

But the monster saw him. And, it stalked him... like a cat trailing a field mouse. Then, the mammoth made a beeline towards lunch. It opened its gigantic jaws and simply inhaled hundreds of gallons of water and swallowed Fern whole. Like a whale inhaling schools of flounder.

Blue Plate Special, thank you very much.

It was the day El Gran Comedor feasted.

Chapter 35

COMMANDER IN CHIEF

EARTH'S MOST FAMOUS home was the White House.

The red, white, and blue!

America had many firsts to brag about.

The First Lady, the First Dog, the First Daughters…

And now, President Chris Powers would order another *first*. "I want the White House evacuated within the hour."

"I'll get it done, Mr. President," Chief of Staff, Robert Laslow, promised. Though, secretly, he wasn't sure an hour was enough time. There were 1,700 employees working the presidential palace who annually trolled $40,000 to $100,000 each from the budget.

Yet, that was chump-change.

It was similar to a millionaire throwing hundred-dollar bills at a stinking, drunken hobo lying on a grubby wooden bench in Franklin Square Park.

Of course, millionaires didn't stroll there. They didn't want anything to do with Franklin Square Park… the rich didn't hand out spare change.

The president frowned at these thoughts. "Don't let me down, Bobby. I'm counting on you to close up shop here at the people's house." *Bullshit. The country doesn't give two-shits one way or the other whether Bob got everyone out.*

In fact, they might applaud a death or two.

Not everyone was a fan of the Powers Administration.

The White House would be the furthest thoughts from citizens' minds when pandemonium erupted.

Then, it would all be about surviving the day.

His people, the poor, who lived in the Pork & Beans section of Miami–*the ghetto*–could care less about his sell out ass. He hadn't kept one promise to any of them.

The African American president blinked aside those crowd screaming memories and led his underlings through the White House's south portico entrance before stepping across the south lawn. In the distance, Marine One waited... along with a single rigid Marine standing sentry at the bottom of six stairs which folded down from the helicopter.

"You'll get it done, right, Bobby?"

"Don't worry, Mr. President," Robert Laslow answered. "We'll coordinate everything on this end before heading up to Camp David."

Beside *The Prez*–a *slickster* nickname FOX NEWS had assigned the president–Lew and Will stared into the screen of a tablet displaying mass evacuation plans for the coast.

Following close behind was Defense Secretary Clark and the National Security Advisor, Steven Richards.

"You guys come with me," POTUS ordered pointing to everyone except Lew and the SECDEF. "We'll talk strategy on the forty-minute chopper ride." It was the length of time it took to get to Camp David.

The engine of the chopper whined to life, and in the background, over the hectic media scene, reporters yelled their questions.

"Mr. President!" Chuck Stodd shouted from behind the press barrier. "Is the country under martial law?"

"President Powers!" a FOX News Correspondent shouted. "Some say you don't have the constitutional authority to mobilize the military on American soil!"

The Prez smiled at the gutsy reporters and turned back to the admiral. "Lew, what's the status of the evacuations?"

Lew glanced to the Defense Secretary. "Clark, what have we got?"

"It's underway, Admiral," the SECDEF answered staring at his handheld device. "The Governors of Georgia, the Carolinas, Virginia, Delaware, Jersey, Connecticut, Rhode Island, Massachusetts, New Hampshire, and Maine are all moving their people from coastal areas."

"I didn't hear anything about Florida in there," the president whispered waving at the reporters.

Composure, that's what I need now.

It was *all about* throwing off the media. Especially FOX News… they waited for telltale signs of anxiety and seized on any variation of the president's expression. So, every prior president had learned early on how to smirk under duress–*even when every ounce of their being wanted to frown*–to avoid being a tidbit of concern on *Rush Limbaugh's* EIB radio network.

Pushing aside these considerations, POTUS looked to Lew. "What's up with the good Governor of Florida?"

"He's not onboard, Sir. He's up for re-election this year and as chairman of the Republican National Committee, he figures any fight with you is a win for the red party."

"What's wrong with these guys in Florida? Get his office on the horn and have his people meet Sam in South Florida to look over the tsunami impact data."

"Yes, Sir," Admiral Brancor answered pulling out his cell phone. "I'll get the meeting squared away."

"And, Lew?" the president added. "You and Clark get over to Newport News Virginia and order the Norfolk Base Commander to get my fleet out of harm's way."

"Yes, Sir, Mr. President, we'll catch a chopper down there right now."

After POTUS stepped onto Marine One, it lifted into the sky, shadowed by two identical twin-engine VH-3D Sea King helicopters flying in and out of each other's paths like leaping frogs. This was so terrorists didn't know which chopper carried the president.

Inside, POTUS thought the swap-out shell game was comical, even ridiculous. He was seated on an oversized recliner staring towards the Jefferson Memorial. Beyond that, a long procession of military vehicles moved along the 14th Street bridges spanning the Potomac River connecting Arlington, Virginia and Washington, D.C. Three of the four-lane bridges were now closed to civilian traffic. They were bumper-to-bumper with National Guard vehicles. At the north end of the bridge in East Potomac Park, three roadways merged and split into two-way bridges crossing Washington Channel into downtown. There, the traffic was brisk north onto 14th Street, stopping dead at I-395 where heavy traffic crammed onto the Southwest Freeway.

The military shutdown of D.C. has begun.

"Excuse me, Mr. President," the Secretary of State interrupted. "I've just gotten word that due to a nasty cloudburst up in the Catoctin Mountains we can't fly into Camp David. So, the flight team will be putting down at the airport in Frederick."

"Really, I am going back into the beast?"

It was a reference to the Cadillac-badged armored limousine often called *Cadillac One, The Beast,* or *Limo One*.

"I'm sorry, Sir."

"Great, Mildred, things are getting off to a rough start, aren't they?"

"They are, Mr. President."

Twenty minutes later, he stepped off the whirly bird, took three more steps, and sat right back down in the right back seat of the Cadillac.

Twenty-eight miles later, he arrived at Camp David.

There… the situation would get hectic.

Some things never changed, not even for a president.

Chapter 36

MILE HIGH CLUB

PERRY WAS READY for a snack, maybe even a beverage and some casual conversation.

With Mark sound asleep in his lounger, the senior producing editor squeezed by his friend, balanced his drunken legs and waltzed up the generously carpeted blue aisle to a staircase. Climbing its narrow steps, he approached a horseshoe shaped bar crowded by tipsy upper-classman.

They huddled around glasses brimming with spirits.

Jack Daniels, Hennessey... Vodka.

It was all here to numb the pain of solitude.

Located on the upper deck of the airbus, two lounges sold first and business class passengers drinks, hors d'oeuvres, and rich chocolates. The lounge also presented five star delicacies and fine wines carefully selected by the airline's picky sommeliers.

"Can I help you, Sir?" a sexy brunette bartender asked, her fine shimmering hair tumbling over soft brown eyes. The eyeballs peeked through a swatch of brown maple mascara that hinted of playfulness.

Perry grinned. *They know how to play the game.* He'd seen this same stare pointed in his direction at the Penthouse Club of Detroit a week earlier. Then, the glare found him in the backroom of the Gentlemen's Club featuring hundreds of the 'Metro Area's Finest Entertainers.'

Entertainers, ha! Perry thought. *Strippers, exotic sweet-asses, that's what they were! Hookers with a license to whatever!*

"Sir?" the luscious, pouty, red-lipped liquor peddler interjected. "Do you want a drink; maybe get yourself something to eat?"

Oh, yeah, Perry considered. *I want something to eat, all right*. But he wasn't sure if this was the place to speak *those* words. That request would be better asked at the Pussycat Club in London. He couldn't wait to stretch out his flesh in their private booth in the VIP Section. Back there, if he were so inclined, the models would play trumpeter on a certain south pole.

Those girls can suck a golf ball through a garden hose.

Staring at his devious grin, the hotshot part-time actress turned transatlantic bartender could practically imagine Perry's filthy considerations unclipping her hot pink bra. She could feel his lips titillating her plump erect nipples and then, god knows what he wanted to do to her. It wouldn't be the first time a passenger pulled her into the restroom and joined the *mile high club*.

But there had to be a payoff.

SNAP OUT OF IT! Charlene thought. *He could be your lonely old grandfather!*

"Hmmmmm," Perry drunkenly sighed deciding to throw caution to the wind. "Let me have a Crown Royal and your cell number? Never know when you might get lonely wandering the streets of London."

Laughing out loud, the Barbie Doll let it rip.

"Har-de-har-har-har! I don't wander the streets. Look at you, grandpa, what're you, like sixty? You're barking up the wrong tree with aging equipment!"

"Oh, well, can't blame me for trying."

She knew the game, having lived in Los Angeles for five years trying to break into the movie business. She found herself in *pictures,* all right. After realizing the flicks were meant for peep-show side street *adult bookstores*, she was devastated. She'd resided in bedbug infested *no-tell motels* and understood the climb to success in Hollyweird meant sleeping with creeps like this guy was par for the course.

That audition couch everyone heard about was just the tip of the methamphetamine shard slicing up her nose.

By the time she realized Hollywood Boulevard was littered with bloody, broken dreams, she found other things had been shoved up her ass.

Pretty Woman, what bullshit! Charlene sighed. *Richard Gere should be nailed to the cross!* It was because of him she thought she could move to L.A. and find success as an actress; maybe her mom and dad would finally be proud.

Bullshit, she thought. *What a bunch of crap.*

"Let me get a burger," Perry asked, pulling the would-be starlet from her sordid memories. "And only put one ice cube in the Crown, okay?"

"What are you, some kind of big producer or something?" she mumbled returning from the torn memories outlining endless meaningless auditions and the dumpster of lies that filled her soul.

"Or something," Perry slurred.

"What have you done? Anything I've seen?"

"This and that," he chuckled. "Name-dropping is never a good idea if you want to make it in Tinsel Town."

"Is that right?"

"That's the name of the game," Perry assured. "Ah, what is your name?" Then, in the middle of his twisted fantasies of screaming with an exploding orgasm, Mark pushed up beside him and ruined everything.

"Perry, you have to see this!"

"Jesus, Buddy… are you kidding me right now?"

"Are you a producer, too?" the hopeful starlet wondered, her tongue seductively dancing behind perfectly aligned white teeth.

"Huh?" But Mark knew the score, he'd been with Perry long enough to know his producer used the station to lure pussy with imaginings of Hollywood producing.

"What is it, Mark," Perry snorted. "Can't you see I'm auditioning this young girl for a part in my next film?"

"Oh, yeah? Well, maybe you'd better come take a look at something for the script." Pulling him over to the plane's windows, Mark pointed to a large, round cloud thousands of feet above the aircraft.

"What the hell is that?" Perry grunted.

Stretching across the horizon was the largest cloud either of them had ever seen.

The dark, thick, rain cloud was unfamiliar.

"Cumulus, cumulonimbus, and stratus clouds reach sixty-five-hundred-feet," Perry recognized. "That has to be somewhere around fifty-thousand-feet."

"How is this possible?" Mark asked snapping a picture with his iPad. "Altocumulus, altostratus, and nimbostratus climb up to twenty-thousand-feet along with cirrus, cirrocumulus, and cirrostratus that usually hover at that altitude. These are way above that altitude."

"So, what the hell is it?" Perry wondered.

"We're flying at forty thousand feet," Mark stated. "What kind of cloud reaches above the altitude of a commercial aircraft?"

Chapter 37

BESSIE THE BEAST

BESSIE WAS ON THE HUNT.

The nickname was one of many assigned by terrified mariners working the Canary Islands waterways.

The Great Eater, Jessie Jaws & Chow Down Darlene!

The names all meant *one* thing. Swimming meant *bye-bye, ¡adios!* They'd be diving dumplings!

Great whites were bloodhounds.

They pursued the scent of blood and didn't let up until the kill. That scent now inundated the seawater and sharks would chase it like a serial killer seeking a warm body.

"Did you see that?" Tish screamed staring towards the spot where the shark had devoured Fern.

Blood now bubbled from beneath.

"Get us the hell out of here!"

The dinghy was more like a lifeboat and capable of holding fifty passengers. Fully loaded, it could do six knots over twenty-four hours.

Tish just wanted it to move. "Come on! Get us to the ship, please!" Glancing across the sea, she shook with fear, her spine tingled. Up ahead, not more than a hundred yards, a helicopter hovered over the Valencia.

The tender roared to life, its engine going full speed as the fiberglass hull bounced through the breakers.

Suddenly, the boat struck something and Tish was thrown to the deck after the boat *stopped dead* and hurled a seaman overboard. For a split second, she couldn't figure out what might have caused the boat to wreck.

And then… she saw the gray dorsal fin.

It surfaced right before her eyes.

Standing back to her feet, the realization hit home. A fin jutted six feet above the surface, and that... she *knew*, meant fright-filled concerns were at hand.

"Look at the size of that thing!" She realized something then. *It's not the same shark that attacked earlier.*

This one was longer, *much bigger,* and it reminded her of the ancient existence of Megalodon. Being a scientist, she knew most of the largest great whites were found in South Australia. The biggest ever recorded was twenty-one-feet and weighed seven thousand pounds. She'd read textbooks proposing the maximum length a great white could grow was twenty-five feet. This shark was thirty-five to forty feet and as round as a greyhound bus.

"Get out of the water!" she yelled at the seaman a moment too late. The gigantic predator moved between the tender and flailing sailor. His eyes were filled with terror... and told everything about horror.

"Jorge," the man overboard hollered. "Dile a mi esposa que la amo!" He knew, deep down where his whispers said goodbye that his blessed days on Earth were ending in a bloody confrontation with the storied monster.

"No!" Jorge responded in broken English. "Carlo! You're going to be all right, just swim to the boat!"

But swimming wasn't going to happen, at least not for Carlo, because just then *something* tugged him beneath.

Tish thought his body went under like a bobber. Just like the ones she used on her childhood fishing line. When the red and white bobber plunged beneath the lake, she knew there was something down there nibbling.

Swiping a bite at the bait, ever so carefully, it chewed around the little shiny hook.

That's what this is.

Except, the bobber today was a man, the bait was his flesh, and the fishing pole... well, that wasn't going to catch this thing swimming underneath the boat.

We're gonna need a torpedo to kill this thing, Tish thought. *With a nuclear warhead attached to the end.*

That's when it hit her! Whatever pulled Carlo beneath the waterline wasn't the beast she was watching. That monster still circled the boat. Then, the shark turned back, propelling toward the tender. When it reached the hull, its huge skull butted the keel and flipped the boat.

"Help!" Tish screamed hitting the water.

But there was nobody to help.

Before her, bobbing on the surface, an amputated human leg floated within arm's reach. Beneath, dark shadows passed her kicking feet.

Then, the two great whites surfaced and circled Jorge.

His jerking flesh seemed to excite the flesh eaters, because just as Tish decided to swim for the ship in the distance... the monsters pounced on the man.

Reaching into the sea and gaging on seawater, she stroked into the rollers, a fright tugging her mind that hadn't stalked her since childhood.

All she could think of was that fishing bobber.

And, the teeth that tugged it under.

At any moment, she expected a bite and then a sudden jerk that would rip away a leg.

Perhaps the fish would crush her skull.

At least then, it would be over before she knew it.

Chapter 38

NOT A PEEP!

NEW YORK CITY'S Office of Emergency Management planned for mega disasters, coordinated the response, and distributed crisis information.

To achieve this, they employed top-tier first responders, brainy disaster planners, and sworn geeks to run artificial intelligence.

"Catastrophes bring out the looters, rapists, robbers..." the Mayor of New York said as he walked through the office. "There'll be punk kids who break windows and steal from their own mothers."

Beside him marched Sam, Gordy, and a slew of FEMA employees. The entourage had been greeted like a band of rock stars. The only thing missing were screaming fans and bursting pyrotechnics.

Nonetheless, Sam was distracted by a cell phone against his ear and Tish's voicemail bouncing off the eardrum.

"It's Dr. Harriet, and if you hear this;
I'm stalking a volcano, so leave a message!"

That was her... an everyday happy-go-lucky researcher taunting everyone not climbing dangerous volcanoes.

But, that's not where she is now, is it? Sam's mind sneered. *Nobody has heard a peep from her since –*

"OEM controls New York City's response to natural and manmade emergencies," the mayor droned while leading Sam through the crisis intervention center located in the heart of Brooklyn.

"Is everything okay, Sam?" Gordy asked, recognizing the familiar look of apprehension in the eyes.

"Huh?" Sam snapped back from his doomsday prophesies. "What's that, Gordy?"

"The phone call," Gordon nodded to the phone. "Is there a problem I can help with?"

Realizing he'd drifted off–that he hadn't heard a word of what the Mayor of New York had said–Sam shrugged and pushed the phone into his pocket.

"Has there been any word from my wife?"

"Nothing, Sam. I can call Homeland Security, see if they have an update, if you'd like?"

Sam had an uneasy feeling in the pit of his stomach. The typical *gut reaction*, that nudging sense of intuition that everyone experiences when something wasn't quite right. That *gut feeling* that hollered... it was panic time.

"Please make that call, Gordy," Sam nodded. "Would you do that? Jingle-up Professor Bill at the Hazard Research Centre? See if anyone has heard from Tish?"

"Dr. May," the mayor asked. "Are you ready to go in and see the Governors?"

As Gordy pushed across the room to grab a secure line, Sam summoned a reserved grin and nodded.

"Sure, let's get moving."

"As I was saying," the mayor continued. "Here, we focus on natural disasters, preparedness, response, and recovery. Our main purpose, of course, is to keep New Yorkers safe and then, following a calamity, we want to help return our citizens to their daily habits quickly."

Sam was mesmerized by the amount of video screens lining the walls. The space reminded him of Grand Central Station–*it was just that big*–during rush hour. Hundreds of civil servants worked phones coordinating the police response throughout the five boroughs of New York.

"When the plan is activated," the mayor continued. "OEM will coordinate city, state, federal, and non-governmental agencies throughout Manhattan, Queens, Staten Island, the Bronx, and here in Brooklyn. We can certainly guarantee the evacuation strategy will be effectively carried out."

Sam interrupted. "Haven't the evacuations started? Time is short!"

"Large scale citywide emergencies like this require collaboration between dozens of agencies and thousands of emergency responders."

Sam placed his hand on the mayor's arm as the entourage arrived at a conference room door. "You need to start the evacuations now, when this volcano..." It was at this instant, in mid-sentence, when he happened to glance up at a news report. There, a replay of the volcano collapse showed the subsequent tsunami barreling through the Atlantic Ocean.

"Balls up! This is it!" Sam grunted. "The wanker is underway! The tsunami will impact your city in..." he glanced at the mayor. "How long ago did this happen?"

"Just around 10:00 a.m. when you were airborne."

Glancing at his wrist, Sam noticed the *Invicta* hands stood at 11:02. That meant they'd lost an hour of precious time.

"What is it, Dr. May?"

"That wave," Sam pointed to the TV, "will crash into Manhattan in just about six hours!"

At that instant, Gordon pushed through the crowd. "Sam, Sam!" he yelled holding a cell phone. "It's Professor Bill at the United Kingdom Hazard Research Centre!"

Sighing in relief, Sam grabbed the phone, held up his index finger to the mayor and barked into the handheld. "Old chap, what've we got ourselves into here, eh?"

"Samuel," Wild Bill's voice boomed. "I am on my way to 10 Downing Street to meet with the Prime Minister and members of Parliament."

"Billy Boy! You have to push them from London, and soon! It won't be long before this monster heads through the Atlantic, barrels up the Thames, and overflows her banks. The underground and London will be submerged!"

"The evacuations are underway, Sam. However, I have troublesome news, my friend."

"What's that, Mate?" Sam grunted.

"It's Tish. Her plane has gone down in the drink!"

Everything faded then.

It was as though the room morphed into a spinning white haze as Sam's body hit the floor. The *last* thing he remembered, just before losing consciousness, was the mental movie offering a glimpse of the Beechcraft Baron barreling towards Earth.

And then... the bloody explosion.

Oh, Sammy? Duktur Maaaaaaay? A tinny echoing voice whispered in the darkness of Sam's mind.

Argh uuuuuuuuuu-ooooooo-kay, chappie boy?

Sam was gone, onto the other side, cheerio!

Chapter 39

THE DEVIL HIMSELF

LEGENDS AND LORE claimed the existence of a living, horrid, lizard-creature chained deep within the damp catacombs of the Vatican.

The demon was said to have influence over world governments, financial institutions, and Fortune 100 corporations. The fiend was alleged to be king of Earth and a non-human race that controlled the planet for hundreds of thousands of years.

Until… the Vatican got hold of him.

This being was believed to be *the force* behind all war, chaos, and destruction of mankind, throughout the entirety of human history.

The lizard-like creature was fluent in every language. It manipulated politics, money, religious beliefs, and was the master of *mind control*.

"Mankind is ready for this news." Cardinal Petrus read from a note Callixtus had written to the Jesuits upon his election. "The healing of minds and hearts cannot occur as long as this species and its plan remains a secret."

There were twelve men listening to Petrus… each having deep roots within the Jesuits of the Roman Catholic Church. And, they were here to discuss what to do with Callixtus. They sat in hand-chiseled stone chairs built around a thousand-year-old block table. The scent of old blood filled the cavern. Power, murder, theft, and horrid secrets were hidden in this chamber beneath the Sistine Chapel.

"This entity has remained locked up in the dungeon for too long," the cardinal secretary continued reading. "After being captured, chained, and imprisoned beneath Rome, it is time we tell the world of *their* presence."

"Good Lord, Petrus," the Franciscan monsignor grunted. "Surely we can silence Callixtus, no?"

That was the issue.

None of these men were convinced Callixtus would toe-the-line of this long held ancient secret.

World changing revelations were at stake.

The confirmation, *that humans were not alone.*

"How did Callixtus get elected, anyway?" a man dressed in a black cassock growled. "This is life and death for the papacy. I thought you had the votes to become Bishop of Rome, Petrus!"

Shuffling around the table, the *man in charge* was *the black pope...* the superior general, the leader of the Society of Jesus, a Roman Catholic order.

"What's the status of Colonel Meeds?"

"Father General," Petrus softly spoke. "He's the best assassin we have and will make contact on your order."

The black pope nodded.

It was a title the media assigned the superior general.

However, the name was shunned by The Order, and was never used by Jesuits.

"These men we're sending to neutralize Callixtus," the black pope asked, "may be counted on by The Order?"

Silence hung over the room.

The air was heavy with thoughts of the conclave's conspiratorial results naming Callixtus their new leader. The black pope had been assured by the world's cardinals that Petrus would be their man. But when the white smoke drifted from the Sistine Chapel's chimney, it became clear the cardinals had betrayed the Illuminati.

"So Meeds will just kill him?" the Franciscan asked.

"Several pontiffs have been murdered," the black pope answered. "Murder is nothing new to us. Killing is a necessary tool of procedure. The circumstances range from the martyrdom of Pope Stephen the First, to a war that took the soul of Lucius the Second. But they all die…a little push *here*, a small hole in the head *there*. Death lingers."

The archbishop leapt in. "That's right. There was the assassination of Pope John the Twelfth. A number of other pontiffs have also died under circumstances of murder, but, for which, definitive evidence has not been found."

"That's the key," Petrus pitched in. "Nothing leads back to The Order, and so it shall be on this deed."

The black pope ran his fingers along the damp stone chamber walls, his nails scraping through centuries of grime. He considered his power-grab scheme, the snatching of life from the stupid trailblazing pope who'd never be anything but a hopeful possibility.

"The people's Pope!" a bishop mocked. "That's what the media is calling Callixtus, you know! They say he's a *champion* of the poor and downtrodden."

Suddenly, the echoes of shoe heels clacking over stone reverberated through the outer passageway.

The Order turned their attention to a heavy, musky oak door, its rusted hinges screeching as it swung inward revealing a thin, tall, Italian.

"Giorgio Napolo," the black pope welcomed the man wearing a William Fioravanti suit and matching Italian suede and leather monk strap shoes. "You're just in time to chime-in on our decision of *sì* or *no* for *sterminio*."

That meant extermination.

President Napolo was a lifelong Italian politician, the current President of Italy, and a prominent leader of the Illuminati. He led the Italian Communist Party, served as President of the Chamber of Deputies, and the Minister of the Interior.

But, it was his appointment as special Papal Delegate to Pope Callixtus that interested the black pope.

Without an inside man, the plan was useless.

"Are we sure Callixtus will let *it* loose?" the president asked standing beside the black pope. "Do we know for sure he will make a *formal* Vatican speech telling the world that *THEY* are indeed here? It's such a shocking story. It might be difficult for people to believe him."

The black pope raised his hand to vote. "There has been evidence of a subconscious movement towards public awareness of the existence of the beast on TV and around the world. Callixtus will confirm their existence."

"And, the American TV show, Ancient Aliens," the Franciscan monsignor added raising his arm. "There will be millions of people who do believe."

"They're becoming familiar to the public," the archbishop offered, raising his gold-ringed hand, "with the ancient stories of lizard-people now coming out."

The cardinal secretary pushed his arm high. "If we're to keep the secret of bygone years, and hold fast disclosure until *we* decide the time is right, we must protect the church from itself."

At that moment, from somewhere in the catacombs beneath Vatican City, an ageless scream resonated through the stone corridors. That brought stares from everyone in the room, all of whom knew exactly what made the shriek.

Fear rarely resided on the faces of men like these.

But this time, terror lined their brows like remnants of an apple pie plunged into their expressions.

The beast understood what they conspired to do.

It knew everything.

So, the President of Italy glanced towards the door, raised his hand and nodded. "Make it unanimous, then. I vote *sì per sterminio*."

They wouldn't have it any other way.

Pope Callixtus would be sleeping with the Saints below Saint Peter's Square; another precious sainthood realized.

As if on cue, a notification alert bleeped from the cardinal secretary's cell phone.

On the screen, he noticed this text message:

Meeds: Contact in five minutes: Yes or No?

Chapter 40

THE VIRGINS

THE ISLANDS lay directly in the path of the tsunami.

"The Virgins and Bermuda will take first impact in the eastern Atlantic," V.I. shouted over the *whining* U.S. Coast Guard chopper waiting on the sandy beach. "The wave will crush Puerto Rico, the Dominican Republic, Turks and Caicos, Haiti, Cuba... and then, the Bahamas before crashing into America."

Atlantis might sink *again*.

There would be *no more* Paradise Island... the dolphins would find freedom and swim back out to sea.

Playtime was over.

V.I. just arrived in St. Thomas after the United Nations declared the East Atlantic Islands a mandatory emergency evacuation zone.

"We'll never get all the islanders out," Port Authority Director, Carl Mottle complained.

"We have cruise ships," V.I. offered. "They can be loaded to double occupancy and sent for the Gulf of Mexico. Ten C-130 Hercules and dozens of commercial planes are waiting at Cyril E. King Airport to fly people to safety in Mexico, Venezuela, Brazil, and the U.S."

"We've only got five hours." The director shouted glancing along the beach of Sugar Bay Resort & Spa. It's where he'd been married, and now, the realization came pounding that it would ALL soon vanish... washed out to sea by the time sunset kissed the beach.

"Let's get airborne," V.I. suggested. "We'll have a better view of the island from 500 feet." Climbing into the chopper, he watched the landscape below.

The Point Pleasant Resort jutted out into the aqua inlet of Water Bay, which now was a ghost town. Scanning the grounds, V.I. recalled working his way into adulthood from this very location. As a young boy, he worked the pool overlooking the Caribbean Sea where he ferried drunken tourists their Bushwacker drinks. And, sometimes, he'd help carry the inebriated guests to their bungalows where things would get crazy.

The Bushwacker was a highly alcoholic drink of Amaretto, Kahlua, Crème de Cacao, Irish cream, and light and dark rums... It tasted like a frozen milkshake.

Staring towards Pineapple Beach, which sat adjacent to the resort's romantic shoreline, he recalled a drunken summer's eve when he lost his virginity at fifteen. Towards the end of puberty, he called this his sexual revolution. It happened after working a long day of beach parties and pool service. That memory pushed forth a mental movie now while gazing at the end of a nature trail on the 15-acre island preserve.

He and his best friend, Tobago, were drunk.

They'd spent all day working, and when the tourists abandoned liquor in the bottom of their glasses, they emptied the alcohol into plastic tumblers for later.

Those containers would eventually hold gallons.

That night, they pushed through a beachfront trail and stumbled onto the ocean side pool. There, with waves rhythmically breaking on the shore, a bombshell American girl stretched out on a cozy hemp hammock strung beneath a pair of Royal Palms.

"Hey, boy," she winked. "What's your name?"

Just like that... *no pretensions*.

That girl became his first lover. She screamed his name beneath a full moon, and later, after a long distance pen pal relationship... Yvonne became his wife.

He moved to Orlando, had four kids...

"Hey? Are you with me, Mon?"

V.I. reluctantly broke from his romantic vision of yesteryear and glanced towards the director.

"Yes, of course. What did you say?"

"Water Bay, Coki, Spring, Tutu, and Sunsi Bays still have residents refusing to evacuate."

"What about Magens Bay?" V.I. asked recalling the district where he grew up. "They're at sea level!"

The man shook his head. "The residents think it's just another flood warning. Nobody can get their heads around a wave crashing into the island with the force of a bomb, even though tsunami sirens are wailing all over the island."

The territory had recently installed dozens of them on St. Thomas, St. Croix, and St. John.

But leading a horse to water...

V.I. was worried about the 100,000 people stuck on the island. Most were in low-lying areas like Frenchtown, Smith Bay, and Havensight. The establishment of the Caribbean Tsunami Warning Program in 2010 by the National Weather Service was a major advancement for the territory. But it was too little, *too late.*

"Put the chopper down in Peterborg," V.I. ordered the pilot and turned back to the director. "And notify the residents of Magens Bay I want to talk to them."

Below, a beach party was underway.

But this festivity would have no morning after.

Chapter 41

SAVING SCARLETT

ITALY'S 9th Parachutist Assault Regiment unit had a distinguished history.

In Afghanistan, they provided support for Italian troops engaged with insurgents. In Iraq, the squad participated in Operation Antica Babilonia, conducting patrol missions and capturing suspects of terrorism.

These were men of honor.

Colonel Meeds had once been honorable. He'd handpicked these men crouching beside him in the helicopter. He knew they'd be capable of operating under any circumstance.

Except one.

They wouldn't assassinate the Bishop of Rome.

Nobody in their right mind would think of such a thing.

Even if they *didn't believe* in a *GOD ALMIGHTY*... a man wanted to keep his options open. Everyone needed a loophole, a reason why they *didn't* believe while walking the little blue planet.

Because... what if, there really was a GOD?

What then?

Killing the pope! That changed things, didn't it?

It painted a huge swath of black paint across *page one* of the Book of Life that said: you were a dirty, low-down motherhumper.

Meeds stared at his men and knew they didn't want to stand before Saint Peter on judgment day and explain why they punched a bullet into the King of Mankind.

There's no coming back from this business.

Meeds imagined his meeting with Saint Peter would go something like this:

Saint Peter: "So, I see you fought for your country?"
Colonel Meeds: "Proudly."
Saint Peter: "Iraq, Afghanistan, Impressive."
Colonel Meeds: "Thank you."
Saint Peter: "You killed the Bishop of Rome, right?"
Colonel Meeds: "That's correct."
Saint Peter: "Alriiiiiighty then. Enjoy the flames."

"What's so funny, Commander?" one of his men asked.

Meeds laughed, imagining the nonsensical meeting within the *Book of Life* room of purgatory. "Nothing, Sergeant, nothing, I was just thinking of something insanely comical."

"We've heaved Shepherd One off the ship's deck with the crane system," the sergeant pointed below, "and we dropped her burned-out frame into the sea. Are you ready for us to land on deck?"

Meeds peered out the jump port at the wooden deck. The planks were burned crisp and resembled charcoal.

"Let's set her down and find Callixtus!"

Across the ship's bow, he glimpsed the outline of a woman stroking through the surf, behind her, chased the largest shark he'd ever seen.

"Figlio di puttanta!" the sergeant yelled.

The commando was astonished.

"Get this chopper down there!" Meeds ordered the pilot reaching for a HK-416 assault rifle. "Hold it steady, I'm going to give that fish a headache!"

The chopper plunged to the rescue hovering above the waterline. The move gave Meeds a good look at the shark charging for the woman's legs.

"That thing must be nine meters long!" the sergeant supposed. It was fifty-yards behind the woman, speeding the waterline and disappeared.

If this were a JAWS movie, the theme music would start right about here.

"That's well over thirty feet," the major pitched in climbing onto the chopper's skids. "I can't believe this. Sharks don't grow this big, do they?"

But apparently... *this one* DID grow that big.

Because, just then, the shadow of the creature came charging to the surface just feet below the woman.

"Hold me steady!" the major yelled while crouching on the skids and reaching for the woman's arm.

Inside the chopper, Meeds sighted his weapon just over her shoulder and began firing a barrage of 5.56mm bullets. They whizzed through the air, punched through the seawater and peppered the fish's nose.

If it gets close enough, I'll let it eat a grenade for lunch!

His weapon was similar to the one that situated a bullet between the eyes of Osama Bin Laden. The gun also boasted a single shot 40x46mm grenade launcher module attached to the rail system.

A grenade will end the shark's hunt.

As the chopper buzzed the waterline, the major grasped the woman's hand and pulled her onto the skids.

Then, just up ahead, another shark surfaced and made a beeline for the Special Forces chopper.

As the chopper rose above the rocking sea, Meeds stopped firing. He was spellbound by the sight of the beast plunging through the surface, its jaws hinged wide. And then, the flesh eater slammed its teeth shut on the shadow of the woman who'd just been where her blood should have poured.

"Tits on a bull!" the sergeant grumbled glancing back to the energy depleted woman they pulled onto the chopper.

"This is your lucky day!" Meeds said.

Chapter 42

GOTHAM

THE MAYOR of New York was rich and his city dwellers forgave him the silk-lined pockets.

Traveling frequently to lavish vacation homes in Bermuda and London didn't stop the constituents from re-electing the non-conforming, bloated idiot.

He was… *really,* a COW.

However, when talk radio commented that *Hizzoner* had purchased a ten-million-dollar Tilt-rotor helicopter, New Yorkers had it up to the eyeballs.

The airwaves were scathing.

> "That S.O.B." a listener bawled. "Who the hell does this guy think he is, *Ironman,* for heaven's sake?"

> "Does Ironman make the suit," the radio host chuckled, "or does the suit make Tony Stark?"

> "That pretentious rich little millionaire prick!" another caller screamed over the airwaves and into the ears of millions.

Of course, *curses* were partially bleeped out by the station, and this caused subsequent hilarity inside every yellow taxi rolling through Manhattan. Cabbies loved *screaming* those exact words out their windows on any given day. It was a measure of the fare… much to the dismay of the *NYC Taxi and Limousine Commission* who received hundreds of complaints weekly from out-of-towners who'd heard a thing or two.

"Turn that crap off, will ya?" the billionaire mayor ordered his assistant who reached over the New Jersey Governor and flipped off the radio. "That jerk *calls me* pretentious?" He stared at the radio and regretted adding the AM station to his FAVE list so he could stay abreast of what THEY were saying about HIM.

"All the crazies are on AM," the mayor complained. "Just listen to these people on WOR Radio 710!"

Sometimes, things were best left unheard.

This was one of those times.

Beside the mayor, Gordy had a great big smile on his face. He was thinking of a way *Priceline* could sell this *joke-of-a-man* as anything except a narcissistic *out-of-toucher*.

"So, what's the plan, Mayor?" Sam asked, his head still spinning over Professor Bill's call informing that his wife... *the love of his life*, might be dead. He entertained visions of her body, lying shattered upon the seabed... left there for feasting by creepy crawlers.

Deep-sea red crabs would rip at her eyeballs first...

He shuddered at the thought and pushed the fright-fest from mind. "God," he prayed. "If you do exist, I ask for a miracle. Please, send an angel to find and save my wife."

The politicians were speechless staring at the storied scientist. Being dumbstruck was a rare event for them; most times, they couldn't shut the holes between their noses and chins. But this time, they just bowed their heads and twiddled their thumbs.

Gordy got it.

He understood pain.

His girlfriend, Jess, had been in a terrible car accident the summer before last. Her Mustang GT 500 was such a mangled mess that Washington, D.C. EMS had to carry out the Jaws of Life to extricate her body from the crushed steel. However, when they cut her free, the body found another kind of confinement inside a body bag and later...

a traditional oak casket. Since she'd served two tours in godforsaken Afghanistan, her honorable remains now rested in Arlington National Cemetery not far from the plot of U.S. Senator Edward M. Kennedy.

Life… *and death*… hit people hard.

Death is what Sam believed Tish faced. Of course, he didn't know she'd escaped her own type of deadly jaws.

"You all right, Sam?" Gordy asked, scooting over to the man who was becoming a friend.

Sam sighed. "I feel like I've been walloped with a Birmingham screwdriver!"

As the helicopter hulked over the East River, he stared towards the Brooklyn Bridge crammed with traffic as citizens desperately tried to escape the city.

Approaching the nearby Ed Koch Queensboro Bridge, everyone saw that it, too, was gridlocked.

"Why is it," the mayor griped… "When I order a state of emergency, we can't evacuate without traffic jams?" Under state law, he had the power to declare a state of emergency.

This included issuing evacuation instructions.

When he issued the order, he did so with insight from the OEM, State and Federal agencies, the National Weather Service, and jurisdictions throughout New Jersey, Long Island, and upstate New York.

Everyone had the same input.

RUN! And, be faster than the wind!

So, with the governors onboard, the mayor ordered the NYPD to stage all-out evacuation from Central Park's Great Lawn.

From there, they'd make: *THE PUSH.*

The plan: cops would line the park from the EAST, WEST, NORTH and SOUTH.

Then, the brigade would push out into the city, ring every doorbell, knock on each door, and literally push the crowds out of Manhattan.

Just like the NYPD did on *New Year's Eve.*

That's where the chopper was headed, Central Park's Great Lawn Softball Field.

From there, the stage would be set.

Chapter 43

THE OLD SUMMIT

SANTA CRUZ de la Palma was demolished.

As the leased CBS Evening News chartered helicopter circled the shattered island, Tom Anderson couldn't believe the images his cameraman captured.

The seaside community had been beautiful, with a colonial historic downtown district. Bleached buildings and island houses once littered the seashore. It was magical, the sound of crashing waves, the calls of gulls.

Paradise resided here. Now, it was little more than a washbasin of devastated wreckage.

Mammoth boulders had rained down onto the city.

What went up… must come down.

It was simple physics.

The seaside community was wiped out. Its wondrous hotels lining white sandy beaches were flattened. What remained of the landscape was unrecognizable. Atop the sea's receding surge, lumberyards of timber, vehicles, and bodies packed the saltwater. These were images of horror.

> "We're witnessing the largest natural disaster in history," the reporter shouted into the camera. "There must be tens of thousands dead; an entire landmass wiped off the face of Earth."

Tom then silenced himself.

The camera took it all in… the pure wretchedness… fragments of what was.

> "This splendid island below leaves behind a shattered legacy of romantic memories."

Ricky, the cameraman, zoomed in on the shore below.

Thousands of corpses crested upon the sea's whitecaps, the bodies ripped to shreds. Blood stained the foaming seawater, and in some patches it resembled an oil slick ruptured from a deep-water well.

"Look!" Ricky said pointing towards survivors.

They were an injured band of zombies, not more than twelve in all. Balancing themselves atop weak splintered rooftops, they were drifting on the tide, their hands waving through the air, screaming for help.

But in the chopper, their shouts were drowned out by the helicopter blades piercing the clear blue sky.

"We have survivors here," Tom excitedly informed the world. It reminded him of Hurricane Katrina's landfall in Louisiana. When that Category 3 storm bore down on New Orleans, more than fifty levees were penetrated by the ensuing swell. That triggered colossal flooding and more than eighteen hundred had lost their lives.

Like New Orleans, the neighborhoods of La Palma were also washed away. Below, the camera recorded the wreckage littering the cruise port.

The capital lay submerged.

Its colonial houses and elaborate balconies… *GONE!*

Bougainvillea draped frontages… *VANISHED!*

One of the biggest volcanic craters… *EXPLODED!*

Nothing was left… except water.

There was plenty of that for everyone.

La Palma would no longer print tourist brochures touting exciting, dramatic sights of the volcano.

The Extra Frisson Tour was closed for good.

From here on out, the only explorers climbing through the volcanic hillside would be those recovering rotting corpses. The smell would carry for miles…

"It's all over here," Tom sadly pointed towards the submerged seaside enclave, "the island is destroyed."

Below, the camera spied men struggling to hold onto a roof rack of a truck as it plunged through the swell.

Suddenly, a squadron of Spanish Navy helicopters swooped over the rooftops and began lowering rescue baskets towards the desperate survivors. As seconds turned to minutes, the crewmembers tirelessly hoisted the stranded... trying desperately to save the marooned.

For the rest of the Atlantic basin countries... terror still headed to their shores.

Chapter 44

HIT MAN HERO!

COLONEL MEEDS felt good.

His men had cheated death.

Once again, as a direct result of their actions, the reaper... *the messenger of death*, with his black robe and razor sharp scythe, was robbed of his mission.

"Th-th-thank you!" Tish shivered lying upon the cold hard-steel surface of the chopper as it hovered above Valencia's deck. "You mmmm-men saved mm-my life!"

She'd been saved from JAWS.

"It's going to be all right, Ma'am," Meeds assured draping a thin survival blanket around her shoulders. It resembled a black plastic bag lined with tin foil. Developed by NASA to keep astronauts warm in space, it was utilized around the world by rescue squads to retain 90% of the human body's heat.

"You gg-guys are rrrrr-real hhh-heroes!" she stated through chattering teeth. "The way the helicopter swooped out of *nnn*-nowhere and pulled me from the water! I was dead, for sure! Did you *sss*-see that shark?"

"Never seen anything like it," Meeds agreed. And that was true. None of them had ever witnessed a shark that enormous. Glaring at the woman, he realized something. He didn't want to explain to Saint Peter why he'd chosen to kill the pope. Then, in the middle of weighing his options, the skids hit Valencia's deck and the chopper's engines shut down.

"Skids down, Colonel!" the pilot advised. "The ship's officer and medical team are waiting."

Meeds carried Tish out the jump port.

Behind him, his men bounded from the machine and stepped onto charred wood.

"Must have been one heck of a fire," the sergeant mumbled reaching down to touch the singed wood.

"Sir?" an officer dressed in white stepped forward. "I'm MSS Valencia's communications specialist. The Captain has asked me to escort you to the bridge."

Beside him, a doctor stepped forward and pointed to Tish. "Let's get her to the emergency room for x-rays."

"Doctor, I'm okay," she answered pointing to the commandos, "thanks to these guys."

"Is the Holy Father injured?" Meeds asked.

"He's quite well, along with everyone in his group."

"Where is he now?"

"He is on the bridge." Leading them from the deck and through multiple hallways, they came to the promenade deck that resembled an enormous park.

"Incredible," Meeds commented glancing around the interior. "How big is this vessel?"

"It runs the length of ten jumbo jets," the officer smiled proudly. "That's about four football fields long. As you can see, the ship follows a New York City theme."

In moments, they walked onto the bridge's expansive command center. Standing at the windows, Meeds saw the captain speaking with Callixtus and his entourage.

"Captain, Sir?" the officer interrupted. "Here are the men from the chopper who've come to evacuate the Pope."

"Welcome!" Captain Maka said. "Where is Fern?"

Tish stared at the captain. The words wouldn't fall from her lips, so she just looked down.

"He is all right, isn't he?"

"I'm afraid your man was killed," Meeds advised. "He was a very brave man."

"Dead?" the captain winced. But before anyone could confirm the fact, an alarm erupted from a panel.

"Captain! Captain!" a navigator shouted. "We have a rogue wave off the starboard side!"

And, seconds later, the ship tumbled in the ferocious barreling surge.

Instantly, thousands were killed.

For the rest, the fright-fest at sea had just begun.

Chapter 45

HER MAJESTY

NUMBER 10 DOWNING Street was headquarters of Her Majesty's Government.

It served as the London residence of the British Prime Minister, and was often an assembly location of members of The House of Commons.

That's where they beat the shit out of each other.

British police had often used OC gas–pepper spray–to break up fistfights in the House of Commons. They were knockdown, drag through the chamber, knuckles on skin brawls! That's how the British governed.

Something similar was brewing now.

So, the Queen of England suffered through the thirty-minute ride in the back of a Bentley. For most appointments, she traveled in a State car.

These weren't commoner cars.

There were eight State limousines, consisting of two Bentleys, three Rolls-Royces and three Daimlers. All were painted in Royal claret livery and didn't have license plates.

Sitting beside the queen, in the left hand seat, her son, the Prince of England, attempted to convince mum a disaster loomed over their beloved city of London.

It was only the second time in sixty years she'd pushed her nose into the business of state affairs and attended a haphazardly rushed cabinet meeting.

When arriving at 10 Downing, she was stern.

"There's nothing about which I am more anxious than my country," she stated to a room full of men. "And, for its sake, I'm willing to die ten deaths, if that be possible. But I must be sure of this calamity facing our Kingdom." Seated in the Office of the Prime Minister, she studied maps of the North Sea, the Thames River, and London.

"The whole of the city is at threat, Your Majesty!" the prime minister argued with representatives of both parties standing at his side.

"It all seems a bit ridiculous, Mr. Prime Minister!" the queen winced. "Won't the surge simply fill the channel?"

She was the longest serving ruler of England. At eighty-years-old, she was the oldest constitutional monarch of the commonwealth realms, their territories and dependencies.

"Mum," Prince Albert submitted. "Isn't it possible these men are right, that the Thames will overflow and drown the city? Do we wish to punt on the hope it won't occur? This surge might track eastward past the north of Scotland and be driven into the shallow waters of the North Sea. Should that transpire, the English Channel will flood the Estuary."

"Albert," the queen scowled. "Don't be such a tosspot."

The prime minister moved beside Professor Bill and formally introduced him. "Your Majesty, this is the second in command at the United Kingdom Hazard Research Centre at University College London."

"Ah, yes," the queen smiled. "That's where Samuel works, isn't that right?"

"Yes, Your Majesty, Ma'am," Professor Bill bowed at the waist in the appropriate greeting. "Sam is caught up in America with the United Nations Global Disaster Alert and Coordination System. It seems the U.S. President has asked Her Majesty's subjects for assistance."

"And, so they shall have it," the queen nodded. "Now, tell me about the predictions in London."

The prime minister's office was staffed by a mix of career civil servants and special advisers.

One of these was Principal Private Secretary, Marv Martin, and he hurried into the room now.

"Your Majesty, Mr. Prime Minister," he bowed pointing to a telly sitting in the corner of the cherry wood molded office. "I would request you flip on BBC to appreciate the calamity unfolding."

The British Broadcasting Corporation was a public service channel providing impartial broadcasting in the United Kingdom.

"Turn it on, Marv," the prime minister ordered.

Picking up a remote control, Marv pointed it towards the screen. What flared to life were aerial images shot from a news chopper.

"As you can see at home," the voice of a reporter boomed from the television, "a passenger cruise ship is being rolled in the wave that plowed into the vessel off the coast of the Canary Islands."

Silence overtook the meeting as everyone watched the Valencia rolling like a toothpick in a street gutter.

"The wave hit this ship when part of Cumbre Vieja volcano collapsed into the sea causing this massive upsurge!"

Then, the screen split into two, and the new window showed a predicted path the surge might take.

"This colossal wave will hit Morocco within the hour. And then, it will crash into the shores of Portugal, France, and the Southern Coast of England."

On the screen, the coastlines of Casablanca, Lisbon, and France were shaded in bright red with these words:

UNDER 50 FEET OF WATER

"The swell will break into numerous smaller waves reaching thirty to sixty meters in height. Those bulwarks of water will travel up the English Channel... Plymouth, Portsmouth, Brighton, and finally... the city of London will lie beneath seawater!"

The queen turned to the prime minister. "Raise the Thames Barrier Gates at once!"

"Yes, Queen Mother!"

However, everyone knew raising the barriers wouldn't stop what they watched on the television screen.

"Evacuate London and the Southern Coastlines!" the queen shouted. "The commoners must be saved!"

Chapter 46

THE DEVIL'S MINIONS

THE CARDINAL SECRETARY was ecstatic.

Today, Petrus Romano considered himself king.

Appointed by the pope himself, the cardinal served as Callixtus' principal counselor. His term was supposed to end when the previous pontiff left office.

"Is he dead?" the bishop muttered to the co-conspirators watching Italian news reports of the overturned ship. "It looks as if the boat is sinking!"

On TV, Valencia drifted inverted on a rocking sea, her steel hull piercing the whitecaps. Its bridge and decks were submerged, and the bow dipped below the waterline.

"Sweet Jesus," the bishop muttered.

"From your lips, to HIS ears," the Franciscan monk said.

The Jesuits were huddled in the Vatican hotel, searching through Callixtus' personal papers and records. Their mission was to find and destroy all information relating to the ancient secrets of The Order.

On the old television, a news reporter said:

> "It's believed the Pope was aboard this Italian flagged pleasure ship. The Vatican confirmed moments ago a Special Forces squad was in the process of a rescue attempt when the rogue wave tipped the vessel into the depths less than thirty minutes ago."

"Let him sleep with the fishes," Petrus snickered. "Maybe now, the foretold revelations will come to pass." At his feet sat dozens of large cardboard boxes containing file folders.

Kneeling to one, the bishop busily pulled printouts from the records and scanned the contents.

"What does he have?" Petrus asked.

"La verità su tutto!" the bishop answered shaking his head and handing over a sheet of paper. It outlined confidential letters and secret communications between prior popes and their personal secretaries. The summary portrayed the Vatican structure as a corrupt hothouse of suspiciousness, conspiracy, and devious discordant fighting.

And then there was this handwritten note:

Holy Father Callixtus:

Cardinal Petrus Romano is head of Project Earth, the Illuminati's incomprehensible scheme hiding the arrival of an alien conqueror.

The Illuminati and the Jesuits are formulating a plan to assimilate mankind under the approaching global shutdown, as predicted by the book of revelations, except this ending is by the hand of an alien god.

Callixtus, we must act to expose this plot now!

Brother Jack Moyland

"The Holy father is exposing The Order," the Franciscan monsignor shouted staring at the dispatch. "We must be certain he is eliminated! He knows the truth about everything," The paperwork defined the organizational structure of the Jesuits, their conspiracy of silence, and the knowledge of ancient life altering secrets.

"Gather everything!" Cardinal Romano ordered while reading a letter from Vatican administrators to three of the last four popes. It begged for secrecy and non-disclosure.

"I have photos of J-Rod EBE..." the monsignor interrupted, a glare of shock filling his stare. He was holding glossy 8x10 photographs displaying a gray alien once housed in section S-4 on the secret base at Area 51.

J-Rod's skin was pasty gray; the head bulbous in shape. *But it was the eyes that stunned everyone.*

The round orbs were huge, black globes... and, they were empty. The stare reminded the monsignor of vampire eyes. They seemed thoughtful, yet devious.

Pure intelligence resided in the stare.

The cardinal secretary moved beside the monsignor and flipped through a stack of documents. When doing so, he came upon diplomatic cables to the United States, Russia, China, and England...all of which explained the necessity for silence on the issue of visitors from outside Earth.

"Not good," Petrus sighed. "If these letters have gotten out, the church will be ruined."

"Leaders of the Earth," the monsignor read from a dispatch. "Between us, the Holy See, world religions, and the governments of the globe, we must admit the existence of alien visitors from other worlds."

Petrus glanced at the letter.

It was written by a priest assigned to the Vatican Observatory near the apostolic summer palace. Leaping from the paper were words confirming his worst fears.

"They're going to release everything."

And, then... there was this news article:

VATICAN ADMITS
"E.T. Phone Home"

"It would be foolish of the church to say there is no life outside of planet Earth!"

Pope Callixtus the Fourth

It was an astounding Vatican approved announcement. The official word from Rome was:

THEY LIVE!

"Quickly, now!" Cardinal Romano griped. "Burn everything in this room and collect the Cardinals! We have a new Pontiff to elect... and fast!"

The monsignor and bishop exchanged nervous glances.

"Cardinal Secretary," the bishop protested. "We don't have confirmation His Excellency is gone to heaven."

"What about, Novendiales?" the monsignor protested.

Novendiales was nine days of global mourning that began when a pope died. The College of Cardinals had declared that no elections would be held until these days passed following a confirmed death.

Petrus Romano turned on the coward. "You want to join Callixtus along his golden sidewalk to paradise?"

It was a threat as clear as the summer afternoon.

"Certainly not," the monsignor stated.

That settled it.

As far as monsignor was concerned, he'd rather be judged by a court than buried by six. Juries sometimes got it wrong... pallbearers always had that hole in the ground.

The grave would forever wait.

And,   so   would   the   hereafter.

Chapter 47

THE CRUISE FROM HELL

THERE WAS NO WARNING.

Just an ear splitting explosion.

It was the sound of bending steel that filled Mikey's ears as the vessel rocked on the sea.

"Mom!" he shouted when thrown from his feet, his cheek slamming onto the hardwood railing overlooking the promenade. He grabbed it at the last minute, hanging three floors above the turmoil below.

Beside him, passengers somersaulted from the walkway, their screaming bodies *falling*, their voices *shrieking* horrible, terrifying cries that dissipated as they plummeted to gory bloody deaths.

The scene reminded him of a YouTube video he'd seen of people leaping from the Twin Towers on 9/11.

They had two choices. Leap to escape suffocating smoke and climbing fire, Or suffer the agony of the inferno.

Those images would stay with him forever.

Now, what played out before him was something similar to Noah's flood… on steroids.

The taking of life occurred swiftly.

One minute, passengers were laughing, kissing, and fantasizing of the day ahead on an exciting scuba excursion, and the next second, the end came calling…

The end found the passengers swiftly.

Glancing to one of those day-trippers, Mikey saw a middle-ager plummet from the walkway and slam into the marble below. Moments later, his heart ceased beating.

Wham! Bam! Thank You Ma'am!

Next up to the plate…

"Daaaaaaaadd!" Mikey screamed, suspended from the walkway railing. His hands slipping; the flesh losing its clutch due to: *Perspiration.*

The details always got us in the end.

Then, an earsplitting impact pierced the ship's hull… and Mikey thought it sounded like a meteor entering Earth's atmosphere… that cracking re-entry boom. It was the sound of iron twisting… and a millisecond later, a ferocious gush of seawater pushed through an enormous hole punched through the steel hull. Central Park Promenade filled with water and passengers struggled against a violent current of debris-filled water.

Many were injured and killed from the rubble.

Blood spurted from passenger's wounds as they slipped beneath the brine, twisted horrid expressions of fear and disbelief frozen on their faces.

This wasn't part of the FAM package…

Surprise! It was a cruise only special!

"Mom!" Mikey yelled above the desperate cries for help. "Dad, where are you?" He scanned the madness of the rising water… bodies plunged through the torrent; the cacophony of fear driven shrieks filled the esplanade.

Human figures… many of them clustered, some *dead,* others *alive…* floated below the railing where his grip now depended upon sweaty fingers.

The scene was out of the *Poseidon Adventure!*

And then, Michael comprehended something.

The waterline had reached his dangling feet and, he could swim. The promenade deck, once a hundred feet below, was now filled with millions of gallons of seawater and the coolness of it tickled his legs. Glaring into the depths, he saw large fish darting through the hull.

With this sight, another realization struck him.

The boat is going to sink.

What Mikey didn't know… what none of the dying passengers *could know*, was a 100-foot wave had crashed into the starboard side of the vessel carrying a boulder-sized piece of the volcano. That's what pierced the ship's casing, dooming the vessel.

"Somebody, help me!" a teenaged girl yelled. She was trapped in the rush of seawater. "I'm going to drown!"

Mikey glanced at her, released his grip on the railing and slipped into the unsympathetic saltwater. Stroking towards the panicking girl, he utilized superior swimming skills to reach her. "I'm gonna save you!" he yelled across the gushing current. "Just hold on, don't give up!"

The ocean liner rocked with a long line of subsequent smaller waves. The sea was heavy and it tossed the superliner into its rollers. The effect was comparable to a bowl of water atop a roller coaster.

"Puh-lease, hu-hurry!" the girl shouted, gaging on seawater forcing its way down her throat. "I can't swim!" She flailed in the water and grabbed hold of a corpse floating nearby. Its head was missing and dark red blood oozed from the neck. As she looked for *something else* to clutch, Mikey seized the girl around the waist.

"I got you," he guaranteed, making for the edge of the waterline for a handhold. Around them, survivors struggled to stay afloat as the water rose. With each inch of seawater, more people slipped beneath the surface.

As more and more drowned, Mikey counted the minutes until the grave would find them all.

There was no escaping the darkness.

Chapter 48

SKYFALL

PERRY WHITSON didn't know what to think.

The cloud is weird.

High-level billows like the one he'd seen did form above 20,000 feet, but since temperatures were so icy at these elevations, he knew the clouds should be comprised of ice crystals. The cloud should have appeared thin and wispy.

That's not what I saw. That thing was big!

After an hour staring at the gigantic cotton ball up in the lounge, Mark and he stumbled back to their seats where the meteorologist nodded off in a throaty, reverberating snore.

"Excuse me, Sir?" a blue-haired centurion begged pointing a gray 14-inch single point knitting needle. "Can you please bump your buddy? I can't focus on knitting my great-great grandson's fall sweater with that noise!"

"They let you on the plane with that thing?"

It looks like an ice pick.

Just because a fragile old woman possessed it shouldn't be reason enough to let the shank through security. Especially since TSA agents wanted to shove body scanners up the asses of business travelers.

"Of course they let it come on, why not?"

"Never mind," Perry smirked nudging his friend. "Hey, Mark! Stop cutting logs, will ya? I'm trying to read up on that strange dark cloud."

Nodding her appreciation… or just recalling a long stored memory, the old woman chuckled. "You two devils have been up in the bar tipping a bottle, haven't you?"

"Maybe one or two," *the producer* snickered and peered back to the computer and 𝕿𝖍𝖊 𝕿𝖊𝖑𝖊𝖌𝖗𝖆𝖕𝖍 news article.

CATACLYSM

History's Greatest Conspiracy Theories

In the piece, it outlined a phenomenon known as Chemtrail Conspiracy Theory. Because of its popularity, world governments had received thousands of complaints from citizens demanding explanations of the zigzagging white trails cutting through the blue sky. The term *chemtrail* referred to floating tracks caused by systematic high-altitude dumping of chemical substances.

Theorists deduced the purpose of the chemicals might be for human population control, or biological and chemical warfare.

Now, how do you like that? Perry grunted.

Reading down into the text, he devoured this:

> "Many conspiracy logicians consider contrails trailing behind airplanes are the result of elements and genetic agents intentionally scattered at high altitude. There is global conjecture that the elements sprayed involve the New World Order directed by sinister services within world governments."

Perry bought into the *cloak and dagger* stuff, he *was* an intellectual and understood governments had their own vicious agenda. His considerations always went back to the Denver Airport and the arguments of underground bases.

Population control seems plausible.

Earth could only sustain so many human beings.

The 18th century philosopher, Thomas Malthus, supposed humans' voracious urge to reproduce would ultimately lead to overpopulating the planet, eating up all the natural resources and causing people to die from worldwide famine.

But what was the tipping point?

How many people were too many?

That was the question!

After finishing the article, he glanced up to see passengers abandoning their seats to stare out the port side windows. It was like watching an episode of Twilight Zone–*not that anyone watched that anymore*–but he recalled an episode where an airplane passenger looked out his window and saw a monster on the wing…

"Look at that thing!" an overweight woman said in shock, rifling through an oversized Chinatown acquired Luis Vuitton knock-off handbag and pulling out a pair of *off-the-shelf* Walgreens glasses. You know the kind, those cheap $2.99 plastic lenses jammed onto displays in the pharmacy.

"I'd say that's one hell of a cloaking device," a bald man hooted. "It must be the size of the Georgia Dome, wouldn't you say, Mabel?"

"M-mmm," Mabel replied. "It ain't anything I've seen before, that's for darn sure. You think it's ours?"

Perry pushed Mark awake.

"What's going on?" the meteorologist grunted.

"Look at this!" Perry pointed out the window.

"What is it?" Mark whispered, aiming his iPad through the porthole. "That isn't an NSA weather balloon."

"It's a UFO," old Mabel cried, her eyebrows raised above wide eyes. This was the *experience* that world governments declared were wild imaginations that never really happened.

But here it is, larger than life, Mark realized. "It's some kind of ship," he mumbled. He now knew that everything Perry supposed about UFO's was true. Snapping off a few crystal clear pictures, the display brought a close up of the gunmetal gray edge of a craft poking through the cloud.

It was an enormous silver metallic disk-shaped mother ship with a classic domed roof.

Jutting through the leading edge of the cloud was a line of dark porthole shaped windows. Above them, the dome spun counter-clockwise while the bottom rotated in reverse.

Rainbow strobe lights burst from the craft and bathed the cabin with bright light.

"We're going to die," someone blurted.

Then, the ship cloaked itself again in the cloud.

Perry was stuck to the window, glaring at the cloaking cloud, realizing there was something marvelous hidden inside the shroud. For him, everything he'd believed about Denver, Roswell, and Area 51 had been confirmed.

But, now… he was scared.

Then, seconds after realizing he'd have to go public on the station about what he'd witnessed and speak of the aliens visiting Earth, the plane was hit by a laser.

The cabin exploded inward, and for an instant, Perry Whitson didn't know what hit them… until the seats were ripped from the floor and sucked out the airplane.

He always wanted to experience skydiving.

But not like this.

Chapter 49

PUERTO RICO
-Does it Better-

SLOGANS... everybody had one.

Puerto Rico is no different from any place else, V.I. thought as he flew over San Juan.

The government wants us to believe they do everything better, but look at this place. It's a virtual ghetto once you abandon the beaches.

Come to Puerto Rico!

That's what the glossy slick commercials begged on American television. The spots insinuated lonely tourists would find wild parties, fun filled vacations and, yes... even erotic, sweat drenched sex on the pearly beaches.

It was a dream of frozen margaritas, the roar of crashing waves pounding the shore... and a suntanned piece of ass riding atop erotically charged, grinding flesh!

That vision enhanced the fantasy.

Orgasms drove industry. *Calvin Klein, Victoria's Secret, Abercrombie & Fitch...* they all used sex to sell their sexy products. Even Old Spice tugged at the minds of women by placing a shirtless swan diving Old Spice man alongside a Komodo dragon on an exotic beach.

Take away the deodorant and the ads stink, V.I. thought while watching the packed shoreline below.

The Isle of Enchantment was a popular tourist destination... however, it didn't do anything better.

"We are proud to be an advertising hub," the official grinned. "Our beaches are featured in ads and on book covers around the world!"

But, the suntanned throbbing sexual escapades the state wanted tourists to believe didn't really exist. This wasn't *Shades of Grey*; Fabio's days were long over. The hundreds of *romance* novel book covers he'd posed for... were going out of print.

Reality reeked.

"There's nothing romantic about this national emergency," V.I. pointed out. "Conditions in La Isla del Encanto are grim and getting worse by the hour."

He'd been touring the island trying to convince local officials the tourist destination was about to join the city of Atlantis. It would be buried beneath the Atlantic Ocean.

Nobody wanted to believe him.

"We have a great location," a disaster coordinator stated. "We're fantastically rich in history and have the best beaches; we'll survive this emergency, too!"

"The entire Caribbean will be gone," V.I. incredulously stated, not wanting to offer *any* sense of false hope. He knew the facts, saw the disaster model predictions and understood that ALL Atlantic Ocean islands would be gone in a matter of hours.

"We're located in the Caribbean," the official went on almost as if V.I. was a tourist and not an evacuation assistance official. "The island lies east of the Dominican Republic and is a mere thousand miles southeast of Miami. The entirety of the island is just one hundred miles long and thirty-five miles wide. We are the smallest and most eastern island of the Greater Antilles. But we're prepared and shall survive this horrendous storm."

"This is not a storm! It's a tsunami! Puerto Rico will be wiped off the map! Cuba, Hispaniola, Jamaica, all of those countries began evacuating!"

"We've survived other natural disasters!"

That was true. Six major hurricanes had wreaked havoc on the island, along with Caribbean floods.

But nothing was comparable to this.

"Look down there!" V.I. pointed to the famous beach and hotel strip of San Juan. "That landscape will be under water, you won't see the hotels, and it will be as if you're looking across the ocean! No land will exist!"

Below, Pine Grove Beach stretched between the Ritz-Carlton and the Marriott Courtyard at the end of Isla Verde. Its crescent white-sand beach was packed with lounging tourists. The scene was tranquil at the moment; the serene ocean was filled with frolicking tourists.

"The shore is protected by an offshore reef from the often rough Atlantic current," the official dismissed. "The shoreline is completely sheltered, and a long sandbar and shallow water stretches far offshore. If anything unusual happens we will have plenty of time to prepare."

V.I. glanced a mile south towards surfers and boogie boarders riding waves. Sailboats and catamarans filled the open water. "Hey, Mon!" he shouted, his island accent rising. He'd often revert to his native tongue when pissed-off. "The President of the United States has ordered evacuations of all U.S. Territory islands!"

The official shrugged. "What happens in America is far from the way things are done here, my friend."

Earlier, they'd flown over Condado and Isla Verde along San Juan's coast. There, Ocean Park's wide beach was also packed to capacity.

"People are swimming in the surf!" V.I. pointed. "You have people down there kite surfing and boating. They'll be dead if you don't act soon!"

"We are not going to evacuate based on a possibility!" the official argued. "Perhaps, if the duly elected Governor notices signs a tsunami is headed this way we will change strategies... but, thus far, nothing more than a rogue wave has hit the Canaries three thousand miles from here!"

Coast to coast, beach to beach, people crowded the shore, as if nothing was happening. In the southwestern corner of Puerto Rico, Boquerón Beach allowed snorkelers to waddle through its waves. The lifeguards were on duty, shops were open, and people surrounded beach picnic tables and barbecue pits. Fried fritters continued to fill their bellies; it was just another day.

Earlier, V.I. watched as government boats refused to evacuate the smaller islands of Vieques, Culebra, Culebrita, Palomino, Mona, and Monito.

"Did you know," the *tape recorder of a man* droned on, "our coasts cover more than three thousand square miles and we're the third largest island in the United States?"

Puerto Rico is in trouble, V.I. realized, *and there is nothing I can do about it.*

Soon, there would be no Puerto Rico.

Chapter 50

IN THE NAVY

NAVAL STATION Norfolk controlled the United States' Fleet Forces Command.

The base provided naval assets under control of the Secretary of the Navy. Its assets were allotted to Northern Command Combat Commanders under authority of the Secretary of Defense.

"Get my boats out of the Atlantic!" SECDEF Clark barked to the base commander. "That's what the President has ordered!"

"Sir, we have nowhere to send 'em," Captain David A. Cullen answered. "The logistics of moving naval assets is proving extremely difficult."

"Why the hell is that?" Clark spat.

Admiral Brancor turned on the Secretary of Defense. "With all due respect, Clark, you answer to the President and Captain Cullen to me. He's not the enemy, the tsunami is... and I won't have you barking at my men like dogs."

"Are you questioning my authority, Lew?"

"Secretary, I serve at the leisure of the Commander in Chief. We both have our orders and mine are to support the mission of Captain Cullen in evacuating the base."

Clark was livid, yet he recognized the problem.

Lew had the president's ear.

He was POTUS' closest confidant and the Chairman of the Joint Chiefs of Staff.

The captain nodded his appreciation to Lew.

"Mr. Secretary, Sir, there are countless explanations as to why the fleet isn't out to sea."

Cullen was second generation Navy with a master's degree in National Security and Strategic Studies.

Following his stint at Joint Forces Command, he reported to Supreme Allied Command Transformation as Counter Improvised Explosive Device Integrated Product Team Leader in support of training. Not long after, the captain was ordered to *Newport News* to assume command.

"What are your explanations?" the SECDEF grumbled.

"Sir," Captain Cullen respectfully answered. "The Fleet comprises 118,000 Navy and Marine Corps personnel serving two hundred ships and 1,300 aircraft. I have an area of responsibility ranging through most of the Atlantic Ocean, North and South Poles, Caribbean Sea, Gulf of Mexico, and the waters of the Pacific, Central and South America. At this base, I have seventy-five ships in port alongside fourteen piers. That's a lot of hardware to relocate in less than five hours."

"And there's nowhere to send the ships," Lew agreed. "There isn't enough time to move the fleet into the Gulf of Mexico, but we are going to try!"

"I know that, Lew!" the SECDEF groused. He knew the numbers. What he had trouble digesting–*the dilemma that shifted his ire*–was the fact everyone *knew* these ships would be lost. There wasn't a safe destination to send them because it would take hours to reach the safety of the Gulf– *time they didn't have.*

"We occupy four-miles of waterfront property," Lew offered looking across the base. "That's seven-miles of pier space, supporting the nation's largest concentration of U.S. Navy forces in the world."

"There's simply not enough time to move everything," Captain Cullen added. "Port Services controls more than three thousand ships and Air Operations traffics one warplane to the runway every six minutes. That's an average of three hundred flights per day."

Norfolk was the hub for Navy logistics and it was now busy with evacuations. In the distance, a gigantic crate was hoisted onto USS Harry Truman. Nobody knew what the bus sized weapon was, but it had been secretly brought onto base, by order of the president, atop a covered tractor trailer. Once on the pier, it was quickly sent out to USS Harry Truman for a secret mission.

The thunderous whine of Harrier Jump Jets drowned out the captain's words as they hovered and landed on USS George Bush. Perfect for use on aircraft carriers, the fighters took off and landed like helicopters.

"Why are we loading the Harriers?" Clark asked.

"Leap frog rescue missions," Lew answered. "We may have wounded after impact, and we'll need the jets to get the seriously injured back to land for treatment."

Scanning the port, SECDEF Clark watched them land on the deck of the Nimitz-class carrier moored at the pier.

"Those are our three available Atlantic Fleet carriers," Lew pointed towards the hulking carriers, "the USS George H.W. Bush, Abraham Lincoln, and my personal favorite, the Harry S. Truman."

"Why is Truman your favorite, Admiral?" Secretary Clark asked, glancing over at the storied admiral. Although he was in charge of executing the president's orders, he wasn't familiar with Lew's service history.

"Since the end of the Iraq war," Lew proudly stated, "most of our carriers have returned to base for maintenance. Truman was *my boat*, under *my command* and it proudly served as the flagship of Carrier Group Two, Strike Group Ten. During my watch at the helm, it was part of the Carrier Battle Group that participated in Operation Joint Endeavor, Deny Flight, Southern Watch, Enduring Freedom, and Operation Iraqi Freedom."

The SECDEF stared at Brancor with pride. He knew the admiral was famous around the pentagon, and now he understood why. *The man is a legend.*

"There are also amphibious assault ships in port," Captain Cullen pointed to the horizon. "Multiple dry cargo ammunition vessels are here, several cruisers, destroyers, frigates, and submarines... practically all of the Atlantic Fleet."

"Christ," Clark blurted. "It's a hell of a time not to be at war, huh?" Staring through the port, he eyeballed a line of Los Angeles Class Submarines. They were nuclear-powered fast attack subs that formed the backbone of the Navy's underwater force. The Los Angeles class contained more nuclear submarines than any other class in the world and they had the ability to wipe out entire countries if so ordered by the president.

"Where are the subs heading, David?" Lew asked.

"ABH," Cullen answered. "Anywhere but here... I ordered them all out to sea, where they'll dive deep. Normal tsunamis are only deadly when approaching land, but this one was caused by a mountain falling *into* the ocean, so it's more like a rogue wave, and those are ship killers. We'll need the subs for rescue operations."

Everyone knew this wave was different.

The captain had been briefed on the incident involving the Valencia and understood his ships would face similar destruction as they made way from Virginia's shoreline.

"You think they'll be safe?" Clark asked pointing towards the subs.

Lew shrugged, "only time will tell."

"Where is the tsunami now?" Captain Cullen asked.

"It's headed for the coast of Africa," Lew answered.

Chapter 51

LAND OF BOGART

CASABLACNCA was Morocco's biggest city with more than three million residents.

The city was famous thanks to the 1942 Hollywood picture, *Casablanca*, starring *Humphrey Bogart*.

"Oh, Mark, you're marvelous!" an elegantly tanned New York literary agent smiled to her lifelong partner flipping through a tourist brochure. "Don't you wish to venture out and visit the Hassan II Mosque?"

"You sure they won't chop off my head, Joy?"

"Oh, stop it. Surely you jest. You love Africa. Remember the last time we came here? You charged across the plains, that rifle in your hands, the scent of lion blood filling your nostrils, the great hunter at work!"

"It was a movie set, luv!" he answered, a grin creasing his middle-aged face. "I was showing an actor how to play his part! Far from the bloodthirsty killer you've made me out to be. I was on my twelfth rewrite, of a great script, for a nickel and dime studio!"

They'd laughed together for days over that day.

That script was the *last time* he wrote for the studios.

Rewriting and *rewriting*, on a script that was *perfect to begin with...* wasn't his idea of a story arc.

It was butchery!

Joy was lounging in *Le Lido Thalasso and Spa's* beachfront bungalow nibbling on an assortment of melons and grapes. It was a luxurious hotel.

Smiling to the love of her life, she glanced back at the brochure and a photo of the mosque. She'd visited the holy structure once before and recalled climbing its 689-foot minaret. The tower was the world's tallest, atop which a laser directed its light towards Mecca.

Joy read while chewing. "The building rises above the ocean on a rocky outcrop reclaimed from the sea. It's one of few Islamic religious buildings open to non-Muslims. In order to see the interior, visitors must take guided tours, be decently dressed, and once inside, remove their shoes."

"You're kidding, right?"

"Come on, grumpy," she grinned.

"How do we get there?"

"It's a twenty-minute walk, from Casa-Port train station. The road is busy with traffic and has few pedestrians."

Mark shook his head. "The hotel says there have been isolated reports of muggings along that route."

"It's better to take a petit taxi from the town center," she agreed. "But, it may be costly."

"Who gives a rat's ass?" he chuckled before kissing her on the cheek. "I'd rather stick an iron up my ass than stomp through Africa's dust filled streets. Plus, I've been up since 5:00 a.m., remember?"

He was sore about being awakened at the crack of dawn by the *Adhan*. It was a call to prayer that blared over street loudhailers. At first, he overheard a soft hum in the distance, and then it increased steadily.

At first the screech was disarming, especially to westerners like Mark who were unaccustomed to the prayer's role in Islam. But after a few days, it was like everything else in Morocco. The screams assimilated into daily life and people had to respect or ignore them.

Ignoring the scream was impossible.

And the Muslims know it, Mark thought.

Although he'd expected some sort of audible notice for the daily devotion, he wasn't prepared for the chaotic cacophony of voices screaming all at once through a speaker just outside the hotel widow.

"Dedicated, aren't they?" he griped. "Why don't they push themselves into a closet, nice and quietly and pray to the drywall… why blurt out their demands along the streets and wake up the tourists? I mean, we are paying a thousand dollars a night for this place, after all!"

Having shook awake, there was no going back to sleep.

So, he huddled up to his MacBook Pro and wrote a chapter of his latest crime novel while Joy worked a long string of e-mails sent by jittery clients across the globe.

She was one of the best New York literary agents to be had, and all the senior editors at the big publishing houses knew she maintained the freshest faces of the storybook future. Nevertheless, with the emergence of the e-book phenomenon, bookstores were going out of style, much like Blockbuster Video and record stores.

The middlemen were being pushed out everywhere.

Direct consumer sales, *downloads…* that was the future.

Steve Jobs, Joy thought. *It was HIS entire fault.*

The creation of the iTunes store is what ushered the end to brick and mortar stores where *real* people walked into physical buildings to browse wonderful record covers.

That was the beginning of the end.

It won't be long before iTunes and Amazon take out Barnes & Noble and Books-A-Million.

Flipping on the television, Joy pushed aside her concerns and stared at a Moroccan news report displaying images of terrified people running through the Port of Casablanca. Their faces lined with fear, and at that instant… screams erupted out on the beach.

Turning to Mark, she asked, "Why are they screaming out on the shore?" Hurrying to the beachfront entry, she reached for the door and pulled it open. On the other side, just a millisecond before the sight revealed itself, she gasped as Mark moved beside her.

In the distance, a wave the height of her New York penthouse hurled itself towards the beach. In its crest, hundreds of sea vessels tumbled through a violent wave.

"Oh, my goodness gracious!" she sighed.

Not a second from then, a violent punch of water flattened the resort and any further thoughts Joy may have had for dinner along the glittering coast.

She'd never discover *the next* Stephen King.

But, someday... perhaps, her agency partner, Joyce Keating, would have their favorite client write the tale of the great *Cataclysm* that hit Morocco.

And, possibly, it would be a *New York Times Bestseller. Ah, the stuff of dreams!*

Chapter 52

LOOSE LIPS SINK SHIPS

HAVING LOOSE LIPS meant this:

Someone had a big fat nasty mouth.

The words from that hole could sink ships.

And, when ships sunk, people ended up dead.

End of story, exclamation point!

The phrase of "Loose Lips Sink Ships" became popular during World War II when sailors on leave yakked incessantly about the warships they sailed on, where they hailed from, and where they were headed.

Snitches needed stitches.

The enemy in WWII was smart. They'd wait in taverns for drunken U.S. sailors to show up, toss back their beer, and voice their seafaring tales. It didn't take long for secret information to somersault from jawbones.

When *that* happened, spies dashed into the night and called in a vessel's position to airfields.

Soon after, propellers spun, bombers took flight, and shells tumbled through the clouds.

Ships would sink.

That's what Colonel Meeds always said.

Now, staring at Cardinal Jonathan heading his way, he didn't show any sign of recognition. They'd come across one another multiple times in Vatican City, knew the same *co-conspirators*, and were both members of the Jesuit Order who wanted Callixtus dead.

"Meeds!" Jonathan whispered.

"Shut the hell up, you idiot," the colonel growled.

The bridge had been upended–*up was down* and *down was up*–the vessel's officers and three commando's lay dead in the rising waterline. They were killed instantly when the bridge's windows imploded in a spray of glass that sliced through their bodies like a thousand knives.

Sloshing through the water, Meeds turned back to the Bishop of Rome. Grabbing him by the arm, he pointed to Captain Maka making way through a doorway.

"Colonel Meeds," Callixtus muttered. What are we going to do? The ship is going to sink!"

"Follow the Captain through the door!"

"Swim for the bridge door!" Captain Maka shouted as water gushed into the bridge. His head was spinning and he suspected he'd been knocked unconscious for a moment.

With the floor now above their head–along with the helm and instrument panel–Callixtus, Cardinal Jonathan, and Tish swam for the exit's archway.

Everyone else on the bridge was lifeless.

Finished! Kaput! Fish Food!

Reaching the flooded doorjamb, Meeds pulled himself through the exit before reaching down for the others.

"Grab my hand! I'll pull you through, one at a time!"

First to reach his grasp was Tish, her frame shivering from another shock of cold seawater.

"What happened, Captain?" Callixtus anxiously muttered. "Why is the ship underwater?"

"A rogue wave hit," the skipper guessed reaching for a handhold. "The force of the wave must have tipped the vessel! We're entirely upside down, which means we're now fifteen stories beneath the waterline."

Tish gasped. "We're going to sink?"

"I'm not sure," the captain answered, his hand wiping water from his brow. "But one thing is certain; we've got to climb to higher decks."

"Can we get out, Captain?" Callixtus queried pulling himself along the edge of an instrument panel jutting from the water.

The captain nodded. "We'll have to make our way to the promenade deck in order to reach the life boats." His voice was wrinkled with uncertainty and it came across loud and clear. "Nevertheless, I'm not sure they'd still be moored after such an impact." Hoisting through the doorway, he found himself standing on the hallway ceiling. Its once hanging light fixtures lay at his feet.

"It's the tsunami!" Tish blurted standing beside Callixtus, his kind stare taking in her terrified presence.

Everyone turned to her then.

"What tsunami?" Cardinal Jonathan inquired, the words plummeting from his mouth like those of a frightened boy hearing of a tragedy for the first time.

"The Cumbre Vieja volcano," Tish informed with an expression of disbelief planted on her face. "Surely you received a warning of the collapse?"

The men glanced at one another in uncertainty.

"You know… the huge earthquake?" Tish insisted.

"Yes," the captain nodded. "We made port in Santa Cruz and found the harbor in shambles. We pushed out of there for Tenerife due to the earthquake."

"Oh, you don't know the half of it," Tish sighed telling the story. Within minutes, she'd laid it all bare, the whole scenario right down to the catastrophic tsunami facing England and the United States.

"Lord, have mercy," Callixtus mumbled. Now, he understood why the soles of his shoes stepped across the ship's ceiling instead of floorboards.

"There will be little help dispatched," Tish supposed. "With the earthquake, volcano, and a resulting tsunami, I'm sure the Spanish Navy has bigger problems than a boatload of ship-wrecked tourists."

"I doubt they even know we're out here," the captain admitted. "Our communication systems were knocked out when Shepherd One crashed on our deck!"

"What?" Tish said in surprise, turning to Callixtus. "Are you all right?"

Callixtus motioned to his soaking-wet cassock. "I'm none worse for the wear and better than most."

Then, the lights blinked out.

"There's an emergency box down the hallway," Captain Maka blurted in the darkness while navigating a damp wall. "There are flashlights and a first aid kit in the strongbox."

But, before they could reach it, the vessel listed to starboard and everyone was tossed off balance.

And with that, seawater pushed into the hallway.

Chapter 53

CENTRAL PARK

CENTRAL PARK maintained twenty-six state of the art ball fields for softball *and* hardball competitions.

Positioned at the center of Manhattan, it occupied over eight-hundred-acres of city-owned land and was the most visited urban park in the United States.

Now, more than 35,000 NYPD cops stood on its Great Lawn awaiting orders from their commanders.

Most had shuffled in by way of the B & C trains at 81st Street. More from 86th Street where they'd hopped off the number 4, 5, and 6 subway lines.

"Are you kidding me?" the mayor griped to the police commissioner while glancing over diagrams for *The Push*. "Can't we move evacuations faster, for crying out loud?"

"There are eight-million people in the city, Mr. Mayor. Clearing everyone out of their workplace and knocking on every door is going to take at least ten hours."

"That's unacceptable! We don't have that kind of time."

"Sam, what do you think?" the N.Y. Governor asked. "I suppose this operation may take twenty-four hours to get everyone out of the city."

Sam pushed his cell phone into his pocket. "The entire Atlantic basin is facing the same situation. I just heard from my guy down in the Caribbean; he has the same problem."

"So, what the heck is the plan?" the mayor asked, staring towards his feet where a map of Manhattan spread across the grass.

Sam ran his finger along nine evacuation zones assigned dissimilar colors. "We've less than four hours to move everyone off the island! This park and everything within thirty miles will soon lie beneath fifty feet of water!"

The mayor was beside himself. "I'm trying to determine how to move eight million New Yorkers, including those without cars, through clogged streets, tunnels and over bridges that connect Manhattan to New Jersey. It's not going to be easy!"

"Easy has nothing to do with it, chap," Sam regrettably argued staring at the map. "Millions of lives are in your hands. Every ferry, bus, train, and bridge must be utilized."

Pointing to the skyline, he swept his arm across it.

"Imagine a wall of water half the height of the Empire State Building moving at five hundred miles per hour!"

"Those buildings are untenable at that speed," the New York Governor pitched-in. "Those buildings were not built to withstand that type of impact!"

Hundreds of cops watched Sam outline New York Harbor. "Imagine, Sirs, the debris field... boats, ferries, tankers... and whatever else that lies in the pathway as the wave comes ashore and impacts the skyscrapers lining the FDR and West Street. The upsurge will bring down buildings and inundate the East River. It will overtake the Brooklyn, Manhattan, and Williamsburg Bridges. And while the water drowns Chinatown and pushes across to the West Village, the pressure will crush the Holland Tunnel."

"We're screwed eight ways from Sunday," the New Jersey Governor grumbled realizing how bad things really were. "The tri-city area will never recover."

Sam hung his head then.

"It's the end!" the mayor mumbled. "There has to be a way to save my people!"

In fact, there was a proposal to evacuate New Yorkers.

After a test run of forty ferries, barges, and tugboats along the East and Hudson Rivers, the mayor's office figured 200,000 people an hour could be saved before the monster wave moved into the bay.

Evacuating eight million would be impossible.

The Police Commissioner sighed. "How is my department going to evacuate Manhattan in less than five hours?"

"You don't," the mayor grunted in desperation. "There simply isn't enough time."

Chapter 54

SHANGRI-LA

CAMP DAVID was in panic mode.

"What are we looking at?" President Powers barked marching into Laurel Lodge. "Now that we're nice and safe up in the hills, let's get down to the people's business."

Located in the hills of Catoctin Mountain Park near Thurmont, Maryland, the retreat was officially *Naval Support Facility Thurmont.* Considered a military installation, it was first known as Hi-Catoctin, a camp for federal government agents. Converted to a presidential retreat by Franklin D. Roosevelt, the retreat was renamed *"Shangri-La"* after the fictional Himalayan paradise.

Later, Dwight D. Eisenhower renamed the woodlands *Camp David* in honor of his father and grandson; both named David.

"I have network coverage," Chief of Staff, Robert Laslow indicated, handing over a remote control. "Rioting has broken out in Boston, New York, and Miami."

"They don't waste any time," the president specified flipping to Boston's WHDH-TV 7 News. On the screen, Boston's Finest hurriedly evacuated residents from an apartment building. That's when the fight broke out.

> "The riots began," a correspondent indicated staring into the camera, "when cops attempted to evacuate residents from this low income housing complex. The event took a violent turn when a rookie officer slammed a teenager to the ground." Behind the reporter, teenagers screamed and tossed projectiles at police. "The violence has not

been confined to this neighborhood. Just
moments ago we heard a National
Guardsman was shot on the streets of South
Boston when his unit entered a housing
project."

The president gawked at the coverage filtering in from
various cities. ABC presented rioting in the Overtown
section of Miami, shoplifters in Georgia, and street fights in
Charleston, South Carolina.

News 4 Charleston was on the scene of a full-scale riot.
A police car was afire; another cruiser was being rocked to
and fro by masked demonstrators.

"Here, in Charleston," another reporter
pointed, "along the well-heeled and heavily
shopped King Street district, opportunistic
raiders are having their go at burglarized
merchandise from looted businesses. For
much of the past hour we've watched as
Charleston Police have battled to take back
the streets of this embattled city."

On the TV screen, the Charleston Police Department
marched down the thoroughfare holding shields while
masked protestors threw Molotov cocktails that landed and
exploded at officers' feet.

"The south is under attack today," the
reporter continued. "This scene is
reminiscent of the Kimani Gray shooting
death that prompted looting and rioting in
Brooklyn, but here... the situation is
growing graver by the hour."

Then, the camera caught sight of a man throwing a
cinder block into a plate glass window of an electronics
store. The glass shattered and sprinkled to the pavement.

Looters jumped through the window frame and dashed away with electronics. The police shot teargas canisters at the scattering looters.

> "And, as tragic as the situation is here, the pillaging has overtaken much of the east coast's major cities. There are reports from Georgia, the Carolinas and, closer to you, in New York, right there in Manhattan."

The President of the United States was in shock. He couldn't believe a national emergency had generated such hate and anger to erupt in the streets.

"What resources do they have available to fight this?"

"Just local law enforcement," the chief of staff answered watching another report from Manhattan. "The National Guard is mobilizing. Remember, Sir, we have a mass evacuation underway while all of this is happening."

On the TV now, NBC's Lester Bolt reported from somewhere in Manhattan.

> "This is a much different scene than we saw just an hour ago, as thieves grabbed anything they could."

The image of the reporter was replaced by a helicopter shot of an NYPD cruiser speeding along Fifth Avenue where it came to a screeching halt in front of the Gucci store. That's where two patrolmen leapt from their squad car and were immediately shot dead by a hoodlum exiting the storefront. The perpetrator stepped over the bodies, got behind the wheel of the squad car and sped down Fifth Avenue.

"Mr. President?" a naval officer presented. "There's a secure audiovisual call coming in from Naval Station Norfolk with Admiral Brancor on hold, Sir."

"Put it up on the screen."

The news was replaced by the grim faces of the admiral, Captain Cullen, and SECDEF Clark.

"What have ya got, Lew?" the president asked.

"We have to send the fleet out for a ditch, Mr. President. Leaving the carriers and battle groups in port will be a threat to Virginia."

"At least at sea," Clark agreed, "the aircraft carriers have a chance. If they're kept here, they will surely be lost."

"Is the weapon onboard?" POTUS asked.

"Yes, Sir," the Secretary of Defense answered.

The president glanced around the room where his advisors nodded their agreement.

"Clark, what do you propose from this point forward?"

The Secretary of Defense motioned to Admiral Brancor. "The Admiral requests orders to command the USS Harry Truman and lead the fleet into the Atlantic."

President Powers walked up to the screen. "Those orders are so authorized, and Lew?"

"Yes, Mr. President?"

"Godspeed, my friend, I'm counting on you. But more importantly, the country stands at your back!"

Chapter 55

PARADISE ISLAND

THE MEGA-RESORT was inspired by the lost city of Atlantis.

It touted itself as a playground built for couples, families, and friends.

Situated a few hundred miles from the United States' southern coastline, the Bahamas once protected rebels, pirates, rumrunners, and runaway lovers.

Then, there was death:

V.I. had just arrived in Nassau and knew that robberies and murders occurred quite frequently here. It was something television ads never mentioned in their marketing ploys. Not long ago, cruise ship passengers were accosted by gun-toting criminals during two separate excursions in town.

Danger lingers around every corner, he understood. *The death toll will only increase if the islands are not completely evacuated.*

"Yah, Mon, jus' so we're clear," he yelled above the shouted commands of the Royal Bahamas Police Force who were busily searching the resort grounds. "The last plane must depart the island by four o'clock!"

"That's less than three hours!" the Bahamian United Nations official griped. "How're we to pull this off in such short time?"

"I don't know, Mon," V.I. insisted. "Nevertheless, the evacuation must get done or people will die."

They stood in the *Water Adventures* section of Atlantis' Paradise Island. Beside V.I., a half dozen government officials and the commissioner of police listened.

"Every inch of the resort has to be rechecked," the Bahamian official instructed the commissioner. "The guests must be quickly shuffled to the airfield and sent back to their countries immediately."

The commissioner shouted to his men. "Check the resort again, and make sure everyone is evacuated!"

"Yessar!" one of his men responded, meaning to respond *yes sir*, but with his accent, what fell from his mouth sounded more like *YASSAR*.

They were searching the manmade *Ruins of Atlantis*. Here, visitors normally watched spotted sea rays and flamboyantly colored tropical fish while sliding down a Mayan temple mock-up and through a plastic tube that ran beneath the shark tank.

The commissioner pointed to the slide now.

"I remember a few years back; we were patrolling the grounds and heard a commotion by the water slide. An eight-foot reef shark slipped over the barrier and onto the slide. It skidded down into the recovery pool at the bottom of the slide."

"Ha!" V.I. grunted in surprise. "The shark entered the glide where people splashed into the pool?"

The commissioner nodded, a smile crossing his face. "It happened about fifteen minutes before opening, so the shark didn't find a tourist for breakfast."

"What happened?"

"The resort workers hopped into the pool to get the shark. However, the fish had other ideas, swam off violently, causing everyone to jump back out of the water."

Walking through the lagoon, V.I. laughed at the tale.

"After five minutes," the commissioner went on, "the hotel staff got the fourteen-year-old female shark onto a tarp and rushed her up back into the salt-water reservoir."

"Nobody got hurt, then?"

"Nah, Mon, but a few days later, the shark perished from exposure to chlorinated water. Imagine... if a hotel guest had slid down that tube when the huge shark got onto it!"

"Now, *that* would have been a true thrill!"

"Yah, Mon," the commissioner nodded. "It sure would have been something to see!"

Glancing at the shark tank, both men had similar thoughts toying with their minds. Atlantis and all the memories created here, would all be mislaid. Soon, the forty-five-foot catamaran used for snorkeling excursions, the shark tanks, the stingrays, the shallow lagoon and sugar sand beaches... would all be a fantasyland memory.

"Another paradise lost," V. I. sighed and glanced across the resort. "Can you show me the evacuation process?"

"Sure," the commissioner nodded. "Let's go through the casino to the lobby and bus departure port."

At this instant, an official appeared. "All thirty-seven-hundred rooms have been cleared, Sir!"

Hurrying through the grounds, they entered an opulent marble lobby and quickly hurried out the front doors where tourists were boarding buses, taxis, and vans.

"We have every vehicle available," the Bahamian official noted. "Everyone on government payroll is busy ferrying residents and tourists to the airport."

"All the islands are being evacuated?" V.I. confirmed, "Freeport, Grand Bahamas, Paradise Island?"

"All of them, Mon," the commissioner promised.

Staring at the exodus, V.I. thought of his family back in Orlando. Breathing a deep sigh of relief, he hoped for the best while expecting the worst.

Maybe we'll survive our appointment with tragedy! Then again, I might die in paradise!

Chapter 56

THE TOMBS

THE VATICAN GROTTOES lay beneath Vatican City.

There, the dead waited for rapture.

They'd been *waiting* for centuries. It was the final resting place of: Saints, Kings and Popes!

Here, in the *Catacombs of Callixtus,* lay the ancient burial chambers of Rome. Deep crypts were carved into solid rock walls that once contained the Crypt of Popes.

The tombs of sixteen pontiffs and fifty martyrs had been here from the 2nd to 4th centuries.

There were spirits here.

In a nearby chapel, a painting hung from latched hooks. It displayed Mary Magdalene's swollen face and according to legend, it bled because a drunken soldier threw a bowl into the image.

Mythology tales were a dime a dozen.

The black pope was lost in his thoughts while standing by a dark grave niche, pointing a flashlight into the damp catacombs. If he got his way, Callixtus the Fourth would end up here with his predecessors by the same name.

Sooner rather than later!

"Making peace with your enemies?" Petrus asked moving into the echoing, narrow chamber. "Or, are you perhaps asking forgiveness for your eternal sins?"

It was shadowy in the underground cemetery, the numbness of death reverberated through the stone chambers like a dentist's drill. It was an empty, excavated, silent burial site. When the relics of antiquity were moved, the catacombs were abandoned; most of the bodies removed...with the exception of Saints Sebastian, Lawrence, and Pancratius.

Their bones still lay entombed in the rock.

Over the centuries, landslides and vegetation had obstructed and hid the entrance to their tombs, so traces of their existence were lost... *and they were forgotten.*

"In the first century," the black pope said turning to Petrus, "Rome's Christians didn't have their own cemeteries. If they possessed land, they buried family members here. Otherwise they resorted to communal graveyards where pagans were buried. That's how Saint Peter came to be buried in the great city of the dead on Vatican Hill."

"Is that right?" Petrus asked, eyeing his leader.

He'd been summoned back beneath Vatican City to meet with the superior general. Here, in the secret of darkness, their words would go unheard by the flocks of Callixtus' faithful.

The leader of the Society of Jesus sighed.

"This boneyard was created by Pope Callixtus the First. He was entombed here until his crypt decayed and its relics were moved to various churches of Rome."

"And why is this important?"

There was a cool draft in the chamber, a wisp of something moving in the air, like a cool hand waved through the tunnel creating a breeze.

"Did you feel that?" the superior general asked.

"I did," Petrus nodded, "a Saint, perhaps, not in agreement with our plan to entomb Callixtus here?"

"Or comfortable in the knowledge this tsunami can't reach us," the black pope realized. "You know, if it wasn't for Gibraltar, Rome would be under water like Morocco."

Their saving grace was the Strait of Gibraltar narrowed between Tarifa, Spain, and Ksar es-Seghir on the Mediterranean coast of northwest Morocco. There a chokepoint of land narrowed the sea preventing the bore from traveling unabated up the Mediterranean.

"The hand of God, perhaps?" Petrus suggested.

"Or the smirk of Satan," the black pope chuckled. Strolling along the narrow chamber, a flashlight illuminating the way, he turned to Petrus, shining the light into his face. "Have you made preparations? Placed calls to Italy's cardinals to voyage to Rome?"

"I have. They'll be here shortly."

Placing his cold hand on the cardinal's shoulder, the superior general smiled. "We shall tell them Callixtus is dead... that we received an emergency message from your man, Colonel Meeds, aboard the sinking ship."

"And what if he isn't killed?"

"Then Meeds will be executed and Callixtus must vanish," the black pope confidently nodded. "You have another man to handle those probabilities, yes?"

"I do, Cardinal Jonathan of the Jesuits."

"And he's prepared to send them both to Heaven?"

Petrus bowed.

"Then, it's settled." Strolling through the boneyard, his footsteps echoed in the stillness of the necropolis. "And when Jonathan returns, perhaps he'll have an accident."

There would be no loose ends.

Chapter 57

THE GREAT EATER

THE RAGING CURRENT dragged screaming passengers out through a gaping hole in the ship's hull.

Seawater rose through the elegant, richly decorated promenade. The sound of bending steel pierced the air and sharks swam into the ship as it rocked on the sea.

Mikey barely made it to the safety of the railing–his arm wrapped around the hyperventilating girl–when the screams started. At first, they were whimpers of fear, just barely audible cries for help.

And then, the beasts revealed themselves.

Two great white sharks arrived, perhaps for a quick look-see at the massive hulking steel dragging itself below the surface. One of the shark's snouts was peppered with holes and it looked to Mikey as though it had been shot.

The second fish circled a woman.

Her movements were frantic, blood oozed from a head wound, and her screams brought Mikey's eyes to the scene of the charging shark.

"Oh, my lord," she yelled watching the dorsal fin looping her position in the water. "It's a shark!"

It sure was.

But she didn't know the half of it.

There are two sharks for sure, Mikey thought, spellbound by the enormous spindle shaped bodies.

They were massive.

"Oh, man!" Mikey groaned with concern for the lady treading water; her eyes glued on the circling shark. If he didn't know better, he'd have sworn the fish was grinning at the woman; a sick sort of momentary grimace that stated he was coming!

"Is it going to attack her?" the girl asked, hugging Mikey's frame. Her flesh trembled with fear, much as it had back home when she watched *The Conjuring*.

Of course it's going to attack!

That's what Mikey wanted to say, but being the polite kid... he shook his head, hugged her tight and whispered this into her ear instead: "It's going to be all right!"

Around them, survivors made their way out of the water, all of whom stared at the woman. One of the survivors was a doctor from Santa Cruz, California, and he spoke up now.

"I won't be able to stitch her wounds if they take a bite."

"They won't eat her," the girl begged, "will they?"

Before the doctor could answer, Bessie the Beast turned in for a closer look at the thin woman going into shock.

"Don't move a muscle!" Dr. Doolittle warned. "They attack by sense. Any slight movement will give up your exact location!"

The treadmill addict wasn't about to wait around for the dinner bell to ring. No sir, what she did then... was stretch out her palms and dig through the water. As fast as she could, she swam towards the band of survivors cheering her on towards safety.

"Come on, lady!" Mikey screamed. "Just a few more feet and you'll be safe!"

"Faster!" the doctor belched, "they're right behind you!"

And they were, too!

The sharks stopped circling and charged for the woman's legs, a blackness filling their stare, the enormous jaws hanging open, the scent of blood in their nostrils. A great white could detect one drop of blood in a million drops of water and could whiff it out a quarter mile away. As water flowed through their nostrils, the fish became more enraged.

"Hurry!" Mikey shouted, watching the two goliaths dive beneath the water. What they did down there was anyone's guess, but surprisingly, they didn't go for the woman.

Dr. Doolittle and the band of survivors reached into the water and pulled her to safety. "You're one lucky SOB! You were a millisecond from becoming dinner–"

Then, just as her feet cleared the waterline, Bessie plunged through the surface, snapped its jaws closed on the woman's torso and dove into the depths with her hips and legs filling its hunger.

Dr. Doolittle and Mikey, holding firm to her arms, stared at the woman's eyes, which hadn't yet perceived her lower body was no longer attached.

"What's wrong?" she said.

Then, she glanced down and knew.

Life was wrong, very wrong.

Chapter 58

POSEIDEN ADVENTURE

USS HARRY S. TRUMAN was a bad motherhumper.

Named after the 33rd President of the United States, its call sign was Lone Warrior.

Lew thought the nickname summed up their desperate lonely mission quite nicely.

"You sure, Admiral," Captain Cullen asked a final time, "that the fleet can make it through the crest of the leading wave and pass into sea?"

"Not sure about anything, Captain."

However, he was sure about death.

Lew had a good awareness what would happen when he steered the massive flattop into the charging wall of water.

"What's the alternative?" SECDEF Clark asked. "In just hours Newport News will be a shadow of Indonesia."

Lew recalled that disaster.

The Indian Ocean earthquake was an undersea mega thrust earthquake that occurred just after midnight on Sunday, 26 December 2004. The quake, known as the *Sumatra–Andaman earthquake*, killed over 230,000 people in fourteen countries, and inundated coastal populations with waves up to a hundred feet high.

It had been the deadliest natural disaster in history.

Cataclysms are happening a lot lately; Lew thought while considering what lay ahead for the fleet.

The voice was like a fragmented whisper, breaking apart in his head like the disassembly of LEGOS.

"Admiral, Sir," Captain Cullen interrupted. "Are you all right? You're looking a little pale around the gills."

Ha! Lew thought, *he doesn't know the half of it.*

Pulling a Cuban cigar from his chest pocket, he thrust it between his teeth and ignited the end. Staring out across the tranquil sea, he considered the boat he commanded.

The one-thousand-foot-long, 257-foot-wide husky mammoth was as tall as a twenty-four-story building. Under normal circumstances, its deck would accommodate eighty aircraft on a four and a half acre flight deck.

With a combat load, the USS Harry S. Truman displaced ninety-seven thousand tons of seawater and accommodated six thousand crewmembers.

"Sir," the captain asked, "Are you okay, Sir?"

Lew heard the Annapolis graduate... but didn't want to answer. He was busy thinking through his options, wondering how Lady Sea would play her hand, how she'd come at them... *violently? Forcing rage filled saltwater onto the bow and flipping the warship into the depths?*

Or perhaps... she'd merely let them thrust through the wall of water; allow them to fight another day?

The voices came when he faced danger.

Always had... they arose in the angered tones of his five prior wives. Each one, nagging and boisterous in their own right.... always there, to offer their two-cents of fury... tugging at the doubts of his mind.

Their yammering could wear on a man.

Sometimes opinions could even kill.

Not Lew!

Not the Navy Man!

He chewed them up and spit 'em out like an old piece of gum that lost its flavor. It would be a sorry day in Hell before he sat in a retirement home wearing blue polyester pants, white patent leather shoes, and a Walmart golf hat.

Lew chuckled at these considerations and looked at the ship's bow. There, he saw two Mark II stockless anchors weighing thirty tons each. The weight would help the carrier cut through the wall of water, and hopefully punch through to the other side.

It would be the ride of their lives.

If… they lived to tell about it.

It is an act of honor, Lew supposed, leading the carrier battle group due east into the vastness. It was his pleasure to serve his country. Although there was zero probability of survival, the mission was to serve the United States.

And, dammit, that's what I'm gonna do.

"Do we have a plan, Admiral?" Clark asked. "What're we gonna do when that tsunami bears down?"

Peering through the rear bridge windows, Lew glanced at the two carriers following him into the Atlantic.

USS George H.W. Bush
USS Abraham Lincoln

"We're going to kick Poseidon's ass, Mister Secretary of Defense. And then, we're going to fire your secret weapon and charge into the horizon for Old Glory!"

Chapter 59

SOCIAL MEDIA

SOCIAL MEDIA was on fire.

Gone were the days of stuffy old *white men* huddling around a white president while filling their pipes.

Kissinger was a has-been; a once upon a time.

Tricky Dick was a faded memory.

His bones turned inside a stinking coffin in a corrupt grave at the library and museum in Yorba Linda, California. Nobody wanted to remember Nixon.

Nowadays, the President of the United States was surrounded by social media twenty-something's who laughed and fist-bumped.

They talked about Beyoncé, Jay-Z, and J-LO.

TMZ was all the rage.

And HIP HOP boomed in the president's ear.

Glancing to his iPhone, he scrolled through a twitter feed showing millions of people commenting on #Cataclysm. It was the official hash-tag for information relating to evacuations and resources.

What a world we live in. POTUS thought. *This is the twitter presidency.* Shaking his head and pushing the phone into a pocket, he wondered if Nixon was in heaven shooting the peace sign and arguing: 'I'm not a crook!'

"Mr. President," Will interrupted, "I thought I'd give you a play-by-play on what we're watching and expecting as the hours grow shorter."

On the TV, a helicopter news reporter pointed to the devastation lining the shore of Casablanca.

"The Hassan II Mosque's minaret is now entirely covered by the tsunami waters. Its

laser perched atop the building is barely
visible through the waterline. The tower no
longer looks out to the Atlantic; it is part of
the ocean now. The shoreline hotels have all
been destroyed."

"Shit!" POTUS grunted switching channels. "That tower
was half the height of the Empire State Building. Is that
what Manhattan faces?"

Will nodded. "It's much worse, Mr. President."

POTUS stared at CNN, where unrest unfolded in South
Carolina, Washington D.C., and Virginia. Stores were
being looted; mobs marched the pavement in protest of the
martial law declaration.

"This is Wolf Blitter here in the Situation
Room at CNN," a middle-aged reporter
stated. "Breaking news is now trickling in
from eastern seaboard states that millions
are moving inland to escape the predicted
path of this wave. But in Florida, we have
word the Governor has refused to issue
mandatory evacuation plans believing the
tsunami will dissipate before hitting land.
We now take you live to Miami."

President Powers turned to his chief of staff. "Robert,
what the hell is the Governor doing down there?"

Mr. Laslow moved beside POTUS. "His office is
refusing our calls for mandatory evacuations. They're still
sore about our public comments on Souls to the Polls."

Florida Republicans hated the White House.

The mutual disregard began when the Florida governor
scaled back early voting in an attempt to hamper the black
turnout for the presidential election. The entire idea of early
voting was to make it easier for people to carry out their
constitutional right. But in Florida, it was nightmarish for

voters who faced record lines in the sun as the Republican Governor closed down early voting hours.

> "That's right, Wolf," an African American correspondent stared into the camera. "Here in Miami Beach crowds have yet to leave the shore; they continue to stroll Ocean Drive and South Beach is packed with foreign tourists."

"Get me the pentagon!" the president shouted. "I want the Joint Chiefs flown in here five minutes ago! Florida will not be run by a backwoods Governor with disregard for public safety!"

"But we have no authority over state evacuations," the chief of staff worried. "The Florida National Guard is run by the state and at the leisure of its Governor."

POTUS winced. "We took those powers, remember? I am the President of the United States and that means two things."

"What's that?" Mr. Laslow grinned.

"One: I run the show!"

"And number two, Mr. President?"

"I have the law on my side!"

"Who am I calling, Sir?"

Smiling, the president pointed to a red phone sitting on his desk. "Get the Chief Justice on the horn and let's see what he has to say about a Presidential Act moving Marines from Camp Lejeune, Cherry Point, and New River to the Great State of Florida."

"I'm on it, Mr. President."

"And find out what Marine recruit resources we have available at Paris Island. We'll get those boys some real time training. I'll show that orange picking hillbilly in Florida who runs the country."

There was some fresh squeezed ass-kicking coming.

And time was getting short.

Chapter 60

AIRPLANE!

THE AIRBUS PASSENGERS were freaking out.

That was the word from the flight crew.

Staring at his instrument panel, Captain Harry Rogers shook his head and flipped his switches. "We have fire!"

It's more than a fire, Harry, his subconscious tugged. *What you have onboard is a mega disaster.* He knew there was engine trouble; the UFO laser had probably punched a gaping hole into the airframe.

Hours into the flight crossing the Atlantic the trip had been uneventful until the spaceship appeared.

Everything after the big reveal was terror time!

Following moments of gawking horror, the flight deck witnessed the laser blast, felt its exploding impact and sensed the plane falling thousands of feet.

Now the A380 was coming apart one rivet at a time.

Behind the pilot, Jeanne strapped herself into the jump seat. "What the heck was that ship? Did we hit it?"

"Looks like we flew into something," co-pilot Skip McGregor lied staring at his gauges. "We're losing cabin pressure!"

"What about Heathrow Tower?" Jeanne worried. "How come we haven't heard from ground control?"

But Harry knew why. *Everyone on the ground is trying to figure out what the mother ship wanted.*

The Airbus plunged through the clouds, descending through ten thousand feet a hundred miles west of Heathrow. Without engine power, the airliner dropped fast.

Harry recognized they'd be lucky to make an emergency landing. Glancing over his shoulder, he attempted to calm Jeanne.

"Maybe this is a result of that erupting volcano we heard about a few hours ago in the Canary Islands. You know the airflow runs west from Africa across the ocean. Perhaps we ran into an ash cloud, like the one in 2010 that grounded four thousand flights from Norway to Denmark."

"That doesn't explain a cloaked flying saucer!"

Skip agreed. "It could have been a mirage; something the mind makes up in times of terror and chaos."

"Do I look like an idiot?" Jeanne spat. "I know what the hell I saw, what everyone saw. That was E.T.!"

The pilot didn't argue.

"We'll be fine," Skip assured. "We probably *did* encounter something."

"The plane was attacked by a laser beam," Jeanne screamed. "Maybe the aliens don't want witnesses!"

The turbulence got worse and smoke seeped into the cockpit from the passenger cabin vents. The billows grew thicker and contained a disturbing scent of sulfur. It was heavy and caused the crew to cough.

The captain pulled on a breathing device.

Glancing out the window, he observed the wing glowing fire red. He knew turbine blades would melt if not for the continuous flow of cool air filtering through tiny holes distributed along the blades. In the middle of these thoughts, the jet shuddered violently and dropped another thousand feet.

"Oh, crap!" Jeanne screamed, her stomach flipping, nausea spinning in her head. It was like riding the Dueling Dragons hanging-coaster at Islands of Adventure.

"We're in a jam, here," Harry griped. "I'm going to dump the fuel tanks."

At this instant, a piercing alarm beeped and a computer generation showed a blinking ENGINE FAIL notification.

"We've got total failure," Harry excitedly shouted, concern mounting in the tone of his voice. "Let's notify Heathrow Control and get emergency clearance."

They were now 50 miles due west of the airport.

"Heathrow Tower," Skip announced into his communication headset, "this is Global Air 2291 heavy. We've lost all engines and request an emergency landing pattern, over? Cross two ZERO left and ZERO three."

"Roger, Global, we have you on radar," the tower responded. "Two seven left, the wind is southwest at ten knots, we have to divert you, the runway is crowded with departing planes."

Looking to his left, the captain stared at a video monitor of the economy cabin. The passengers were all strapped into their seats; turbulence shook their flesh while the overhead compartments jostled open, spilling their contents.

The airbus was coming apart.

"Mayday!" the captain shouted. "Heathrow Tower, we are declaring an immediate emergency!"

Chapter 61

KILLER ELITE

C OLONEL MEEDS was close.

I could send him to Cherubland.

The colonel could have jerked out his sidearm, pointed it at Callixtus' head and pulled the trigger.

Bam-Bam... hole in the head.

Within seconds, the Bishop of Rome would've been singing with the angelic choir.

He'd be walking the golden roads of paradise.

But instead of completing the mission, Meeds shook his head in disgust. He wasn't sure if he could carry it out.

This is murder, his conscience mocked. *There's no coming back to the altar and professing your sins after killing HIM.*

"I got it!" Captain Maka grunted popping the lock on the strongbox. Reaching in, he pulled out three Nebo Treadline Select flashlights and shined one into Meeds' stare.

"There we go!" Cardinal Jonathan chuckled awkwardly. "Now everyone can see the path ahead!"

"Smartass," Meeds growled grabbing a light. "C'mon Captain, shine that beam along *our path* so we can traverse this sinking bucket!"

"Thank God!" Callixtus sighed.

"Watch your step," the captain warned before handing over the last flashlight to Tish. "Be wary of the fixtures, paintings, and debris; remember we're walking on the ceiling and the ship is upside down in the water!"

An earsplitting roar of gushing water reverberated from ahead as they paced towards a stairwell at the ship's bow.

"We need to climb stairs," the captain stated, pointing his light into the flooding shaft. "But the steps are useless because the vessel is upside down!"

Tish gazed into the inverted staircase. "It's a ladder! We can climb the newels like rungs of a stepladder."

The captain shone his light over the ascending stairwell. The waterfall stairwell was bordered on either side by mahogany bannisters supported by 55-inch fluted box newels. "It's more than fifty feet to the Promenade Deck."

"Not a problem for me," Tish offered. "I've been climbing volcanoes my whole life, this should be easy."

"Tough girl," Meeds grunted.

"I can make it, too," Cardinal Jonathan offered.

They turned to the pope.

"What about it, Callixtus?" Meeds asked. "Is that cassock of yours going to get in the way?"

The Bishop of Rome reached down to his vestments and unbuttoned the lowest buttons. "I'll make it."

He was in amazing shape for a Holy Father.

In fact, Callixtus could win Rome's Marathon.

"Let's do it, then," Jonathan urged, grabbing the bottom newel and leading the climb.

"Don't look down," Meeds warned. "A fall from this position would mean certain death."

Slowly, they climbed, hand over fist, step by step, and within minutes, they'd made progress.

Meeds stared at Callixtus while considering his circumstance. *Perhaps he'll lose his grip and plummet to death, should that happen, I won't answer to Saint Peter after all.* It would all be a tragic accident. With his crew out of the way, there were no longer any obstacles.

Then, almost as if Meeds willed it into reality, Callixtus suddenly lost his solid grip due to the sodden wood.

"I'm falling!" he bellowed.

Cardinal Jonathan peered down from above. "Carlos! Hang on! Don't you let go of that wood!"

This is it, Meeds thought. *I can grab his legs and pull him down, say it was an accident!*

There would be no inquiry.

"Help me, Jonathan!" Callixtus howled, his fingers hastening the death clock's arrival to sainthood.

At that instant, Meeds made his decision.

I'm all in, this is action time!

Reaching above, he grabbed for Callixtus' shoes.

Chapter 62

BAHAMA MAMA

NASSAU'S BUSIEST lure was the Queen's Staircase.

There were sixty-five steps to climb.

Carved from solid limestone by slaves in the late 18th century, they were forced to cut through the rock with axes and hand tools.

V.I. thought they should've strung up their masters.

The hundred-foot staircase was named to honor sixty-five-years of Queen Victoria's reign. The monument was still regarded as remarkable.

"The tourists come from all over the world to climb those stairs," the commissioner pointed. V.I. and he were seated in the helicopter buzzing the rooftops of Nassau making sure there were no stragglers to be plucked to safety. "Fort Fincastle, is just ahead sitting on Bennett's Hill. It's just a few minutes' walk from downtown and there may be tourists stuck there."

"What's the fort used for?"

"Like Fort Charlotte, this fortress proved useless in preventing assaults because Nassau was never attacked. Therefore we used it as a lighthouse and signal tower."

Flying over the hill, V.I. stared at old rusted cast iron cannons sitting on tracks along an ancient wall. Surrounding this, patches of trees lined the property and in the distance, a dozen cruise ships crammed the port.

"You want to set down in port?" the commissioner asked, nodding towards the pier.

"I'd like to see how the ship evacuations are coming along. It looks like every cruise line from here to America has joined the rescue."

"They have. Virgin Caribbean, Elegant Seas, and Atlantic Cruise Lines all have ships here, along with the United States Navy, Coast Guard, and major shipping corporations."

V.I. scanned the port and noticed long lines.

Hundreds of thousands of residents and tourists waited to enter the terminal and climb aboard a ship. He had been here many times and knew downtown bordered the cruise terminal. It was here, along the waterline, on *Woodes Rogers Walk* where he'd purchased dozens of knock-off Rolex, Breitling, and Guess watches for $50 apiece. One Christmas, he handed them out to friends and family like candy back in Orlando.

Of course, they broke a few days later.

Screw 'em if they couldn't take a joke.

He loved Nassau; it was a quick get away from the hustle and bustle of the U.S. When arriving by ship, the wife and he would get the party going by stopping at Señor Frogs. There, after a few strong margaritas, they'd dance the tango while Bahamian boys poured shots down their throats with a hose.

Nassau was definitely a party town.

But the merrymaking was over.

As the chopper buzzed Festival Place–a shopping mall normally filled with cash spending tourists–V.I. noticed a man leaning out the window of a yellow and white port tower pointing to a cordoned off spot on the pier.

"They have a place for us to put down!" the pilot indicated. "Do you want to land and meet with the evacuation coordinator?"

"No," the commissioner answered, "get to the airport."

As the chopper sped over port, V.I. noticed their arrival had caused people to stare heavenward. Moving through the sky, the cruise-port faded and the airport appeared on the horizon. Planes bounded from the runway and the taxiways were packed with aircraft.

"There are over a hundred planes on the airfield right now," the commissioner counted. "Every airline from here to Miami is assisting with the evacuation!"

V.I. saw jets everywhere and imagined the air traffic controllers pulling their hair out. "Let's get on the ground and see how departures are going."

They landed beside a modern white terminal, hopped out and were met by Karin Soma who'd flown down from New York to personally oversee the massive operation on behalf of the United Nations.

"Oscar," she said hugging her friend. "It's good to see you! Thanks for your efforts in Puerto Rico and the Virgin Islands, looks like they're almost evacuated because of you and the advance team."

"Just doing my job!"

"Ha!" Karin waved him off. "You're doing more than that, my friend. Follow me, will you?" Hurrying towards a tent, she pointed to six C-130s sitting at the end of the taxiway. "Lockheed Martin Corporation and the U.S. Military sent those in a few minutes ago. They'll allow us to evacuate thousands more."

"Amazing," V.I. marveled. "They're huge, huh?"

"We're moving a hundred thousand people an hour," Karin stated handing over a Samsung tablet. "Destinations range from Chicago, Dallas, Indiana, and Ohio."

"I bet the tourists aren't too happy about that."

"No, they aren't. That brings me to you."

V.I. glanced to his boss.

"I need you in Miami. Between Key West and West Palm Beach, we need to move over six million people."

V.I. stared at her, "That's a lot of people."

"Besides, it's your home state, the fourth most populated in the United States. And there is a plus."

"What's that? So far all I see are negatives."

"You'll be meeting up with your new friend, Dr. May."

V.I. smiled. He'd developed a soft spot for the British researcher. "When do I leave?"

"Right now," Karin answered pointing to a United Nations jet. "Sam will meet you at Miami International Airport. He's flying in from the northeast. From there you guys must educate the Miami Mayor on this."

Jogging to the plane, V.I. looked back over his shoulder. "When I get back to Manhattan, I want a promotion!"

Karin hoped there would be a New York after all was said and done. "You got it, kid, anything for you!"

Stepping onto the plane, V.I. took a seat and strapped himself in for the twenty-two minute flight.

Chapter 63

EXECUTION

VATICAN CITY tensions ran high among Rome's Catholic Cardinals meeting to discuss Callixtus' fate.

Few believed he was dead.

Others just weren't sure.

Press conferences were underway and discussions of the pontiff's supposed death became heated.

Rome's Cardinals refused to agree on a start date for conclave, where a hundred fifteen electives would cross the globe to name a successor to Pope Callixtus the Fourth.

"We have no proof Callixtus is dead!" one argued.

"We're not following tradition!" another griped.

Like the church itself, the process of choosing the Bishop of Rome was a blend of modernism and old-fashioned traditions.

There were canons to be preserved.

First: There should be proof Callixtus was dead.

Second: A secret vote should be taken.

Although cardinals swore an oath not to reveal details of their conversations, the Vatican Press Office had already given its take on the situation.

> "We've never elected a new pope before the deceased father has been pronounced. We'll need time to decide who might be best suited to become Pontiff."

An hour after that Vatican briefing, the spokesman was found dead in his study with a knife in his back.

The cardinal secretary soon followed with his own press conference at St. Peter's Basilica.

"Conclave will proceed in weeks!"

It was the official line spoken to 7,000 journalists.

Flocking to Rome, the media wrote their stories and accepted the tale confirming Callixtus' death.

Inside a conference room above Saint Peter's Square, the statement of Cardinal Secretary Romano had ruffled the feathers of nineteen Jesuit cardinals seated in red velvet backed chairs. These were hardline Italian diehards who felt Callixtus should be found before proceeding.

"Without a body," Cardinal Raffael Farina protested, "there can be none of this nonsense of conclave." He was the 88-year-old overseer at the Vatican Secret Archives.

He was somebody in this town.

"We're not going to play games today," Petrus informed the men hunkered around a five-hundred-year-old walnut table. "We must send a strong message to the world that the Holy See is in control."

The See was the *episcopal jurisdiction* of the Roman Catholic Church in Rome. They branded its bishop... *the pope...* the global spearhead of the church. Since Rome was the central Episcopal See of the apostolic, it acted as a government. Recognized by international law as a sovereign entity; it was a régime without a leader.

"What is the meaning of this?" Cardinal Farina asked, pointing a crooked finger to Petrus. "You think I don't know what's going on here? We know you want to be named successor to Callixtus!"

"If that be your will, Cardinal," Petrus nodded.

"Over my dead body!" he scoffed.

Petrus stared at the old man. "I know about you, and your lowly foot soldiers who conspired during the last conclave to ensure I was not named Bishop of Rome."

"You know nothing, Peter!"

"I know everything, Cardinal," Petrus grunted rising to his feet. "It was I who should've been named pontiff, and it is you and the reformers who conspired with thirty-three other cardinals to prevent my elevation."

"You don't deserve to be the world's leader," the old cardinal spat, "you'd leave the church in ruins should the Illuminati grasp control of the papacy."

Sighing, Petrus nodded to a servant who poured each cardinal a glass of sparkling water. "It is to the church's benefit that we proceed with courage and agree among ourselves that we, *the Roman Cardinals*, will sway the conclave vote to one of our own as Bishop of Rome."

"Never!" the old cardinal protested.

Picking up his glass, Petrus made a gesture. "May we all agree to drink the fruit of our lord and ask for his guidance in electing a new leader?"

They bowed in reserved agreement and drank the water. It signified life and played a central role in the purification of worldly things.

The sound of a glass shattering filled the room.

Glancing to Cardinal Farina, everyone appeared horrified. His body convulsed, an expression of agony occupied his stare, and then... *there was nothing.*

A final gasp, the jerking of his body... and then, it was over; the end had found the old man.

The Vatican Archivist was dead.

At that moment, the creaking hinges of a heavy door pulled the cardinals' attention to the devious grin of the black pope stepping across the ancient stone terrazzo floor.

"Disagreements rarely lead to progress, wouldn't you all agree?"

Glancing to one another, the realization hit the cardinals that murder had occurred right before their eyes.

"When the conclave meets," the black pope ordered, walking to Cardinal Romano. "Perhaps it is Petrus you'll name as our new Bishop?"

The command was as vibrant as St. Peter's bell.

One at a time, the men rose from their seats, marched past Petrus and placed a hand on his shoulder.

It was a signal they would each vote YES.

With eighteen of Rome's most powerful cardinals voting him the new pontiff... the world would follow.

Fear could sway everything.

Even for those who believed in God, or the alternative...

G.O.D. – Good Orderly Direction.

Chapter 64

A BLOODY MESS

TOWER BRIDGE was crowded.

Originally, the only crossing for the River Thames, more bridges were built as London grew.

Today, the view had changed dramatically.

Tower Bridge was a joint bascule and suspension bridge and an iconic symbol of London. It consisted of two towers jointed at the upper levels by horizontal walkways.

The nearest London Underground station was Tower Hill on the Circle and District lines, and the nearest Docklands Light Railway station was Tower Gateway. All of these were now the focus of great concern for the throne.

The only way out of London was over its bridges.

Contrary to widespread acceptance, the tune *London Bridge Is Falling Down* had nothing to do with Tower Bridge, but referred to the failures of others.

Nevertheless, on this day, many secretly knew this:

When the surge plowed up the English Channel, knocking ships to shore, the energy created by the deluge would wreak havoc on the bridges.

That's what now caused sirens to shriek.

Their wails carried through rain-splattered streets as British police cars weaved through two lanes of congested traffic. Speeding onto Tower Bridge Road, the cruisers joined a rush of traffic through Southwarks streets before arriving at Waterloo Station, the central railway terminal of the London Underground located in Lambeth. One of seventeen locations in Britain, its underground tracks lay near the Thames South Banks.

Waterloo was England's busiest station.

CATACLYSM

"Get yer rumps into the tubes and clear her out!" a British police commander shouted to his men who hopped from the cars and dashed through the goliath stone entrance. Leading them through crowds of commuters, he ran for the main ticket counter. "Out of the way, this is a national emergency!"

Before him, a digital DEPARTURE board hung from the wall. It was as long as a soccer field and exhibited hundreds of train departure times and platform locations.

On the opposite side, an identical ARRIVAL board flickered with trains scheduled to pull into the tubes.

"By order of the Prime Minister!" the commander shouted to a confused ticketing clerk, "you must close the Underground!"

"But, that's impossible! The station is full."

"We've plenty of room in lockup, should you wish!"

The clerk's face drained of color; he'd spent a sleepless night in the clink last summer on a drunk and disorderly charge. He wasn't prepared to repeat the experience.

Picking up a phone he dialed a number and shouted into the mouthpiece. "Suspend the rail lines at once!"

A second later, a loudspeaker blurted:

> "Attention, attention! All Waterloo passengers! We apologize for the inconvenience, but on order of the constabularies all trains are cancelled from the station. Please proceed from the tubes to the nearest exits.

And then in French:

> "Attention, les passagers, nous sommes désolés pour ce désagrément, mais tous les trains sont annulés à partir de la gare de Waterloo. S'il vous plaît procéder à la plus proche des sorties."

The commander glanced through the station where crowds frantically moved towards the exits. Turning back to the clerk he nodded his appreciation. "That's a good lad. I trust you don't fancy the Queens porridge?"

Shaking his head, the clerk glanced to a monitor. "There are still a dozen arriving trains down in the tubes!"

Looking to his men, the commander formulated a plan.

"Get into the subways and evacuate all passengers from the trains! We have very little time now!"

Sprinting from his location, he dashed through a sea of panic-stricken passengers to the platforms below ground.

Only a miracle would save them.

Chapter 65

JET EXPRESS

Dr. SAMUEL MAY stared out the jet window towards a dozen battleships charging through the Atlantic.

Beside him, Gordy pointed to three aircraft carriers. "It looks like President Powers ordered the fleet to sea. He's trying to save the ships from certain destruction."

They were twenty-seven thousand feet above the ocean, twenty miles southeast of Virginia Beach.

"There must be fifty ships down there," Sam counted, scanning the water for as far as the eye could see. "Is that the entire American fleet?"

Gordy shook his head. "No, we have more carriers assigned to Naval Station Norfolk, but the rest are probably on active duty tours in the Middle East." Pointing to the ships, he seemed lost in a memory. "Those carriers are the *Abe Lincoln, Harry Truman,* and *George H.W. Bush.*"

At this instant, the co-pilot appeared through the cockpit door. "Gentlemen, the Captain requests you tighten your seatbelts, he's going to offer the boys below an aerial salute on behalf of the President."

Gordy nodded. "Yes, Sir, we'll strap in."

"What's an aerial salute, Mate?" Sam asked.

"It's the ultimate sign of respect from the air. Known as a *flyby* or *flyover,* the plane will buzz the top of the vessels and our pilot will *wag the wings.* You might've seen this at sporting events in the United Kingdom or on television. It's akin to waving to a friend, and is accomplished when the pilot partially rolls the airframe from one side to the other."

Sam grunted. "Indeed, Mate, I've seen it many times."

"Tighten your seat belts," the co-pilot reminded turning back to the cockpit. "We're going to drop rapidly and circle the fleet to show respect."

"Sam, are you secured?" Gordy asked. "This might get bumpy coming through the cloud cover."

Clicking his seatbelt, Sam scrutinized the horizon as the jet suddenly descended allowing a closer look at the Atlantic Fleet. "They're brave men, your countrymen," he recognized eyeing the ships.

"Do you suppose they'll make it?" Gordy asked. "When the giant wave hits?"

The plane dipped to starboard and Sam saw the entirety of the flotilla. It was like staring through a window on hell. For as far as his vision allowed, tall gray steel structures protruded from the sea, each vessel crowding out the tranquil blue water.

"I'll be *gobsmacked* if they don't find their knickers in a twist. It's not going to be pretty."

Gordon peered over Sam's shoulder and caught a glimpse of the USS Harry Truman leading the warships into disaster. For a brief second, he imagined the brave group of men who'd be huddled on the bridge attempting to plot a course to safer waters.

War would be safer.

As the jet leveled off, there was a sudden roll to the right and left, completing the aerial salute. Then, over the loudspeaker, the captain's voice boomed.

"God bless our heroes out there."

"Hoo-yah," someone in back yelled.

"Ooh-Rah," another grunted.

"Hoo-ah," Gordon muttered.

There were veterans on the plane.

Mumbling these words meant something.

No matter how the words were uttered, they all meant that you'd seen your country through.

HONOR -- DUTY

BROTHERHOOD

Gordon recalled his squad members echoing through the hallowed halls of Annapolis. He recollected the utterances at formations, repeated before, during and after each training mission. He'd heard the grumbles a million times shouted by Air Force Security Forces, Pararescue, and Combat Controllers.

Ooh-Rah was muttered proudly by his team in the SEALs, and by friends in the Marines!

No matter how it was spoken, with a U instead of two Os, the word was a manifestation of morale, strength, and confidence.

"What does it mean?" Sam asked.

Gordy smiled. "It tells the world we're warriors and that we serve our country every day, fighting all the way, until dirt covers our bodies."

Sam stared back out the window and wondered:

How many heroes will die this day?

Chapter 66

THROWING A WOBBLY

BOB THE KNOB-HEAD stood listening to Professor Wild Bill's voice emanating from a speakerphone.

Sitting on a desk, Bob was surrounded by research students stunned to silence by the recognizable terror held in the professor's far-a-way voice.

"It's bloody bonkers on the streets. The Queen, Prime Minister, and Prince are said to be on the run, the country is moments from devastation and I haven't a clue how to find safety."

The researchers stared at one another.

"Where are you, Guvnor?" Bob shouted and stared at a color-coded map pinned to the wall.

There was a second of silence… and then:

"I'm headed towards the Chunnel Tunnel. Authorities are evacuating London, so I hopped on the Eurostar at St. Pancras to Lille, France. We're about to enter the tube."

The thirty-one-mile undersea railway linked the United Kingdom with northern France beneath the English Channel at the Strait of Dover. At its lowest point, the tunnel dove 250 feet… and at twenty miles, the passage was the longest undersea burrow on Earth.

"You're right barmy, Professor!" Bob recognized drawing his finger along the map. "You've placed yourself directly in the path of the surge! The water has already overtaken the shores of Plymouth, Portsmouth, and Southampton. It will find the Chunnel any minute now!"

Glancing to the huge television screen, he saw the English Channel had widened by more than a mile.

"How long," Bill asked, "until the surge hits London?"

Glancing to his colleagues, Bob scowled at their cold stares of hopelessness. "It'll be mere minutes, Chap, before it passes over the Chunnel. From there, it'll thrust down the Thames and drown the streets of London."

On the TV, the cliffs of Beachy Head loomed.

It was a chalk bluff in Southern England, close to the town of Eastbourne in East Sussex. The rock face was the highest chalk sea cliff in Britain; rising more than five hundred feet above sea level allowing views of the coast from Dungeness to the east, and Selsey Bill to the west. It was also one of the most famous suicide locations the world over. People traveled from every corner of Earth to leap to their death.

Now, the surging swells reached the cliffs apex and the chalk disappeared beneath the waterline.

"Fiddle sticks!" Bob swore watching the destruction of the shoreline. "The Kingdom is about to fall!"

"I'm holding my gonads here," Wild Bill's terrorized voice interrupted. "Bobby, pray I make it through to Calais before the Chunnel is inundated."

That's when everyone in the room saw what they couldn't bring themselves to tell Wild Bill.

The upsurge overtook the shores of France.

Goliath mountains of water pushed aground, toppling everything in its path. The waves knocked antique buildings from their stone foundations and crumbled wooden framed houses like twigs. The towns of Calais and Dunkirk were below the saltwater. The images on the TV displayed nothing but water... the Chunnel entrance was gone, buried somewhere deep beneath the tide which now hunted for a train barreling through the tunnel.

"Bobby?" Bill snipped. "Why is everyone so quiet?"

They were stunned to silence by the images.

The video on the *screen* changed then to people dashing through the streets of London as sirens wailed over the chaotic scene. Police blew whistles, trying to clear a path for a Bentley leaving the Palace of Westminster.

A reporter stood yelling into the camera.

> "The city of smoke and fog is only moments from annihilation," he nervously gestured to the mayhem. "The Square Mile is predicted to fall beneath the weight of the River Thames as she peaks over the barriers and swamps the sunken city."

Panic filled the screen, the end seemed imminent, and hopeless screams of concern filled the air.

> "Behind me, you can see the Queen's Bentley leaving the palace where a meeting just ended in Parliament. Sources close to the network are reporting the government has all but abandoned the city to the devastation flooding the English Channel."

Commonly known as the Houses of Parliament, the Palace sat on the Middlesex bank of River Thames in the City of Westminster. Its name, derived from Westminster Abbey, referred to the Old Palace, a medieval building complex destroyed by fire in 1834.

Now, the palace would be a big fat zero.

It'd be another abandoned structure of brick.

There was nothing royal about a pile of dirt.

As the queen's Bentley sped from the palace under a heavy police escort, the constable cars plowed into and *ran over* crowds of people running for their lives.

> "This is bonkers!" the reporter yelled pointing to mangled bodies strewn across the pavement. "The Queen Mother has just

abandoned her people in a pool of blood as
her cars ran them down like dogs!"

As a long line of Rolls-Royces and Daimlers exited the palace joining the motorcade, a security officer leaped from the tail car, punched the cameraman in the nose and threw the camera to the ground.

The last thing Bob saw on TV was a concrete road an instant before the news camera shattered.

Chapter 67

STAIRWAY TO HEAVEN

CARDINAL JONATHAN thought the end had finally found the pure intentions of the pope.

Good riddance!

The flow of seawater pounded the stairwell, and the barrage felt like needles piercing his skin as the freight train of H2O drowned the climb.

Just below Callixtus, Colonel Meeds reached for the Holy Father's red Morocco leather shoes.

Get him, Jonathan thought. *Send his Jesuit, downtrodden loving, inmate kissing ass to hell!*

Before the ship had rolled into the sea, a text message leaped alive on the screen of the cardinal's cell phone.

"When you have the chance," Cardinal Romano's text message advised. "Take out the liberal idiot should our friend, Colonel Meeds, fail to meet the mission!"

Wiping water from his brow, Jonathan surveyed Callixtus hanging by one hand while struggling to gain a foothold. At any moment, it appeared he'd fall fifteen stories to the bottom of the stairwell.

"Jonathan!" Callixtus begged. "Reach down, grab hold of my hand!"

Jonathan was astounded.

Why on God's good Earth would I help him?

"Jonathan!" the pope howled again, "please, help me!"

The cardinal stared at Callixtus. He was prepared to witness a murder, and imagined Meeds yanking the pontiff from the wooden newels.

Do it! His mind whispered. *End it now!*

Just as he thought this, Meeds sent a shockwave through the cardinal. The Special Forces assassin didn't pull Callixtus from the bannister. What he did was… strain against the cascade and shove the pontiff's feet back onto the newels.

What the hell is he doing? Jonathan wondered. *He just saved the reformer from certain death!*

"Up you go," Meeds shouted above the din of gushing water. "Grasp hold of the wood; you're almost to the top of the bannister!"

Traitor! Jonathan's considerations shouted in the depths of his thoughts. *You've forsaken the orders of execution!*

That's when a loud crack sounded beneath.

"Oh, no," Tish screamed, "the wood is splintering!"

"Quickly," Captain Maka shouted. "Climb!"

The wood bannister started to give way under the weight of the climbers. Tons of seawater pounded its construction like a heavyweight boxer hitting a side of beef in a meat locker.

"Come on, Cardinal!" Tish begged. "Move your Roman ass up those newels before this ladder is the end of us!"

Jonathan forced himself to abandon his condemning thoughts of Meeds. He couldn't believe the colonel had missed the opportunity to let the pope die. *What's this? Why did the assassin not let the bishop drop to death?*

"Jonathan!" Callixtus shouted. "Hurry and climb the few remaining footholds!"

Staring back into the downpour the cardinal quickly climbed a half dozen more newels before arriving at a landing. Regarding Callixtus, he reached out a hand and pulled the leader of the Catholic Church to safety.

There'll be time enough for killing, he supposed, *when nobody is turning an eye to witness the deed.*

Meeds was last to climb onto the landing.

When he did so, Jonathan stared him down as the others moved down a hallway towards the esplanade.

"Why didn't you end it?"

"The time wasn't right," Meeds whispered. "What would you have me do, kill him right in front of those witnesses?"

"You had the golden opportunity."

The colonel grimaced. "Don't pretend to inform me how things must be done. I'll take out the target when the circumstances favor our situation."

"But this was perfect," the cardinal argued.

Then, the waterlogged staircase gave way in an exhausted, splintering collapse. It twisted in a cacophony of snapping screws and quickly... the thick newel-ladder simply snapped free of its fasteners and buckled into the void like wooden matches tumbling from a matchbox.

"Just in the nick of time!" the captain exclaimed from up ahead. "Follow us, Colonel! The promenade is this way!"

Moving through waist-high seawater, the piercing sound of bending steel occupied the hall, and in the distance screams were lined with fear.

"Help! We're over here!"

Sloshing through debris-filled water the captain led his band of survivors into the Times Square promenade.

It was nothing like Meeds had seen when coming onboard. Now, it was a huge tank of water with passengers clinging to railings. On the far side, a huge hole had been punched into the hull. Through the gaping steel, they could see the vast ocean and blue sky.

Then, Meeds saw the fin of Bessie the Beast.

Chapter 68

FLAMINGO LAND

MIAMI WAS PARADISE.

Known for its pristine beaches, flamboyant art deco vibrancy, and the neon lights illuminating Ocean Drive, it was the melting pot of Earth.

Tourists from North and South America, Europe, and the essence of humanity all flocked here for a sense of elegance and the hope of spotting celebrities.

Home to Hollywood's biggest stars, *Flamingo Land* was mostly known as the backdrop of the 1980s TV show Miami Vice. The drama starred Don Johnson and Philip Michael Thomas. But even they wouldn't have wriggled out of this disaster facing the Magic City.

Sam knew few destinations were as romantic as Miami.

There was a sense of urgency that amplified its shimmering seductions. It was exotic too, with architectural styles bounding into heaven, transforming its scrubby maritime landscape into a semitropical utopia.

"There's a sense of swagger in the air," Sam stated stepping off the plane and shaking Oscar's hand. He knew populations living close to the ocean blithely ignored the fact an energetic wave could wipe the beach clean.

"This is the American example of denial!" V.I. tiredly agreed. "The stage is set for the biggest event in history. Disaster is headed for this barrier island of sand and coconut palms along the *Gold Coast* of the Atlantic."

The nickname came from the large amounts of gold salvaged from shipwrecks off the shores of Palm Beach & Fort Lauderdale.

Walking across the tarmac, Sam stepped to a Humvee on loan from Florida's National Guard.

Miami Soldiers and Air Force personnel made up the 2nd Battalion, 111th Aviation Regiment.

Sam peered at a guardsman standing sentinel beside the armored vehicle. "Thank you, Mate, for everything you undertake for this ripe world of ours!"

The soldier nodded.

Since 9/11, the Florida National Guard had called on over seventeen thousand inactive members to serve.

"Do you have a name, soldier?" Gordy asked.

"Major Emmett, Sir."

Gordon saluted. "Bless you, Major. I served with the Second Platoon, Airborne Brigade Combat Team."

"Sir," the major stood at ease. "We hear a shit storm is headed our way, huh?"

"Did the Governor send you?"

"No, Sir, we're here directly on orders from the Commander In Chief."

"Well, I'll be dipped in shit," Gordon hooted. "How in God's good country did that come to pass?"

The major grinned. "The U.S. Supreme Court, Sir. Base command received an executed declaration from the Chief Justice backing orders by POTUS."

"The Governor told us not to evacuate citizens," another guardsman pitched-in. "But ultimately we take orders from the President. We've been deployed overseas four, five, six times... so we've developed quite a few experienced soldiers who know for whom they serve."

"Eighteen members of The Florida Guard have died while serving their country since 9/11," the major sighed. "Some perished in combat, others from accidents and natural causes. We like to think our ultimate sacrifice means something."

"I know how you feel, Major," Gordy agreed. "I was over there fighting Haji when 22-year-old Army Specialist Jeffrey M. Wershow was *killed in action.*"

"Who's Jeffrey Wershow?" Sam asked.

"A red blooded hero, that's who," Major Emmitt affirmed. "Jeff was the first Florida Guardsman to die in combat after September Eleventh. He was shot at Baghdad University while conducting military operations after being called to serve while studying at Santa Fe Community College."

"Sorry to hear that," Sam grunted.

Suddenly, Gordon's cell phone rang. Looking to the caller ID he smirked and pulled it from his belt: "Yes, Sir?"

"Gordy? Did my boys meet up with you down there in the Sunshine State?"

"Yes, Mr. President, Major Emmett is standing ready."

"Tell the Major to thank Southern Command; we'll handle the bald bastard in the Governor's Mansion!"

"Yes, Sir," Gordon smiled.

"And, Gordy?"

"Sir?"

"Tell our British friend to kick his royal ass into high gear down there! We have millions of people to save."

With that, the president was gone.

Yet, just before Gordy pressed the end-call button he could've sworn he heard POTUS chuckling. *Well, why not? He just shoved a banana up the governor's ass.* Climbing into the Humvee behind Sam, he knew what lay ahead was deserving of that banana and maybe even a bitch slap.

Politics... you have to love it.

Chapter 69

INTO THE VASTNESS

USS GEORGE H.W. BUSH was big.

The CVN-77 was the tenth and final Nimitz-class super-carrier of the United States Navy.

That just reads *BAD ASS!*

Named for the 41st President of the United States, "No New Taxes" former WW II aviator, and former Director of Central Intelligence, the carrier's call sign was *Avenger*.

The Pentagon named it for the TBM Avenger fighter flown by then Lieutenant Bush.

Now, the carrier sailed alongside USS Harry Truman and USS Abe Lincoln, just off her starboard side.

A flotilla of nuclear subs surrounded them.

"Avenger," Admiral Brancor boomed into an open radio channel, "you got your ears on over there?"

"I've got you, Lew," Rear Admiral Craig Hastings stated. He was commander of Carrier Strike Group Two. Under his command, the George H.W. Bush Carrier Air Wing Eight departed on their first deployment on 15 May 2011. They sailed across the Atlantic to Britain to assist in *Exercise Saxon Warrior* in the Western Approaches culminating in the *Thursday War*.

"There's an old saying by Woodrow Wilson," Lew said. "We shall take leave to be strong upon the seas, in the future as in the past; and there will be no thought of offense or of provocation in that. Our ships are our natural bulwarks."

Staring through the binoculars, he saw his friend standing steady on Georgie's bridge staring through his own glasses.

"And like that old quote," Lew continued. "We stand ready to battle not an enemy of the human race, but a *cataclysmic* event sent to us from the depths of hell."

Putting down the glasses, he turned to a skeleton crew crowding him on the hi-tech bridge.

"We're going into that monster wave, men. We won't put our tails between retreating legs and run for the Gulf of México. The waters we serve on won't shake us in the face of certain death. We'll stand ready to die as men of honor."

Beside the USS Harry S. Truman cruised its Carrier Strike Group consisting of guided-missile cruiser USS San Jacinto, USS Gettysburg, and guided-missile destroyers USS Mason and USS Bulkeley.

On every ship of the flotilla, the battle ready men heard Admiral Brancor speaking his words of encouragement.

Now, in the stillness of those words, the sailors came to deck and saluted the storied war-tried admiral and the Chairman of the Joint Chiefs.

"We're ready to serve the President, Lew!" Admiral Hastings replied over the open radio channel.

Lew picked up his binoculars and scanned the men standing ready on their ships. It was a sight to see; the saluting hardened war torn soldiers ready to die for their country. Glancing to the bridge of George H.W. Bush, he smiled at the sight of Hastings, a Cuban cigar clenched between his teeth, chomping through the tobacco as a plume of smoke rose around his head.

Those puffs, Lew knew, were stoked by the blood of hardened sailors across the world's oceans.

The stogies were outlawed in the United States.

Screw 'em if they didn't like it, Lew thought.

As far as he was concerned, fleet commanders had to fight the bloody wars; their men died for freedom and what they smoked was their God given right.

The carrier group had just returned to Norfolk following a seven-month deployment supporting operations with the U.S. Navy's 5th and 6th fleets.

They were the best that they could be!

Today they'd be tested, yet again.

Staring at his flight deck, Lew watched six Sikorsky SH-60 Seahawks he'd ordered loaded on each of the carrier's decks. His plan was simple. When the wave came, he'd load his men into the choppers and send them above the tsunami.

Then, he'd aim the top-secret laser into the wave.

If all worked as planned, the weapon would vaporize the monster and punch a hole through the surf.

After all hell broke loose, the choppers would descend on the aftermath and look for survivors of the fleet.

They'd find one of two things.

The carriers might make it, or the fleet would be gone.

His battleships and strikers were sure to be lost at sea.

But… anything could happen.

This was the vastness of the deep.

"All hands," Admiral Lew Brancor ordered. "Ready the fleet, secure all hatches, batten down the ships. We're going into the bright blue yonder!"

Chapter 70

THE BLACK POPE

IT WAS ONLY a matter of time now.

With Rome's Cardinals in his pocket, the leader of the church's invisible secret society knew two things.

He would finally control the Vatican…

And, the world would be his playground.

The superior general was invested with extraordinary power over members of the Society of Jesus, and had more power than a bishop, clergy, or diocese. So, he decided to call in a favor to ensure Callixtus found fate in the bottom of the Atlantic.

Reaching for a wireless phone, he dialed a number.

"Palazzo del Quirinale," a voice answered.

The Quirinal Palace was a historic building in Rome and the official residence of the Italian President. Located on Quirinal Hill, it had once housed thirty popes, four kings, and eleven Presidents of Italy.

Now, a traitor ruled the land.

"Put him on," the black pope ordered.

"Right away, Your Excellency."

Since Saint Ignatius was elected superior general in 1540, black popes were elected for life by the General Congregation of Jesuits representing provinces from around the world. His mission entailed running *The Order* according to constitutions, norms, and guidelines of the general congregations that he controlled.

And sometimes, power guided evil.

The Order was like a black program.

It was invisible, a virtual black hole. Its activities were hidden. By constitution, the superior general absolved priests and workers of sins, and overlooked the wickedness of murder and espionage.

And, this demon ran the show.

Jesuits could murder Monday and be absolved Tuesday.

According to Decree #3 of the general congregation, servants of Christ worked towards helping individuals in the struggle to find meaning in a governing philosophy of subjectivism, moral policy, and practical greediness.

Hogwash! The black pope thought pacing the hardwood floor. *People want iPod's! They desired... Computers! CARS! Money!* Humanity wasn't interested in maintaining spiritual dialogues or reflecting on relationships, morality, or faith! They favored things.

"Hello?" another voice came onto the line.

"My friend!" the superior general muttered. "I come before the altar of man seeking illumination."

"Speak this and so it shall be done."

Moving to heavily draped windows, the black pope pushed aside heavy fabric curtains and stared towards the thousands of worshippers packing the square begging a miracle on behalf of their pope.

Saint Peter's Square was a massive plaza located directly in front of the basilica by the same name. At its center rose a four-thousand-year-old Egyptian obelisk, surrounded by massive Tuscan colonnades accommodating one hundred and forty statues of saints overlooking twin granite fountains.

Below and to the right, he stared at the weathered stone statue of *Petronilla*–the legendary Virgin daughter of Saint Peter, which silently condemned him now.

Glancing to the pulsing crowd, he smiled. To be loved by them is what he wanted. *Idiots, lining up to be fleeced of their valuable wool and hard earned wages for the hope of redemption.* Releasing his bony grasp on the fabric, he shuffled across the dark room and reclined into a plush leather couch beneath a massive oil painting of Jesus.

"His Excellency?" the tinny voice interrupted.

The black pope was stunned to silence by the painting depicting the face of Christ.

It burned into his throbbing skull.

Where had it all gone wayward?

His teenaged beliefs that maybe, possibly, there was a true God in which he could believe.

Now... *he knew the truth.*

There was no God... except for the keepers of Earth.

Those who'd taunted society for longer than memory served, etched in drawings and paintings dating back centuries, ominously hanging just below dark clouds.

These were the secrets he had to protect.

"Superior General?" the voice asked again.

He asked his favor. "Make plans to feed the Shepherd. Bring down the Hammerhead!"

It was a name of death and destruction.

"Is this what you want?" the unhesitant voice queried.

"It is," the black pope sighed.

Chapter 71

CHUNNEL TUNNEL

EUROSTAR'S HIGH-SPEED railway connected London, Paris, and Brussels.

Traversing the Channel Tunnel between the United Kingdom and France, people could climb on in England and step off at Disneyland Paris, southern France, and the Alps in winter.

Cars were out of style in Europe.

OPECs stranglehold on oil wasn't welcome here.

The train service was operated by eighteen coach class Pullmans running at 300 kilometers per hour on a network of high-speed lines.

They redefined transportation.

Rail service was the *fastest* way to travel.

And, it carried more voyagers between terminals than all airlines flying the same itineraries.

The only priority now was this:

Getting far from London!

"I'm telling you," Professor Wild Bill shouted into his cell phone. "London is doomed!"

The coachman was packed to capacity; expressions of concern lined the faces of refugees fleeing the land they so loved.

"The Chunnel is doomed!"

That's what Bob's voice pounded into Bill's ears… just a millisecond before the connection dropped.

Glancing out the train's window he saw flashes of light as they hurtled through the Chunnel, speeding past lights attached to the reinforced concrete channel.

CATACLYSM

Sitting in *Business Premier* Coach, he thought it was equivalent to lounging in first class on a jumbo jet. Collapsing back into a large, plush gray seat, he fastened his seatbelt, pulled out a laptop and quickly plugged in the power cord. Crouching over a table, he connected to WIFI and punched in these keystrokes:

http://www.mylivestreams.com

From the landing page, he typed "London" in the search widget and selected Trafalgar Square. Normally, there'd be a continuous trail of double-decker buses shuttling tourists through central London and Westminster.

That's not what he saw.

At the center of the screen, he stared at Nelson's Column, a monument built to commemorate Admiral Horatio Nelson, who died at the Battle of Trafalgar in 1805. It was adorned by four bronze relief panels cast from captured French guns. The spire rose 169 feet from its base to the top of Nelson's hat. Defended by four lion sculptures at its base, there were multiple statues and sculptures in the square, each exhibiting varying pieces of modern art.

Now, there was nothing but pandemonium.

The entire square was packed with nervous Londoners lining up for buses evacuating the city. In the background, a fountain gave passersby a taste of what would soon come.

Bill typed "River Thames" into the widget and pressed the play button ○ to access live feeds of the river.

If it's flooded, he supposed. *I don't have a knobs headed chance of escaping this tunnel.*

On the screen, a *live London HD* web-cam *faded into* various views of the River Thames normally pushing beneath The Albert, Chelsea, and Battersea Bridges.

The camera overlooking Battersea Power Station and Cheyne Walk was hectic, but showed no hint of flooding.

Then, searching the widget for "The English Channel," Bill pressed the play button again and found his disaster.

This feed overlooked Sandown Bay Beach, a seaside resort on the southeast coast of the Isle of Wight.

"Crikey Moses!" he mumbled taking in the scene.

The shoreline was gone; houses, buildings, and boats raged through a violent, powerful, surge... rushing over the banks of the channel. Then, a yacht barreled towards the camera, riding high on a gush of water, which sent the video stream to blackness.

Wild Bill stared in astonishment.

"Can I assist you, Sir?" an attendant moseyed up staring into his terrified green eyes, obviously concerned with the expression of utter fear on Bill's face.

Abruptly she was thrown from her feet and soared through the cabin slamming into a wall. Passengers flew from their seats as if the train had impacted a wall.

Bill's neck snapped violently against the headrest and he immediately felt a spiking pain. Turning to the window, he saw water plowing through the Chunnel.

Then, the train's windows cracked, the passengers screamed and everyone stumbled from their seats.

But, there was nowhere to go.

This is it, Bill thought, just an instant before the windows shattered and water pushed through the empty window frames.

Then, everyone onboard drowned, their lungs gasping buckets of water while clutching for an escape that would never come.

Last stop: Purgatory!

Chapter 72

COMING IN HEAVY

HEATHROW WAS IN SIGHT.

Sitting twelve nautical miles west of central London, its twin east–west runways stretched into the horizon.

"Repeat, Heathrow Tower," Captain Harry Rogers called out. "This is Global 2291, requesting an immediate landing pattern, over?"

"Negative, 2291," the tower responded. "Our runways are congested with outbound traffic. You've been dark up there about what's happened since the volcano erupted. The ridge of that mountain fell into the ocean and caused a surge to push through the English Channel flooding London. There's nowhere for you to land down here."

"They don't know about the UFO?" Jeanne asked.

"Doesn't sound like it," the co-pilot said.

"You're not going to tell them?"

No freaking way, the captain thought. "They'd ground us in a minute, say we're all crazy. Let the passengers articulate that story on the news. You know what happens to flight crews who admit seeing UFOs."

"Repeat, Global 2291," the tower called. "Heathrow is heavy with runway traffic; you must go around, over?"

When instructed to *go around*, a pilot was required to loop the airport until receiving clearance to land. Under normal circumstances, pilots would apply power to the engines and adopt appropriate climbing attitudes. The landing gear would be retracted, the flaps would be withdrawn and the plane would climb to necessary altitude in anticipation of further instructions from the tower.

Going around is not going to happen.

The Airbus utilized a fly-by-wire system with go-around modes that automatically set power and pitch for best performance, using a *TOGA* button.

With the engines out, the electrical system was useless.

Skip also realized going around wasn't an option. "Heck. We've got to set down somewhere. There's no power to circle the airfield; we're dropping like a rock."

"You want to tell them?" the captain asked.

Pressing the communications button, Skip called out to the tower. "Global 2291, Tower Heathrow, do you have another immense radar signature at our one o'clock?"

"Negative," Heathrow replied. "Your ping is the only inbound heavy on radar, over?"

The tower couldn't see the spaceship.

Harry shook his head and checked the navigation screen. "Heathrow is out of the question, we need to find a flat surface to put down safely."

Peering through the windscreen, he observed the congested runways. Landing on either of the two airstrips wasn't possible... unless he wanted to cause the biggest aviation accident in history.

"Five thousand feet," the co-pilot informed.

"Put down in the river," Harry suggested. "The span in Woolwich is fifteen hundred feet across; we'll ditch east of the Thames Barrier Gates!"

"C'mon, Captain," Skip scoffed. "Are you kidding? This isn't the Hudson River and you don't have the luck of Captain Sully Sullenberger." Sully was a heroic pilot who crash-landed US Air flight 1549 departing New York's LaGuardia Airport. That Airbus struck Canada Geese during takeoff, lost engine power, and ditched into the Hudson River.

"Not sure I can even pull it off," the captain stated while feeling the aircraft coming apart behind him. "But we have to put down and the river is the only safe place."

Skip nodded. Silently, he understood this was the right call. "Four thousand feet and falling," he noted while pointing to the altimeter. Placing his hand on the control stick, he retracted the landing gear by pushing the lever forward. Instantly abandoning any thoughts of Heathrow, he peered towards the winding, snake like Thames River cutting a path from Twickenham to Hurlingham Park.

Beyond, London's skyline jutted into the sky.

Within seconds, the plane skimmed the trees of Southward Park and lined up for ditching on the most famous river in the world.

"One thousand feet and descending," Skip informed, his eyes locked onto the shining metal domes of the Barrier Gates. "We're gliding in Captain, coming through five hundred feet."

They were approaching London's Millwall Dock.

From the air, the development once resembled a U, with the Thames running around its banks. It sat near the center of the *Isle of Dogs*, just south of the Canary Wharf commercial business area.

NOW, it all lay beneath water.

"Blazing saddles!" Skip shouted. "It's all gone; everything is drowned on either side of the river." The dock was once home to the West Ferry Printing Works, the largest newspaper printer in Western Europe. The only thing visible now was the upper floors of office towers housing small companies.

Before either pilot had time to think of the implications of what they were seeing, the plane dove towards disaster.

"One hundred feet, Captain!" Skip yelled.

On the riverbanks, barges had been pushed to shore, resting atop factories, ships had crashed into buildings and many had collapsed. On the northern shore, Thames Barrier Park was wiped from Earth.

"Look at the top of the gates!" the captain pointed.

Their gigantic steel gateways were submerged. Built to prevent floods from reaching London, only the domes were visible above the waterline.

Flying inches above the barriers, the captain pushed forward the yoke and braced for impact.

"We're going in!" Jeanne yelled a moment before the goliath airframe plunged into the river.

Chapter 73

BESSIE BABY

Tɪsʜ COULDN'T MOVE.

Her legs were rubber; the soles of her boots seemed stuck to the waterlogged hallway by crazy-glue.

"Righteous mercy!" Colonel Meeds muttered.

Before him, slicing through the water was the familiar gargantuan dorsal fin. Pulling the HK-416 assault rifle from his back, he scanned the water. "Did anyone else see...?"

"You're darn right, I saw it," Tish interrupted, staring at the captain. "It was the same Carcharodon Carcharias that attacked the tender and killed the first mate and–"

"Almost ate you for dinner," Meeds cut in while aiming the weapon for the water. "We're going to have to keep an eye out for that thing."

The captain didn't see Bessie.

None of them did except Meeds and Tish.

The others were like actors in a horror movie... where someone detects a monster coming, but the others are oblivious to the deadly deal stomping through the darkness.

"Carcharodon Carcharias?" Jonathan asked. "What in God's name is that?"

"A shark," Meeds answered. "It's the largest man-eater in the ocean."

Jonathan peeled his eyes from the pope who was offering last rites to the dead. "Look at him, we're on the verge of demise and he's blessing those who've already gone to freedom." Glaring back at the hired assassin, he seemed puzzled. "What makes you think there's a shark?"

"Not just a shark," Meeds grunted. "This fish is a Great White eating machine, Cardinal."

"Huh?" Captain Maka spun to the conversation. "Colonel, did you say a great white shark?"

"Help us!" a voice yelled from somewhere out of view.

Tish scrambled to the breezeway ledge and glared towards a man, a boy, and a girl hanging from a balcony railing just a foot above the waterline. "Hang on! I'll climb down and get you!"

"Please, man!" Mikey yelled. "Don't let jaws get us!"

Behind them, the man peered to the water, waiting for the giant sharks to reappear. Back in California, he was the Director of the Santa Cruz Shark Research Center.

There, he oversaw a crew of marine biologists who studied aggressive sharks and tracked the ongoing attacks occurring in the Monterey and San Francisco Bays.

Currently on a two-week vacation, this was supposed to be a relaxing trip before he headed home to research great white behavior, biology, and ecology.

Funny… how things worked out!

"Come on," Meeds yelled climbing the balcony.

The words snapped Doolittle's attention back to the misadventure.

"Keep climbing," Meeds urged Mikey. "Just continue hand-over-hand, one step at a time, I'll meet you half way!"

A violent swirl of water caught Tish's attention and when she glanced to the surface, she saw tiger sharks ripping into a body.

"We've got to get to the tender boats!" Captain Maka suggested. "This ship will be underwater within an hour."

"Where are the boats?" Tish queried.

"Attached to the exterior of the ship, we have to navigate these deadly waters and make it through the hole in the hull."

Dr. Doolittle stared to the giant, jagged hole and imagined swimming under the surface and out to safety.

"Do you have scuba gear onboard?"

The captain nodded.

"Where is it–"

"Are you mad?" Tish interrupted pointing to the seawater. "Those fish will rip us apart!"

"It's the only way out!" the skipper stated. "We either die trying to get out, or go down with the ship!"

Tish screamed in annoyance. "Are you crazy?"

"It'll be one hell of an excursion," Jonathan mumbled.

The Great White Shark Experience!

However, Jessie Jaws wasn't their only problem.

The tiger sharks would WANT their human asses, too.

"We better suit up," Meeds ordered. "Our great adventure to freedom waits below the surface!"

Chapter 74

LONDON BRIDGES

THE QUEEN ELIZABETH II Bridge was:

Falling down!

The River Thames swelled and overtook the four-hundred-foot structure. The ferocious current brutally swept hundreds of vehicles from the span… like ants being hosed from a sidewalk.

Tumbling from the cable-stayed bridge connecting the southbound section of Dartford Crossing, the motorized coffins charged through the congested river with an ear-splitting screech of bending steel.

Battered and bloodied citizens hysterically scrambled from sinking cars. Once in the river, they struggled to swim from death's merciless embrace.

Some managed to reach the bridge's pylons.

Others sank beneath the tideline with a final gasp.

Thousands gagged on the briny water, congesting their lungs before stiffening in death's embrace.

Along the Thames' banks, hundred-year-old structures warped beneath tons of water… and now, it would depend on the Thames Barrier Operational Area to halt the swell before London found annihilation.

Then, a helicopter appeared above the river.

Inside, a pilot bellowed into a VHF radio. "Elevate the gates! The surge is heading downriver towards London!"

He was a London Metropolitan Police Officer assigned to support the Marine Policing Unit during the evacuation. Responsible for patrolling the river between Dartford and Hampton Court, he'd already scooped hundreds of screaming people from rooftops.

"Will do, Bennett!" a voice responded from the radio.

"I'm one minute from the barrier!"

"Jolly good, Mate!"

Staring below, the pilot surveyed the waterway pushing into Rainham Marshes Nature Reserve. It was one of few ancient scenes in London.

Following a looping river channel, the raging water charged straight through the natural habitat.

"It's the end of the Monarchy!"

Piloting the chopper over his hometown of Erith, he scrutinized a forty-foot upwelling crashing into the *All Saints Church* on Hempstead Road.

It was here, on Sunday mornings, where the wife and he prayed for peace and prosperity for their three kids.

"Oh, my dear," Bennett trembled.

Everything he'd come to love about the town lay submerged. The pubs, restaurants, and retail outlets: Eardley Arms on Woolwich Road, the Vic on Victoria Street, the Royal Standard in the heart of the village... and The Fox in Belvedere village.

It was all gone.

Choppering over the river, he saw the barrier gates. *They can't stop this monster.*

Both gateways lay beneath water.

On the other side of the barrier, a British police patrol boat chased behind a ditching commercial plane.

"That bloke has lost his peanuts!"

Watching, he surveyed the super jumbo jet falling from the sky, literally silent in its approach as it loomed above the water. Helpless to do anything, he considered skimming the brackish river to look for survivors of the eventual crash. But just then, the radio crackled.

"Bennett, boy, pick it up mate!"

"Go on, I've got my listeners on!"

"Kittyhawk and Unicorn need evacuation!"

"Blimey!" Bennett offered. The codenames were the MI-6 call signs for the Queen and Prince of England.

Chapter 75

BOCA CHICA

KEY WEST was the land of Jimmy Buffett.

The islands included Fleming Key, Stock Island, the Overseas Highway, Sigsbee Park, and Sunset Key.

Life here was all about sunsets and margaritas.

Then, there was Boca Chica Naval Air Station.

It was a beehive of activity.

Planes leapt for the sky and service personnel sped from the base in jeeps and Humvees.

They were getting out of dodge.

Base Commander, Steven McAlney, was on the phone.

"Captain," Sam's voice shouted through the receiver. "This is definitely an actual emergency."

"So, let me get this straight," McAlney replied, walking the airfield with FEMA personnel. "My men must evacuate everyone from Key West to Key Largo?"

"That's right, Mate. And it must be accomplished in less than three hours. It's all the time you have."

"Impossible," McAlney grumbled staring towards a squadron of VFC-111 Sundowner jets. "Unless we get every passenger plane in Florida down here," he suggested glancing at the idiots from FEMA, "the best way out of the lower Keys is by a strategic operational motorcade along the Overseas Highway and then over to western Florida!"

"Sir," a FEMA man interrupted, we really must get–"

"Boy!" Captain McAlney screamed. "Stand your pussyfooted bones ten paces behind my ass and shut your lackluster, government fed, mouth."

He was a no-nonsense, Annapolis graduate who knew how to put fear into the hearts of men.

"Where can we place an evacuation zone in the middle of Florida?" Sam's voice moaned. "It'd have to be west of Miami, out in the middle of the everglades somewhere."

The captain called out to his chief petty officer. "Pass me the RE-CON tablet."

Stepping beside his commander, a tough-as-nails naval chief handed over the electronic mapping device.

On its screen was a satellite image of Florida.

Running a finger along Interstate 75–*Alligator Alley*–the captain outlined a route running northwest of Miami to a section of swampland baptized *Billie Swamp Safari*.

"There!" McAlney pointed. "We can take over this encampment on 2,200 acres of untamed Florida Everglades on the Big Cypress Seminole Indian Reservation."

Sam's voice trembled. "How far is it from Miami Beach and the Atlantic Ocean?"

"Eighty-nine-miles northwest of Fort Lauderdale," McAlney answered tracing his finger along the map.

"That's farther than the flood will travel," Sam sighed in relief. "Make that swamp our evacuation base camp."

"Evacuate the base!" McAlney ordered before turning his attention back to the phone. "Dr. May, NAS Key West is located five miles northeast of Key West on Boca Chica Key. Do you know what that means?"

"You're in quite a cock-up!"

The captain laughed. "It means the keys are right in the middle of hell, Sir! But on order of the President, we're going to move Heaven and Earth… see you in Miami!"

Sprinting to a command chopper, he pushed the cell into his fatigues and ordered the airframe skyward.

"We're flying navy boys!"

Sunuvabitch, he thought. *This is gonna be one crack-up of a trolley train of misfit civvies!*

Below, an endless string of cars stretched along U.S. Highway One. The mass evacuation was underway.

The only questions McAlney had were:

Do we have hours?
Or will the tsunami come early?

Chapter 76

MEGALODON

DR. TISH HARRIET was NOT getting in the water.

"Those *things* almost killed me," she reminded Meeds. "Now, you expect me to swim into their jaws?"

"We have to get out of this boat!" Captain Maka stated. "If we hang around here, worrying about what's beneath, the ship will eventually sink and we'll drown anyway!"

"I don't care," Tish argued. "My Texas flesh ain't swimming into shark infested water to be gobbled by Megalodon's gnawing choppers."

"Megalodon?" Dr. Doolittle grinned, an expression of disbelief filling his stare. "They've been extinct for millions of years."

"What's Megalodon?" Mikey asked.

"It's what would have eaten your ass," Meeds chuckled, "if I didn't save you and the girl."

"It's a vanished species of shark," the marine biologist corrected. "Regarded as one of the largest and most dominant flesh eating predators in vertebrate history, fossils suggest it was bigger than the great white shark."

"Jaws?" Mikey probed.

"Exactly," Captain Maka agreed. "However Megalodon is supposed to be an extinct species!"

"Apparently not," Tish asserted. "I was rescued from its chomping incisors after my plane ditched." She couldn't shake her memory of Megalodon's Jaws. They hung in Manhattan's American Museum of Natural History on Central Park West at 79th Street.

As a volcanism teacher at the museums' David S. and Ruth L. Gottesman Hall of Planet Earth, she'd recently participated in a lecture entitled:

Mitigating Disasters
Earthquake Responses in the 21st Century

After the speech, she wandered through the Hall of Vertebrate Origins where jaws from the 100-million-year-old fish Carcharodon Megalodon hung above her head.

"I once held a triangular tooth of Megalodon," she told Mikey. "It measured more than a foot long and was lined with jagged serrations."

That caused the boy to stare at the water.

"Jagged what?"

"Sharp, uneven notches," Tish grinned flashing her pearly white choppers.

Lawdy, lawd! Have some mercy!

She imagined what *might transpire* should similar jaws find the tenderness of their pink flesh.

"You've seen those daggers at work once before," Meeds chuckled. "And it wasn't make-believe."

"Did I say thank you for saving my ass?"

Chuckling, Meeds winked. "You could have given me a kiss on the cheek, or a tight appreciative hug!"

"Get stuffed," Tish joked flipping him the bird.

"ShaaaaaaarK!" Mikey yelled, interjecting terror into the group while pointing to a fin breaching the water.

"Stand back," Meeds ordered shouldering his rifle. "Come on, come to daddy!" Peering through the titanium scope, he thought the swooped-back cartilage resembled the tail of a '59 Cadillac Eldorado.

"Take the shot!" Cardinal Jonathan exclaimed.

The fish charged; its dorsal fin climbing from the water as it approached. For an instant, Meeds thought the eyes broke the surface, it's dead, black eyeballs sizing him up...glaring into his soul for a sign of weakness.

"Come on!" Tish urged. "Shoot the bloodstalker!"

The moment Meeds decided to pull the trigger, it was a second too late; the beast slipped beneath the water.

"Unbelievable, Meeds!" Jonathan mocked. "What are you, some kind of Greenpeace, PETA loving idiot?"

The colonel turned to the sniveling cardinal and punched him in the nose. There was a distinctive snap as either the bone or cartilage fractured.

"You broke my nose!" the cardinal whined, a moment before he fell to his knees like a desperate child who'd lost his warm cuddle puppy.

"It's just a bridge fracture," Meeds grunted turning to Callixtus. "He'll have a couple black eyes in a day or two, maybe next time he'll keep his offensive mouth bolted."

Callixtus nodded in agreement. "Jonathan, the Lord does not excuse bad behavior because of fear."

"Jeez!" the cardinal spat. "That thug assassin breaks my nose and you're lecturing me on manners?"

"Now, Jonathan," Callixtus warned. "The next time the colonel might wash out your mouth with soap!"

"Then again," Meeds said pulling out a knife.

"All right!" the cardinal surrendered scooting a few paces back. "I'm sorry, what are you going to do, kill me for mouthing off?"

"That's a good boy," Meeds smiled.

"Now," the captain pitched in, "let's start thinking about getting off the vessel."

Meeds sheathed the knife, reached out his hand, and pulled Jonathan to his feet. "No hard feelings, buddy."

Chapter 77

LET'S GET HUMBLE

ASPEN LODGE was the president's hideout.

Thirteen former presidents had occupied the olive green cabin at Camp David. Initially christened *The Bear's Den* by President Franklin Delano Roosevelt, it was *the* place where presidents enjoyed the most privacy.

No cameras allowed.

Reporters weren't present at Aspen Lodge.

The Prez didn't have to worry about lenses capturing his every move, or correspondents asking trick questions. It was just him and his wife, Vanessa.

"What are they telling you, Chris?" she asked. "Will we be able to return to Washington?"

The president grabbed her hand.

"It's not good, Darling," he mumbled, pursing his lips, and shaking his head. "We're going to have a lot of people who need our help along the east coast... Washington, as we know it, will probably be destroyed."

"Will the country be able to help everyone?"

"I'm not sure. Citizens are rioting, looting, and taking to the streets in protest of being forced from their homes. In Miami, we're overriding the Florida Governor who hasn't moved on mandatory evacuations."

"You have to be kidding!"

"It's a fight for the military to get everyone to safety."

Stepping across the room, they emerged onto a screened-in porch hosting a flagstone patio.

Glancing to the pool, the president recalled a water gun fight he'd had with his twin daughters on their 18th birthday. Beyond the pool, were a one-hole golf course and the woodlands of the Catoctin Peaks which formed the eastern rampart of the Appalachian Mountains.

In the distance, secret service agents roamed the birch and oak timberland–*their heads swiveling*–constantly at a state of readiness watching for timber rattlesnakes, black bears, raptors and, human predators.

"I'm going to head down to the bunker," POTUS advised. "You want to come along, watch the turmoil unravel across the country?"

"No. I think I'll call the kids at Harvard."

Pulling out her cell phone, she punched in a number.

The girls had just returned to Cambridge to prepare for the first day of fall classes. But with the university lying close to the Charles River, evacuations were ordered and the secret service wanted the girls out.

After a few rings, The First Lady's expression grew in concern. "They're not answering, Christopher!"

"I'm sure they're fine," the president shrugged and kissed her cheek. His gut, however, wasn't so sure. It wasn't like them not to answer, especially during a time like this.

For Vanessa, any deviation from the norm meant things were *anything but fine*. Then, after the voicemail picked-up, her panic set in. Turning to POTUS, her voice cracked with uncertainty.

"Can you contact their security detail?"

"Of Course," he nodded. Motioning for an agent, the president watched him hurry over. "Get a hold of my kids' away team and find out their location, will you?"

"Yes, Sir, Mr. President."

Slapping the agent on the back, POTUS hugged the love of his life. "Keep me posted on what they find out."

Stepping across the patio, he hurried through the cabin and entered an awaiting elevator at the front door. Pressing the down button, he descended 200 feet before arriving in the underground bunker and communication facility.

Rushing through the maze-like complex of busy offices, POTUS entered an executive conference room.

"Mr. President!" A marine saluted.

"Good to see you, Jacob."

Walking across the room, the Commander In Chief stared at a wall of flat screen televisions displaying the disaster unfolding along the Atlantic shoreline.

Codenamed *Orange One*, the bunker connected Aspen Lodge to a six-mile tunnel burrowed into Raven Rock Mountain Complex–also known as *Site R*–a massive underground shelter hosting the Alternate Joint Communications Center (AJCC) that served as a backup to the Pentagon in times of national emergency.

"Mr. President!" his national security advisor stated. "We have reports coming in from various countries, and none of them are good."

"Take it from the top," POTUS barked.

Chapter 78

DEADLY SKIES

THE AVIANO AIR BASE was a secret installation.

Sitting in northeast Italy, it bordered Austria to the north, Slovenia to the east, and the Adriatic Sea.

Nobody cared of the west.

There, the highlands made access impossible.

This was Italy's Area 51! At the foot of the Southern Carnic Alps, the Italian Air Force hosted NATO and an American Fighter Wing.

It was the only U.S. presence south of the Alps.

The strategic location made fighting operations in NATO's southern region conceivable.

And, there were whispers of black ops.

Creepy, X-FILE sorts of things…

Underground bases, UFO activity,

And, witnesses who found early deaths.

The story went like this: A hiker once happened to point a video camera skyward. Suddenly, two fighter jets appeared escorting a saucer shaped UFO over the Alps. Climbing the summit, the man watched the craft land at the base where it entered a black hanger. Talk of the disc belonging to Project Blue Beam whispered throughout town. The locals hypothesized that the United States, NASA, and Italy conspired with world governments to implement a New Age religion with the Antichrist at its head. Anyway, not long after the report hit the news, the Italian journalist who reported the incident died from a rare brain infection. That heated the conversation of cover-up conspiracies supposing murder.

Nowadays, nobody dared to trek the mountains.

There were things up there…

So, when the orders came to Aviano Command to arm Italy's new Hammerhead Drone with heat seeking missiles, that's exactly what transpired.

Once airborne, the silent, unmanned missile-shooter would climb to 45,000 feet, making it invisible to anyone on the ground.

There was a target on someone's back.

"Why're we arming this?" an American Specialist queried his Italian counterpart. "I thought these hotdogs were strictly for Italian ground surveillance?"

"Piaggo," the Italian shrugged. "He's-uh the Base Commander, and runs-uh the Aeronautica Militare." It was hard understanding the Italian as every few words ended with a grunt-like uh. Attaching the Hammerheads, he checked the drone's integrated sensor operating system and cleared the airframe to prosecute Italian airspace.

From here, nobody knew where the drone was headed.

"Clear-uh!" the Italian shouted and waved to a command tower above the airfield. Speaking into a handheld radio, he gave the okay. "Romeo-uh is TANGO-uh for Project-uh Sainthood!"

Tango for Project Sainthood? The American considered. *What the hell is this, some Rambo wannabe movie set?* At that moment, right in the middle of his contemplations, the drone sped along the tarmac, blasted down the runway and burst into dark gray clouds.

A storm was brewing.

Within seconds, the white drone disappeared from sight and rocketed through a classified course firing over the Alboran Sea off the coast of Spain.

That's where drone control was handed off.

"What the heck is project Sainthood, Mariano?" the specialist nudged his Italian buddy.

"Who-knows-uh, Jeremy?" the Italian shrugged. His face was lined with an expression of discomfort.

"Somebody knows," the American quizzed.

"It's-like-uh, mission impossible, no?"
Whatever this mission was, it was hush-hush.
And, somebody had to be in control.

Chapter 79

BUMPER TO BUMPER

THE SEVEN MILE BRIDGE was dangerous.

Featured in the twisting plotlines of movies like *True Lies* and *License to Kill... the* locals called the Spanaway *Soul Snatcher*.

The reaper collected bodies here.

Vehicle accidents snatched lives every week.

Connecting Knight's and Little Duck Keys–islands of the Florida Keys–the concrete overseas span was among the longest and deadliest bridges in existence.

To either side, the calm aqua sea shimmered, mullets leapt from the water, pelicans crowded cell phone towers, and seagulls dove to the coral for unsuspecting fish.

Drivers couldn't resist glancing at paradise.

Often, it was the *last thing* they saw.

Now... the bridge was a fright-filled purgatory... a desperate two-lane escape route from a killer wave.

Impact was in hours

Captain McAlney was flying above U.S. Highway One in a navy helicopter when he saw the smoke.

Headed to coordinate an evacuation battalion staging on the islet of Islamorada, this was an unscheduled emergency.

Hit by the Labor Day Hurricane of 1935, this well-heeled shoreline had the best evacuation plans of Florida.

Glaring through a cloud of thick black smoke, the captain glimpsed bumper-to-bumper traffic below.

"We'll be lucky to get these people across the bridge," the pilot blurted. "Let alone evacuate the lower keys."

The bridge was a sea of overheating vehicles.

"Look!" McAlney pointed. "There is a fire somewhere down there and everyone is abandoning their cars!"

Near the span's center, a frenzied horde hiked up the Moser Channel Arc… a steep curvature usually providing clearance for boats.

Hearing the helicopter, the panic-stricken crowd pointed skyward.

"Over here!" a Cuban man waved.

"Hey! Get us outta here!" Another begged.

Buzzing the structure, the chopper looped the scene.

Spanned by the Seven Mile Bridge this section of gorgeous teal seawater was *one of four* predominant channels in the Florida Keys. It exchanged seawater with the Atlantic waters of Hawk Channel and the Florida Reef.

"Look at that small island," the FEMA man pointed out the window. "There are pink flamingos along the shallows!" It was officially called Pigeon Key, a small, exclusive, five-acre Island at mile marker 45. Originally known as *Cayo Paloma*, it was named for large flocks of white-crowned pigeons, which once roosted there.

Now, along the shallows, pink flamingos were feeding.

Glancing back to the bridge, McAlney peered to smoke billowing from the roadway. A raging fire engulfed the northern downward slope of the passage where a tractor-trailer had crashed into a double-decker Greyhound bus.

"Get Boca Chica's ears on," he ordered, "and have air support send a Chinook to tug the truck off the highway."

"Murphy's law," the pilot mumbled.

"What's that?" the FEMA man asked.

"Murphy's Law," McAlney repeated. "Anything *that can go wrong* will go wrong!"

Swooping over the fire and landing on the north end of the highway, the men hopped from the chopper with portable fire extinguishers.

"These aren't going to stop this fire!" the FEMA man shouted breaking a red plastic sealing tie on the handle.

Rushing to the Greyhound, the captain observed dozens of dead bodies burning in their seats. The windows had disintegrated, and through the raging flames…the fleshless, eyeless skulls grinned into eternity. The skin and muscle had burned away, leaving blackened rows of gaping teeth that looked like smiling skulls.

The scent of roasting flesh occupied the air; a sour, crisp stench, which reminded everyone of burned bacon.

"I have a survivor!" someone yelled.

Glancing to his chief petty officer, McAlney watched as the lucky bastard limped away from the fire. Peering back to the inferno, he knew the coroner would need dental records to make positive identifications.

Dousing the fire with a handheld extinguisher and watching as the final flame flickered out McAlney watched a Boeing CH-47 Chinook landing on the highway.

"Attach a towline!" he ordered soldiers rushing out from the chopper's rear ramp. "We need to pull these vehicles off the bridge!"

"But there are bodies inside!" someone argued.

"And there'll be thousands more," McAlney answered staring into his soul, "if we don't get these vehicles over the bridge and out of the Florida keys!"

Chapter 80

PANIC STATION!

THE STAMPEDE had begun.

Waterloo Train Station was a tomb waiting for bodies.

Perched between Westminster and Waterloo Bridges, the subterranean railway was a frenzied hive of turmoil.

Misfortune headed its way.

"Move along," a constable urged hundreds of hysterical passengers stepping from the train platform. "Mark your steps with haste and get up to the street."

Sprinting along the walkway, commuters rushed up a set of stone stairs flanked by black steel handrails.

This was the way to freedom!

Water would soon fill this tube!

Climbing, they had very little time to escape.

"Hurry!" the constable urged. "Step hastily now, run up to the lobby!" His thoughts jolted back to summer 2005 and the nightmarish memory of the London bombings. Like the cowardly attacks on Manhattan and Boston, Britain suffered its own assaults.

These were a series of coordinated bombings targeting public transportation during morning rush hour.

Four terrorists had detonated four bombs... three in The Underground trains and another on a bus in Tavistock Square. Fifty-two civilians were slaughtered and hundreds more severely injured in London's first terrorist attack.

The world was turning into a nightmare.

As the constable recalled that day and his service to the crown, he tilted his head toward the shadowy tube in the distance. At the far reaches of earshot, he perceived the sound of gushing water.

It was a *pounding, whooshing* rhythm…

Like a waterfall crashing over a cliff.

Peering into the dark tunnel, he witnessed a train barreling into the station. Its speed was faster than anything he'd ever witnessed.

And then, he glimpsed the black water.

Its nastiness propelled a Eurostar Pullman through the concrete tunnel like a bullet bursting from a handgun.

The hulking steel locomotive was on its way to glory!

"Ruuuuun!" the constable yelled. The train seemed to slow down in his mind.

It's a SLO-MO sequence of death and destruction; his face imitated a Saturday Night Live comedy act of horror.

"Ruuuuuuuuuuuun!"

However, before the commuters could react, the torrent slammed the train into the platform and through hundreds of fleeing bodies. The subway car lifted from its track and crashed through the station's concrete beams. With nothing supporting the ceiling girders, the entirety of the structure collapsed onto the platform.

Absconding up the stairs, those who survived the impact trampled one another as water gushed at their feet, washing many back down the stairs and through the tube.

Swimming through a sea of bodies, people begged for mercy, their arms slapping the water, reaching for a handhold to keep them afloat.

But there was nothing.

Hugging a handrail, a young girl clutched a teddy bear. Her eyes holding fright, the pupils locked on the pandemonium and death flowing down the stairwell.

Swimming to her, the constable grasped her arm and kicked back to the stairwell… the force of the water pushing them up into the concourse.

"Mum!" the girl cried, "I've lost my Mum!"

Struggling to gain his footing, the constable pulled the girl onto the concourse's marble landing. Behind him, the water rose into the station from the tubes beneath.

In the main concourse now, it was bedlam.

Commuters ran for the exits, stampeding, pushing one another, in some cases, to death.

Lifting the girl in his arms, the constable sprinted through the feverish scene, dodging those who'd fallen.

His eyes were trained on one thing.

The double doors of the exit.

Then, just as he reached them, the water blasted into the station and lifted everyone into the violent surge.

Within seconds, the depths reached twenty feet and the train departure boards were at eye level.

"Help!" the constable shouted as the upwelling trapped him in a massive crowd of drowning people.

But assistance would never come.

Chapter 81

SALVATION DIVING!

VALENCIA OFFERED passengers an amazing deep-water scuba excursion when ported in Tenerife.

Those days were over.

, *Finished! Caput! Sayonara!*

Stocked with dive gear, the program was baptized:

Fate of the Deep Snorkel Adventure

They'd be diving for death!

"Why don't we all go into the deep together?" Captain Maka argued. He'd just spent the last twenty minutes searching for scuba tanks, wet suits, flippers and goggles.

Colonel Meeds wanted to take the plunge.

He didn't want *them* to chance being eaten alive. Slinging an oxygen tank over his broad, muscled shoulders, he stared at the bloody water.

"Listen, Captain, we know what waits below. At least two great whites have attacked, countless other sharks are feasting, but someone has to take a chance on getting help. I'm the most qualified."

Staring about the promenade deck, the captain found it almost totally submerged and he had no choice but to let someone enter the bloodbath. The screams of dying passengers had become whispers of finality amidst the loud groaning sounds of sinking steel.

The ship would be underwater in less than an hour.

"What's the plan?" he asked.

"Jesus," Tish sighed. "I can't believe you're agreeing to let anyone get in the water with Jaws!"

Jessie Jaws waited!

"I'll be the scout," Meeds offered. "Maybe I'll end up in the stomach of a large fish, or perhaps I'll make it through the graveyard and find help outside."

Cardinal Jonathan scoffed. "Why do you get to escape this sinking ship?" Pointing to Callixtus, he grunted. "Isn't your job to protect His Holiness? Why would you strand him and us here?"

"If you enter that bloody water," Dr. Doolittle assured Meeds, "you'll never be heard from again. Dinner bells will ring down in the darkness and the man eaters will find you before ya know what hit you."

Decisions... decisions!

"Why not draw straws?" the captain suggested.

"Huh?" Jonathan asked.

"Straws?" Mikey asked. "Draw straws?"

"What are you talking about?" Meeds queried.

"You know," Captain Maka answered. "Cut straws, and whoever picks the shortest will scuba out for help."

"That's ridiculous!" Tish argued glancing at the hole in the ship. "It would be fifty yards of uncertain swimming to reach the hull and then the open ocean."

"Where do you plan on getting straws?" Jonathan asked. "In case you haven't noticed, Skipper, there isn't a bar anywhere in sight."

"It would be a fair way to choose who goes into the water!" the shark researcher suggested. "I'm in if we can find something in place of the straws!"

"I am not playing this game," Jonathan objected.

"It's not a game," the captain spat. "This is life and death, Cardinal. And, you might find you've been hoodwinked your whole life."

"What's that supposed to mean?"

"I'm just suggesting death might be final, no winged angels or roads paved with gold."

"How dare you!" Jonathan growled.

CATACLYSM

"Easy, Jonathan!" Callixtus interrupted, pointing to the giant hole in the hull. "We're all in this together. It's a matter of whether we have faith of making it through shark infested waters to escape safely through the hole."

At this, the kid's pride kicked in, or perhaps it was the foolishness of youth. That undeniable invincibility that teenagers felt; the sense life would *never end.*

"I could do it, send me out there, I'll get help!"

"You're not going into that water alone," Doolittle argued with Meeds ignoring the boy. "Just because you're some kind of Italian G.I. Joe doesn't mean you have to suffer gnashing teeth on my behalf."

"You're not dying for me, either," Tish instructed, grabbing the colonel's arm. "I don't want that shit on my head for the rest of my life."

"We should all decide who risks death," the girl beside Mikey stated. "Let's take a vote, or something."

"I agree," Callixtus nodded. "The drawing of straws seems like the fair way to go about it. Any ideas?"

Meeds sighed, shook his head and shrugged off the scuba tank. "Okay, all right! If you want to vote, it has to be done fairly!" Reaching into his pocket, he pulled out a pack of wet Italian cigarettes. "We can use cancer sticks." Shaking smokes from the blue pack, he broke them into dissimilar lengths and pushed them into his closed fist. "It's simple, everyone grab one, and whoever ends up with the shortest will strap on a scuba tank and go for help!"

Walking to Meeds, the pope grabbed his.

"The Shepherd must always lead his sheep through the valley of death." Glancing to Mikey, he smiled. "If you're the chosen, young man, it will be God's will, not yours."

Following his lead, everyone drew a cigarette.

"My Lord!" Cardinal Jonathan sighed in defeat as everyone else displayed longer cigarettes.

"Looks like you're going swimming," the captain nodded at the red-faced cardinal. "Let's get that scuba tank on your back and get you into the water."

"I guess you got your wish," Meeds smiled. "I'll be with Callixtus while you go for help."

Chapter 82

THE BUNKER

TELL ME what's happening, Steve.

That's what the President of the United States had said to his national security advisor before we peeked in.

"It's bedlam, Mr. President! Rioting and looting have broken out in Jacksonville, Charleston, Philadelphia, New York, and Miami. The National Guard in many states can't stem the tide of violence and civil unrest."

"It's bedlam," POTUS agreed.

"And then some," the vice president added.

"Then, we have the media," the national security advisor continued while pointing to a bank of huge video screens equal to those in a NASA mission flight control center. "The networks are slamming us for being unprepared."

"They're comparing our administration to George, *Mission Accomplished,* Bush," the VP chuckled, "and the Louisiana disaster caused by Hurricane Katrina."

"Seriously?" the president moaned and shook his head. Glancing towards the TV screens, he watched numerous live reports from around the world. "Is there any word on the whereabouts of my kids?"

"Not yet, Sir," the national security advisor responded. "My people at NSA and agents from the secret service are working on that right now."

"Priority mission, Steve, I want to know they're safe."

"Yes, Mr. President," the NSA boss replied rushing off to call the Director of *The Service.*

Tracking her down, however, would be another story, as her DC office was under mandatory evacuation orders.

Realizing this, he approached a nearby agent. "Have the boss call POTUS, pronto."

"Yes, Sir," the young agent nodded pushing his finger against an ear. "Notify Honcho ASAP for POTUS."

Depressing the earpiece activated a two-way radio strapped to the agent's belt. The ear bud resembled an iPod earphone with a curly wire running down the neck and under the shirt. The microphone was concealed just under the shirtsleeve, explaining why agents spoke into their wrists.

Returning from his mission, the VP rushed back to POTUS who stood staring into the televisions.

There, a plane headed for the Thames River.

> "For those of you watching our live coverage at home," a reporter's voice boomed over the live shots. "The scene playing before your eyes is Global Air flight 2291 from Atlanta to London. We are told the plane is going to ditch into the Thames."

On the screen, the Airbus plummeted towards the river.

> "Sources close to the network say that somewhere over the Atlantic Ocean, the super jumbo jet, carrying hundreds of passengers, lost power to its engines. After requesting an emergency landing at Heathrow, the pilot was denied clearance by the tower because the runways were packed with departing jets."

"Mr. President," William interrupted and pushed forward a cell phone. "It's Sam. He says the Florida Governor has issued evacuation orders."

"Finally, the man has done the right thing."

"He also says the state will never be evacuated in time."

Grabbing the cell, POTUS grunted. "Sammy, what the heck is going on down there?"

"With only two bloody hours until impact," Sam's voice answered, "there's no way to get everyone out."

The president stared at the TV and a shot displaying the destruction along the French shores of Nantes, Cherbourg, and Le Havre. All were beneath water. Houses were pushed from foundations, cars, buses, and trucks rode atop gigantic swells and crashed into buildings.

> "We now take you live to Washington, DC, where government workers are in a rush against time to move hundreds of historical artifacts, including the Declaration of Independence, Rob?"

The screen changed to an image of a reporter standing on the steps of the National Archives near Constitution Avenue, a stone's throw to the National Mall.

> "That's right," the reporter answered. "We're standing outside the National Archives where crates containing the Declaration of Independence, the U.S. Constitution, and the Bill of Rights are being evacuated. The Archive is charged with preserving and documenting all the government's historical records. Today, officials are indeed working against an unstoppable deadline to get these historical documents to safety, along with the Louisiana Purchase Treaty, the Emancipation Proclamation, and numerous important photographs, paintings, and historical cultural relics."

Behind the reporter, men heaved wooden crates into armored trucks. Around these, soldiers watched bystanders.

As the president handed the phone back to Will, he glanced to another TV screen. On it, a helicopter hovered over Buckingham Palace.

On the screen was headlined:

Queen Mother Trapped in London!

"Mr. President," the secret service agent interrupted. "Your daughters have ditched their security detail again."

"Christ! Where are they?"

Hurrying to a group of agents seated at a satellite monitoring station, the president leaned over their shoulders. "Pull up the GPS tracking chips embedded in their clothes."

After a few keystrokes, two red dots blinked on with an address listed.

"72 Vesey Street," the agent pointed to the screen.

"Vesey Street, Manhattan?" POTUS grumbled.

"The Freedom Tower... Mr. President."

Chapter 83

DRAMA QUEEN

THE WESTMINISTER BRIDGE was gridlocked.

Even for the Queen of England.

The arch bridge stretched eight hundred feet across the River Thames, linking Westminster to the north and Lambeth to the south.

It was the road to perdition.

Painted green, the bridge was identical in color to the leather seats in the House of Commons and contrasted by the red Lambeth Bridge matching the House of Lords.

"Poppycock!" the queen muttered from the rear plushness of the Bentley, its soft lambskin seats stitched magnificently with the finest materials. "Both parties of government should be thrown out on their bums. Legislators! They're a load of tosh, the whole lot of them!"

"What's that, Mum?" Prince Albert asked, placing his hand on his mother's royal quilted knee.

Realizing she'd uttered a private thought, Elizabeth waved off her son and stared out the window. "I've erected more than fifteen bridges in this Kingdom, and this one I like the least."

"Why is that, Mum?"

"I've articulated before. It's the conduit to nowhere, of course. Nothing is done in parliament." Peering through the windshield, she eyeballed the Coade Lion perched atop its stone rostrum.

On the lion's paws was inscribed: W.F.W. Coade 24 May 1837.

"I should've ordered the etching altered on that magnificent stone creature. The verses ought to vaunt of England and our prominence."

"And misplace its antiquity?" Albert chuckled. "You'd rather perish than have modernism smear that imprint from the stone."

"I presume you're correct," she sighed, taking in its splendor. Constructed from Coade Stone, the lion was a guardian of London. Its thirteen tons had survived World War II and were later preserved by King George VI.

Relocated here at the south end of the Westminster Bridge, it was twin to another erected at a brewery in Twickenham.

"The deprived object has seen time fade," Albert stared with pride through the curtained windows. "We should've relocated it to Buckingham Palace and mounted it at the primary frontage at the east facade."

"Now it'll be mislaid," Elizabeth groused.

Glancing beyond the lion, Albert saw the London Eye Ferris Wheel. Loved by millions, it hulked four hundred feet above the river's south bank. The tallest in Europe; it was the most popular paid tourist attraction in London.

"What's the issue?" Elizabeth urgently queried the chauffeur. "Can't we make way through this foolishness?"

The man shrugged. "Your subjects are all trying to escape London, and, I dare say, I can't blame them."

For as far as he could see vehicles lined the bridge.

Horns blared and attitudes flared.

Then… this came over the radio.

"This is Mark Forrest at BBC London's 94.9 FMs coverage of the god-smacking devastation in Her Majesty's Kingdom. A fifty-foot surge is presently carrying over the Millennium and Blackfriars passages, and is tearing up the Thames waterway straightaway, heading for the Waterloo Bridge and then presumably both houses of Parliament."

"We must abandon the coach, Ma'am," the chauffer insisted glancing upriver. "We're instants from being ensnared on this lethal crossway!"

Then, suddenly, chilling screams erupted outside the Bentley as hundreds of commoners left their vehicles and ran across the bridge.

Unexpectedly, the door jerked open and the royal security detail pulled the queen from the car. "Make haste, Queen Mother, we must gallop across the channel!"

"What's the import of this?" she griped.

But, before quarreling further, the detail pushed her and the prince into the mob of Londoners sweeping across the pavement with frenzied glances upriver.

Sprinting in distress, and enduring the pain of age, the queen pushed along the crowded bus lane. Peering into the distance, she cried at the spectacle of Hungerford Bridge collapsing under a mountain of wreckage.

Behind her, Big Ben gonged.

"Look at that!" the queen yelled.

Not more than a mile away, boats tumbled into the upwelling and crashed onto shore demolishing everything!

"Mother!" the prince shouted, understanding that within seconds, the gush would hit the bridge, its impact shaking them off the bending steel, their bodies ripping apart, limb by limb. And then, it would all be over.

Suddenly, a helicopter swooped down and landed.

"Hastily," the pilot directed, "hop in Queen Mother!"

As the chopper lifted over London, Elizabeth watched the swell reach to Big Ben's face while washing everything down river. "Oh, no!" she cried, her body slumping into the future King of England. "We've lost everything!"

"Don't fret, Mum," Prince Albert comforted. "The commoners will toil night and day to reconstitute London."

And they would, too, just like the Egyptian slaves busted their backs for their beloved pharaohs.

Look where it got them. Some people never learned.

Chapter 84

BILLIE SWAMP SAFARI

NAVAL COMMANDER McAlney was proud.

His men had cleared the Seven Mile Bridge and some of the stranded evacuees were loaded onto the Chinook for the thirty-minute chopper ride into Swampville.

The Chinook could carry up to forty-six souls, depending on configuration and cargo.

In combat situations, there were jump seats for thirty-three hard-core warriors.

But today it carried fifty civilians jammed on this *bus run mission*. Two rows of twenty-five red jump seats ran along the fuselage and were filled with refugees who weren't sure they'd ever see Key West again.

Their faces were drawn with uncertainty.

Marching along a steel and rubber footpath, the captain glanced at the nervous civvies. To his flank, and over the thundering chopper blades, a baby cried in the arms of a young Cuban woman.

Beside her, an elderly couple looked on.

"What's his name?" McAlney asked.

Nervously smiling, and with a broken English accent, the brunette looked into his face with frightened eyes.

"Carlos Alberto Del Castillo Cabeza De Vaca."

"That's quite a name."

"He has grandpa's name," she smiled with pride. "Papa came to Miami from Havana on a rubber raft in the eighties and almost lost his life for America's freedom."

The captain nodded. "We'll be landing at Camp Exodus Six in just minutes."

"Where is that?"

He looked out the porthole behind her. "On the grounds of Billie Swamp Safari in the Everglades."

The elderly man leaned over. "Will we be safe there, Sir, in the middle of the Everglades?"

The captain placed his hand on the man's bony shoulder. "You'll be safer than the President of the United States."

He didn't know how true that statement was.

Continuing down the aisle, he entered the cockpit and looked over the crew. Through the window, he glimpsed *Alligator Alley*. Officially called I-75, it began its journey from Hialeah and snaked its way westward across Everglades Parkway and northward to Georgia.

"It's busier than Route Irish," the pilot said, staring below to traffic snaking westward. Route Irish was Baghdad Airport Road, a seven-mile stretch of highway in Iraq, stretching east from the airport.

"That was one *helluva* shit hole," the co-pilot recalled. "No Hadji here stateside, though. No towelhead camel herders hiding AK-forty-sevens." He'd done six tours in the desert and was glad to be home. Too many friends had been killed in action over there for nothing.

Changing the subject and trying to wipe bloody visions from his angry memories, he turned to the commander.

"How're the civvies holding up in the back of the bus?"

"They're doing all right."

Swinging north of the road, the chopper put down on a blacktop parking lot packed with military vehicles.

Stepping from the chopper, McAlney jumped to the sticky tar and aided the evacuees in exiting the whirlybird.

Surrounding the Chinook, Florida National Guardsmen came to the rescue with bottles of water.

Over a loudspeaker was this:

"Please move along, we have food and water
for everyone. Please remain calm; you are
located a safe distance from the coast of the

Atlantic. We have set up telephones in the rec center if you need to contact family members."

Hurrying through the crowded camp, the elderly couple found a building with *amphitheater* painted in white above the doorway. Pushing through the entrance with a group of worried migrants, they glanced towards a TV displaying a helicopter shot of Miami Beach.

"We'd like to welcome our national viewers at home. You are now observing a special report of WSVN Channel 7 News here in Miami. We want to bring in Skyforce 7 reporter, Ralph Clayburn, who is hovering over South Beach. Ralph, I understand the beaches are still not clear. What's going on?"

Sitting in steel backed folding chairs of the amphitheater, the elderly couple watched the helicopter scene unfold. Ocean Drive was packed with tens of thousands of people lined up at rows of helicopters.

"That's right," a voice boomed over the image. "People still pack the streets of South Beach here as officials set up a command post on the McArthur Causeway. With very little time until impact of a life ending tsunami, you have to wonder what the holdup is."

Back at the Chinook, Captain McAlney went airborne again. This time he'd been ordered to McArthur Causeway to assist a high priority official, Dr. Samuel May.

There were people to save.

And, very little time do it.

Chapter 85

SECRET ARCHIVES

WITH THE OLD MAN DEAD, it was *game on*.

It's time to raid the secrets, Petrus thought.

"What do we seek, Cardinal?" a monsignor asked.

"Deep, ancient confidences are held in this brightly painted chamber," Petrus replied. "Most could shake our planet to its knees. We must not allow *certain things* to be made public, lest fear and turmoil erupt!"

They were in the Vatican Secret Archives, marching along black and white checkered tile. On every inch of the walls, hand-brushed portraits of history's popes stared down at them.

Their eyes seemed to judge the cardinal's words.

"Yes, but what are we looking for?" a bishop pushed.

"The Third Secret of Fatima," Petrus stated with a deadly glare. "It's hidden away in an envelope and must be here somewhere!"

"But that was revealed in the year two thousand," the bishop scoffed. "Eighty-three years after the first apparition of the Lady to the children in the Cova da Iria. The secret spoke of the 20th century persecution of Christians concluding with the unsuccessful assassination attempt of Pope John Paul II in 1981, on the 64th anniversary of the first apparition at Fatima."

Petrus chuckled; *they would believe anything!*

"Was that not the secret?" the monsignor scoffed, sensing the flock had been misled all these years.

The cardinal secretary peered down several rows of lengthy dim isolated corridors. They were packed with miles of ancient shelving holding one million books, documents, and dispatches of the Holy See… one of which stretched back to the eighth century.

"Petrus," the monsignor begged. "What is this about?"

"It was a diversion," Petrus off-handedly admitted, "a public sham to divert the public eye from the real third secret. The revelation was so profound for the church and our beliefs that the Holy Father decided to conceal the genuine message until *they* forced our hand."

"What are you saying, Petrus?" the bishop pleaded.

"Who is they?" a friar asked.

"Find the Third Secret Miracle of Fatima at once!" the cardinal secretary ordered the army of monks standing before him. Their dark brown habits offered heavy hoods, which were pulled over their heads hiding emotionless stone cold stares. "Callixtus ordered the dead Vatican archivist to lock the real text away in one of these secured bookshelves until he released the contents to the public!"

Nodding to the monks, the monsignor sighed. "Do as the Cardinal Secretary wishes; break the seals of the ancient secrets and find the papal envelope."

"Yes, Brother," the large burly friar answered turning to his men. "Break the shelf locks; rifle the editions page by page until you've discovered the sacred sachet!"

Securing shelves of ancient weathered books were brass links secured to brass ringlets welded onto long steel bars. They were meant to safeguard the scripts and resembled a library bookcase encased with vertical bars.

That's the feeling the friar felt when entering the dead silent hall, and he often wondered why books needed to be chained in place like a bicycle to a rack.

Now he knew.

Pulling bolt cutters from a nearby table, he watched his monks spread throughout the library cutting free the bookshelves' chains. As the links fell from the volumes, their weight collapsed to the tile floor in a sigh of freedom.

Normally, only the pope controlled the document graveyard. The collections contained here were considered his personal property. But with Callixtus slapped aside like a swatted fly, none dared argue this point with the cardinal secretary or his conspiring minions.

Staring away from the checkered floor, the monsignor glanced to Petrus and considered where Callixtus might have hid the precious document.

"Everyone holds beliefs of what past pontiffs have stashed in these secret archives," the monsignor supposed. "Some whisper there is a hidden time machine here baptized *The Chronovisor* that was supposedly constructed by Benedictine Monk, Father Pellegrino Ernetti. The rumors say he traveled back in time and filmed Jesus Christ's crucifixion. Is this true as well as the third secret?"

Some alleged the Vatican had the tape!

Described as a television-like device, the time machine could supposedly tune into the past and allow Father Ernetti to see, hear, and record important historical occasions that occurred centuries before.

The cardinal secretary grinned. "Of course it's not true, Brother. How could you believe such nonsense?"

But Petrus knew the story and he was the principal Vatican disinformation specialist on the actual incident. He knew the time machine viewer really did exist and was one of the few in the church who knew of its hidden location.

"Another story running rampant," the monsignor went on in a hushed tone, "is that we're in contact with aliens who've threatened to destroy the world. The whispers suppose that beings from another planet will soon implant silicon chips into mankind and force humanity into slavery."

This is very near the truth, Petrus thought.

And, it was all outlined in the Third Miracle of Fatima.

The story went something like this. According to three children, Lucia, Jacinta, and Francisco, the Virgin Mary appeared to them and provided a message in a sequence of apparitions at Fatima, Portugal in 1917. The messages held precise predictions and warnings concerning the Catholic Church and the world. There were three chief enigmas, two of which were revealed at the time… while the third was kept in an envelope by the Vatican and not revealed until the year 2000.

Petrus knew that release was a fake.

What his monks now searched for was the real deal.

"I found it!" a friar shouted rushing over to the monsignor and handing over a hemp envelope fastened with the wax seal of Pope Callixtus.

On its face was etched this:

Terzo Segreto di Fatima

"The third secret of Fatima," Petrus read aloud before ripping open the envelope and staring at the long awaited message written in Latin.

Staring over Petrus' shoulder, the monsignor read the shocking communication. "Project Earth and Humanity is nothing more than a galactic science project which shall soon end in natural cataclysmic disasters erupting around your world."

Gasps went up amongst everyone.

"Earth a science project?" the friar scoffed.

"What is this?" another monk growled.

"It is no joke," Petrus confirmed. "The next pontiff elected by conclave will be the Last Pope. For centuries, we have hidden the truth from the public that a race from another universe has created mankind."

Then, a knock at the heavy door brought a bishop.

"Yes?" Petrus called.

Stepping forward, the man nodded. "The cardinals are assembled in the chapel and await your arrival."

"Of course, I'll be right there."

Turning back to the monks forming a circle around him, he assured their faith.

"This doesn't mean there is no God. It only means the creator is something other than what we have thought. Imagine what would've become of the church over the last two thousand years if the world knew this fact?"

"I think we've always known," the friar offered. "Genesis 1:26 was always an enigma to us where it reads: *'Let us make mankind in OUR image, in OUR likeness'*... Clearly, this is quoting more than one creator?"

Petrus affirmed this. "You've all seen the church's artwork dating back centuries illustrating spacecraft hovering in Renaissance Era paintings. *The Crucifixion* hanging above the altar at the Visoki Decani Monastery in Kosovo was painted in 1350. On either side of Jesus are spaceships, one chasing the other with aliens working controls. *The Madonna* painting from the fifteenth century has the glowing saucer with a man and dog regarding the ship. *The Annunciation* painted by Carlo Crivelli in 1486 on display in the National Gallery in London shows a ship shining a beam of light onto Mary's head. This is recorded history."

"What do we do now?" a monk asked.

Petrus shrugged. "We continue living our lives and directing society, but most importantly, we do not disrupt the belief and efforts of ordinary people living their peaceful lives. It's not like they don't know about these spacecraft; the UFOs appear in the sky over Earth daily."

"We stay silent?" the monsignor asked, "about the end?"

"What is the alternative?" Petrus scowled. "Surely chaos would erupt; the church would be done. Yes, Brothers, we must never reveal this to the world's population."

"Cardinal?" the bishop again interrupted, "the Roman Cardinals await."

Walking from the secret archives with the Third Secret of Fatima, Petrus would use this information during his argument to be named the Last Bishop of Rome.

Then, he would make sure Callixtus was dead.

Chapter 86

SAVING SOULS

CAPTAIN HARRY ROGERS had practiced emergency water landings in Atlanta's airbus flight simulator.

The simulator artificially re-created flight environments for training. It included replicating calculations governing *how* aircraft flew, the reaction to flight controls and influences like air density, turbulence, wind shear, rain, and emergency landings.

But, nothing prepared him for this.

After raising the plane's nose fourteen degrees, the tail hit the river at a speed of one hundred sixty feet per minute.

It seemed like a textbook ditching.

Then the engines plunged into the water.

And, mayhem ensued.

The impact pushed the nose under, its effect violently shaking everyone in their seats. It was like driving an F-12 Berlinetta Ferrari 150 mph into a lake.

"Evacuate!" the captain shouted into the intercom.

Unlatching their safety harnesses, the crew leapt from their seats and pushed to the reinforced cockpit door. It was designed to flex at the bottom, allowing pilots to evacuate in crash landings just like this one.

It worked just as planned.

Bursting through the door, the captain found death.

In business class, a huge hole had been punched through the port side of the plane; rows of seats were missing.

Perry Whitson and Mark were gone, along with the fifty other passengers who'd pushed to the windows to glare at the UFO. The rest sat in their plush seats, their necks clearly broken. The bones were twisted grossly and the scene reminded the captain of turkey necks his wife tossed aside on Thanksgiving Day.

"Jesus, how the hell did that happen?"

Glancing away from several bright red pools of blood staining the gray carpeted aisle, he peered towards screaming frantic survivors on the opposite side of the aisle.

"The space ship did it!" a businessman screamed.

"A laser cut through the cabin," another cried. "Then a bright light ripped out the entire section of the plane."

"They were abducted!" someone else shouted, fear and uncertainty crackling in the voice. "I watched as the poor bastards were carried right out the plane!"

"Oh, my God, no!" a passenger screamed.

"Get us out of here!" another begged.

"Open the escape hatches!" Jeanne pointed.

"Reach under your seats," the captain ordered everyone while moving to an emergency exit on his right, "and put on your life vests!"

Glancing over his shoulder at the missing seats, he now believed what they saw in the cockpit.

There was no dismissing *them* now.

Pushing the heavy exit door outward, he glanced to his co-pilot who was busy opening escape hatches back in economy. He knew there were fourteen emergency exits on the *Airbus 380*; flight attendants were now pushing each open throughout the cabin.

Except for these three exits on the port side.

They were removed by something else…

Reaching to the *slide bustle* of the door, Captain Rogers pulled its lever and watched as an inflatable slide expanded over the river.

"Everybody out!" he shouted, placing a hand on each opposing bicep. "Hold onto your shoulders, jump onto the slide and glide into the water."

CATACLYSM

As the first passengers bounded from the aircraft, slid down the rubber, and splashed into the gushing water the aviator thought of his teenage kids back in Falling Water Point, a suburb of Atlanta.

Ironic, coming from a place called FALLING WATER and ending up crashing into water. I fell into it, all right!

"Skip," he shouted to his co-pilot. "I'm heading up to first class to assist with evacuations!"

Bursting down the narrow aisle, the plane suddenly shifted and he was knocked from his feet. On the way down, his forehead slammed into an armrest.

Slipping to the floor in semi-unconsciousness, his mind soared to childhood and a memory of falling into the family pool. The drain had sucked his loose fitting shirt into the out take pipe causing his arm to get caught. His lungs burned, he wanted to breathe! Death was coming!

Then it was over.

A neighbor had pulled the future captain to safety. But, not before introducing a fear of water.

"Captain! Captain!" Jeanne called out slapping his face. "Wake up! Come on! The plane is sinking."

He was out cold.

Pulling him onto an empty seat, she shook him awake.

"What the heck?" Harry mumbled faltering to his feet.

"We have to go!" she ordered.

Glancing about the cabin through blurred vision, the captain found the plane empty; everyone had gotten out except the poor bastards in business class. The rich died just as well as the poor... Shit happened and then you died!

Stumbling to the escape slide, the captain leapt for glory and found hope at the bottom.

His fear of water was cured.

He'd saved the day!

Take that, Sully Sullenberger!

Chapter 87

CONFESSION

ONE HOUR passed since Cardinal Jonathan dove beneath the depths and disappeared.

He was nowhere to be found.

Captain Maka gathered the scuba gear. "Does everyone know how to dive? If not, just follow Colonel Meeds' instructions."

"It'll be a first in Papal history," Callixtus smiled, "the leader of the Roman Catholic Church diving!"

"Never done it before, huh?" Dr. Doolittle chuckled.

"Oh, sure," Callixtus answered nonchalantly. "Where I come from in Spain, a boy doesn't turn the age of ten before venturing into the sea. I learned young how to navigate the deep blue waters."

"How come nobody's come for you?" Tish wondered. "They sent Colonel Meeds to save you and the Vatican must know something has happened. Shouldn't they have dispatched another team to rescue you?"

"They think he's dead," Meeds unexpectedly confessed.

"You have something you want to tell me, Son?"

Meeds stared to his feet in embarrassment.

It was *Man Up time*.

He could continue as a ruthless contract killer, or come clean and ask forgiveness.

The Truth will set you free!

That voice booming in his head was clearer than a chirping bluebird on a spring afternoon. The angelic mental order spoke rhythmically, pronouncing *Truth & Free* with forceful indignation.

Forgiveness will be yours!

"I came here to kill you, Papa," Meeds muttered, glancing into Callixtus' squinting eyes. He observed pain there, an agonized expression that reminded him of an instance twenty years before when he admitted to his dying mother he was a cold-blooded assassin.

"Huh?" Tish asked. "What do you mean?"

"My goodness," the captain scoffed.

Dr. Doolittle backed away, "I knew there was something not right about you. A black cloud of doom surrounds you; gives me a feeling of dread and evil."

Shielding Mikey and the girl, Callixtus kept his gaze locked on Meeds' stare. He knew there were enemies in the church who wouldn't mind if he wasn't pope.

But, murder?

"Forgive me, Papa," Meeds pled. "My heart won't allow your death on my bloodstained hands."

Kneeling, he bowed his head in shame.

"The Illuminati wants you out of the picture, starting with the Italian President, the Superior General, and his foot soldiers of the Society of Jesus. One of these is your personal assistant, Cardinal Jonathan."

Callixtus was shocked, "My Jonathan?"

"Who are the Illuminati?" Tish probed.

"They're mostly Jesuits, similar to the Knights Templar of history. Many in the ranks have been twisted by the Illuminati to overthrow and disrupt the church."

Mikey stepped around Callixtus. "Are they killers?"

Meeds nodded. "Some are, but many in *The Society* are good, faithful men. However, the devious among them are powerful, vengeful demons who've lost sight of their souls; the essence of what it means to serve Divinity."

"Why kill me?" Callixtus mumbled.

"You're the first Jesuit elevated to Pope who was going to reveal everything," Meeds recognized. "And, you aren't *one of them*; you're a true outsider who embraces the downtrodden. The conclave was fixed, you should never have been named pontiff, but for a small group of loyalists who secretly conspired to prevent Petrus from gaining the votes to take over the Vatican. And, now, the illuminated ones know you're planning on exposing one of their dirty little secrets."

"But the Cardinal Secretary is a Jesuit!"

"Yes, and much of the church is Jesuit," Meeds acknowledged. "But you're not one of them, you aren't illuminated."

Staring at the assassin, Callixtus knew exactly why they wanted him out of the picture. "How much do you know?"

"I've only been told you're going to expose a great secret which will bring down the Holy See."

The pope stared at the killer. Irritation tore at his humanity… yet, his soul cried out to his lamb in heaven for guidance and the strength to love.

"Please, forgive me," Meeds begged. "I would do anything to atone for my sins and serve you."

"He's a killer!" Tish shouted, pointing a finger of accusation into Meeds' face. "Forgiveness, are you out of your mind? You came here to kill the goddamn Pope!"

"Easy, Sister," Callixtus mumbled.

Dr. Doolittle laughed. He couldn't help himself. The scene was something of a Shakespearean tragedy.

"I know who the conspirators are!" Meeds admitted. "I can reveal every one of them for you."

Stepping to the colonel, Callixtus nodded. He understood he'd need this man to route the church of the deceivers. "For all have sinned, and according to the book of Romans, all fall short of the glory of God."

"What?" Tish protested. "The bible says not to kill."

Smiling at her, Callixtus placed a hand on Meeds head and glanced to Tish. "One of our prior Popes once said, 'Let us not forget this word, God never tires of forgiving us, but we sometimes tire of asking Him to forgive us. Let the one among us who is without sin be the first to throw a stone at this man.' Thus I must forgive the colonel."

Closing his eyes, he whispered a prayer.

When completed, the pope smiled at those surrounding him, and offered his hand to Meeds. "He who is greater than I have heard your plea, and, he finds you guiltless."

Rising to his feet, Meeds kissed the papal ring.

"Grazie, Eccellenza. I shall help you bring these scoundrels to justice before the Lord's throne."

"Ridiculous," Tish spat. "In the great state of Texas they'd have hung his ass out back for the rattlers."

Then, the ship rocked violently.

"Quickly," Captain Maka ordered, "sling on your scuba gear, attach your headlamps and let's get off this sinking tin can!"

When they'd strapped on the equipment, Meeds led everyone into the water and beneath the surface.

There, they'd find danger of another sort.

Into the darkness they dove, their eyes scrutinizing every shadow, each ripple, for hulking giants.

There were hungry things down here.

And religion aside, people were just fish food.

The Lord did work in mysterious ways.

Chapter 88

LONE WARRIOR

EIGHTEEN SIKORSKY SEAHAWKS.

That's what lifted from the flight decks of the USS Harry Truman, Abe Lincoln and Georgie Boy

Battle gray steel filled the air.

"It's show time, fellas!" Admiral Lew Brancor barked to his men while peering through his binoculars towards a protracted line of ships taking up his flank.

Strapped into forward command seats, he was skirted by the SECDEF and Captain Cullen.

Directly below, the flight deck dwarfed their position in the aircraft carrier's bridge–*the crow's nest.*

Lew watched the twin-turbo-shaft choppers lifting into heaven. Their engines roaring like thunder, causing him to recall a fragmented memory of a downdraft.

Years before, while stationed in the Persian Gulf supporting air missions over Iraq, a landing signal officer caught the ride of his life. As a squadron of Seahawks lifted from the busy flight deck, the chopper's downdraft knocked him to the deck.

They called him Fall-Down Joe after that!

The Seahawks were multi-mission, battle worn hogs with the ability to engage in anti-submarine and air-to-surface warfare.

They'd come in handy now.

Just like the ship's motto stated. The buck stops here!

Behind the carrier, other ships lined up like dominoes.

They were *Single File Line* just like kindergarten.

The plan went something like this:

When the tsunami was 100 yards from impact, the Secretary of Defense would order the White House's ultra-secret weapon to engage.

It had been fitted for just this emergency.

The Tactical High-Energy Laser (THEL) weapon was secretly installed on Truman's bow just hours before departing Newport News. Resembling a telescope, the armament was designed specifically to obliterate a water source from an enemy's country.

Lew recalled a headline he'd recently read.

RUSSIAN VILLAGERS
BAFFLED BY MISSING LAKE

The story associated with the headline was quickly taken down by most U.S. news organizations.

But, if someone went to *Google* and typed in the *above caption*, you'd find the mystery lingering out there like a sci-fi conspiracy.

The admiral knew THEL had been in secret development for years and was a joint operation between the United States and Israel. It had successfully shot down twenty-eight Katyusha Artillery Rockets and five artillery shells. The weapon contained a telescope for tracking and chemical lasers utilizing rotating mirrors to bounce rays towards targets.

It was the stuff of science fiction.

But here it is, Lew thought, *sitting on Truman's bow.*

Looking away from the laser, he considered the rumors, shook his head and glanced to the secretary of defense.

"Is it true about the Russian lake?"

"It should work, Admiral," SECDEF Clark answered, avoiding the question with a statement.

Ah, Lew thought, *no answer from Mr. Top Secret.*

"Son of a bitch better work," Captain Cullen grumbled.

The SECDEF grunted. "You guys know this is above your security clearance."

Bullshit, Lew thought. He was sick of the top-secret eyes-only nonsense coming out of the pentagon. "This is shit. You know I'm aware of the technology onboard and where it comes from. I was at Vandenberg Air Force Base the day the UFO shot down our missile."

"C'mon Lew," Clark grunted in defeat. "This has nothing to do with the threat heading across the Atlantic!"

"Will the THEL vaporize the wave?" Lew asked.

The secretary of defense reluctantly gave in to the angry stare of the admiral. "Lew, I know you're aware we've been experimenting on laser technologies and Directed Energy Weapons since 1988. We use 'em on our satellites and they're the backbone of our national defense."

Off the bow, the nuclear subs submerged.

It was the signal that impact was incoming.

"Here we go, men!" Lew barked grabbing the binoculars and peering at the horizon where a wall of water appeared.

"Ready the laser!" the secretary of defense ordered.

Captain Cullen nodded to his men. "Direct the bastard right for the center of this monster."

Bracing for eternity, the men watched as the barrage of seawater sped toward them.

"Five hundred yards," Captain Cullen stated.

"Boys," Lew said, placing his binoculars on the command console. "It's been a pleasure serving beside your honorable, terrorist fighting asses!"

"One hundred yards!" the captain shouted.

"Engage the laser!" SECDEF ordered.

On that order, an invisible beam of energy hit the seawater, vaporized hundreds of tons of water and exploded in a violent spray of steam.

Then USS Harry Truman rode towards its appointment with history.

Chapter 89

MAGIC CITY

SAM WAS GETTING FRUSTRATED.

Meeting with Miami's Mayor, he'd been briefed on the evacuation routes leading to Billie Swamp Safari.

Now, huddled beside Gordy and V.I. at American Airlines Arena, he stared at the burgeoning crowd.

Before him, enormous Royal Palm trees sprouted fifty feet from brick sidewalk pavers. The pale white tubular stadium *usually* served as a sports and entertainment venue nestled on Biscayne Bay. It was home to the Miami Heat and sat close to the Metrorail at Government Center Station on the Metro-mover Omni Loop.

Think an electric train on tires.

Glancing across the concrete complex, Sam saw reporters shouting into cameras to viewers across the globe. He thought the complex looked like a war zone.

> "We're standing on the hallowed grounds of the World Champion Miami Heat, where hundreds of thousands of Miamians are being corralled from pristine beaches just a mile east of here. Officials are telling WSVN News that when the wave hits South Beach, more than a million people will die."

"Codswallop!" Sam griped pointing to the reporter. "He's hyping the entire city into a nest of hornets!"

The major chuckled. "That's WSVN for you!"

Sam shook his head in disgust, "Leeches."

"Agreed!" Gordy conceded. "They're troublemakers!"

Hurrying to the Humvee, Sam was worried. "With kooks like that reporting the news it's a wonder you Americans haven't started world war three!"

Glancing to the reporter, he watched him pointing towards the traffic.

> "Biscayne Boulevard is backed-up for miles, looting in the urban neighborhoods of Overtown, Little Haiti, and Liberty City has occupied the Miami Police Department and the evacuations are going so slow, one official told us, he believes the east coast of Florida will be gone!"

"Stop it, man!" Sam interrupted the reporter. "You're panicking the citizens of Miami!"

> "Who are you?" the reporter asked shoving a microphone into Sam's face. "Are you part of the federal evacuation team invading Dade County? Aren't you concerned with the gridlock clogging this main artery in Miami? U.S. Highway One runs from Key West to Georgia and nobody can get out!"

Sam slapped the microphone from the reporter's hand. "What's wrong with you, Chap? Aren't you concerned people will die because of the panic you create?"

> "How many people are escaping Miami-Dade County?" the reporter asked picking up his microphone and pointing to the mammoth concrete stadium. "With everyone in Miami Beach evacuating to this stadium and over five million residents in the city, things seem to be going way too slow."

Staring to the arena, Sam squinted at the team's logo of a flaming basketball swooshing through a basketball rim. Beside this, a mesh outline of a player dunked a ball in mid-air, like a Michael Jordan logo. Under that, the entrance was hectic with National Guardsmen guiding frightened evacuees towards Metrorail's Government Center Station. It was one of twenty-three train-like stations peppered along an elevated rapid transit system, which now directed everyone to Miami's International Airport.

This thought reminded Sam of a TV show he liked.

AIRPORT 24/7 MIAMI

Touted as an all-access pass to the intense and dramatic world of Miami International Airport, the experience was told through the eyes of employees whose jobs were to keep America's largest *category X* airport–*a prime target for terrorists*–safe and running around the clock.

They've got their work cut out for them now, Sam knew. *Wait till they see the stresses of getting 100,000 passengers an hour through the airport.*

"Answer my questions!" the reporter interrupted. "Are you going to get everyone out of Miami alive?"

"Get stuffed!" Sam spat and hurried down two sets of concrete stairways to the Humvee waiting at the curb.

Then, Major Emmitt's cell phone rang, "Hello?"

"I'm five minutes out!" a voice informed.

"Ten four," Emmitt affirmed, glancing to Sam who climbed into the vehicle. "The chopper is coming."

"We're putting down on McArthur Causeway," the voice stated. "Have your guy meet us there."

"Roger that," the major agreed flipping the phone shut.

"Who's that?" Gordy asked as the Humvee sped along a guarded emergency lane and swerved under a green sign displaying an image of an airplane and highway 836-West.

The airplane imagery was added to Miami street signs after German tourists had gotten lost and ended up driving a shiny new rental car two blocks west into the crack-infested ghettos of Miami.

Some had been killed.

Welcome to paradise.

"Commander McAlney is coming to pick us up," Major Emmitt said leaning over to the driver. Pointing to the road ahead he said, "Get us onto the causeway."

Merging onto the empty eastbound lanes of MacArthur Causeway, Sam peered at miles of westbound traffic heading in the opposite direction... away from the beach.

"How long do we have until the wave hits shore?" V.I. asked with urgency.

Turning his attention to Gordy, Sam knew time must be running short. "How about it, Agent Holland?"

"Not very long," Gordy answered glancing to a tablet displaying the time to impact.

Staring to the causeway arch, Sam observed two massive cruise ships moored at the Port of Miami. Jamming the waterway were pleasure boats of every type. Some crashing into one another as they sped inland to escape the inter-coastal waterway.

"Look at them," Major Emmitt agonized.

Behind this hoisted the skyline of Miami. It's skyscrapers of glass and steel gleamed in the afternoon glare of the sun. To the left, jutting against Miami Bay sat the abandoned Miami Herald building... and just north of this, waterfront property for as far as the eye could see.

"It'll all be gone soon," Sam said.

Up ahead, from somewhere over South Beach, a slew of Black Hawk and Chinook helicopters buzzed the sky.

"We're getting twenty thousand people an hour out by chopper," Major Emmitt offered, "another fifty thousand by trains, buses, trucks, and cars."

"It's not enough," Sam realized.

"Not long to impact," Gordy confirmed.

"Where's Sylvester Stallone when you need him?" Sam joked. "We need an Arnold Schwarzenegger or Bruce Willis hero right about now!"

Speeding along the road to paradise there was a sense of doom hanging over Miami like a mushroom cloud.

Chapter 90

BLOODLINE

PRESIDENT POWERS was on the move.

Before him, Marine One waited.

"Mr. President," the VP protested. "I've got to urge you against going to Manhattan."

"They're my kids, Foster," POTUS waved off his second in command. "Notify New York City's Mayor I'm headed straight for the Freedom Tower."

"Forget it!" Will argued. "You'll never make it in time. A hundred foot wave is going to impact lower Manhattan and devastate everything!"

"At least take the SEALs," Foster begged.

Glancing to four men standing beside the V.P., POTUS relented. "Are you men up for an adventure?"

Stepping forward, they nodded.

"It's settled, then," POTUS glanced to the V.P. "I've got the best outfit on the planet watching my back, you satisfied?"

"Do I have a choice?"

"Not from my POV!"

"Mr. President," Will stepped in. "Your point of view will change drastically when the wave charges up New York Bay and flattens everything in its path, there's no guarantee anyone will survive. There's a great chance you'll be killed in due course!"

"If that happens, Willie, then Vice President Logan will move the country in the right direction. My girls need their father now, and I'll be darned if I won't give everything I have to save them!"

"But what about the country," Chief of Staff Robert Laslow grumbled, "what do we tell the press corps?"

"Tell them to go to hell."

Will realized then what it must mean to be a father, how everything in the world seemed irrelevant when the blood of a child was on the line. He wondered if he'd ever have the opportunity to feel such love and dedication.

Being single had its perks, but in the end, who surrounded the coffin mattered.

"You're coming with me, Willie," POTUS ordered hiking beneath the chopper blades. "I need all the information I can get about this bastard heading our way."

There was no hesitation on Will's part. The SEALs and he followed POTUS up Marine One's six metal stairs. Passing the Presidential Seal attached to the nose of the olive green airframe, he grinned. It was one of those moments that stuck with a man his entire life. He'd tell this story for years, and isn't that what life was about... the experiences, shared struggles and accomplishments?

This day would go down in history.

Once inside, everyone took seats around the president for the ride to Manhattan. Time was running out, and as the chopper cut a path over the Catoctin Highlands, Will wondered how a leader prepared himself for these events.

On the satellite-linked television, POTUS watched a news report showing hundreds of super jumbo jet crash survivors treading water in London's river.

In the background, the A-380 bobbed on the waterline.

> "It's a catastrophic scene here in London," a
> reporter's voice bemoaned the scene. "With
> the Thames Barriers Gates destroyed, the
> surge has pushed up the river where
> hundreds of thousands are presumed dead or
> dying. As you can see, the bridges have all
> collapsed as shipping containers, boats, and

barges have crashed into the super-structures. Now, there are hundreds of jet passengers fighting to stay afloat as their plane will surely sink into the abyss of history."

"Is there any word from the Prime Minister?"

"No, Sir, Mr. President," Will regretfully answered. "However, we've received dispatches notifying the Queen and Prince landed safely at Buckingham Palace."

"God did save the Queen, then?"

"Yes, Sir."

"Amazing how phrases like that eventually come true." Flipping the channel to WABC New York, the president was confronted with scenes torn from a Hollywood blockbuster. People were running west through Manhattan's congested streets, where traffic crammed the George Washington Bridge.

Over the whapping of the news chopper's blades, POTUS swore he heard screams of terror from those sprinting for their right to survive.

"This is WABC Reporter, Brian Keene," a voice said. "We just received word that the Mayor of New York has ordered all New Yorkers to enter the closest skyscraper and climb as high as possible. With time running out, we're being told it has now become clear evacuating everyone from Manhattan is impossible."

Picking up a phone, POTUS connected with the pilot of Marine One. "Major, get this bird to the Freedom Tower, lightning fast!"

It would be a cold day in hell before he allowed the city to consume the dreams of his kids.

Today would be a new kind of Independence Day.

America would not flinch in fear.

We must survive, he thought. *Nothing beats a failure except a try, and hell if I won't try!*

Chapter 91

PLUNGING DEEP

THE MURKY SEAWATER was dark.

Leading the way, Meeds pushed bodies from his path.

Attached to his head, a yellow CREE XPG Q5 LED waterproof headlamp lit the way.

Made in China of course!

But, the colonel didn't care about that.

What did matter were the ravaged bodies blocking his path. One of which was Cardinal Jonathan. The expression frozen on his face told a tale of terrorizing death.

Huge chunks of flesh had been chomped from his body, reminding everyone of an ice cream container after the scoop had dug deep.

Beside Jonathan, a skeleton floated in an orange life preserver. Its white skull revealed the eyes had been sucked from their sockets. The once fleshy cheeks and lips were gone; chewed away by the gnashing teeth of blue fish.

Sonuvabitch! Meeds thought.

A school of painted Parrot Fish were gorging themselves on remnants of Jonathan's flesh.

Glancing over his shoulder, the colonel saw everyone followed close behind. Amidst a pocket of air bubbles escaping the scuba regulators, the group pushed into the darkness and through the hole in the hull. With a quick kick of the scuba flippers, they thrust for the surface.

Pulling the scuba *demand valve* mouthpiece from his lips, Meeds took in the sight before them.

Human carcasses were everywhere.

For a mile in either direction, pockets of survivors clutched anything that allowed flotation.

"Tragic, about Jonathan," Callixtus mumbled to Meeds. "He may have been a conspirator, but nobody deserves to die by the jaws of fish." *It's just the beginning,* he thought, *compared to what lies ahead for mankind.*

If the prophesies were true, these disastrous events were going to get larger and worse around the world.

"There's our skiff!" Captain Maka excitedly shouted. We have a satellite phone stowed onboard!"

Fifty yards away, a small six-seat dinghy sat tethered to the inverted cruise ship. Utilized for *man-overboard* drills, the crew often rowed into the sea to save passengers.

"Come on!" Mikey shouted, swimming away.

Stroking to the dinghy, everyone climbed aboard as Meeds cut the tether and Doolittle grabbed the oars.

Moving to the bow, Callixtus bowed in prayer for Jonathan and the thousands of dead filling the sea.

Then, *from out of nowhere*, The Great Eater surfaced beside the dinghy and violently rammed its snout into the sideboards, knocking everyone to their knees.

"Look!" Mikey screamed, pointing ten yards off the bow. "It's the other shark!"

Cutting through the surf, Bessie the Beast quickly circled the dinghy as El Gran Comedor dove beneath the skiff and disappeared in the depths.

"They're teaming up," Doolittle recognized pointing to Bessie eyeballing the boat. "Look at that monster lifting its snout above the surface to gaze at us. This is pack behavior, very similar to what wolves do."

"It's spy-hopping, all right!" Tish agreed.

The behavior of staring towards their prey had been seen in blacktip reef sharks, and was learned from interaction with humans. At Seal Island, great whites attacked in *clans* of two to six individuals.

Meeds shouldered his HK 416 assault rifle and armed the single shot 40x46mm grenade launcher.

Suddenly, moving quicker than anything he'd ever seen, Bessie stopped circling and charged for the boat.

"Kill it!" Tish shouted. "Take that bastard out!"

Sighting the scope, Meeds lined up its crosshairs between the shark's large black eyes.

"Come on you big beast!" he whispered –

Then, the skiff was struck again from beneath.

Meeds turned to an enormous splash.

As he did so, a gargantuan set of jaws opened for a bite of the boat.

In seconds, the mammoth shark hurled itself from the water towards Meeds.

"Go to hell you fat bastard!" the colonel whispered and fired the grenade. On impact, the detonation ripped apart The Great Eater and rained bloody flesh into the boat.

Then, with the scent of blood in its shout, Bessie the Beast charged for the carcass of El Gran Comedor and forgot all about the skeletal humans.

Rowing for their lives, Doolittle and Callixtus joined forces and rowed two hundred yards. At that moment, from somewhere above, a jet engine whined.

Before anyone could react, two Hammerhead missiles impacted Valencia and detonated in quick succession.

The repercussion knocked Meeds to his knees.

"Holy shit!" Callixtus grunted, his face reddening in embarrassment the moment he realized his words.

"If I didn't see all this," Doolittle said, wiping sweat from his brow, "I would've never believed it."

"That's why we call 'em fish tales," Meeds chuckled.

Staring at the destroyed ship, Tish didn't understand what she just saw. "What the hell was that?"

"Missiles," Meeds answered. "They were probably Italian; a death blow to make sure the job would be done."

The pope glanced to Meeds. "The Illuminati really wants me out of the way, don't they?"

"They do, so did Jonathan. He's with his secret society in hell begging for ice water."

"So, what do we do now?" Callixtus asked.

Meeds pointed to land. "I say let's row this boat right up their ass and expose the entire plot!"

Captain Maka handed the pope a satellite phone retrieved from the skiff's lockbox. "It's about time to get the cavalry marching."

Chapter 92

THE FREEDOM TOWER

ONE WORLD TRADE CENTER was redemption.

For those who died in the Twin Towers and in honor of the recovery accomplished by the City of New York.

America was proud!

The skyscraper's *one hundred and four* stories were a marvel of the American spirit. Spiraling symbolically 1776 feet into greatness, its height mirrored the date of the country's historic Declaration of Independence.

Payback was sweet.

Now, with Manhattan's destruction imminent from another sort of horror, Ground Zero became an evacuation of Manhattan refugees. Jamming the complex were thousands rushing for the high-rise buildings located along Greenwich Street.

Each would become Noah's Ark.

"Come on!" Latisha Powers urged her twin sister. "We've got to get to the Freedom Tower's roof."

"Why?" her twin, Sara grunted.

"Remember what the Secret Service told us? In an actual emergency, climb to the rooftop of the nearest building and activate our panic buttons." The button was actually a RED iPhone APP located on the home screen of their phones. All they had to do was log off Facebook and press the red square button. It was hard; social media was a drug.

The Mexican Mafia had nothing on *status updates.*

The girls navigated hordes of international tourists visiting The National September 11th Memorial. It was a tributary park honoring the lives of three thousand slayed by terrorists on September 11, 2001.

More than ten million visited the park since it opened.

Passing a swath of Swamp White Oak and Sweet Gum trees separating twin granite reflecting pools, the girls heard falling water created by the largest manmade cascades in North America. They plunged thirty feet into the footprints where the towers had stood.

Glancing to one of the pools, Sara thought of the lives lost and why something so tragic had to happen. Locking her gaze on a bronze parapet surrounding the vast clear pool, she saw *FLIGHT 93* inscribed here.

It was the reason they had snuck away.

A friend of Sara's was on the United Airlines jet hijacked by al-Qaeda as part of the attacks. Boarding in Newark, New Jersey, her BFF never came home. Instead, she found winged angels in a field near Diamond T. Mine close to *Shanksville, Pennsylvania.*

Grabbing her sister's arm, Sara stopped cold.

"What is it?" Latisha asked following her gaze. But, before her sister could answer, the vision of the bronze letters paralyzed her. A chill crept up her arms at the sight of *FLIGHT 93...* embedded here forever, like the stone faces chiseled into Mount Rushmore.

"I can feel her," Sara gulped.

It was true. The memorial held a spiritual presence, an envelope of energy that wrapped visitors with love and compassion in remembrance of what once was... *and yet... the holes in the ground would always remind....* some things could never be again.

Things had changed; innocence was lost.

"Move it," an NYPD cop yelled, "get up into the buildings!" Then, he recognized the twins. Some things a man forgets... but a cop never forgot faces. "What the hell are you two doing here?"

"We just got sidetracked," Latisha lied.

"Yeah, officer," Sara nervously shrugged. "The Secret Service ditched us at Harvard and here we are!"

"Jesus H. Christ!" the cop grumbled. "Do you have any idea how pissed your dad must be right now?"

Then, an NYPD helicopter flew overhead.

"Attention! Attention! Attention! Everyone climb into the Freedom Tower! The city will be impacted soon by the tsunami! Attention! Attention! Everyone needs to get as high into the building as possible!"

Then, the chopper was gone.

"Come on, you two," the cop ordered leading the way.

Rushing behind thousands of fleeing people, they entered the steel structure and climbed twenty flights.

There were just eighty-four floors left to hike.

It would be the race of a lifetime.

Glancing up the stairwell, the NYPD officer hoped this act would satisfy an Internal Affairs Investigation into his conduct towards a pair of tourists earlier this year.

Screw it, he thought. *Headquarters will be gone soon.*

Sara heard her iPhone ringing.

Reaching into her jeans, she pulled out the white device and pressed *speaker*.

"Hi, Dad, sorry we ditched the detail!"

"You girls are in so much trouble!" President Powers shouted. "Where are you?"

"We're climbing the Freedom Tower stairs." Latisha shouted into the phone. "But don't worry. We have one of New York's Finest protecting us!"

"Hello, Mr. President," the cop introduced. "This is NYPD Officer Raymond Burns, and I assure you, your daughters will be safe!"

"Get them to the roof, Burns," POTUS ordered. "I'll have a commendation awaiting you in Marine One!"

We'll be there, Sir," Raymond assured. "But, I don't see how you will be able to land with all the people up there."

"Just get them there, officer," POTUS said, just before the cell service went out in all of New York.

Chapter 93

SMOKE & MIRRORS

CARDINAL PETRUS ROMANO walked through the Apostolic Palace with a devious grin wrinkling his cheeks.

The Palazzo Apostolico was the official residence of most popes. Known as the Palace of the Vatican, it contained offices, the Papal Apartments, the Holy See, the Vatican Museums, and the *library*.

Petrus had riffled through more files to ensure no more ancient secrets were hidden here before heading to the Sistine Chapel for an unofficial Roman cardinal vote.

He knew something the others didn't.

A dirty little secret! The fix was in, and the votes had already been counted! The white smoke that would billow from the Sistine Chapel's chimney in weeks confirming a new pope would be a mere formality, like raising the flag on the White House lawn or down the street. Nobody ever thought twice about doing it, or why it's done... they just carried their old popping bones out the creaking front door, walked across the yard, and pulled up old glory, day after day.

It was routine.

The cardinal secretary knew the votes to elect HIM pope had already been wrangled by threats of denouncement, excommunication, or a fate like the Vatican librarian.

Elect Cardinal Secretary Petrus Romano... or die.

That was the edict told to each of the cardinals.

"You'll never know how death arrives," the black pope threatened the world's cardinals.

Poison in an innocuous glass of water?

A bullet punched into the head?

A knife's edge slashed across the throat?

Strolling through the chapel doors, Cardinal Secretary Romano saw Rome's Cardinals seated at long tables running the length of the hand painted chapel.

This was just a dry run on eventuality.

It's my time, Petrus thought, *I'll be King of Earth.*

Scanning the men, he took in their stony stares. The hatred in their eyes penetrated his soul. And he knew, right then, standing beneath the brightly painted ceiling by Michelangelo, he had to cull the herd.

He glanced up to the nine finely painted scenes depicting the Book of Genesis and showing The Creation of Adam. The paintings were of numerous figures, both clothed and nude.

It was beautiful.

As Petrus walked through the chapel, his shoe heels echoed through the hallowed chamber. *Each footfall,* he thought, *brings a hammer strike upon the nail of Christ's cross. I am walking in the lord's house!*

Then, just as he was about to turn to his place, the Franciscan monsignor ran into the chapel with Swiss Guard by his side. "Cardinal Secretary!"

Turning to his servant, he nodded.

"It's the Holy Father," the monk frowned. "The Spanish Navy has Pope Callixtus! He is alive!"

The cardinals jumped to their feet with cries of glory.

"It can't be!" Cardinal Romano stated, his legs losing strength, the blood draining from his face. "What are you saying, Brother? Callixtus is dead. He was killed when his chopper went down!"

"No, he isn't," one of the guards confirmed. "I just spoke to him from a rescue chopper in the Canary Islands. It's confirmed, he's alive! He's with the Spanish Navy!"

The cardinals embraced one another, shuffled from the chapel, and cried with relief.

"The drone missed," the monk whispered to Petrus. "When His Holiness returns we'll be tried for treason!"

It was too much for Petrus.

He collapsed to his knees and bowed his head in defeat.

I have to get out of here. Pack my things and run to the ends of the Earth!

First, he had to find the strength to get off the floor.

In his thoughts rhymed this:

> Petrus, Petrus, Pope Defeater,
> Had a God but Couldn't Keeper,
> Put Him in A Place Called Hell,
> And, there he suffered Very Well!

The word *suffering* stuck in his head.

Rising from the floor he ran for the door, not knowing where he was going, just that he had to flee Vatican City.

Chapter 94

SHALL NOT PERISH

IT WASN'T LOOKING GOOD.

Not for the trailing Atlantic Fleet.

United States Naval Aviator and Seahawk Pilot, Jeff Myers, couldn't believe his staring eyes. The USS Harry Truman's secret laser had punched a hole through the leading wave, allowing the carrier to advance through the surf and survive initial impact.

But, the wall of water restructured over the stern, climbed above the flotilla and slammed onto Abe Lincoln's deck, knocking the carrier to stern.

For a moment, the ships disappeared.

A two hundred foot upsurge crashed over the entire fleet and he imagined the ocean had swallowed the mighty hulking warships.

There would be lots of sinking on this day.

Especially for those aboard USS George Bush and its straggling battle group that was violently hoisted into the gigantic wall of water. Tumbling bow to stern, a half dozen battleships crashed into one another and were lost to the eastward push.

Georgie Boy was riding a wall of H2O heading for land. The seawater churned itself desperately, pushing to the sundrenched beaches of the coast. The trajectory of the carrier depended on the southwesterly thrust.

Where it might crash ashore was anyone's guess.

Jeff wasn't a guessing man. *But if I were,* he thought, *Miami and Fort Lauderdale are in for a big surprise!*

He was a sea rescue operations specialist. As part of Helicopter Maritime Strike Squadron based at Naval

Station Mayport, Florida, he'd served ten years in the Strike Wing of the Atlantic Fleet. When not on tour in the theater of war his assigned mission was to provide superior chopper training to fleet replacement pilots so they could fight and win at sea.

And, sometimes... save lives.

"Air Boss, Truman," Jeff called into his COMM to Admiral Brancor. "Sir, we've lost carrier George H.W. Bush and we've got more waves barreling towards your position at twelve o'clock!"

No answer.

The ship was busy riding the bull.

Staring east, Jeff eyeballed five additional smaller waves rushing towards the surviving carriers. He knew enduring the initial tsunami impact wasn't the end. There were often several more breakers that trailed the leading wave.

Those could be more deadly than the first.

Looking to the horizon, he was amazed at the leading wave stretching to the limits of his vision. A tsunami didn't resemble normal sea breakers, because its wavelength was longer. Rather than acting like a breaker, tsunamis resembled a rapidly rising tide. This one was a wall... reminiscent of a glass plate, reaching hundreds of feet and stretching north and south like a string in either direction.

Behind this, were more giant waves.

It's a wave train, Jeff thought, *just like Indonesia.*

The Japanese symbol for *harbor wave* stuck in his head like a timestamp. The day after Christmas, 2004, he was ordered to Indonesia to participate in the rescue mission following the Indian Ocean tsunami.

Jeff's attention was snapped to a huge explosion.

Below, he watched in desperation as the tsunami pushed guided-missile cruisers USS *Jacinto* and *Gettysburg* into the path of their accompanying destroyers, USS Mason and Bulkeley. In one heaving collision, the four battle machines exploded in a diesel fireball.

Then, as the successive trailing waves bombarded the flotilla, only the *Truman* and *Lincoln* remained.

Surrounding them, bodies littered the rocking sea.

Manipulating the Seahawk's controls, Jeff radioed the other choppers flying formation at his six o'clock. "Let's get down there boys, save as many as we can!"

"Roger that!" a response crackled over the COMM.

Skimming the surface, Jeff glanced to his airmen lowering rescue baskets. As survivors were hoisted to safety, he looked west at the wave heading for the coast.

Loss of life, he thought, *will be more drastic than anyone has guessed.*

They'd been briefed that a wave one hundred feet high would demolish the fleet. *Its size is double that.*

"Notify Southern Command," he shouted into his COMM, "a two hundred foot wave is headed for the East Coast of the United States!"

Chapter 95

HIGHWAY TO HELL

THE MACARTHUR CAUSEWAY was a six-lane highway connecting South Beach and downtown Miami over the cobalt Biscayne Bay.

Sam thought it was the road to survival.

Glaring at the concrete lanes stretching over the shallow intercostal waterway, he recognized it represented the only escape from Miami Beach.

There is no PLAN-B for evacuating the coastline.

This bastard wave will kill them quickly.

"The road is empty," V.I. noticed. "Why is there no traffic flowing along the westbound lanes?"

The road ahead was blocked east of Star Island.

The island was a small manmade islet hosting a neighborhood of ninety-eight residents.

Sean "P-Diddy" Combs, Gloria Estefan, Don Johnson, Rosie O'Donnell, and Shaquille O'Neal had all lived on the privileged guarded landmass.

Pointing to a group of Miami Beach Police Officers blocking westbound traffic, Sam was firecracker hot.

"The copperheads are budging up evacuations!"

"We're getting a lot out," Major Emmitt offered. "But the police have shut the road for a few minutes to evacuate celebrities who reside on Star Island."

Stretching across a small white concrete bridge sat a procession of shining limos: Bentleys, Mercedes, and a black two-million-dollar Bugatti Veyron.

Sam was disgusted and pushed open his door. Stepping to the pavement he pointed to a long line of cars halted at a red light. "Let the lot through the causeway, this is an emergency, don't you know?"

"Get back in your truck," a cop threatened.

Sam imagined the Bugatti might hold X Factor boss, Simon Cowell. He certainly wasn't shy about flaunting his expensive toys. The music mogul had been seen zipping around South Beach in a similar car. Then again, it could have been Stallone, Madonna... anyone, really.

This was the city of Miami Vices.

What a monster, Sam thought, taking in the beauty of the vehicle. Knowing that behind the tinted glass probably sat one of America's most famous entertainers.

"Get back in the car!" the cop threatened again.

"Excuse me?" Sam protested. "Celebrities get special treatment in a national emergency? The city is allowing those knotweeds to evacuate separately?"

"I said get back in your Humvee," the cop angrily ordered pulling out a nightstick. Then, as V.I., Major Emmitt, and Gordy stepped from the armored vehicle, the officer realized this was the president's emissary he'd been briefed would arrive. "This is a police emergency," he stated changing his tone. "It's the only road out and the superstar residents of Watson, Palm, Hibiscus, and Star Islands have priority access to evacuate across McArthur before anyone else who lives along the waterway."

"Nevertheless," Major Emmitt reminded, "Miami Beach P.D. does not have authority to stop traffic for them."

Behind the Humvee, a squadron of military vehicles arrived and the military took control.

"You are relieved of your command, officer," an Army general notified the officer handing over a federal decree.

Poo! Hoo! Hoo! V.I. thought, watching as soldiers removed the roadblock and allowed traffic to flow west alongside the celebrity vehicles. He imagined the *STARS (enter gagging sound here)* flinching on their pig leather seats, forced to drive beside the common residents.

"Word is,' Major Emmitt joked, "J-Lo was stuck in gridlock trying to hustle out of town to her jet."

"Madonna would ride it out," Gordy smiled.

"She sold the Miami house," Emmitt stated glancing to a Police Deputy Chief arriving on the scene. "She packed her bags and moved to London, just like Johnnie Depp, much safer over there."

"Doesn't Justin Bieber have a place here?" V.I. asked.

"Nah," Emmitt dismissed. "The jail is full."

It was a sarcastic remark referencing the pop star's very short visit to the County Jail for a drunken driving arrest.

Are you effing kidding me? Sam thought.

In the middle of the thought, the Chinook swooped overhead and landed a quarter mile ahead on the empty highway at Terminal Isle.

It was a command post for the military evacuation.

"Just under the bridge," Major Emmitt hollered to Sam, "leading to Miami Beach, the Coast Guard operates a base of Sentinel Class Fast Response Cutters. These are the boys who chase down cigarette boats filled with Columbian white powder on its way to nostrils across America."

Not today, buddy! Sam thought.

"The patrol boats are gone," the Miami Beach Deputy Chief stated, stretching out his hand. "The Coast Guard is now deployed on ferry missions moving evacuees through a network of our Miami waterways west and out of the path of the surge we expect inland."

"Who are you, mate?" Sam asked.

"Rico Martinez," the chief introduced. "Sorry about that idiotic move on the part of my guys stopping traffic. We kowtow to the *a-listers* down here in the Sunshine State."

Squinting at the hard-nosed cop, Sam believed he'd heard the name somewhere before.

"Samuel May," he responded shaking hands. "Have we met before, chap?"

"No, Sir," Rico replied. "I don't believe so."

But, Gordy knew the cop and wasn't afraid to say so.

"Detective Rico Martinez, Manhattan South Homicide, a celebrity murder cop who moved his tired ass down to Miami like everyone else in their golden age."

"Que pasa, Gordy?" Rico grinned hugging his friend.

He'd met the president's bodyguard when the secret service traversed New York City on quite a few occasions.

"You're that New York cop," V.I. realized placing the name with headlines, "the detective who caught *The Santa Claus Killer*, right?"

Everybody knew about it.

The case was a worldwide sensation.

Nobody could run amok in Manhattan dressed as Santa Claus and murder people during Christmas without gaining global media attention.

Rico shrugged away the notoriety. "Well, now I'm just Deputy Chief of Miami Beach P.D. We hand out jaywalking tickets to old folk in walkers."

It wasn't true. The beach was a haven of violent crime. Four-hundred robberies, forty rapes, and five murders had been committed on South Beach this year.

The Miami papers just named recent murders the Miami Beach Bodies.

"Well," Sam said, bringing Rico's attention back to the present disaster. "You're about to retire for good."

"I should have stayed in New York," Rico said.

"You'd be dead there, too," V.I. shrugged.

"Sumbitch," Rico grunted. "I can't win no matter what."

Chapter 96

A BLOODY RESCUE!

THE AIRBUS WAS DESIGNED TO FLOAT.

Nobody knew for how long.

There had *never* been one ditched on water before.

Co-pilot Skip McGregor had managed to toss thirty inflatable rafts to passengers treading water in their life vests. Each blowup would fit twenty passengers under extraordinary circumstances.

This was beyond extraordinary.

After clearing the plane and finding it evacuated, Skip bounded onto the slide, thrust down its slick surface and splashed feet first into the River Thames. When he surfaced from the plunge, he found his captain barking orders to hundreds of passengers.

"Pull the release cords, the rafts will inflate!"

Swimming to a group of passengers holding onto their flotation devices, Skip reached for a yellow plastic bag with a red handle jutting from its side. Yanking it, a bright orange raft rapidly inflated to the size of a yard pool. Slanting his gaze to the middle of the plane, he observed Jeanne assisting passengers into the rafts.

Stroking to another inflatable, he pulled the ripcord and watched as it expanded.

Moments later, a loud creaking sound erupted from the airplane and it tipped to port.

"It's going to sink," Harry shouted. "Everybody get in the rafts and paddle away from the jet!" He was proud to be skippering the A380; knowing the only other serious emergency was Qantas Flight 32, which suffered uncontained engine failure before making an emergency landing at Singapore Changi Airport.

It was the first of its kind for the A380.

Watching the rafts fill, the captain was euphoric; his crew was successful at evacuating the survivors safely.

The Airbus was a good plane.

No, he thought, *it's a great plane.*

Climbing onto a raft, he grabbed a pair of plastic oars secured beneath a zipper compartment. In the distance, yellow *search and rescue* choppers raced in their direction. Painted on the airframes was the bull's-eye insignia of the Royal Air Force:

Captain Rogers whispered, "Per Ardua ad Astra."

That was their motto. *Through Struggles to the Stars!*

On one of his trans-Atlantic flights–*of which there were too many to count*–Harry hung out with a British Air Captain in a hotel bar. He recalled a tale his friend told of his time serving in the Royal Air Force.

Somehow or another, the subject changed to UFOs and Captain Rogers got this drunken diatribe.

"I once was assigned to the RAF at Woodbridge in the United Kingdom," the pilot drunkenly recalled, seemingly lost in a haunting memory. "I was at Rendlesham Forest the night lights descended from space and a saucer landed in the woods. I was an eyewitness to all the events over that three-day period."

Harry wasn't a believer back then.

He previously thought tales of UFOs were bullshit hippie hallucinations and regarded anyone claiming to have seen one a psycho.

Nonetheless, he nodded and listened.

"It's now one of the most famous UFO events in Britain, ranking with Roswell and hanger 51. You know that guy on the history channel, Nick Pope? I met him last year at the UFO Congress at Fort McDowell Resort in Fountain Hills, Arizona."

"No shit, a UFO conference, huh?" Harry interrupted cracking up with laughter. "Sometimes, I think of jumping into the cockpit of my jumbo jet and flying it right into Buckingham Palace; your stories are crazy!"

Glancing to his watch and feigning a yawn, he glanced to his grinning friend and smiled.

"Well, my dear British friend, I've got an early morning transatlantic. Nice seeing you again."

Finishing his Guinness, the pilot nodded goodnight to Harry and carried his aching bones to bed.

He loved messing with the British

A few weeks later, Harry learned his friend was killed by a rare and mysterious illness. The man's wife claimed he walked through a storm of red rain and became extremely sick within days. Now, he wondered if maybe he should have given his friend a little more support.

"Grab hold of the ladder, Captain!" a British voice pulled him from the memory. Snapping from the considerations, he glanced about the life raft, and was surprised to see everyone gone.

Better get my head examined, he thought.

In fact, he now realized his head was throbbing, pounding actually, like a drummer on stage with his favorite teenaged rock band, Guns and Roses.

"Captain," the winch man again shouted.

Reaching out, Harry grabbed a plastic climbing ladder and hiked up its swinging footholds.

In the background, the A380 sank beneath the Thames.

The wide body had done her due and kept the passengers safe.

As Harry climbed, staring into the face of a twenty-year-old RAF service member, he knew one thing… he believed his drunken pilot friend.

There are aliens in the skies above.

But he wouldn't be the one to tell that tale.

Not in a million years.

Chapter 97

GIVE 'EM HELL

THE ATLANTIC FLEET was gone.

And, if USS Harry Truman's onboard newspaper, the *Give 'em Hell Herald,* could have reported so, they would've summed it up like this:

It Was The Fight of Honor!
Atlantic Fleet Decimated!

But, Harry Fights On!

The carrier always brawled to the end.

"Dewey Defeats Truman" was a legendarily erroneous headline printed on the front page of the Chicago Tribune on November 3, 1948. It was published the day after TRUMAN won an upset re-election victory over New York Governor, Thomas E. Dewey.

The headline was a classic mash-up.

Turned out, Dewey wasn't a glad-hander like Truman.

Sometimes people jumped the gun.

Whenever twenty-eight-year-old Senior Medical Officer M.P. Matthews found insurmountable circumstances, he carried himself up to the carrier's library and stared at the newspaper headlines.

The words reminded him to hold his mud.

They screamed: think before speaking.

Seeing those headlines did something else too:

They offered hope.

The message was: no matter what people said, nothing was written in stone! There was always an alternative; something else which the *universe defined!*

There was only one certainty for Matthews.

His existence on a carrier was hard, it was a disciplined way of life, and the daily grind molded the manner in which a man carried himself.

Matthews was all in… ready to die for *the life*.

The Fleet was his anchor of self-respect.

The medical officer was a natural leader and technical expert on emergency medicine and natural disasters. He'd studied major cataclysms that occurred over the last century.

This is something un-natural; he thought. *It speaks of something bigger than a volcano falling into the ocean.*

But he couldn't put his finger on it.

When this was over, he might film a report for Truman's weekly television newscast, *Tru North*.

But, now, thinking this, he double-timed his ass onto the bridge with an emergency medical bag.

"Here I am, Commander!" Matthews urgently grunted, scanning the ocean and taking note of the Sikorsky Seahawks filling the sky.

He couldn't believe his eyes.

The Fleet was gone.

The cruisers, destroyers, and frigates were capsized and sinking. The nuclear subs had surfaced and were now conducting rescue operations assisting the Seahawks in plucking survivors from the water and shuttling them to the decks of Truman and Abe Lincoln.

"Get pressure on the wound!" Admiral Brancor urgently hollered, bringing Matthew's attention to the secretary of defense flat on his back.

"He has a large gash on the forehead," Lew barked. "When the initial wave hit, my binoculars flew off the command console and slammed into his skull."

The SECDEFs eyes rolled in their sockets.

His skin was pale, the body jerked in an epileptic fit.

"Hold him down!" Matthews ordered a petty officer.

Matthews knelt to the SECDEF.

His skin felt cool. The fingers, earlobes, lips, and nail beds had a bluish hue to them. The hands were a blotchy red-blue indicating death was near.

Lew looked to Captain Cullen. "We've lost the battle group, everything except Abe Lincoln."

"And one of the subs," the captain pointed while turning to his executive officer. "Tom, what's the status report?"

"Seventy sailors suspected lost in the fleet. Forty-seven injured have been recovered. Our carrier has sustained minor structural damage."

"Are any of my men deceased, injured, or missing?"

"We don't think so," the executive responded. "We're taking roll call right now."

"Looks good, then?" Lew asked.

"Yes, Sir, we did pretty well with the engagement of the Tactical High-Energy Laser. We're undertaking recovery operations with the surviving subs."

"What about the other ships?" Cullen asked.

"Abe Lincoln's crew was hit pretty hard when the initial wave closed over our hull and crashed into their flight deck. But, thanks to our preventative measures, survival rates look pretty good."

"George Bush?" Lew queried. "Anything coming in?"

"No response, Admiral," the executive answered.

Matthews interrupted. "Admiral, the Secretary of Defense is deceased, Sir! There's nothing else I can do."

Glaring at the body, everyone removed their hats and saluted the leader in a moment of silence.

Then, with the snap of a wrist, Lew pulled out a cigar, placed it between his teeth and grunted.

"Prepare honors. We'll have a Burial at Sea since we don't know what conditions on land will look like after the tsunami hits." Staring to the rescue scene below, he hoped there'd be a Virginia, but from what he'd just experienced, he wasn't sure anything would exist after impact.

Either way, his job was done.

He'd seen his men through the wave.

However, knowing the details of Project Cataclysm, Lew knew this was just the beginning of the crisis.

The president had quite a road ahead.

Chapter 98

FINDING HOPE

VATICAN CITY HELIPORT contained a round concrete landing pad circled by a single painted yellow line and the brightest green grass known to man.

After looping the dome of St. Peter's Basilica, the Spanish Navy Helicopter hovered over the landing pad.

Pope Callixtus was anxious.

The Swiss Guard normally awaited his arrival with trumpets and harmonic instruments.

Today, they were armed to the teeth.

Nestled two hundred feet above sea level in the Vatican Gardens, the landing zone was situated at the westernmost section of Leonine Wall on the border of Vatican City.

"They're not going to let you do it," Meeds informed Callixtus while staring at the Swiss Guard. "And, even if they do, the church's hierarchy will bring in more executioners to take you out of the equation."

Callixtus wasn't having any of it. "I'm a trailblazer," he replied when the chopper landed. "Haven't you been listening to the things people say about me? It's time for the church to tell the truth about our place here."

"Oh, I know all about trailblazing, Your Eminence. But, this blazes unexplored secrets trailing back to Saint Peter."

Callixtus stepped to the landing pad. "Today, we're going to buy humanity some time."

During the chopper ride, they received word that Italy's President, the black pope, and Petrus had fled Rome with a band of co-conspirators.

"Papa!" one of the Swiss Guard bowed.

A group of cardinals stepped forward.

"Get me to the catacombs!" Callixtus ordered.

With the Swiss leading the way, Callixtus and Meeds entered a secret door hidden behind a thick shrub.

Once inside, they descended a steep set of ancient stone stairs burrowing under the city.

"Callixtus!" an old bishop stated blocking the path. "I urge you not to free the demon."

"Arrest him!" Callixtus ordered the guards.

Hurrying along the prehistoric stone tunnel, the leader of the Catholic Church knew this was the only way. The rumors of a creature held captive beneath Vatican City were true, and he knew about it.

What he didn't know was this:

Why did they want to wipe out the planet?

How could he prevent the termination of humanity?

"Release what demon?" Meeds asked as they hurried along the echoing hallway. "What is the Bishop talking about? What's with all the secrecy?"

Tell him, the pope's mind whispered, *lay it out.*

"There is a creature beneath Vatican City," Callixtus stated glancing at Meeds. "Chained in the catacombs... its existence has been intentionally hidden from the world. When elected by conclave, I was immediately taken to the Room of Tears where I was handed a box containing a letter written by Jesus outlining the end of the world. It stated the truth about the illuminati and the end of mankind. The letter has been passed down from Pope to Pope."

"Are you serious?" Meeds asked, stopping in his tracks.

"Anyone can *Google* the *Room of Tears* or the *Pope's Box,*" Callixtus said pulling Meeds down the hallway. "Other pontiff's have talked about it. Reading the letter, I was stunned. Then I became angry. That first night, when I retired to the papal apartment, I found a file at the foot of my bed explaining the existence of the creature and what to do to release it."

Meeds was shocked, "Are you out of your mind?"

"I was going public," Callixtus went on. "You say the Illuminati sent you to kill me? This creature is the force behind everything throughout human history. His race is planning to wipe out Earth by a series of natural cataclysms over the next year."

"Is that why you were in Candelaria, Spain?"

"The La Palma volcano disaster and resulting tsunami is the first major cataclysm," Callixtus admitted. "I thought if I went to Spain, there would be some way for me to stop the beginning of the end."

Entering the catacombs, he pointed to a prehistoric iron door built into a stone wall.

"Behind that gate is said to be the leader of *the others*."

"The what?"

Callixtus pulled a loose stone from the wall and removed an old iron key. "The *others* are *beings* who control and manipulate this world. They will put the human race into slavery if their leader is not released."

"Their leader?" a Swiss Guard interrupted.

"The High Priest," Callixtus confirmed. "He is the spearhead of the Great Old Ones." Pushing the key into an enormous modern lock, he was interrupted by a voice.

"Stop!" a monk called out. "Do not release it! The entity has been confined here since the time of Peter!"

But Callixtus stayed the course.

Surrounded by cardinals, priests, monks, and nuns... he pulled open the creaking dungeon door and stepped onto a black and white checkered floor.

Immediately, his thoughts were bombarded with images of the destruction of Earth. Earthquakes, plagues, polar shifts, weather changes, cities on fire... all this playing out on the projector of his mind... it was like watching a mind movie.

Let me out, Carlos of Barcelona! A voice boomed in his considerations. *The time for this to end is now!*

"Give me light!" Callixtus ordered.

When Meeds handed one over, the pope pushed forth the light and the beam illuminated a deep stone dungeon.

"What is it?" Meeds asked.

"The Ark of the Covenant," Callixtus knew. "It disappeared before the destruction of King Solomon's First Temple. Priests anticipated the coming destruction and moved the ark to Ethiopia. The last anyone knew, King Josiah had the Ark put into Solomon's Temple in 623 B.C."

"It's been here the whole time?" Meeds asked.

"Sweet Jesus!" Callixtus moaned. "I have always believed the Solomon Temple objects were taken by Romans and hidden down here in the catacombs."

The sound of trembling chains emanated from the darkness, and then... an ear-splitting shriek of rage assaulted everyone's ears.

Then, the light exposed a veiled life form.

Its wrists were heavily chained to crooked ancient glowing obelisks with pictographs chiseled into the stone. The ankles were shackled to the floor.

The bones of a dead goat sat nearby in a pool of blood.

Callixtus was shocked... it wasn't a dragon or lizard or some bizarre monster as the ancient texts had described.

This was a four-foot-tall, frail, skeletal, dark gray-skinned humanoid being. The non-muscular elongated body stood on short legs, jointed differently than humans. Its thighs were the same length as its forearms and shins.

Callixtus had seen this race of beings a million times. On television, in newspapers... the media called their existence a hoax, their crashed ships... weather balloons. The thousands of sightings had been labeled preposterous.

And, yet, the pope thought, *here it is.*

Release the chains, an authoritative voice pounded into Callixtus' thoughts. *I mean you no harm.*

Stepping to the creature, the Bishop of Rome stared at the alien's elongated large skull.

Just like those found beneath the Vatican.

There was no hair.

No ears or nose… just small openings.

The creature was small but beautiful at the same time.

"You're a gray alien!" Callixtus realized moving closer.

We are much more than this, the being answered with telepathy. *We're the beginning, the middle, and the end of all things in the universe. Your expiration will come, much like the end humans have suffered on Mars, and other planets we seeded with mankind. Your race is doomed to destroy itself; fighting one another for inarguable reasons. We must terminate our project here on this planet.*

Callixtus stared into its unblinking large opaque black eyes. There wasn't an iris or pupil. Yet the stare locked on the pope like a riflescope targeting prey.

Instantly, upon gazing into its stare, the pope was bombarded with mental images of nuclear war, cities on fire, people dying, and then the earth exploding.

He was shown the end of Earth.

"We can change," Callixtus begged. Moving to locks securing the alien's ankles, he unconfined the legs and then moved to the wrists. Almost immediately, the force field holding the alien captive abated. "You have to give us a chance to alter our destiny, to find the strength within ourselves."

As the chains fell from the alien's wrists, it placed its four-fingered hands together like a prayer.

Keeping those hands apart is what hindered its strength.

Instantly… it shape shifted into a divine entity.

A gasp went up from everyone present.

There, standing before them was something of another world, appearing as every God described by the people of Earth throughout the centuries.

And then, it did something breathtaking.

Callixtus stared at the entity as it displayed the kind forgiving image of Jesus Christ clothed in a white robe and worn leather sandals.

Walking across the cavern, it presented splintered palms where ancient holes had been hammered into the flesh. The scabs reopened and blood poured onto the floor.

"And now you know," it verbally spoke, placing a bloody hand on Callixtus' shoulder. "Humanity kills things it doesn't understand. You are a race of useless murderers."

The Bishop of Rome fell to his knees.

Behind him, Swiss Guard, cardinals, priests, monks, and nuns all fell to the floor with sobs of disbelief and terror.

"Just give us a chance to change," Callixtus pled. "We *can be* better! Don't destroy us now, I beg you! Give me time to tell our world leaders what they face!"

"And those who have kept me here," the entity questioned. "What shall become of them?"

"We'll find them. Mankind will chase them to the ends of Earth and bring them to justice."

At that point, the entity stepped back, pushed its hands onto the Ark and turned into a blinding white light. "Time is running out," it warned. "The next time you see me, it will be the end of Earth. If your people do not change the course they've set, this volcano will only be the first of many disasters to end this world."

The chamber suddenly trembled and the stones collapsed. It was as if the greatest earthquake on Earth occurred right in this cave beneath Vatican City.

"Callixtus!" Meeds yelled pulling the pontiff from the chamber, "we must evacuate the catacombs!"

Then, just as they fled the chamber… the alien and Ark disappeared in an implosion of stone and concrete.

Trembling from the experience, Callixtus stumbled to his feet. "We have mighty work to do."

"What was that thing, Papa?" Meeds nervously asked. "Did we just see our creator?"

Nodding, Callixtus blinked back a tear.

In his heart, he felt the weight of the world.

Convincing Earth's leaders to change their stripes wasn't going to be easy.

And yet, that was the task ahead.

"I have a mission for you," Callixtus informed the colonel. "It is of the highest priority!"

"Anything, Papa, anything you want."

"We must begin cleaning our own house. The future depends on it."

Turning to his order, he saw the clergy staring at the alien's bloody handprint on his shoulder.

It would be all the proof he needed going forward.

"Put out a dispatch to the world," the pope ordered. "Inform the media, the time to disclose the future is now. Tell them I'll speak at the United Nations… and make sure to tell them… their lives depend on it."

That should get them moving.

Chapter 99

THE ARRIVAL

SAM HEARD THE SCREAMS.

They were spikes of terror wrapped in panic.

"Everybody run for your lives!" V.I. yelled.

Across the bridge, leading to Miami Beach, a wall of water hulked over the horizon. It carried an aircraft carrier at its apex and could be seen speeding towards land. The water was so tall people supposed the wave might touch the clouds.

Running won't solve anything, Sam thought as he glared to the USS George H.W. Bush heading for the art deco hotels lining Ocean Drive. *We're done. This is so long and see ya later, hop aboard the elevator!*

Going up!

The wave would not enable escape; the act of panic driven sprinting wouldn't keep death at bay.

Everything now happened in slow motion.

Like in the movies, when a film director desired the audience to focus on a sliver of time; to glance momentarily towards that important element of the story.

This was that scene.

"Get in the helicopter!" Major Emmitt yelled.

However, before the words left his mouth, the Chinook abandoned the concrete causeway without picking up its passengers. Hundreds of distressed people ran for the machine, grabbed hold of the landing skids and caught the last ride out!

Sam just stood there.

He was frozen in awareness that a full house beat a pair every time. Everybody loses in the end. Some find death in the bottom of a bottle, others find the reaper during accidents, and those lucky enough to wither in old age are usually surrounded by loved ones.

This was something else. It was a mass end of life event.

Then, just as the two hundred foot wave was about to destroy South Beach… something extraordinary happened.

A sonic boom exploded above the causeway.

The sound was so powerful a reverberating pulse wave shook the concrete bridge and threw everyone off balance.

That's when Sam saw the spaceship.

"Oh, good God!" Gordy exclaimed.

"That isn't God," V.I. whispered.

Sam couldn't move his eyes off the ship. It blocked out the sky for as far as the eye could see.

Hovering not more than five hundred feet above ground, a hatch the size of a 747 opened and a bright light impacted the wall of water. For an instant, the beam penetrated the depths and then, it was over. The wave collapsed on itself and didn't hit shore.

It just flattened into the ocean as if it had never been.

"What in the hell am I looking at?" Gordy asked.

Deputy Chief Rico Martinez put his hands on his hips. "That, my friend, is a mother ship from outer space!" It was no surprise to the lawman that he was looking straight up the ass of an extraterrestrial spacecraft.

Sam glanced to Rico, thought of saying something slick and British, but then realized he was speechless.

All his years as a scientist never prepared him for this.

This was science fiction come true.

It was as good as landing on the White House lawn.

E.T. existed, and they saved mankind.

"Come on!" Major Emmitt shouted. "We've got to get over the bridge and see if there are survivors."

Hiking to the top of the Fifth Street Bridge, they ran to South Beach and were stunned at the sight.

Sitting perfectly on the sand were hundreds of cargo ships and pleasure boats... set down harmlessly as if stranded on a sandbar. Just off shore, the USS George H.W. Bush rocked upon the normal rolling tide.

In minutes, the sky was packed by news choppers.

But the spaceship didn't move.

It just hung there, beneath the thick cloud cover, waiting for something, maybe giving the human race time to comprehend what they were witnessing.

Then, Sam's phone rang.

"Hello?"

"Sam? Honey?" Tish's voice begged. "Are you allright?"

"Bonkers," he retorted holding back tears. "You're alive! I thought I had lost you in a plane crash!"

"I thought so, too, Sam."

He was relieved. Emotion poured over him, his knees felt weak and for an instant, he thought he'd cry in front of everyone standing beside him.

"Sam? Are you there?"

"I'm here," he answered fighting the tears. "Just realizing how happy I am to hear your voice."

"Are you watching what's happening in Miami? It's something isn't it?"

Composing himself, he realized... *It is something...* this was an occurrence ancient alien proponents had been predicting ever since an object crashed on a ranch near Roswell, New Mexico.

"Now, there's no denying it," he said. "The Martians are really here."

"Sam? Are you all right?"

"Yes. Now that I know you're safe."

Safe? His mind toyed. *Nobody is ever really safe, are they? This party is just getting started, dear boy!*

Chapter 100

CHASING DEMONS

LUCERNE SWITZERLAND was a good hiding place.

It was Jesuit country.

It had been a week since Meeds began the Vatican's manhunt to find the black pope, Cardinal Romano, and Italy's now deposed ex-president.

They were hunted men.

The entire world was stalking them.

Britain's MI-6, the CIA, China's MSS, the FSB of Russia, and even Israel's Mossad jumped into the pursuit.

With alien spacecraft hovering above every continent of Earth, Meeds understood Callixtus had very little time to change the course of human history.

In a matter of days, the Bishop of Rome would address the United Nations with a blueprint for the road ahead.

"We got them," Meeds mumbled to his team of six highly trained killers. Initially the trail led him to the northwestern tip of Zürich. Having discretely inquired about town, he learned of newcomers appearing around the Fraumünster Swiss Reformed Church.

It would be a perfect hiding place.

But the trail went dead.

Now, stalking the cobbled streets of Lucerne, Meeds had eyes-on Italy's ex-President Napolo walking across Lucerne's Jesuit Church Bridge.

This is where the traitors are hiding.

Pulling out a small pair of spyglasses, he zoomed in on Napolo. *There's no question; we've found the traitor.*

The Jesuit Church was a major tourist attraction. People milled about everywhere, allowing the conspirators to have a false sense of security and the belief they could hide in plain sight in civilian clothes.

Following Napolo's trail, Meeds' team spread into the thick crowd surveying the target's destination. Within minutes, two more men appeared and sat in yellow chairs at a sidewalk café.

"We have confirmation," a voice crackled in Meeds earpiece. "I see Cardinal Romano and the Black Pope, meeting with ex-President Napolo. You were right, Colonel, morning coffee time."

"Stand by, I'm moving in," Meeds ordered.

Pulling out his cell phone, he stared at his reflection.

A black wig, mustache and beard disguised his true appearance. Wrapped around his waist looped an orange apron borrowed from the café's owner the previous evening. Finding a gun pointed at his head, the owner promised he'd cooperate.

Besides, if these were the guys who tried to kill the pope, the owner said he was game.

Blending into the café's foot traffic, Meeds adjusted his matching shirt and trousers, and then moved to the table.

"Good morning, Gentlemen, what is your order?"

The black pope glanced at the menu dismissively.

Petrus stared at Meeds. *There's something familiar about this guy.* Being overly paranoid, he was seeing secret agents around every corner and behind every tree. *Yet, the eyes don't seem right.*

The Italian President glanced up from a menu printed in German. "I'll have a large Café Crème, and a plate of Fotzel Slices."

"I think we'll all have the same," the black pope said.

It was something like French toast.

Using day-old bread, the café sliced twelve thick sections of dark wheat bread and sprinkled them with a concoction of milk, eggs, butter, sugar, and cinnamon, before browning in a conventional stovetop pan.

"I'd like mine served with fresh apple purée," the Italian stated handing over his menu.

Watching the waiter, Petrus was uneasy and decided to test the waiter's heritage.

"Haben Sie sich damit beschäftigt gewesen, heute?"

"Very busy, indeed," Meeds flawlessly answered the German language. "We sold more coffee this year than last! Switzerland, as you know, is the third biggest coffee drinking nation in Europe, with only Finland and Norway consuming more."

"Yes, yes, of course," Petrus answered in English.

Hurrying off towards the storefront, Meeds knew the cardinal was a suspicious character. He was known to keep a stranglehold on the Holy See when he was in control of Vatican City, almost as if he had a sixth sense… but this time would be different; he'd lose the game.

Reaching an old oak tabletop, Meeds prepared three cups of espresso infusing it with steamed milk. Pulling a clear cylinder from his pocket, he poured in lethal doses of poison.

It would work instantly.

Next, the café owner handed over the poisoned Fotzel.

Whether they drank the coffee, or ate the food, the traitors would die in a matter of seconds.

Meeds had learned they ordered the same thing every alternating day. Thus, when they sat at the tables today, everything was prepared for their arrival.

They were so predictable.

Carrying their breakfast out the glass doorway, Meeds approached the table with a smile. "Here you go, enjoy!" Walking away, he couldn't help but peek over his shoulder as the traitors sipped their coffee.

Almost immediately, they dropped dead.

Chapter 101

SAVING HUMANITY

POPE CALLIXTUS knew time was short.

The alien ships were everywhere.

Worldwide newscasts displayed the dark metallic hulls lingering above the clouds. They were here, and unless earthlings met specific demands, the human race would be wiped from the face of the planet.

Playtime was over.

Millions trekked to The Dome of The Rock where glowing orbs hovered in Jerusalem's skyline.

In Egypt, circular objects descended over the pyramids.

In Ethiopia, believed to be the location of the Garden of Eden, UFO enthusiasts shot video of landing ships and posted them on the internet–*proving once and for all*–that aliens existed and were invading nations across the globe.

The extra-terrestrials didn't exit their ships.

They just landed occasionally, maybe as a show of force, to reinforce the idea that mankind had lost control.

Just minutes earlier, the President of the United States had gathered superpower leaders in a private conference room to discuss the demands mentally infused into the Bishop of Rome.

Now, standing just off stage, Callixtus prepared to address the U.N. General Assembly and the world.

Thousands of television cameras focused on a gigantic stage specially built to hold the most prestigious religious leaders the world had ever known.

Thousands more crammed into the room.

This is what they've been waiting for.

It was the path to survival.

"It's time," agent Gordon Holland stated.

He'd been appointed head of the pope's U.S. security detail by POTUS and was quickly approved by the Secretary General of the United Nations.

"Thank you, Gordon," Callixtus smiled.

Pointing ahead, Gordy showed the King of Mankind his entrance point. "Knock 'em dead, Your Holiness."

Walking to the podium, Callixtus waited as hundreds of leaders packed seats behind him; a concrete display of solidarity. It was no longer Jew against Arab, Christian versus Muslim. This was a united human race.

Nobody disputed land of the West Bank.

Everyone realized Earth wasn't theirs.

As Callixtus cleared his throat, clicking cameras pierced the hushed room. Before him, lying on the lectern was a folder stamped:

PROJECT CATACLYSM
Top-Secret-Eyes Only

It had been hand delivered by the President of the United States and outlined decades of intelligence the CIA had gathered from crashed UFOs.

They knew all along what lay in the future.

Now, camera flashes erupted in brilliant white bursts.

Callixtus smiled, recalling the meeting with his surviving shipmates, Tish, Dr. Doolittle, and the teenager, Mikey. The pope was present when the boy had been reunited with his mother and father, both of whom were picked up by another Spanish Navy ship.

He imagined that now they were huddled around a TV somewhere, like everyone else on the planet, wondering what came next.

On a teleprompter, the words 'you are now live' appeared followed by prepared statements.

Who decided on these words was up for debate.

CATACLYSM

Most said the message came directly from *The Others*.

"People of planet Earth," the pope read. "We mean you no harm, unless you fail to meet the following conditions and implement all aspects of Earth saving methods immediately and without argument."

Glancing to the front row of spectators, he nodded to Meeds, the leaders of the U.K., America, Russia, China, and Europe.

"We'll never surrender!" someone yelled from the back.

"Go back to space!" someone else shouted deliriously.

Watching as the men were removed from the crowd, Callixtus wished those two statements could be true.

But the sad reality was that Earth existed as nothing more than a fishbowl, a science project started centuries before by a people called The Anunnaki.

They were a group of gods in ancient Mesopotamian cultures. *The Others* had told Callixtus they were Sumerian deities of an old prehistoric line; immortals of fertility, linked with the underworld where they were judges who took their name from the old sky god Anu.

In the week since the aliens had revealed themselves, the people came to know *The Others* resided inside most of Earth's tallest mountains and volcanoes.

There was even a base on the dark side of the moon, that's why humans never went back after the 1960s.

The aliens were unconcerned with heat or cold.

Some speculated they had been hiding in plain sight.

They were mentioned in *The Epic of Gilgamesh* when Utnapishtim tells the tale of Noah's great flood.

Now, everyone knew the story.

The Annunaki came to Earth when hominids populated the planet. Infusing them with alien genes, the entities altered our DNA which created modern humans.

They had wanted slaves to mine gold.

There was the missing link.

Later, one of the strongest aliens caused the great flood, to rid the planet of the humans they'd manufactured.

But alas, some of us escaped the deluge.

And we survived with the help of other aliens.

"Today is the beginning of the end for humanity," Callixtus read from the screen. "The aliens have terminated their interest in mankind and now give us specific instructions on how they'll shut down the planet if we do not comply."

A gasp went up from the room.

Behind the pope, a large HI-DEF display burst alive with images of the sky turning gunmetal gray, the oceans were barren and plant life withered. The entire Earth was a wasteland of death and destruction. Animals lay wasting beside human bodies, cities were destroyed, and nothing survived.

"This will be your destiny," the pope continued. "Or, the human race can dismantle all nuclear capabilities, share global wealth, and cease killing one another for petty differences." Glancing to the worried chamber, he was distracted by the scene of arguments and erupting chaos.

That's when an alien arrived.

It appeared on the stage for just a moment... merely long enough for the cameras to glimpse the seven-foot creature layered in gold hieroglyphs.

It had the face of a lizard, and the body of a man.

Around its wrists wrapped bands of gold and silver.

And then, it was gone...

This was one of the Watchers, a race of ancient aliens who controlled the planet and first introduced mankind to knowledge. First described in the Book of Enoch, history described them as angels.

Now, everyone knew they were better.

The hall became quiet for a moment, and then, there was nothing. All eyes stared to Callixtus.

"We must survive," the pope begged his worldwide audience. "There's no other way, no amount of fighting will change our circumstance, we must go back to our countries and work out the differences which make us hate. When that happens, we'll find the only thing that matters are the bonds we share."

Stepping off the stage, the pope knew there was much work ahead. He'd need an INTERVENTION to save humanity from certain destruction.

But, he believed in humankind.

Sometimes that's all one needed.

THE END

AFTERWORD

There are hundreds of alleged UFO conspiracies involving the Roman Catholic Church.

More pepper ancient civilizations.

Extraterrestrials have been here for a long time.

Every early society speaks of 'gods' descending from the clouds and mingling with Earth's inhabitants.

Almost always, our ancestors have etched history with tales of "angels" and "star people" thrusting back to the heavens after imparting knowledge to mankind.

Clearly, we've been visited throughout history.

Why can't we admit this fact?

As a young boy, my mother used to drag me to Mass every Sunday morning where I'd accept communion right along with everyone else.

The priest would place a wafer on my tongue.

"This is the body of Christ."
"AMEN," my young lips whispered.
"Good boy," Mom smiled down at me.

Ah, life was good... innocence was wonderful.

Ignorance was bliss.

I often wonder, what might have happened if I just revolted? What would the church have done if I didn't drink their grape juice? What if all my friends (many of whom were altar boys) said, *sorry... not buying into it!*

No wafer for us, thank you very much!
Nope, we don't like grapes, anyway!

What would've happened?

I remember, as a curious lad, I wanted to believe in God so bad, but could never put a finger on why.

Now, looking back, I think that youngster just wanted to follow everybody else.

Doesn't every child?

It takes courage to swim upstream, doesn't it?

I'm not the first author... nor shall I be the last, to suppose there are fantastic secrets hidden in the Vatican.

The stories I tell in *Cataclysm* are a few of the most horrific whispers hushed in chambers around the globe.

In many cases, information on the existence of aliens is readily available for anyone willing to open their mind.

Just research the tales I suggested.

The Room of Tears, Project Lucifer, and the Lizard Creature chained beneath the Vatican.

I didn't make up this stuff.

My accounts of UFOs brushed into history's religious paintings are real. The disc-shaped images were in fact painted by artists who desired a record of what they saw.

The paintings exist.

With surprising little effort, one might find much more than I have put forth in this volume.

There are underground bases in Colorado, Ohio, Nevada, and god knows where else.

Are they all connected through Denver International?

It's alleged the subterranean bases are linked by 300-mile an hour Maglev Trains... running through clandestine tunnels throughout America.

Just take the time and research these allegations.

Like anything in life, one may eat from the apple of the tree of knowledge, or simply turn a blind eye.

That's for you to decide.

But you don't have much time.

I choose to stare into the sacred halls of possibilities.

It's my job to enter a dark room and throw open the heavy curtains to splash light onto a subject.

Sometimes the truth is frightening.

Often... where there's smoke... a fire rages.

Personally, I don't know what to believe anymore.

Is there seriously an Almighty, all knowing, heavenly God judging mankind from the clouds?

Is it *any less likely*... that aliens also exist?

Why do we believe in the existence of an invisible Divine being from an undetectable place called Heaven?

And yet, we shun the possibility of an alien race visiting Earth from another planet?

I'm torn between two robust beliefs... one in a higher power, and another in the existence of aliens.

Isn't it possible both might exist?

Does one cancel out the other?

Maybe, just possibly... Earth IS a science project.

And, if that's true, we're in for quite a ride.

It's been proposed that climate change and the extreme weather on Earth is *the beginning of the end.*

Some claim the underground bases are an attempt by E.T. to save humanity from a cataclysmic pole shift.

What do I know? I'm just a messenger!

Yet, I'm not stupid... I have a doomsday bunker.

If I end up dead after this is published, I suppose you'll know there was something to the tale.

Stay tuned, my friends. I've got my ear to the ground and my eyes to the heavens.

Something tells me I've been tuned in.

I'm just saying...

RJ Smith

MAY 15, 2014

Turn the Page

COMPLIMENTARY PREVIEW

RJ Smith's

The Santa Claus Killer

TH€ BUZZ

Not Your Typical Serial Killer Book
September 30, 2013
By Kat Yares (Clinton, AR USA)
This review is from: The Santa Claus Killer: Volume 1
(FBI Serial Killer Task Force) (Kindle Edition)

Tired of run of the mill Serial Killers? RJ Smith will thoroughly help you break that mold. In The Santa Claus Killer, you get to meet one of the most unusual serial killers I've ever met in a work of fiction. Superbly well written and plotted, I guarantee you will keep turning the page to find out what happens next. And by the last page, I promise you won't have seen the ending coming. Want a good read - this is it. Go for it, what are you waiting for?

I received a copy of this book for a Hellnotes professional review.

A Unique, Compelling Writing Style
July 20, 2013
By Carol G Hovsepian – Hollywood Producer
This review is from: The Santa Claus Killer (FBI Serial
Killer Task Force) (Volume 1) (Paperback)

I have to say, the brilliant, unique writing style that author R.J. Smith uses to suck you in, is compelling in itself. It's clear the author knows NYC inside-out which makes us visualize we are not only following bad Santa ourselves through Times Square, but also makes us aware that we, as readers, are being followed as well. And that's creepy. The author's chapters don't follow a traditional flow as found in most fictional books. He deviates to focus on a specific character or two that really pulls us into their minds and motivations. I love that! You feel you know these characters and the murderous world they partake in even if you've never been to NYC.

Satisfying Read, Full of Grit, Witty Twists
September 29, 2013
By Paso Palmer – California Reviewer
This review is from: The Santa Claus Killer: Volume 1 (FBI Serial Killer Task Force) (Kindle Edition)

No, it's not sugar and spice and who would want that? This crime thriller made me lose sleep, both because of the subject matter and also because I just couldn't put the book down. If you enjoy smart tough dialogue, the characters will not disappoint you and the plot twist are imaginative without suffering from gimmicks employed by lessor writers of the genre. My wife is afraid to read it, but I've warned her, if she gives it five minutes, she'll be engrossed enough to have to finish. I'm looking forward to RJ's next book, Cataclysm.

Edge of your seat, THRILLER!!!
September 29, 2013
By Sean Kennedy New Fan of RJ Smith
This review is from: The Santa Claus Killer: Volume 1 (FBI Serial Killer Task Force) (Kindle Edition)

So, I am not one for trying to read a whole book in one day but........ The Santa Claus Killer was the exception!!!! Calling this incredible read a "Page-Turner" does not bring justice to such an intense edge of your seat thriller! RJ Smith has hit a homerun with an incredibly fast paced tour de force!

R.J. SMITH

ACKNOWLEDGEMENTS

To all who continue the good fight… *tramping through the ditches of dreams…* and refusing to surrender their faith in the fantasy of storytelling.

For Friends: Steve Blauvelt, Kainoa Maka, Trisha Cook, Oscar Thomas, Darren Langford, and Gordon Holland.

To my beta-readers, Linda L. Barton, Carol Hovsepian, Debbie Vandyck, and Paul Swearingen, your steady stewardship was well pondered.

As well, to my Facebook acquaintances who listened, engaged, and strengthened the ravings of a dramatist.

This book would've <u>never</u> been written if not for of the encouragement my awesome Literary Agent Joyce Keating.

And also: for my UK Proofreader, Robert Snow.

BUT, *finally,* to that pint-sized boy I once was,
Who crisscrossed the depths of hell,
Yet somehow became a man,
I say these long-past-due words…

Well done, kid... You did just fine getting me here!

R.J. Smith
The North Pole
Christmas Day

FOREWORD

WHERE I COME from, Santa Claus would've killed to be in my book... those auditioning would have lined their fat asses up around the block of Woolworths to audition for the part.

Now, they carry their bones down to Walmart and shake barbered heads in feigned disgust.

People have asked:

"What's gotten into you, RJ? Why did you write this horror involving the King of Christmas?"

I say, screw it... if Mr. Chris Kringle has time to keep a naughty list, then my name is número uno to receive coal! Let fatso track me down between deliveries and drag my lazy carcass to the graveyard; good for him.

Everybody has to die sooner or later.

Why not now?

For everyone else, those of you who think the guy behind the beard might have something to hide, this tale is for you.

Growing into my teens on the streets of Manhattan, I wasn't invested in Christmas. The shiny new toys didn't call to me from Macy's glittering windows. The season's opening of Rockefeller Center ushered in the Upper West Side kids... and yes, Christmas was fun for them... it was special...

They bought the scam and drank the Kool-Aid.

I guess, as a young boy, I recalled sitting on HIS lap one winter and tugging on the beard. Then, I knew the hoodwinking I'd received. I understood the con job and how it all played out. So, when I got older, I filed my complaint with the jolly old fat man! He laughed and smiled, and didn't give a crap.

And, that's when I knew something wasn't right.

There was a secret.

Thus, the gang and I kept a close eye out for his appearance along the sidewalks and in every store right after the parade on Seventh Avenue. There, he rode into town atop his official red and green glittered sleigh on Thanksgiving Day.

The city would dance, and cheer, and sell their Christmas toys.

But, deep down, I knew a monster lurked under that façade, and, that one day... he would show his real face.

That day is today.

That's what carried you, dear bookworm, to this nightmarish tale of murder, horror, and fright.

Nobody, after all, gazes into the blackness of a shadowy graveyard expecting to find a love story.

You know why we're here!

You stared at the book cover of Santa dragging his bloody sack through Times Square, accepted the premise, and then bought the book recognizing damp, sticky blood would soon fill your stockings!

However, let's not get ahead of ourselves here…

The particulars of how we get through Christmas rests in the pages that follow.

For there, amongst the sleigh bells sounding in the dead of night, a snowstorm is brewing, and just around the corner, a murderer rings his bell.

R.J. SMITH

This Is

NOT

Sugar & Spice!

WELCOME TO THE SHOW

JUST ANOTHER SNOT-NOSED KID, a lousy orphan, an abandoned morsel, left here to die at my feet.

You better watch out, you better not cry,
You better not pout, I'm telling you why,
Santa Claus Is Coming To Kill...

That was his anthem, the tune that got his rocks off better than a five-and-dime hooker. It was also the lone miniature melody he couldn't shake from his throbbing skull. The twelve days of Christmas were heading down the pike like a freight train–Tick; Tock, Tick; Tock–Father Time was stomping through the dead of winter, waiting to turn the calendar of another rotten year.

"Please," a streetwise white boy begged. "Just let me go and I promise to live my life right!"

He was flat on his back staring up at the face of a monster; the kind that Mommy warned would stalk him one day.

"Too bad, so sad," the slaughterer scoffed. "Take your five-finger discounts to the pits of hell."

The boy trembled, fear gripped his spine and urine pooled beneath his hips.

"Just give me a chance!" he bawled, sensing the Fat Lady was about to sing.

"Time's up!" the killer cackled. "There's no more time to lie, cheat, or steal!"

"I wasn't meant to die this way," the boy cried, his arms and legs flailing for freedom. "I could have been somebody!"

Yet, escape was useless; the assassin had him pinned to the sidewalk in the middle of Times Square. To either side, hundreds of people milled about… watching the strangulation, waiting for the moment when they'd witness a murder.

New York was every man for himself.

"But you ended up a fucking nobody!" the murderer growled. "Shit happens and then you die!"

Death, the boy reflected, *will end the pain. It will pinch away all hopes and dreams… and then, my life-force will blink out... like the lights on a Broadway marquee... popping off, one at a time, goodbye, so-long, and farewell.*

That darkness of finality would bring the end to his nightmarish life.

Good Golly! Jolly Molly! A disembodied voice cackled in the recesses of the slayer's mind. *I do believe that boy is about to cry like a bitch!*

Stefan might've sobbed, had his childhood memories not flooded the blurring vision of the killer's face.

I'm on my way to heaven!

But death took time. It never happened like actors portrayed in the movies.

Committing homicide required some doing.

It took muscle, and every once in a while, this murderer knew he had to drag their naughty souls kicking and screaming into their graves.

Chapter 1

The Master Poser

MANHATTAN NEVER SLEEPS.

It gives birth to dreams and stamps them out like cheap, harsh cigarettes.

Frank Sinatra once sang that if you could make it here, you'd make it anywhere. What he failed to mention was the boogeymen who stalked the streets in search of blood.

That's where Richard Blake slouched; ringing his bell at the entrance to Macy's on 34th Street where miracles were replaced by the gore and mayhem that plunged through his mind.

"Bastards," he grumbled. "Good for nothing squares." Every year, he'd shrug on a Santa outfit and watch the fools scurry into the store for their spoiled little brats nestled safe and sound at home. It angered him that while he, the main attraction, stood out here in the freezing cold, panhandling for pennies, those fat little piggies were nestled in the warmth of their beds.

"Nasty little disease carriers, that's what they are!" Grumbling, he reached into his coat and retrieved a pint of Mad Dog 20/20. He adored the red grape flavor—better known as Bum Juice—an inexpensive, low-end, fortified wine that had an alcohol content of 18-percent. It packed one hell of a wallop and washed away his pain and misery. It excited him to drink the Mumble Juice right there in front of the silly fat cows as they dropped their meager coins into his bucket. He called it Mumble Juice because if he drank too much of it, he wandered the streets mumbling to people who weren't really there.

And that was just crazy.

Besides, if he really wanted to be one of the bums he hunted, he had to play the part and drink their Kool-Aid.

First impressions meant everything.

Tossing back a gulp, he scowled at the shoppers. "Ho! Ho! Ho! Have a merry, fucking, Christmas!"

The bargain hunters gasped, covered the ears of their youngsters, and rushed into the night.

"Hey, pal," a fatherly type muttered, shoving his finger into bad Santa's chest. "What's your problem, huh?"

Santa sniggered, and took another swig. "This whole damn city's my problem! You're all stinking gatherers, nothing but spenders!"

The man shoved Santa to the ground, shook his fists, and stormed down the street. "You drunken, stupid idiot, ya need a New York ass-whipping, that's what you need!"

"Asshole wannabe," a passing woman sneered. "You're not Santa Claus at all; you should be ashamed of yourself!"

I should be ashamed of myself. What am I doing wearing this itchy costume again this year? Damn naughty or nice, how many more will piss on my lap and step on my toes?

He staggered to his feet, spat on the ground and stared at a passing Camaro and a teenager who hurled insults from its open window.

"Yo! Dickhead! Where's your lousy reindeer?"

"Rotten thug," Santa answered. "It's because of pricks like you that I'm in this situation to begin with!" Stepping from the curb, he reached to the ground and gathered a snowball. "I'll show you bastards, I'll teach you a lesson or two!"

To those interested enough to stare at the drunken Santa Claus stumbling from the sidewalk and flinging his snowball at the passing car, they might've wondered what had become of the King of Christmas.

But Richard knew exactly what had become of himself… what his mission was, and why he stood out here in the snow to draw in the bums who begged for money and harassed the herds.

So, as his anger tracked straight and true, exploding in the face of a Puerto Rican boy, he smiled triumphantly.

"It's a present from Rudolph, with my compliments from the North Pole!"

Suddenly, the Camaro spun on an icy patch of road and slid towards the place where he stood. What headed his way were four wheels of death and destruction; a horn desperately warned the innocent of its destructive approach. However, for those who knew better, horns and whistles were merely comfort warnings that cautioned the shit wagon was headed their way.

Nothing stopped the candy man when he jingled up your number, calling.

The car crashed into the windows of Macy's just moments after the shoppers leapt to safety.

They screamed in horror as three teenaged boys sprung from the car, attacked Santa, and taught him about street justice.

"You stinking deadbeat fraud!" a white boy shouted, swinging his fist with all his might, striking Santa on the chin.

"Get off me, you little prick!" Santa sniveled a moment before the boy smashed a bottle against the side of his skull. Stumbling to a knee, he reached to the boy's neck, grabbed a crucifix hanging from a chain, and collapsed to the street.

"Kill his sorry-ass, Mighty Whitey!" the Puerto Rican boy begged. "Send his phony ass back to Mrs. Claus in a body bag!"

And that's what might've happened if a black kid hadn't pulled Stefan away at the cacophony of approaching sirens.

"Come on, Stefan! Let's get out of here before you kill him!"

"I got to find my chain, Darius," Stefan yelled. "The lousy deadbeat ripped it off my neck!"

"There's no time," Darius urged pointing to an NYPD cruiser turning the corner. "We have to haul ass!" And so, they abandoned the poser in a puddle of his own blood and hightailed down the dark street and out of sight.

As for the Grinch who stole Christmas, the last thing he remembered were the voices in his head.

Chapter 2

Ushering in the Season

THE NEXT DAY, wind battered the cheeks of three-million spectators lining Macy's Thanksgiving Day Parade.

The tradition began in 1924.

Back then, they released the balloons at the end of the parade until one brought down an airplane.

Now, they fold them up for next year.

Crashing planes are a touchy subject.

The smart viewers lounged at home watching televisions, their feet digging into plush shag carpets, their mouths watering from the turkey roasting in the oven. Nobody wanted to venture into the blustery wind just to welcome a jolly ole fat man from the North Pole.

But, staying at home was for chumps.

Any kid worth his weight in Bubble Yum would tell you, in order to one up their friends, bragging rights came by freezing their balls off while hot chocolate warmed the hand. Boasting that they came, saw, and conquered, meant watching from a heated living room wasn't going to cut it.

Stefan whistled as the Spiderman balloon soared overhead. "Look! It's Spidey!"

The boys went crazy as the masked marauder soared past Macy's followed by the Late Night Float.

"Look," Stefan pointed to the rock and rolling band on wheels. "It has a giant Les Paul guitar on it."

"Imagine that!" Darius grunted, nudging Stefan.

"You think it's a sign?"

"Maybe, why not?"

Marco couldn't refuse. "Maybe the universe is warning us not to steal one." It was a reference to an upcoming heist they'd planned.

"Maybe it's a sign?" Stefan again asked.

"Take it easy, Mighty Whitey," Darius giggled. It was a nickname they'd given Stefan.

Then, they cheered louder as the Air Force Marching Band appeared.

"Damn!" Stefan exclaimed. "Those are some ass kicking brothers!" Cheering, he didn't know what war was, but liked the drums just the same.

After a long procession of bands and television stars, pandemonium broke loose and an emerald and gold sleigh appeared. From high upon the float, Santa and Mrs. Claus waved as tickertape fluttered over the scene like a blizzard.

Christmas had officially arrived.

"Can you imagine," Marco joked, "that fat slob screwing the hookers on Forty Second Street? He'd be pawning his toys to buy those girls their crack."

"Yeah," Stefan chuckled. "Liberty Pawn and Jewelry would put his sleigh in the window with a big fat Santa mannequin sitting on it."

"Red-light special," Darius threw in. "Pawn it or sell it!"

After a moment of hysterical banter, the boys picked up bottles and hurled them at Santa. It was a display of anger that presents weren't delivered to street kids like them.

"Put these in your stockings," Stefan shouted and threw his bottle.

"Hey!" a city cop yelled hurrying through the crowd. "You guys throwing the bottles! Hold it right there!"

But, holding it there wasn't part of the plan.

Before anyone knew what happened, the friends ran through the horde with police hot on their trail.

It was just another day in the city of dreams.

Chapter 3

The Belly of the Beast

STEFAN WAS PISSED at how he'd been treated by New York's finest jerks.

When criminals were arrested in the County of New York, they were searched, degraded, and sometimes beaten before being locked into holding cells pending transport to Rikers Island Jail.

That's where Mighty Whitey now sat with petty thieves, drunks, and most likely, murderers.

He was losing his patience.

The corrections officers had already changed shifts once... and none of the detainees had been shuffled upstairs to the housing units. As far as the prisoners were concerned, the only difference between them and the guards was that the guards hadn't been caught.

Stefan stared through a Plexiglas barrier and cursed knowing the morons weren't actually working. He didn't remember much of the parade, save for throwing the bottle and running for his life. Everything else was beaten from him by the flatfoots who chased him down and taught him the consequences of getting on Santa's naughty list.

"What are you, some kind of tough guy?" they'd barked, daring him to argue. "We have a place for idiots like you."

And they did, too, he found out–a meat locker of freezing human flesh.

Bodies in the morgue are warmer than this, he thought. *My friends are nice and warm back at the apartment, probably resting on the flea-infested couch having a laugh or two.*

"Shit," he moaned, pinching his nose against the putrid stench of urine. It was so rancid he could taste it.

One of these lowlifes is going to vomit on my two-hundred-dollar kicks at any moment.

It was in the middle of those thoughts, that the cell door clanged open and Johnnie Law appeared. In his hands were wristbands, the type found on hospital patients.

"If I call your name, exit the cell, place out your right hand and keep your lying mouths shut."

"It's cold in here," an elderly man protested, his bones rattling from the chill, obviously drunk from one too many.

"This," Johnnie Law sneered, showing the man his wristband, "was your ticket outta here. But now, old man, you wait." He smiled vindictively, pushed the wristband deep into his pocket, and glanced around the room.

"Does anyone else have a hearing problem?"

There were no takers; everyone understood there were no magic numbers in a hat, no prizes squirreled away behind door-number-two.

They knew who the king cobra was in this pit, so they gave nothing–except their rapt attention.

When a snake threatened to strike, you had to avoid the bite.

Stefan was led to a blue payphone hanging on a dingy wall.

"One phone call," Johnnie Law mumbled.

Considering his options, and balancing the odds, he wondered who to call.

"Can I call two people?"

"What're you deaf, kid? You get one phone call and you better make it count."

Putting the receiver to his ear, Stefan dialed the one person who could pull him from the dungeon, his criminal defense lawyer, Terry R. Woodward.

Chapter 4

The Defender of Justice

TERRY STOOD SMOKING a Partagas cigar on the wind chilled terrace of his posh 5th Avenue penthouse overlooking Central Park.

The terrace was his getaway.

Creeping out here late at night, the crisp air cleansed the muck from his lungs. Having danced with demons, he'd whiffed their unpleasant odor and was glad to simply be an observer.

Then, there was Mirabel, his lovely wife.

Yes, indeed, he considered, glancing across the snow-blown scene below. *Life is good.*

He walked amongst the nightmares of society and rubbed shoulders with the worst people in Manhattan. A criminal defense lawyer, he was in tune with the pulse of the real world; he recognized the heartbeat of the street, knowing sometimes, it was a cold-blooded monster.

Years of defending the guilty had born down on him. Yearning to believe in justice again, he wanted to gain that fervor of hope he once held as a young defender of justice. Yet, the lawyer understood those hopes of innocence were lost.

Terry knew justice and truth had nothing to do with actual verdicts. Jury trials were a game. Innocence and guilt depended on which side weaved the best story for a jury. If a lawyer got the jurors to trust them, it didn't matter what the facts were; it was all in the storytelling.

Most defendants were chips to be traded for a later date. The object of the game was to hold other people's chips for that one case which came along every once in a while; the defendant he wanted to save.

But those cases are few and far between, Terry supposed turning to Mirabel who stepped through a sliding glass door carrying Henri IV Dudognon Heritage Cognac.

"Hey, rock star," she said, pouring them a glass, "its celebration time for winning your biggest case yet."

It was true; this was his biggest case.

His client, Pablo Rivera, was arguably the city's most fabled drug dealer, independently ruling the city's crack cocaine and heroin trafficking trade. That meant two things: Rivera was bigger than John Gotti and controlled more cash than Donald Trump.

Terry grabbed the glass and stared into its liquid. "This is two-million-bucks a bottle, a hell of a bonus from the city's most dangerous man."

"Don't beat yourself up, my love, you kept your oath and paid your dues."

"Nah, the jury did the dirty work. I merely told them a fantasy of innocence."

Mirabel sighed, pushed against her husband for warmth, and raised her glass, "To our little white bunny rabbit, then?" It was a reference to a long-ago witticism they shared, that one day he would acquire a cottontail to hop about the office as a reminder of their fairy tale.

"To all things magical," he agreed, placing his arm around her waist and staring into her eyes. "You know I love you, for better or worse."

"I prefer the better over the worse." She lived for moments like this, alone with her man, just sharing the same space. It was magical. This was where she wanted to be–forever. Shivering in his warm embrace and staring into the night skyline, she recalled their humble beginning.

Her husband had climbed the Legal Aid ladder, clawing his way from the depths of nothingness, slaving through eighteen-hour days in the swamps of the criminal courts, defending the poor who couldn't afford an attorney. He had a desire to make a difference, to save them from themselves. But, she knew it was the horse and water tale: Sometimes he just couldn't make them drink.

Today was her husband's day.

It culminated this afternoon in the Federal Courts and Terry was the center of attention. He had beaten back the United States Attorney's Office, the snakes with the longest fangs. A jury of five men and seven women had acquitted his client despite overwhelming evidence of guilt.

And yet, Mirabel knew, the acquittal weighed heavily on the love of her life.

"Why do I feel so guilty? I've let Pablo out to prey on the suckers who buy his dope."

She kissed him. "Your client is free tonight because of your oratory skills and dedication to the law. Right or wrong, innocent or guilty, the United States Constitution guarantees people like Pablo their day in court… to appear before a jury of their peers when accused of a crime. That's the nature of the beast. It's how the system works."

"It doesn't mean I have to feel good about it," he said sipping the cognac."

"No, you don't."

He stared into her bright green eyes and rubbed a palm against her cheek. "On this cold day, the system worked just fine for Pablo Rivera, accused, but acquitted, and most assuredly, New York's most renowned gangster."

She giggled and hugged him.

Then, just as the world seemed bearable again and things were perfect once more, his cellphone rang.

"God damn it!" he growled staring at the display. "It's the payphone from county jail."

Chapter 5

Nightmares & Dreamscapes

AFTER HIS PHONE CALL, Stefan was locked into an eight-foot cinderblock cell.

There, in the frigid loneliness, he stretched out upon a wretched, threadbare mattress and pulled an itchy blanket over his head. It was similar to those utilized by stables to warm horses in the dead of winter.

He fell into a recurring nightmare.

They'd intensified recently, pushing him from slumber into a clammy, panicked sweat.

Nobody escaped the lunacy of dreams.

This particular frightscape extracted a memory of years before when his twelve-year-old eyes watched helplessly as his father beat him to a pulp.

And, his mother got revenge.

"You good for nothing little brat," Daddy Dearest screamed in a violent rage. He was delirious with drunkenness and had slammed Stefan's head against the wall.

"Please, Daddy, stop!" But, he understood father's motives. Once monsters like him got their hooks into you, they stomped and stroked and sometimes…

Off came the belt, "I'll show you who the man of this house is!"

That belt seemed twenty feet long and Stefan knew it was going to hurt... he'd felt its leather slicing into his flesh many times before.

His dad was a butcher and parked his refrigerated truck down the street.

Inside, treats waited for later pleasures.

In the dream, he covered his eyes with trembling hands, helpless to avoid peeking through his fingers at the preview of things to come.

"No, Dad. Please, don't hurt me."

Then, suddenly, his mother appeared through the bedroom door with a knife in her hands.

She's going to shove that knife into his heart, he thought; cowering in the corner, he watched as daddy moved closer, raising the thick leather belt over his head.

Crack! Whip! Crack! Snap!

"Mommy!" he screamed, the leather biting into his pale white skin. "Mommy, help me!"

The strikes stung, the belt leaving a raised red welt across the cheek. And then, his right eyelid began to swell and his vision blurred.

Mother lunged. Her face twisted in fury the moment the monster had grabbed her boy's legs towards the bed. She was quick... swinging the knife with all she had... allowing it to find its mark deep inside his chest.

Cruuuuuuuuunch!

A splash of bright red blood drenched her face and jogged along her neck as it spurted from the wound.

"I told you," she said. "I warned you!"

Yet, that isn't true, Stefan thought. She had never cautioned father that a knife would slam into his ribs. This was something new.

One thing was for sure, Daddy wouldn't drive his meat wagon another night. He'd run out of tokens and the turnstile of life would no longer rotate for the psycho.

His mom was making sure of that right now.

"Get away from us!" she screamed, yanking the blade from dad's chest and watching as consciousness faded from his eyes.

Stefan imagined she'd rip the heart from the chest and take a big old bite, like chomping on a New York apple.

Then a voice woke him from dreamland.

"Wake up, come on, get out of bed!"

Emerging from the dream, he tried to grasp where the words originated, yet there was only darkness.

"Stefan Berks," the voice barked. "Wake up!"

His eyes flashed open and he realized... there was no killing zone; gone was his demonic father who attempted to take his life. And then... it all came crashing back. The barking voice in dreamland was a guard standing in the jail cell.

"Court time, get yourself together."

Stefan swung his trembling legs off the steel bunk, glad that nightmares had an ending. Little did he know; the frightscape had just started.

ABOUT THE AUTHOR

RJ Smith is an American Screenwriter & Novelist who blossoms in the Contemporary Horror and Thriller genres.

He enjoys twisting the mind of readers while bending the reality of his characters.

The author's been noted in multiple national writing & screenwriting competitions: The Page International Screenwriting Awards, Francis Ford Coppola's American Zoetrope Studios and the Sundance Film Festival Table Read.

He lives in Florida

RJ Smith's Website

www.ingramcontent.com/pod-product-compliance
Lightning Source LLC
Chambersburg PA
CBHW060144260626
47160CB00001B/114